"What do

Us. Love. Forever. Sight.
Zaccaria Angelino could

"What do you want?" Sa
defeat in

He we

"I wan
and held

But he
better."

So she
one step
with love

"Zach." She cupped his face like she had in her apartment, her warm, dry palm closing over his scar. "I don't want better."

He just looked at her.

"I want you," she said. "Just like you are."

He couldn't speak, couldn't utter a word that was in his heart.

But Sam didn't notice, because she was still touching him. She inched up on her toes and kissed his good cheek. Then his scarred cheek. Then his mouth. Heat coiled up inside him, his body betraying his brain, his need so much bigger than his pride. "I want to make love to you," she whispered.

———

"Hot, fun, fast, and fearless! I want one of these bodyguards."

—**CHERRY ADAIR**, *New York Times*
bestselling author on *Take Me Tonight*

PRAISE FOR
ROXANNE ST. CLAIRE

———————

"With Roxanne St. Claire, you are guaranteed a powerful, sexy, and provocative read."
—**CARLY PHILLIPS,**
New York Times **bestselling author**

———————

"Roxanne St. Claire delivers unforgettable heat with nonstop action."
—**LifetimeTV.com**

———————

"Sexy, smart, and suspenseful."
—**Mariah Stewart,**
New York Times **bestselling author**

ROXANNE
ST. CLAIRE

EDGE OF
SIGHT

FOREVER

NEW YORK   BOSTON

Copyright © 2010 by Roxanne St. Claire
Excerpt from *Shiver of Fear* copyright © 2010 by Roxanne St. Claire
Excerpt from *Face of Danger* copyright © 2010 by Roxanne St. Claire
All rights reserved. Except as permitted under the U.S. Copyright Act of 1976, no part of this publication may be reproduced, distributed, or transmitted in any form or by any means, or stored in a database or retrieval system, without the prior written permission of the publisher.

Book design by Giorgetta Bell McRee

Forever
Hachette Book Group
237 Park Avenue
New York, NY 10017
Visit our website at www.HachetteBookGroup.com.

Forever is an imprint of Grand Central Publishing. The Forever name and logo is a trademark of Hachette Book Group, Inc.

Printed in the United States of America

First Printing: November 2010

10 9 8 7 6 5 4 3 2

For my nephew, Captain Anthony Roffino,
who is all the extraordinary and amazing things
an Army Ranger hero should be... and so much more.
I'm proud to be your Aunt Rocki.

ACKNOWLEDGMENTS

As always, I have a legion of amazing individuals ready and willing to help make sure my books are as close to accurate as possible. My research sources are generous and patient, so if there are errors on these pages, it's my fault, not theirs.

I call in a team of specialists for every book and would be lost without them. They are: Los Angeles Police Officer Kathy Bennett, my go-to girl on police procedure; the "gun guy" Roger Cannon, making sure the characters shoot straight; and former FBI agent Jim Vatter, who brings the Bureau to my doorstep on an almost daily basis.

A few individuals were particularly helpful with this story: U.S. Army Officer Jessica Scott, the hero(ine) who took time out from fighting a war to answer my questions and help assure military accuracy; dear friend and fan Rossella Re, for being my Italian girl connection— *grazie, amica mia*! I plan to give you your own branch on the Angelino and Rossi family tree.

And a special nod to the impressive group of attorneys and public affairs professionals at the Innocence Project, with gratitude for the fact checking and detailed information regarding witnesses, exoneration, and the law.

Thanks to all my dear writing friends, too many to name (lucky me), but most especially to Kresley Cole, Louisa Edwards, and Kristen Painter, who keep me sane, focused, and laughing. And not in that order.

The entire team of publishing professionals at Grand Central Publishing, most especially my editor, Amy Pierpont, who hands me a shovel, forces me to dig deeper...and somehow makes me think I'm having fun.

Lastly, always and forever, my deepest love and gratitude to my husband, Rich, and our children, Dante and Mia. You three remind me every day that there's no station, only the journey...and we're on the best trip ever.

EDGE OF
SIGHT

CHAPTER 1

I understand you got into that little law school across the river."

Samantha Fairchild scooped up the cocktails from the service bar, sending a smile to the man who'd been subtly checking her out from behind rimless glasses. "Our trusty bartender's been bragging about me again."

Behind the bar, Wendy waved a martini shaker like a sparkler, her eyes twinkling. "Just a little, Sam. You're our only Harvard-bound server."

Sam nodded to the light-haired gentleman, not really wanting to start a conversation when Paupiette's dining room was wall-to-wall with a Saturday night crowd. Anyway, he wasn't her type. Too pale, too blond, too...safe.

"Nothing to be ashamed of, a Harvard law degree," the man said. "I've got one myself."

"Really? What did you do with it?"

The smile widened. "Print money, like you will."

Spoken like a typical Harvard law grad. "I'm not that interested in the money. I have another plan for the future." One she doubted a guy dripping in Armani and Rolex would appreciate. Unless he was a defense attorney. She eyed him just as two hands landed on her shoulders from behind.

"I seated Joshua Sterling and company in your section." Keegan Kennedy's soft voice had a rumble of warning in it, probably because she was flirting with lawyers in the bar when her tables were full. "I'll expect a kickback."

"That sounds fair." She shrugged out of his grip, balancing the cocktail tray.

"I bet he's a generous tipper, Sam," the lawyer said as he placed two twenties on the bar and flicked his wrist for the bartender to keep the change. "You'll need it for the Con Law texts alone."

She gave him a wistful smile, not too encouraging, but not a complete shutdown, either. "Thanks..."

"Larry," he supplied. "Maybe I'll stop in before you start classes with some first-year pointers."

"Great, Larry." She forced a more encouraging smile. He looked like a nice guy. Dull as dry toast, but then he probably wouldn't kick her in the heart with an... army boot. "You do that."

She turned to peer into the main dining area, catching a glimpse of a party of six being led by the maître d's second-in-command.

Joshua Sterling's signature silver hair, prematurely gray and preternaturally attractive, glistened under the halogen droplights, hung to highlight the haute cuisine but casting a perfect halo over this particular patron.

It wasn't just his tipping that interested Sam. The last time Boston's favorite columnist had dined here, they'd gotten into a lively debate about the Innocence Mission, and he ended up writing a whole article in the *Globe* about the nonprofit. The Boston office where Sam volunteered had received a huge influx of cash because of that story.

"Good work, Keegan." Sam offered a grateful smile to the maître d', who had vacillated between pain in the ass and godsend since he'd started a few months ago. "Count on ten percent."

He laid a wine list on her cocktail tray, threatening the delicate balance of the top-heavy martini glasses. "He tips on wine, so talk him into something from the vault. Make my cut fifteen percent and I promise you we will not run out of the tartare. It's Sterling's favorite."

She grinned. "Deal, you little Irish weasel."

After delivering the cocktails to another table, she headed toward the newly seated party, nodding to a patron who signaled for a check while she paused to top off the Cakebread chardonnay for the lovers in the corner, all the while assessing just who Joshua Sterling was entertaining tonight.

Next to him was his beautiful wife, a stunning young socialite named Devyn with sharp-edged cheekbones and waves of golden hair down to trainer-toned shoulders. Two other couples completed a glossy party of six, one of the women finishing an animated story as they settled into their seats, delivering a punch line with a finger pointed at Joshua and eliciting a hoot of laughter from the rest. Except for Devyn, who leaned back expressionless while a menu was placed in front of her.

Joshua put a light hand on his wife's back, waving casually to someone across the dining room. He whispered to her; then he beamed at Sam as she approached the table.

"Hello, Samantha." Of course he remembered her. That was his gift, his charm. "All ready to tackle *Hah-vahd*?" He drew out the word, giving it an exaggerated Boston accent.

"Classes start in two months," she said, handing over the wine list, open to the priciest selection. "So, I'm ready, but nervous."

"From what you told me about that volunteer work of yours, I think you've got more legal background and experience than half that first-year class. You'll kick butt over there." He added a smile to his laser-blue gaze, one that had been getting more and more television airtime as a talking head for liberal issues on the cable news shows.

No one doubted that Joshua Sterling could hit the big time down in New York.

"I hope you're right," she said, stepping aside for the junior maître d' to snap a black napkin on Devyn Sterling's dark trousers. "Otherwise I'm going to give it all up and go back into advertising."

"Don't doubt yourself," Joshua warned with a sharp look. "You've got too much upstairs to push computers and burgers. You need to save innocent victims of the screwed-up system."

She gave him a tight smile of gratitude, wishing she were that certain of her talents. Of course, doling out bullshit was another gift of his. "What's the occasion?" she asked, wanting to get the conversation off her and onto a nice big drink order.

Joshua waved toward the brunette who'd been telling the story. "We're celebrating Meredith's birthday."

"Happy birthday." Sam nodded to her. "We have two bottles of the '94 Tattinger left."

"Nice call for champagne," he said, "but I think this is a wine crowd. You like Bordeaux, right, Meredith?"

The woman leaned forward on one elbow, a slow smile forming as she looked at him. "Something complex and elegant."

Sam waited a beat, as the woman's gaze stayed fixed on her host. Devyn shifted in her seat, and Sam could practically taste the tension crackling in the air.

"Let me get the sommelier," Sam suggested quickly. "I bet he has the perfect Bordeaux."

"I know he does." Joshua handed Sam the wine list back without even looking at it. "Tell Rene we'd like two bottles of the 1982 Chateau Haut-Brion."

"Excellent selection." Was it ever. "While I get that, can we offer you sparkling water or bottled?"

They made their choices, which Sam whispered to a busboy before darting down the narrow passage from the dining area to the kitchen, her shoes bouncing on the rubber floor as she left the gentle conversation and music of the dining room for the clatter and sizzle of the kitchen.

"Where's Rene?" she asked, a smell of buttery garlic and seared meat rolling over her.

"I'm right here." The door to the cellars flipped open as the beefy sommelier hustled toward her, carrying far too many bottles. Two more servers came in right behind him with similar armloads.

"Rene, I need two bottles of '82 Haut-Brion, stat."

"After I help with the upstairs party," he shot back.

"Then give me the key and a general idea where I can find the '82s."

"You're not getting the '82s, sister." The faux French accent he used with customers was absent as he deftly set bottles on the prep deck. "One slip of the hand and you just cost us both a month's pay."

"Come on, Rene. I can get two bottles of wine, for crying out loud."

"You can wait like everyone else, Sam." He started handing bottles to one of the other servers, who gave her a smug look of victory.

The doors from the dining area swung open, and Sam squinted down the hallway, just in time to get a glimpse of Joshua strolling across the room, reaching out to greet a gorgeous former model and her date sitting at the deuce near the bar. So he wasn't in a huge rush for his wine. She glanced at the plates on the stainless steel pass, calculating exactly how much time she had to get this wine poured before her four orders for the old Brahmins on ten came up.

Not much. She wanted the Haut-Brion delivered first or she'd lose her whole rhythm.

One more of the waitstaff came up from the cellar, several bottles in hand. "This is the last of it, Rene. I just have to go back down and lock up."

"I'll lock it," Sam said, snatching the keys.

"No." Rene sliced her with a glare. "I'll get them, Sam. Five minutes is all."

"Come on, Rene."

The door from the dining room flung open and Keegan marched through. "Sterling wants his wine," he announced, his gaze hard on Rene.

"Then you get it," Rene said. "Not Sam."

But Sam was already on her way. "Thanks, Keegan," she said quietly as she passed. "You know I'll slather you with payola tonight." As she opened the door, she called back to Rene, "The Bordeaux are in the back nests, the Haut-Brion on the lower half, right?"

"Sam, if you fuck this up—"

"I will dust the bottles! You can watch the video tomorrow," she added with a laugh. As if that prehistoric camera was ever used.

"I will!" Rene shouted. "I just put a new tape in."

She hustled down the poorly lit stairs, brushing by one of the sous-chefs carrying a sack of flour from the dry storage pantry. Farther underground, the temperature dropped, a chill emanating from the stone walls as she reached the heavy door of the wine vault.

A breeze blew the strands of hair that had escaped her ponytail, making her pause and look down the dark hallway. Was the alley exit open again? The busboys were always out there smoking, but they sure as shit better not be taking lung therapy when Paupiette's was this packed.

Tarragon and rosemary wafted from dry storage, but the tangy scents disappeared the moment she cranked the brass handle of the wine vault, the hinges snapping and squeaking as she entered. In this dim and dusty room, it just smelled of earth and musk.

She flipped on the overhead, but the single bare bulb did little to illuminate the long, narrow vault or the racks that jutted out to form a five-foot-high maze. She navigated her way to the back, her rubber soles soundless on the stone floor. Dust tickled her sinuses and the fifty-eight-degree air finished the job. She didn't even fight the urge to sneeze, managing to pull out a tissue in time to catch the noisy release.

Behind the back row, she tucked into the corner where the most expensive wines were kept and started blowing and brushing the bottles, almost instantly finding the distinctive gold and white label of Haut-Brion.

Sliding the bottle out, she dusted it clean, and read the year 2000. In racks stocked chronologically, that made her a good eighteen years from where she wanted to be. She coughed softly, more dust catching in her throat. Crouching lower, she eased out another, 1985.

Getting closer. On her haunches, her fingers closed over a bottle just as the door opened, the sound of the brass knob echoing through the vault. She started to stand but a man's hushed voice stopped her.

"I'm in."

Freezing, she worked to place the voice, but couldn't. It was low, gruff, masculine.

"Now."

There was something urgent in the tone. Something that stilled her.

She waited for a footstep; if he was another server, he'd walk to a stack to find his bottle of wine. If it was Rene, he'd call her name, knowing she was down there, and anyone else...

No one else should be down here.

Her pulse kicked a little as she waited for the next sound, unease prickling up her spine.

Nothing moved. No one breathed.

Praying her knees wouldn't creak and give her away, she rose an inch, wanting to get high enough to see over the stack. As she did, the knob cracked again, and this time the squeak of the hinges dragged out as though the door were being opened very slowly. She rose a little higher to peek over the top rack of bottles.

A man stood flattened against the wall, his hand to his chest, inside a jacket, his head turned to face the door. In the shadows, she could hardly make out his profile, taking in his black shirt, the way his dark hair blended into the wall behind him. Not a server. No one she'd ever seen before.

He stood perfectly still as the door opened wider, and Sam tore her gaze from the stranger to the new arrival. The overhead bulb caught a glimmer of silver hair, instantly recognizable. What the hell was Josh—

The move was so fast, Sam barely saw the man's hand flip from the jacket. She might have gasped at the sight of a freakishly long pistol, but the *whoomf* of sound covered her breath, the blast muffled like a fist into a pillow.

Joshua's face contorted, then froze in shock. He folded to the floor, disappearing from her sight.

The instinct for self-preservation pushed Sam down behind the rack, her head suddenly light, her thoughts so electrified that she couldn't pull a coherent one to the forefront. Only that image of Joshua Sterling getting a bullet in his head.

She closed her eyes but the mental snapshot didn't disappear. It seared her lids, branded her brain.

Something scraped the floor and her whole being tensed. She squeezed the bottle in her right hand, finding balance on the balls of her feet, ready to pounce on whoever came around the corner.

She could blind him with the bottle. Crash it on his head. Buy time and help.

But no one came around the rack. Instead, she heard the sound of metal on metal, a click, and a low grunt from the front of the vault. What the hell?

Still primed to fight for her life, she stood again, just high enough to see the man up on a crate, deftly removing the video camera.

The security camera that was *aimed directly at the back stacks*.

She ducked again, but it was too late. She heard him working the screws in the wall, trying to memorize his profile. A bump in a patrician nose. A high forehead. Pockmarks in a grouping low on his cheek.

Dust danced under and up her nose, tickling, tormenting, teasing a sneeze. Oh, please, *no*.

She held her breath as the camera cracked off the wall, and the man's feet hit the floor. In one more second, the door squeaked, slammed shut, and he was gone.

Could Joshua still be alive? She had to help him. She waited exactly five strangling heartbeats before sliding around the stacks and running up the middle aisle.

Lifeless blue eyes stared back at her, his face colorless as a stream of deep red blood oozed from a single hole in his temple. The bottle slipped out of her hands, the explosion of glass barely registering as she stared at the dead man.

God, no. God, *no*. Not again.

She dropped to her hands and knees with a whimper of disbelief, fighting the urge to reach out and touch the man who just minutes ago laughed with friends, explained a joke to his wife, ordered rare, expensive Bordeaux.

This couldn't be happening. It *couldn't* be.

The blood pooled by his cheek, mixing with the wine.

The smell roiled her stomach, gagging her as bile rose in her throat and broken glass sliced her knees and palms.

For the second time in her life, she'd seen one man take another's life. Only this time, her face was caught on tape.

CHAPTER 2

Sam hatched her entire escape plan from the floor of her bedroom closet. There, with her laptop and phone, she figured out how to fashion a disguise, sneak out of her apartment in the middle of the night, and maybe not get caught and killed in the act. Maybe.

Until that very moment, though, she didn't know where she would go once she got out. She needed a friend, obviously, but more than that, she needed someone who could help her find out just how close the police were to catching Joshua Sterling's killer. 'Cause they sure as hell weren't telling her anything.

And then, surfing through news stories on her computer, hidden in her closet with her apartment door barricaded, she saw the name and instantly had her answer.

Vivi Angelino. Normally, she would not be high on Sam's list of friends—former friends, in this case, since they'd grown so far apart in the last three years—who could help in this particular jam. But seeing her byline as the author of the lead story on the *Boston Bullet* crime investigative website catapulted Vivi to the top her list.

Vivi, a relentless reporter with a nose for news and an inquisitive streak that didn't know the meaning of the words "no comment," was the perfect person to help. She would know what was going on inside the Boston PD, she would know if they had any suspects in custody or under investigation, and she would understand exactly why the police weren't offering any protection to the eyewitness.

She knew Sam's history with the local cops. She also knew...no, they'd just keep *him* out of it. The man had done enough damage to Vivi and Sam's friendship. She wasn't about to let the hurt of hearing his name keep her from getting the help she needed.

She opened her phone and scrolled down the recent calls. Now she understood why Vivi had called her twice this past week after several months without even a hello. Sam hadn't considered returning the call—she hadn't really talked to anyone but the police this past week. But Vivi probably wanted to interview Paupiette's employees if she was covering the crime. Well, Sam would give Vivi the scoop of a lifetime...if she could give Sam some inside information.

She tapped the keypad of her phone and sent the text. *Hey. Saw your story on* Boston Bullet. *R u home?*

That was innocuous enough in case anyone was tracking her calls or texts.

She hit Send and let her gaze linger on the headline. *Police Hit Brick Wall in Sterling Case*.

The headache that had started in the wine cellar a

week ago clobbered Sam's temples with every word Vivi had written.

No break in the case.

No clues to the killing.

No evidence, no motive, no suspect...no witnesses. Police suspect professional assassin at work.

Two words stood out at her. *No witnesses.* That meant the police still hadn't released the fact that there was an eyewitness; at least they'd kept their word on that.

What other information were they withholding? Sam had to know if they had anyone in custody or on a suspicious persons list. And, despite the man who'd come between them, Vivi was definitely the person to help her find out.

But she couldn't risk having this conversation on the phone. This would have to be in person.

Requiring her escape plan to work.

In her hands, the BlackBerry vibrated, flashing Vivi's name like a lifeline.

Wow. Long time no hear from. How are you?

Yeah, really long time.

How to respond...how was she? Scared to death, in hiding, desperate? She went for direct. *Can I come over?*

She squeezed the phone, willing Vivi to understand that she meant *now*, and not ask why.

Sure. Come on over.

She stared at the response, affection and appreciation swelling her heart. Now that was a true friend. No questions asked—a minor miracle considering this was Vivi Angelino, and every sentence started with who, what, when, where, and why.

Thanks, she wrote back, then turned the phone off

before a barrage of questions lit the screen. Sam would answer in person. If she had the answers.

Staying low so she didn't make a shadow, she crawled across her bedroom floor for the wig and sneakers. She'd found the black wig in the back of the closet, a leftover from some college Halloween party costume when she'd gone as Cleopatra.

Well, Cleo was about to buy Sam some air and information and, she hoped, a disguise that would get her right past anyone watching for her. Right past *him*.

Assuming he was out there. She had to make that assumption; it was the only way to stay alive.

She stuffed her hair under the wig, itchy where the cheap netting clawed her scalp. Still low enough not to be seen through the windows, she shoved her feet into a pair of Nikes, tied the laces, and duckwalked to the bedroom door. She moved stealthily through the windowless hallway, then crawled through the living room and made her way across the linoleum floor to the kitchen door.

Now came the tough part. Leaving through the back door from the second floor of a house... with no back stairs.

As quietly as possible, she stepped out to a small wooden deck overlooking the Brodys' fenced-in backyard. In all the time she'd rented the place, Mr. B. had promised that he was going to build a little stairway so Sam could have access to their yard. He hadn't gotten around to it, but Sam knew her landlord would move heaven and earth for her, after what the Innocence Mission had done for his cousin in Arizona. When he'd learned Sam volunteered at the organization, he'd actually lowered the rent.

But he still hadn't built the stairs. Even though he knew damn well that the place didn't meet fire code. But that turned out to be a good thing. Anyone who'd staked out her place would focus on the front, the only exit from the upstairs apartment.

No one would watch the fenced-in backyard, or the dilapidated second-floor porch that was home to her plants and a place to catch some rays. No one would suspect that she would put on a wig and dark clothes, jump off a second-story deck fifteen feet off the ground, then slide through a secret opening in the fence, follow the alley to the corner of Prospect and Somerville Ave, where cabs were always parked outside to take drunks home on a Saturday night.

No one—especially not the man with the bump on his nose, the pockmarked cheeks, and the deadly pistol, who, right this minute, could be parked in a car across the street—was waiting for her to leave.

She crawled to the railing, glancing at the houses on either side, both dark for the night. In fact, the entire Somerville neighborhood was pretty quiet, but it was summer and most student renters were gone now. Leaning over, she gauged the drop. Maybe not fifteen feet. Maybe twelve, and if she hung from the side, only about seven to the soft grass below. A little risky, but not exactly skydiving without a chute.

The other option was using the drainpipe and windowsill, which looked really easy in the movies, but probably didn't execute so well in real life. Plus, Mrs. Brody was a light sleeper and that was their bathroom window. Close enough to the bedroom to be heard. Lights would come on; questions would be asked. Anyone staking her house would be on red alert.

She opted to hang and drop, climbing over the railing, then shimmying into position, a splinter of wood stabbing her finger. Ignoring the sting, she peeked down to the ground, her breath caught in her throat.

She could break a leg.

Damn it, Sam, stop second-guessing and move.

A car drove up Loring, ambient light falling over the yard and the side of the house, moving slowly. Way too slowly. Slowly enough to take pictures of her house, maybe? To plan how to break in and shoot the witness in the head?

Hell yeah, that slow.

She let go, falling for a second in a surreal kind of slow motion, air whooshing past her ears, almost blowing the wig off. She landed with a soft thud, rolling right, then stayed perfectly still, waiting for the stab of a broken bone.

Everything moved. Stashing some stray hairs back up under the fake wiry ones, she took off to the back corner of the yard, to the broken boards where she'd watched the neighbor's kids come in and out playing hide-and-seek a few weeks ago.

Back in the good old days when she could sit on her own balcony and not wait for a sniper's bullet to hit.

The boards lifted easily, as they had for the kids. On the other side, the alley was nothing more than the back fences of the houses on the next street, a holding place for garbage and Dumpsters, barely wide enough for a car. She broke into a slow jog, not fast enough to get someone's attention, not slow enough to get shot.

Following the route she'd mentally mapped out in advance, she tore through the first intersection, even though there were no cars in sight. The streetlights of the main drag beamed beaconlike, the first glimpse of a yellow cab earning a satisfied "Yessss" through her teeth.

As she approached, the driver sat straight, probably waking from a nap. When she opened the door and he turned to her, for one horrific second she half expected to see *him*. Beak nose. Pockmarks. Silenced pistol.

But only a sleepy black man looked at her, nodding as she threw herself into the back and yanked the door.

"Brookline. Corner of Tappan and Beacon in Washington Square." She slid deep into the seat, cloaking herself in the darkness.

"You runnin' away from somebody, miss?"

Somebody. "Just, please, I'm in a hurry."

He got the message, driving silently down Mass Ave over the Charles, where the thud of her heart matched the clunk of the wheels on the bridge. By the time they were on the Boston side of the river, her pulse had started to resemble normal.

She put her hand on the phone in her pocket, but she resisted the urge to take it out, turn it on, and read any texts Vivi might have sent. She'd tell her everything once she got there. Now, she had to remain on high alert.

At every turn, she checked behind them, the lanes next to them, the oncoming traffic.

"No one is following, I promise," the driver said with a quick smile. "Seriously. You can relax. You are safe."

Relax? Safe? He had no idea.

She'd never relax or be safe until they caught, convicted, and imprisoned the guy who killed Joshua Sterling. And as long as *she* was the only living witness, half the cops in Boston wouldn't care if the killer made her his next victim. They were laughing their asses off at this one; she just knew it.

Of *all* people to witness a murder.

The cab rumbled over the train track and brick bumps of Beacon Street, side by side with what had to be the last Green Line car for the night. It stopped at Tappan, blocking them from making a turn.

Sam leaned forward and squinted up the block to the redbrick apartment complex she'd once called home, a wave of nostalgia hitting her. She'd had some fun in that building, working at the ad agency, making friends—including Vivi. Going to Vivi's parties...

Don't go there, Sam.

But wasn't that the reason she hadn't been back here to see her friend for so long? And that was wrong. She shouldn't have let what happened—or didn't—come between them. And considering that she had, Vivi was an angel for opening up her home at one in the morning.

All that history was just that... *history.* Women should never lose a friendship over a man. No matter who he was or what he did.

Just as the trolley car rolled away, a man stumbled out from around the corner waving helplessly at the back of the train, teetering on the edge of falling over.

"There's my next fare," the driver said. "Even if he's dead broke."

Sam smiled. There were good people left in the world.

"Just drop me here, then," she said. "I'm going right up to the first building. That way you can pick him up." She stabbed into her pocket and pulled out a little leather case, handing him two twenties, twice the fare. "This'll cover him, too."

"Thanks." He turned to look at her, the sleepy gaze replaced with warmth now. "Hope the son of a bitch doesn't find you."

"Me too."

"Here." He handed her a card. "Call me if you need a ride somewhere else tonight. I won't be far."

She took it and nodded thanks, then slid to the door and threw it open. Waiting for one car to pass, she crossed Beacon, securely under the streetlight and well within sight of the bright red lights of the Star Market.

The entrance to Vivi's apartment was less than a hundred feet ahead, but with each step, it seemed to grow darker up that hill. Jogging the rest of the way, she looked to Vivi's fourth-floor corner unit, but didn't see a light.

Her heart dropped. Hadn't she waited up?

She slipped her phone from her pocket, touching the screen to life. No new texts.

Slowing her step, she considered the possibilities. Vivi fell asleep. Vivi wasn't alone. Oh, she hadn't thought of that.

The front of the building was always dim, but Brookline was such a safe area, it hadn't really seemed to matter before. Now, the shadows seemed ominous and threatening, with one pathetic light from inside the locked entryway. At the callbox, she reached for V. Angelino in Unit 414.

Just as her finger touched the plastic, a hand clamped over hers. From behind, a man's body slammed against her, stealing a gasp as her wig was ripped off and strong, large fingers slid into her hair.

"The wig's a waste of time, Sam." His breath was as hot as his voice. "I'd recognize that ass anywhere."

CHAPTER 3

I guess this means you're not dead."

He squeezed a little tighter. "Is that what you thought?"

"A girl can hope."

"Not dead." Far from it. In fact, Zach's whole being crackled like a live wire as Samantha Fairchild's body molded to his one more time. He fought the burn and kept her locked into position, careful not to let her turn. Not that he expected her to wrap her arms around him in a hero's welcome, but he had to have control here.

"Well, that's a shame," she said coolly. "Because it would have been a great excuse for inexcusable behavior."

Whoa. That didn't take long. "Sorry to disappoint, Sammi. I'm alive and..." He curled a booted foot around her ankle as if he could knock her off her feet. *Again.* "Kicking."

"What are you doing here?" she demanded. With each

word, her muscles coiled so tight she felt as if her body would unravel if he let go. So he didn't give an inch, his face pressed against the honeysweet silk of her hair, smelling a mix of citrus and sweat. And something else he recognized all too well. Fear?

"I'm visiting Vivi. Just like you are."

"How do you know what I'm doing?" she demanded.

"I got your texts."

"They weren't sent to you." She ground out the words.

"She forgot her phone." And while he was thumbing through the texts trying to figure out where the hell Vivi had gone, the little device brightened with Sammi Fairchild's name the same way she lit a room when she walked in. At a thousand watts, alive with energy, brilliance, expectations, confidence.

At one in the morning, alone in Vivi's apartment, Zach had succumbed to the temptation of Sam. But now, reality set in. She was about to see him, and his midnight fantasies about a booty call suddenly seemed flat-out stupid. His lower half, however, thought it was a great idea, stiffening against one of the world's most excellent backsides.

"Let me go, Zach." She jerked again, more angry than scared now.

"Not yet." He buried his cheek deeper into her hair, almost groaning at the mix of pleasure and comfort and soothing, sweet softness.

"Forget it." She jerked her head away. "I did."

"I'm sure you did." That's exactly how he wanted it. Right? Forget it. Forget her. Forget them.

Like that was possible. He stepped back, taking her with him, into the shadows.

"What are you doing?" A little note of panic broke her voice, and the sound kicked him in the gut.

"Just getting out of the light."

"Why?"

Good question, but he didn't answer, because "taking you to the darkest place possible so I don't scare the living crap out of you" probably wouldn't fly. "You'll see." All too soon.

"I need to talk to Vivi," she said, fighting for calm in her voice, but keeping her body remarkably steady.

"She's not here."

"And you told me to come over?" She went from panicked to incredulous. "After three years of radio silence? You just say 'come on over' without even warning me you'd be here?"

"You'd never have come."

"No shit." She spat the words out, fury giving her so much strength she almost managed to turn around. "Let me go. What the hell is wrong with you, Zach?"

"The list is long, Sammi." He relaxed his hold, letting her breathe, expecting her to spin around, but she didn't.

Without making a sound, he put his lips against her hair and kissed it so softly she could never have felt it. Just once, to remember. Then never again.

He finally let go, taking a slow step backward, down two stone stairs, which would put them at the same height, face-to-face...eye to eye. It was time.

"Turn around, Sam."

She did, drew back, let her mouth open. "Oh."

Yeah, *oh.*

Her reaction confirmed two things: Vivi had kept her promise and never said a word to Sam, and he was even buttfuck uglier than he thought. Otherwise that one little syllable that opened her mouth the way it used to open when she kissed him wouldn't have been packed with pity. And surprise. And, damn, disappointment.

"Nice to see you haven't changed as much as I have, Sam." He couldn't help it. He reached to brush his knuckles over her velvety skin, burning his hand with the memory of that beautiful face.

"You...were injured...over there." She lifted her hand to do the same, but he instinctively drew back, leaving her fingers to flutter in midair, her look telling him she misread his reaction as shame. "I'm sorry."

"It's only an eye and I got two," he said quickly. "Believe me, I saw guys lose a lot more."

She stared at the patch, then the scar on his cheek, then zeroed in on his one good eye. "Is this why you never called?"

"One of the reasons." The rest were just so fucked up, he'd be keeping them to himself. So let her think he was that vain. "I figured...too much time had gone by."

She didn't respond, but her look was enough. Disgust, distrust, dismay. At least that's what it looked like, and he'd been waiting in the dark for her long enough that his night vision was sharp, despite the patch that covered half of his sight. He could easily make out the streaks in her burnished blond hair as it fell out of some kind of hastily made ponytail, the pallor in her skin, the bruise of sleeplessness under indigo eyes.

A car passed behind him, and she backed deeper into the shadows, her gaze suddenly divided between his face and the street, tension and fear pulling at her fine features.

"What's the matter, Sam?"

The lights faded as the car disappeared onto Beacon, but her expression stayed taut. "I told you, I need to talk to Vivi."

"At one in the morning, in disguise."

"It's complicated."

"Obviously."

She glanced toward the street, clearly torn. "When's she coming back?"

"No clue. Don't even know where she is."

She frowned. "Do you live here, too?"

He managed a shrug. "I'm between places, crashing here."

A couple of college kids climbed out of a car, heading for the Star Market on the corner, and Sam's posture subtly changed, growing even more guarded and wary. The store closed at midnight, so what were they doing?

"I guess I have to go back, then," she said.

"Your cab left."

She gave him a sharp look. "You were *watching*?"

"Waiting."

"To ambush me?"

"Once I knew you were coming, I just thought it would be polite to meet you at the door."

"From behind," she noted scathingly.

"You used to like it that way."

Her eyes flashed, not in insult or anger, but in fear again. "You were out here waiting for me and I didn't even see you." She sounded angrier at herself than at him. "You could have been anyone. You could have been..."

She jumped a foot at the sound of a car door. He'd seen that reaction to a loud noise before. He'd *had* that reaction. "C'mon. Inside." God damn it all. What else could he do? He'd been the idiot who said "come on over."

But she reached for her phone. "I'll call a cab." But that little tone of desperation in her voice squeezed his chest.

He nudged her toward the door. "Put the phone away and get inside. Whatever has you all jacked up won't get you there."

"Really, I...I can't."

The two men who'd just gotten out of a pickup walked directly up Tappan, within eye contact range, which they made, looking directly at Sam.

"Okay, let's go inside," she said quickly, the words running together as she bolted for the door, scooping up the wig he'd knocked off and stuffing it in the front pocket of her hooded jacket.

"You going to tell me what happened to make you like this?" he asked as he unlocked the entry.

She looked up at him, her gaze dropping over the scar that ran along his cheek, the flesh burning with each second she stared. It always stung, always hurt. But this kind of scrutiny just made the pain more intense.

The entryway light might as well have been a thousand suns blasting on his face, deepening the crevices, spotlighting the handiwork of a grenade that he had deserved to swallow on account of sheer stupidity.

"Are you going to tell me what happened to make you like that?" she countered.

For a beat, he said nothing, fighting the natural instinct to turn away. "Wrong place, wrong time."

Seconds ticked by as he stared as hard as she did.

Funny, he might not have recognized her face as easily as he had her body. It was Sam, of course, the same proud, straight nose and extra-full lower lip that always looked pink, as if she'd been gnawing on it. Or he'd been. She'd never been much for makeup, just flat-out pretty in a disarmingly straightforward way, but tonight her complexion had a sallow tone, and her brows were drawn into enough of a frown to put a line where none should be on a thirty-year-old.

She didn't look older, but more mature, wiser, maybe not so...confident. No longer the carefree career girl he'd met at his sister's party three weeks before he went wheels up.

Sam looked as if she'd waged her own private wars while he was fighting the country's battles. For a split second, he got suckerpunched with guilt, then put it away and headed down the hall to the back stairs, expecting her to follow.

It wasn't his fault if she was miserable. He hadn't made any promises he didn't keep. He hadn't made *any* promises, period. No declarations during tearful good-byes. Therefore, he had no reason to feel guilty. No reason to feel anything, which was his preferred state of mind.

"Just so you know," she said, close behind him. "I have no intention of picking up where we left off."

"I can't remember where we left off." *Liar, liar*.

"Then maybe I should remind you." She grabbed his elbow and forced him to turn and face her. "I was flat on my back, in the position I spent the better part of three weeks from the night I met you until the morning you left. If I recall correctly, you were stuffing your feet into boots. And I told you I loved you."

Yep. That's where they left off, all right. He just stared at her.

"And that's exactly what you said in reply." She snorted softly. "Nothing. Not then, not when you got there, not when you..." She flicked a finger toward his scar, making him wince. "Not a phone call, Zach. Not an email." She jabbed his shoulder with a finger. "Not a letter." Another poke. "Not a fucking postcard." Jab, jab, jab. "Nothing."

He closed his hand around her finger and removed it like a knife from a wound. "There was nothing to say." Nothing she wanted to hear, anyway.

And that much hadn't changed in three years.

Nothing to say?

She watched him walk down the hall, vaguely aware her jaw had fallen into the vicinity of her chest. Nothing to say?

Why? Because once the three weeks of bone-melting sex ended...so did their relationship? Of course. That much was obvious, and Sam could not let herself forget that.

She kept her distance behind him, gritting her teeth, forcing herself to stick with the decision she'd just made. No, she didn't want to follow Zaccaria Angelino into an empty apartment—the very apartment where she'd met him and launched that unforgettable interlude of lust and laughter—but those men had made her nervous, and right now, Zach was the lesser of two evils. But still, an evil.

And his *face*. Her insides had turned at the sight of the jagged scar that ran from under a menacing black eye patch, ripped over the skin of his cheekbone, and then disappeared into three days' growth of beard stubble. Oh, Lord above, why hadn't Vivi told her that he'd been hurt in Iraq? Or Afghanistan. Or… wherever he'd been.

Because she and Vivi had hardly talked in the past year or so, their friendship as damaged as his face. Vivi had always been loyal to her twin brother, and never once, even in the early months of his deployment, had she whispered where he was, what he was doing, or when he was coming home. She'd only said "it's classified," which Sam eventually interpreted as "he lost interest in you the minute he got on that plane for Kuwait."

From the way he positioned himself ahead of her, all she could see was his right side—which was as freaking perfect as she remembered—and the locks of long black hair that curled down his neck, shaggy and uncombed.

This was Zach Angelino, Sergeant First Class, Army Ranger, military hero, blistering-hot lover who brought her to her knees with his very first kiss? Not that he couldn't make a girl's knees weak. He was muscular to the point of distraction, but now a vicious-looking black and purple tattoo of thorns encircled one of those thick biceps. He was still impossibly larger than life, but that flirtatious, audacious, delicious man who'd followed her into the bathroom at Vivi's party, pushed her up against the wall, and kissed the holy hell out of her… was gone.

In his place was someone dark, brooding, and dangerous. Could war change a man that much? Or had it just brought out a side of him she hadn't been willing or able to see when she was blind with lust and falling fast in love?

Something told her he wasn't going to answer those

questions, so she opted for a more innocuous one. "How long have you been back?" she asked as they climbed the stairs.

"A while."

She slowed her step, still processing how he'd changed. Was this the same man who could *talk* her into an orgasm? And had. On several occasions.

He turned, half facing her. The unscarred half. "You coming?"

Like she had a choice at this point.

On the fourth floor, he unlocked Vivi's door to incessant clawing on the other side. "It's just Fat Tony," he said, putting a hand on her shoulder. "Vivi's cat."

"I remember him," she said. "I met Vivi right after she got him. Tried to talk her into 'Snickers' or 'Whiskers.'"

He snorted. "This is Vivi we're talking about." He opened the door as the black and white cat looked up and purred, clearly not happy they weren't who he'd been expecting. "Be happy it's not named Aerosmith."

Fat Tony, who wasn't really that fat, ambled to Sam, sniffing her jeans. She reached down to give his neck a rub while Zach headed down the narrow hall, disappearing to the left, to a darkened living room. Sam followed, passing Vivi's bedroom on one side and an office on the other, where an air mattress filled most of the floor, covered with a mess of sheets and blankets.

She got a little dizzy at the thought of Zach in that makeshift bed, tangled up in linens and sweat and *her*. The night they'd met she'd ended up in that same spare room; it had been a sleeping bag then, not an air mattress, that had been his crash pad while he waited to deploy. The next day, the action moved upstairs to Sam's old apartment and a real bed, where sometimes it seemed like they stayed for the whole three weeks before he had left.

Then, he was gone. Until tonight, when she was least equipped to deal with the emotional impact of seeing him.

In the living room, he was draped over a navy blue sofa against the wall, his feet propped on a coffee table overrun with mail and magazines and clippings and papers. A mountain of newspapers teetered on an end table, vying for space with Vivi's collection of framed pictures of their enormous, adopted American family, the Rossis.

"What kind of trouble are you in, Sam?" The question was delivered with a clear subtext—*no more bullshit; we're inside now*.

"Nothing that concerns you." Because nothing in her life concerned him. Hadn't he assured that?

She dropped onto the armrest of a chair, not willing to get too comfy and relaxed, but also giving in to the bliss of relief. Sanctuary and safety enveloped her for the first time in a week.

Not that Zach was safe…but no one who wanted her dead at the moment knew where she was. She was so grateful, she decided to be civil.

"When do you think Vivi'll be back?"

"I have no idea." The only light was a golden glow from a distant streetlamp that filtered in through the rounded bay windows that faced Tappan and Beacon streets. From this angle, his scar was in the shadows, and she could barely make out the darkness of his eye patch. His gaze did follow her, though, black as his hair, somehow twice as intense as it used to be, not half, as one might imagine.

Still, a little piece of her broke off inside. His damage was obviously irreparable and permanent, robbing the world of one of its most incredible faces.

"Not like her to leave without her phone," she said, nodding toward the BlackBerry on the coffee table between them.

"Yeah, I was surprised when I saw it there. But, if you said she filed a story, she has her laptop. You can email her or you can—"

"No. That's not…" Safe. "A good idea."

He leaned forward, threatening in a different way than he'd been outside. "Why not?"

"It's just not." She stood, crossing her arms and pacing the room, avoiding the windows out of habit, stealing glances at him, still unable to reconcile the man she saw with the one she had known so briefly. "Are you out of the Army now?"

"Yeah. Don't change the subject. Who're you running away from? A boyfriend? A lover?" His lip almost curled. "A husband?"

She didn't answer.

"You're married?" Was that a note of disappointment in his voice? That took a lot of nerve, seriously.

"No. Please don't ask any more questions." *Like how I've been. And if I missed you. And did I wait for word that never came?*

"You know, Sam, I've been at war a long time, and all it's done is hone my ability to pick up signals, subtle or otherwise. Terror is rolling off you in waves. What the hell is going on?"

She looked at Vivi's phone, black screened with a red light flashing to indicate a message, the edges of a ragged

black and white sticker that Sam knew was probably a logo
for some skateboard or guitar company curling around the
plastic.

"Maybe I should email her, and use that phone instead
of mine."

"Be my guest." He dropped back on the sofa, scratch-
ing the cat, who'd climbed up next to him and pressed
against his thigh.

"Then, if she's not coming back…" She was not
spending the night alone with him in this apartment.
She'd take her chances and get home. "I'll decide what
to do."

He lifted an uninterested shoulder. "Suit yourself."

His indifference cut. But, what did she expect? "Oh,
Sammi, please stay here and let's talk about all that's happened since we've been apart"?

Get real, Sam Fairchild. He wasn't interested. He
wasn't making a play; he hadn't even looked hard at
her except outside when all he did was scrutinize her
bedraggled face. He hadn't tried to reach her in three
years, after that mind-blowing three weeks. That ship had
sailed, sister, and sunk.

"Why do you need her so bad it can't wait for morning?" he asked.

She paced the room, turning in case the hurt showed
on her face. "Because she's the only person I think can
get me what I need."

"At one in the morning?"

She glanced at him, trying to interpret the rueful note
in his voice. "Yes, at one in the morning."

"So you must need information, Vivi's stock in
trade."

"I do. And fast."

He clasped his hands behind his head, the position exposing a well-toned bicep. She let her gaze move down over his stomach, still hard and flat, and his jeans, tight and worn right where they should be, down to bare feet on the coffee table.

Her mouth went dry, and a tendril of very female response twisted through her lower half.

God, could she not even be in the same room with him? Was she that weak?

"As much as it pains me to admit this," he said, pausing just long enough that she dreaded what he could possibly say next. "Sometimes my sister doesn't always come home at night."

Sam frowned. "Is she involved with someone?" The last she knew, Vivi was single and happily building a résumé as an investigative journalist.

"She's married to her job."

"And that keeps her out all night?" She abandoned the pacing and went back to the chair across from where he sat, this time sinking into it, beaten by the week and the worry and the realization that she could be in this apartment a long time, alone with Zach.

Slowly, he stood, towering over her, his knees close to hers, his hips and that worn bulge on his jeans right in front of her face. Heat coiled through her as she gritted her teeth and looked up. What the hell was he trying to do to her? Test her resolve?

The jackass. Did he think she couldn't resist him?

"I like to go with her when she's out at night," he said. "But she says I scare her sources."

"You probably do."

He got one centimeter closer. "Do I scare you?"

There were no words for how much. "Not in the least."

He placed his hands on the armrests of the chair, trapping her with his body, locking her knees with his and leaning over. "'Cause you seem kind of scared."

"Not of you," she shot back.

"You sure?"

Right then, she wasn't sure of anything, except that the sense of smell really was the strongest memory trigger in the body. And with each slow and unsteady breath of Zach-infused air, the mental images firing off in her head got...dirtier.

Zach laying her down...kneeling over her...his erection bursting and ready...lowering himself to start what they could never seem to stop.

"Of course I'm sure." The words stuck in her bone-dry mouth.

"You don't sound sure."

His face was inches from hers, his body just as close. All he had to do was relax his knees and he'd be right on top of her.

They'd done it in a chair once.

For one insane second, she couldn't even remember what they were talking about. That's what he did to her. Every single time she looked at him, common sense and intelligence got trumped by hormones. She could *not* let that happen again.

She flattened her palm on his chest, not sure which surprised her more, the impact of how hard it was...or the heartbeat that slammed against those muscles. "Get away," she said coolly. "I'm not interested."

"Neither am I." But he didn't move. "I'm just trying to figure out what's wrong with you."

"I can't breathe, that's what's wrong." She pushed harder. It was true. She couldn't breathe. At least not without inhaling some wildly erotic memory. "Move it. I'm leaving."

He straightened suddenly. "You are?"

For a nanosecond, he sounded disappointed; then the uninterested body language took over again, and he walked away, toward the kitchen. "I'll tell her you stopped by."

Just like that. *See ya, Sammi.*

She smacked her hands on the chair with more force than was necessary and pushed herself up. In the kitchen, she heard the pop and hiss of a beer bottle.

"Want a Sam Adams?" he asked. "They're your favorite."

Her heart wrenched. He remembered that? "Not anymore," she said quietly, pulling the wig out of the hoodie pocket. "I've moved on."

Wordlessly, she headed toward the hall, pulling Cleopatra's hair over her ears. She had made it far enough to get her hand on the knob, when one landed on her back.

"You forgot to say good-bye."

She closed her eyes, swallowed, and turned. "You forgot to call or write. So, we're even."

"I told you I couldn't have contact with the outside world."

That was his excuse? What kind of man couldn't just say, hey, it was sex. Wham, bam, thank you, ma'am. She shrugged out of his touch and opened the door. "Bye."

She slammed the door behind her before he could answer, breaking into a run toward the stairs before he came after her.

Yeah, right, dream on, Sam. He's not the run-after-you-and-beg-for-a-second-chance type. As she navigated the stairs, tears burned. Good God, hadn't she cried enough over Zach Angelino?

Wiping a stray tear with her sleeve, she made it to the main floor, hating herself for hesitating when she reached the door. Hesitating…and listening. Was he coming down those stairs to stop her from leaving?

Silence.

Of course he wasn't. And she could get home the same way she got here and talk to Vivi in the morning. It was worth the risk just to get away from him.

Stepping out of the stairwell, she reached into her back pocket and pulled out the cab driver's card.

"Please, buddy," she whispered as she dialed the number into her phone with disgustingly shaky hands. "Don't be taking some drunk to the North End right now."

A man answered on the first ring.

"Hi, I need a cab in Brookline. Tappan and Beacon. You dropped me off earlier, remember?"

"I gotta send someone, sweetheart. Gimme the address again."

She did. "How long will it be?"

"Five, ten minutes. Sit tight."

"I'll be in the front lobby," she said, heading that way.

Once more, she glanced at the door to the stairwell, hating herself for hoping Zach would come after her and hating him more for not. Of course Zach had let her go out on her own, even though it was obvious she was scared and in trouble. The only thing that could have gotten her sanctuary with that son of a bitch was sex.

If he still even wanted it from her.

Giving the wig a good tug, she headed to the front doors to wait, leaning against the wall, staying in the shadows. What would she do when she got home? There was only one way into her apartment. One door, in the front, where anyone parked on the street could see her.

What was she thinking to have left Vivi's apartment?

She was thinking that one more minute with Zach looming over her and she might have...

No. Never again. She would never, ever do that again.

Plus, he didn't want her even if she were willing to forget what had essentially amounted to a three-week-long one-night stand.

A yellow cab drove up Tappan, moving slowly. She put her hand on the bar to open the door, waiting to make sure it was hers. He passed the building and continued, moving very slowly, as if he were searching for the address. It might be hard to see in the dark.

He kept going up the hill.

Damn, was he going to drive right by? She pushed the door open to see where he was going, not willing to get locked out. She leaned far enough out to catch the driver lowering his window to get a better look at addresses. Yeah, this had to be her cab. If not, she was taking it anyway.

She stepped out, letting the door lock behind her. At the top of the stairs, she waved, trying to stay in the light so he could see her. But he just hit the gas and zoomed right up the street, disappearing.

God *damn* it.

More mad than scared, she was looking at her phone to

redial and plead with her original driver just when a black and white cruiser appeared on the left at the top of the hill, moving slowly toward Beacon Street. For a moment, she thought he stopped, but then he picked up a little speed and got close enough for her to see the colors and lettering.

Thank God. Not Boston PD but a Brookline cop. If they asked for ID, maybe this guy wouldn't recognize her as persona non grata in the department. She rushed to the street so she could flag him down, but just as she got to the sidewalk, he flipped on his lights and the siren wailed, sending her back a step in surprise. He never saw her, flying right by and practically soaring over the T tracks to turn left on Beacon and chase some baddie.

"Oh!" She slammed a fist against her thigh in frustration. For one miserable second, she considered dialing Vivi's phone and asking Zach to let her back in.

But no. She had her pride.

Unfortunately, pride wasn't going to drive her home. She walked across the street, phone in hand, headed for the lights of the Star Market. Even though it was closed, there would be workers in there, cleaning and stocking. At least she'd be relatively safe under the neon lights of the building waiting for her cab.

This wasn't the worst part of town, but it wasn't completely safe either. Her pulse jumping, she walked toward the path she knew ran down the hill from Tappan to the market lot, a path she'd used a thousand times when she lived in the building she'd just left. There was one section of dark in the trees, but faster, easier, and less out in the open than going all the way to Beacon to get from this street to that lot. She didn't think anyone had followed her here, but she wasn't going to take any chances.

Still, her heart thudded to the same beat as her nervous footsteps as she ran across the street and ducked under the branches of an oak to get to the path. She slipped into that one section where the trees blocked most of the light, dipped her head to see the Star Market sign, and—

Whoompf.

The blow to her back came so hard and fast, she couldn't take her next breath as she fell to her knees.

A hand slammed over her mouth; a man's body pressed against her.

For one insane second, she thought it was Zach. His idea of a—

"Pretty far from home, aren't you, Samantha?"

Not Zach. No. It was *him.* He'd found her.

CHAPTER 4

Jesus, he was a lucky sonofabitch. Timing was everything, and Teddy Brindell had a magic touch for being in the right place at the very right time. He tossed the dirty apron in the back bin, glancing around the kitchen to make sure no one was near, then pulled the roll of bills from the front pocket of his waiter's pants.

Holy shit. The grass was in bloom at Paupiette's that night, and he'd mowed it down. Tell the cops...get hassled and dragged downtown. Tell reporters...make a bundle. Who knew a little inside information could pay so well?

He flipped through the cash, a slow grin growing on his face. There were freaking Benjis in this pile, man. In the darkness of the dining room, he'd thought they were slipping twenties, not hundreds, every time another customer pretended to gesture him closer and ask about a special.

But the only Saturday Night Special they were interested

in was the one that was fired in the wine cellar a week ago. *Did you wait on him that night? Did you see the body? How'd his wife act? Did she freak out? What did he eat? What do you know?*

And he hadn't told anyone a single "real" fact. Yet. His information, his rock-solid, good-as-gold, heard-with-his-own-ears information was too valuable to hand over to some dick customer. No, he wanted the right reporter, one willing to part with thousands, not hundreds.

He pulled out three twenties and a ten to declare as cash tips, and just as he stuffed the wad back in his pocket, the kitchen doors swung open and in walked the triumvirate of assholes—chef, maître d', and sommelier—already smoking and getting ready to pour wine and discuss the moutard.

The little maître d' stepped closer and looked accusingly down his nose at Teddy.

"What?" Teddy asked. "I'm not stealing anything." He waved the seventy bucks. "Just counting my cash tips so I can figure out your percentage."

Keegan snapped the money out of his hand. "This will work."

"Hey!" Teddy made a lunge for it, but Keegan was too fast.

"You've got ten times this much in your pocket," Keegan said, looking pointedly at Teddy's pants pocket. "Unless you're just glad to see me."

He wanted to step on the little worm, but Keegan made the schedule and Teddy wanted good shifts.

"Just keep that, then, dude," Teddy said with a quick smile. "You gave me some great tables tonight. And, uh, my station's clean, so can I go?"

Rene walked closer, his reading glasses perched low on a ski slope of a nose. "You're not talking to customers, are you?"

Teddy did his best to look dumb as dirt. "Only about the specials, sir."

Keegan came up on his other side. "You know what he means. About the . . . incident."

"Oh, no, sir. I just tell them I can't say a word, and I don't."

Rene narrowed his eyes to distrusting slits. "I saw you plenty friendly with the customers tonight."

"Just doin' my job," he said, giving them his best Boy Scout grin.

"You know the rules," Keegan said. "You talk about the incident, you're fired. We have no intention of profiting from this tragedy."

Right. Like the restaurant wasn't overflowing with curious customers. "Of course, sir."

"You have a ride?" Keegan asked suddenly. "The T's done for the night and I didn't see your dad out there in front."

He hated the rise of color to his face almost as much as he hated the fact that his dad still had to drive him to and from work because he didn't have a car and still lived with his parents in Chestnut Hill. But with the right person to pay for the information he had, all that could change.

"I'm cool. I'm taking a cab," he said. His old man had sounded a little toasted when he called about the pickup, so he figured he'd spend one of his newly acquired twenties on a nice leisurely cab ride for a change.

But, Christ, he needed that car.

"See you tomorrow," Keegan said.

He nodded good-bye, though the chef and Rene were already deep in conversation. But he'd gotten the message with that little exchange. They were on to him.

So maybe he couldn't hold on to his hot information for long. Maybe tomorrow night, he'd find that guy from the *Herald* again. They loved trashy stories. Or that hot chick from—

And there she was, as if he'd conjured her up with the thought. The little babe with a nose diamond who was in the bar tonight. They hadn't talked, but Wendy told him she worked for some investigative website. And Wendy knew everybody and everything. He had no doubt the bartender had made as much as he had in fake information tonight.

But Wendy didn't know the one thing *he* knew.

He eyed the young woman again, liking what he saw. The rock star short black hair was so sharp at the edges it looked like it could cut...when he slammed his hands on her head and she sucked off his cock.

Yep. Money wasn't *everything*.

As he got closer, she locked on him with sharp, dark eyes and pale skin. Under her arm, a skateboard.

Holy shit, that was sexy.

She wasn't a kid, either. Probably late twenties, but smokin' hot. And damn, something told him she was ready, willing, and just standing there waiting for him.

"Hey." He gave her a lazy smile. "I remember you."

She tilted her head to one side, added a brief smile. "Thought you might." She reached out her hand. "Vivi Angelino with the *Boston Bullet*."

"You don't look like the media," he said, making a

show of checking her out. "You look too cute to be much of a reporter."

She gave him a vile glare. "Looks are deceiving." She stepped under the streetlight, and he got a good view of her body. Slender, fit, maybe five foot five at the most, a pair of cargo-style khakis hanging loose, a white T-shirt filled out, but not slutty looking. Not exactly trolling-for-sex clothes, but that little bit of indifference was kind of a turn-on, too.

"So what're you doing on St. Botolph Street at two in the morning, Miss Looks Are Deceiving?"

She moved the board from one side to the other. "I want to talk to you."

Oh, yeah. Now they're getting somewhere. "So, you noticed me, too." He gave in to a smile. "I thought we had a little eye contact earlier tonight."

"Not exactly. I understand you were working the night Sterling was murdered."

So she was playing hardass. That was okay. She'd soften up when she found out what he knew.

"Yep. But I'm not allowed to talk about it." He started walking down Botolph toward the Colonnade just to see if she'd follow. She did.

"That didn't stop you when you told Mr. Alvechio that Sterling's wife seemed pissed off at him."

He slowed his step. "Alvechio?"

"The older man at the table by the window, the one who nursed a gin and tonic and only had appetizers. And works for *Boston Magazine*."

"Oh, him. Yeah. Well, I did mention to him that she wasn't, you know, all happy and fun that night."

"And how about when you told that nice woman

sitting alone near the hostess stand that Mr. Sterling was kind of drunk and loud that night? Does that count as not talking?"

"She was from CNN," he said.

"She was not," she shot back. "She was just another rubbernecker. How much?"

He stuck his hands in his pockets, letting his fingers close around his wad of cash. "How much what?"

"Did she pay for that tidbit?"

He stopped, right under a light that caught the glint of that little diamond. She had more in her ears, and a silver chain with an electric guitar charm at the end. This was going nowhere fast, and if he didn't start to work her, he'd be in that cab going home to Mom and Dad. Alone.

"You play guitar?" he asked, letting his eyes linger on the charm and the nice rise of small but firm titties below it.

"Some."

He got a little hard staring at her chest. "You wanna know something, Vivi?" Vee-vee. He liked the sound of her name on his lips.

"That's why I'm stalking you, dude. You got anything to tell me you haven't sold off to the highest bidder yet?"

He gave her what he hoped was a sexy smile, but it was probably just sweet, like his mother said. "Depends."

She didn't look amused. "On what?"

"What you're bidding."

"I don't pay for stories, sorry."

He let his eyes drop to her chest. "Not cash, maybe."

"Forget it, pal. Wendy the bartender told me you were acting pretty cagey the night of the murder."

He stepped back, a different kind of rush going through him. "What the fuck? You think I did it?"

"I didn't say that. She said when the cops were there and everyone was being interrogated, you were acting… weird. Like you knew something. Do you know something, Teddy?"

Wendy noticed that? Why didn't she say anything? "I might."

"Have you told anyone this something you know?"

One person, but he quit the next day. Like Samantha Fairchild and a couple of other creeped-out servers who didn't want to work in a place where a guy was killed. Not Teddy; this was a golden opportunity and he intended to mine it. "No," he lied. "I'll tell you, though."

She looked right at him, and for the first time, she smiled. And, crap, she was really pretty then. "Okay."

"If you fuck me."

She snorted softly, her eyes closing a little. "Points for honesty, but, no, sorry, can't do that either. You're too young for me."

"I'm twenty," he said.

"I'm thirty-one, and listen, Teddy. Tell me what you know. I'll keep your name out of it."

He considered that for a second. "You don't look thirty-one."

"I told you—"

"I know, looks are deceiving." He laughed at his joke, but she didn't. "But, sorry, I got something worthwhile, and I'm not just giving it away for nothing. Someone will pay for this information." He started for Huntington, more embarrassed than pissed. "I'm going to catch a cab at the Colonnade."

But she stayed with him. He wasn't dumb enough to think she was having second thoughts about sex. He'd just dangled that carrot to see what she'd do.

"So, this thing you know, would it tell me who killed Sterling?"

"Nobody knows that," he said.

"Somebody does," she fired back.

"I thought you were following the story," he said. "The killer was a professional; at least that's what the police say."

"Speculation," she replied. "And they're not very forthcoming with information on this case, especially considering the victim was a member of the media."

She said it as if they were something special.

"It was a paid assassin," he said, unable to keep the certainty out of his voice.

"No one is sure of that."

"I am." Shit, that was more than he should have said.

She matched his step as they crossed the back parking lot of the Colonnade, heading toward the covered area of the lobby. Beyond that, only one cab waited in the taxi line.

"How's that, Teddy? How do you know?"

He glanced over at her, fighting a smile as he put his hand on her back. "I just do."

She eased out of his touch and switched the board to her other hand, managing the clumsy longboard as if it were an extension of her arm. "I'm just trying to write a story and get something in it that hasn't been published umpteen times before. Do you have anything?" she asked.

"How 'bout a blow job?"

She looked a little amused. "How 'bout you give me what you got, Teddy? Then I won't tell your bosses how you're bartering information for sex and money."

His smile faded. "I won't tell you everything, but I'll tell you something. And if I lead you in the right direction, will you sleep with me?"

She tilted her head, closed one eye, and assessed him. "You know, you're a cute kid. Nice eyes, good smile, and a pocket full of money. This town is jam-packed with coeds. You can get laid, Teddy. You're selling yourself short."

The words hit a soft spot and tightened his throat. Damn if he didn't need to hear that, and from someone who was clearly no bullshit.

"Meet me here tomorrow night."

She blew out a breath and shook her head, ready to drop the board. "Never mind."

"I'll tell you tomorrow."

She let the board hit the concrete, then put one foot on it and looked over her shoulder, right before she kicked. "Thanks anyway, kid."

"Taylor Sly!" he called.

She slammed her back foot down, bringing the board to a stop, popping it up, and whipping around. "What?"

"You heard me. Tomorrow night." He bolted for the cab, because one more minute and she'd get the whole story out of him. At the taxi, he yanked open the back door and stole a glance at her. She was still standing there, staring at him.

He climbed in and slammed the door shut. "Chestnut Hill." The driver flipped on the meter and pulled out toward Huntington, and Teddy resisted the urge to turn around and take one more look at her.

But the driver tapped the brakes and glanced into the rearview mirror. "Uh, sir, looks like someone wants to share this cab with you."

A slow smile stretched over his face. Bingo. But he refused to give her the satisfaction of letting her see him turn around in anticipation. That wouldn't be cool. "Fine. You can stop and let her in."

The door opened and Teddy looked up, expecting the dancing brown eyes, but seeing a man's face instead.

He opened his mouth to protest, but the guy was already in the seat, a gun pointed directly at Teddy's gut.

"Get on 93 south," the man said to the driver.

The driver looked confused, frowning at Teddy for permission, obviously unaware of the gun.

"It's okay," he said slowly.

"What did you just tell her?"

All Teddy could see in the shadows were icy-cold eyes. "Nothing. I didn't tell her a thing."

"It didn't sound like nothing. It sounded like you saw something you shouldn't have."

"I made it up, man. I thought she'd, you know, be impressed."

"Did you now."

It wasn't a question. Was this the guy he saw in the basement? The one who'd talked to that model chick in the hallway where the bathrooms were? He couldn't remember. That was the truth. He'd barely noticed the guy, and it wasn't until all hell broke loose a few minutes later that he even put two and two together and remembered the dark-haired guy who shot out of the basement and practically knocked Teddy down while he was smoking.

"What exactly did you see that night, Teddy?"

His bowels turned to water as the driver rolled toward the Southeast Expressway. Where the hell could they be going?

"Nothing. I swear, nothing." A cold sweat formed on his forehead. The guy didn't move. He was like a freaking statue, holding that gun. They were on the expressway, and each mile and minute Teddy got more scared. "Where are we going?"

"To see some friends."

That didn't sound good. More miles, more minutes. More sweat. Nobody said a thing.

"Get off here," he said to the driver.

Teddy looked at the exit. Holy crap, this was the worst of South Dorchester. Was this guy going to leave him here? He'd be dead in an hour.

"Right here's fine," the man said to the driver.

It was an underpass from the expressway, a hole of darkness and shadow. "Here?" the driver asked, looking around nervously.

"Pay him," the guy said, using the gun as a pointer. "Now."

Shaking, Teddy reached into his pocket and tried to grab just the top bill, but the whole roll of cash came out, fluttering in his shaking hands. He stuffed whatever the top bill was through the little hole in the plastic glass.

"Give me the rest."

He handed the cash over. "Listen. Please . . . don't leave me here, man. This is a bad part of town."

"Very bad." He stuck the gun in his side and Teddy braced for death. "Get out."

He did, half amazed that the guy followed him. The

second he closed the back door, the cab peeled out. What the fuck?

Something moved in the shadows. A footstep scuffed. Another. Every hair on the back of Teddy's head stood up as men stepped out of every dark corner. Two, three, four of the them, surrounding him.

"Please..." His voice cracked. "You have all my money."

"There's a price for seeing what you shouldn't have seen, Teddy. You're about to pay it." The man held out the cash to one of the others. "Roll him." Then he walked away to a black SUV parked a few feet away. He opened the back door and threw one last look at Teddy, then disappeared.

As the circle formed around him and closed in, Teddy started to cry.

CHAPTER 5

Zach went ice cold at the sound of Sam's muffled cry. He couldn't *see* her. But nothing was wrong with his hearing, and that sound was a body hitting the ground.

He vaulted out of his hiding place next to the building and raced across the street to the break in the trees.

"Help!"

A thud of fist against flesh was the only answer to her call, enough to guide him to the path. All he could see was a dark figure, on Sam's back, holding her head and saying something in her ear.

Rage rocked him as he dove forward with a grunt, punching the guy's head and rolling him off her.

"Run, Sam!" he ordered, already pouncing for his next attack. The guy was fast, rolling and jumping to his feet, a ski mask covering his face. Zach threw a kick at his stomach that doubled the man over, so Zach could slam a knee into his nose and take another swing at the side of his head.

That was enough to make the man stumble down the

hill, almost to his knees. Zach stole a glance over his shoulder where Sam stood, watching in horror.

"Go!" he told her. "Run."

"He...he..." She pointed at the man. "Get him. Zach, we have to stop him!"

But her assailant had found his footing and ran like the wind, already in the supermarket parking lot.

"Go get him!" she insisted, running toward Zach and pushing him out of the way.

"Are you fucking nuts?" He grabbed her shoulder and held her, stunned by the stupidity of the request and the power of her determination. "Let him go!"

She shook her head, her eyes wild. "It was him!" she exclaimed. "It was..." She watched him disappear across the lot, behind a ten-story apartment building.

"Who?" Zach demanded, still clutching her. "You *knew* that guy?"

"He knew me." Her words were raspy with defeat. "He knew me." No, not defeat. That was stone-cold fear that quivered in her voice. It matched the look in her eyes when she finally dragged her gaze from the parking lot to Zach. "He found me."

His instinct had been right. Sam's trouble was no ordinary fight-with-a-boyfriend kind of thing. That sixth sense that she was in serious danger had been the only reason he'd sneaked out the back of the building and down the side street to make sure she got into a cab. The only reason he'd gone after her when everything else in him said *let her go*.

"Thank Christ I followed you."

"Yeah, but you let him get away."

He snorted out a disgusted breath. "Hey, yeah, you're welcome."

"And the cops." She looked in the direction the cruiser had gone. "They were just here."

"And they were a really big help."

Her shoulders sank. "They never are when I'm involved."

"What exactly *are* you involved in, Sam?"

She took a breath, that juicy lower lip sucked into her teeth, almost distracting him from the raw pain in her eyes. "Murder."

For a second, he didn't breathe. "What?"

"You heard me." She pushed past him, back to the street. "I'm going to have to stay here tonight. Believe me, I don't want to."

"And I don't want you to."

"Got that, Zach. Loud and clear."

He ignored the comment, but put a hand on her back, looking up and down the street for any sign of trouble as they crossed. "You better be prepared to explain."

"I don't owe you an explanation."

He practically kicked the glass door in, but managed to turn the key and usher her back into the building. "I just saved your ass. You owe me an explanation."

She marched toward the stairs, shoulders square, head up, looking left and right at each door they passed as if her attacker might jump out at any minute.

She brushed her hair back, but missed a leaf sticking out of the side. For some reason, that leaf just got him. She could have been killed. If some goddamn intuition hadn't sent him out there...

He plucked the leaf, making her jerk when he got close.

"You wanna keep this as a souvenir?"

She snapped it from his hand and whipped it to the floor, silent. She stayed that way until they were back in Vivi's apartment, not relaxing until he'd double-locked the door. Then, in the living room, she dropped into the chair, the adrenaline dump almost visible.

Vivi's phone sat blinking on the table next to his nearly untouched beer, a stark reminder that he didn't know where his sister was at damn near two in the morning, but wherever she was, she was as vulnerable as Sam.

He took the sofa across from her. "Start at the beginning, Sam."

She looked up at him, her face pale and drawn. "I witnessed a murder a week ago."

"That Sterling guy?"

She nodded, her lip hidden under her front tooth, turning white from the pressure of her bite.

"How the hell did you witness that?"

"How did you put it? Wrong place, wrong time."

His scar twinged at the reminder, burning as it always did, but before he responded, her eyes lit up. "I know that guy out there had a mask on, Zach, but did you see his eyes? Did you see what color they were?"

"No. I wasn't looking at his eyes. I was trying to kick the shit out of him and get him off you."

Her expression softened for one quick second. "And I appreciate that, but..."

"But you wanted me to cuff him and bring him in for questioning."

"Yeah, actually. That's exactly what I wanted."

So he'd saved her life, ostensibly, but fucked up. "I had no idea he was anything but a common mugger, rapist, or killer. My usual course of action is to protect the victim."

She nodded. "I know. If I had told you—"

"But you took off before we talked about anything of substance." And he hadn't exactly begged her to stay. Because ten more minutes with Sam, and he'd be hard, hot, and hungry for another taste. No way, not again. He wasn't putting either of them through that again.

"What were you doing there, anyway?" he asked. "Having dinner at that restaurant, Paupiette's?"

She gave him a funny look. "I work there."

She did? "Oh, Vivi didn't..." Of course not. The subject of Sam was off-limits. He shrugged as if her employment meant absolutely nothing to him, even though it begged a million questions. "The police are saying that was a professional hit. What happened?"

"Oh, he was no amateur," she agreed. "And he has my picture."

"What?"

"My face was caught on the security camera that was in the wine cellar. It was pointed right at me as I stood up and saw him pull the trigger. He dismantled and took the camera that was aimed directly at me. And obviously..." She glanced in the general direction of the street. "He's following me."

"He didn't follow you up here, so relax. And, Sam, hasn't anyone told you that's not how security cameras work? You have nothing to worry about. A closed-circuit TV is just a camera lens, no video or film. If someone has your picture, it's whoever monitors the restaurant security. I'm sure the cops have that tape as evidence."

"Well, you're wrong, and yes, the police originally

thought that, too. But it wasn't that kind of camera. It was, like, a video cam, only there to stop employees from walking off with a thousand-dollar bottle of wine. It's been in there forever. I didn't think it even worked anymore, but right when I was going downstairs, the sommelier said he'd just put a tape in it. The killer took the whole camera."

"I take it the police know all this."

"I've told them everything." She dropped her head back and closed her eyes. "Not that it matters, but I've tried to cooperate. Now I'll have to tell them that he's found me. Which will mean nothing."

"They'll give you round-the-clock protection."

"In your dreams," she said bitterly. "They'd give *you* round-the-clock protection. They'd give that cat round-the-clock protection. Me? They escort me to and from interviews and give me vile looks of hatred."

"Why?"

She just shook her head, then sat forward, reaching toward the beer. "May I?"

"Help yourself. It's flat and warm."

She put it to her lips. "Just the way I like it." He let her take a drink, ignoring the little blast of heat when she put her mouth where his had been.

Vivi's phone vibrated with a call, dousing his personal fire and reminding him of his missing sister.

"How much does she know?" he demanded, flicking his gaze to the phone.

"That's why I'm here. To find that out."

"Jesus." He grabbed the phone, realization dawning. "She's covering this story. Does she know you're a witness? Does this guy—"

She waved her hand to stop the questions. "No one knows anything. They haven't even announced there was an eyewitness. The only person, other than the police, who knows what I saw is…him." She closed her eyes. "The man who just attacked me."

"Are you sure it was him?" he asked. "A woman was raped behind that Star Market three months ago. He might have just been—"

"He knew me. He said my…" She frowned, thinking. "Did he say my name? No, he said, 'Pretty far from home, aren't you?' But did he say my name?" She gave the armrest a frustrated tap. "Damn it, why can't I remember? No wonder the police don't trust my judgment. *I* don't trust my damn judgment."

"Because you can't remember what the guy said when he jumped you?" He was already scrolling through Vivi's incoming calls, clicking on her calendar. "Nine out of ten people couldn't, Sam. The adrenaline rush shuts down brain cells and you go into survival mode. That's why witnesses in criminal cases are unreliable."

"Trust me, Zach, I know."

His attention was on the phone. "If Vivi's not back in five minutes, I'm going out to look for her."

"Where?"

"Her phone memo said 328 St. Botolph Street. Mean anything to you?"

"Yes," she said with a soft choke. "That's Paupiette's. Where I work. Well, worked."

He started stabbing in an email to her other address, on the off chance she was sitting in some twenty-four-hour Starbucks with her laptop open. *Where are you? Get home or call.* He almost hit Send, then added *NOW*.

He tossed the phone on the table. "Why the hell don't they have you in protective custody if you witnessed a murder and the killer knows who you are?"

"It's a long story."

"I have time." Five minutes, anyway. He glared at the phone, willing it to buzz with a return email.

"Do you happen to remember me telling you that I once put a man in jail?"

Did she even have to ask? Of course he remembered. "I remember that something happened when you were a teenager. You saw a shooting in a convenience store."

"Right. When I was sixteen, almost seventeen, I witnessed some guy kill a clerk. I saw the whole thing from the back of the store, got a good look at the killer." She shook her head. "At least I thought I did. It was my eyewitness testimony that convicted him."

"Hard to believe that would happen twice in a lifetime," he said.

"Especially when the first time I was wrong."

"What?"

"The real killer came forth just a few months after you left. He had some kind of life-changing religious epiphany and confessed to the crime. DNA testing proved his confession was valid, and Billy Shawkins, the man I helped convict, was guilty of nothing but..." She added a wry smile. "Wrong place, wrong time. And he'd been on the cops' radar for some petty crimes in the neighborhood. They wanted him convicted and my testimony sealed the deal."

"He's out now?"

"Yeah, he is. But when I found out, I just..." She

shook her head. "It was really hard knowing I put an innocent man in jail. It rattled me, down to the bone. Everything I thought about myself, about always being right? Now I'm never sure if I'm even in the ballpark of right."

That would be a change in her personality; she'd been confident to the point of cocky when they first met. But this girl in front of him? Not so much. "So, what did you do? Anything to help him?"

"You bet I did. I found out about this organization that does nothing but help people like Billy, called the Innocence Mission. I worked with them, and..." She let out a sigh. "I basically turned my life upside down, quit my job in advertising so I could spend all my time helping this brilliant pro bono attorney get Billy Shawkins exonerated. And we did." She smiled, but her eyes were sad. "Billy's a free man today."

He studied her, putting it all together. "Just because you made a mistake doesn't mean the cops shouldn't protect you if you happen to have the misfortune of seeing another person murdered." *Shouldn't* being the operative word when dealing with law enforcement.

"Except that in the process of getting Billy exonerated, I opened up a can of Boston Police Department worms. There was an investigation, and two cops lost their badges because of how they handled evidence, specifically my statements and ID of the suspect. The repercussions went through the whole department. I am not a well-loved citizen at the Boston PD."

Now that made complete sense. He knew from his cousins, one a cop, one a former FBI agent, they were as tight as the men in his platoon.

"So you quit your job in advertising for this whole Shawkins thing and work as a waitress now?"

She narrowed her eyes at him. "This 'whole Shawkins thing' was my entire life for the past few years." Was that a note of indictment in her voice? What was the subtext? *If you cared, you'd have known that.* He just rubbed the cat and gave her a little nod.

"Anyway, I didn't go back to advertising, and right now I work as a waitress because in September I'm starting law school," she added softly.

"Law school?" He couldn't feign indifference to that.

"I guess Vivi never told you."

More like he'd refused to ask. "And here I thought it would take an act of God to get you off the corporate career ladder."

"It did," she said simply. "Getting Billy Shawkins out of jail was nothing less than a miracle, and the whole thing changed my life and my ambitions. It consumed me, and really opened up my eyes to some injustices. I want to work for the Innocence Mission after I get out of law school."

"Well, good for you for finding...your passion." He sounded like an idiot. He took the beer she'd put on the table. He sounded like an idiot who knew *squat* about passion. "Where are you going to school?" he asked right before taking a swig.

She hesitated a nanosecond, then smiled. "Harvard."

He choked, the beer trapped in his throat.

She laughed softly. "You don't have to be that shocked. Although, I admit, I applied on a lark and still can't believe I got in. I'm sure the work with Billy made the difference."

"You're going to Harvard." It was like a steel-toed boot in his belly. Harvard Fucking Law School. She was amazing. But then, he'd known that three years ago. He'd known that after the first night they were together. She was amazing and deserved…more than he could offer. "That's…" *Harvard.* "Wow. Really, good for you."

She nodded thanks. "Anyway, I made that mistake once, identifying the wrong suspect. Although, I do try to *learn* from my mistakes," she added, this time the sarcasm unmistakable. "And I try not to repeat them. As far as Billy, well, I was responsible for ten years of his life spent behind bars. But, now, he's one of my closest friends."

Man, this girl was full of surprises. He sipped the beer, swallowing, saying nothing. What could he say? She'd put her life together pretty damn fine without him, as he knew she would. Hit her bumps, and triumphed. Found her passion and…

Well, at least she wasn't married. That might have been too much to take. But she would be, soon enough. Probably had some lawyer boyfriend already. Although, wouldn't she be with him tonight?

"I'm really proud of—"

"You should be," he cut her off.

"Of Billy," she finished. "He's a model citizen who's found Jesus, lives in Roxbury with a lovely woman, and holds a steady job at a paint factory up in Revere."

Remorse gnawed at his gut. He'd missed all these changes in her. She'd done all that while he was on mission after mission after mission, blowing up caves and tracking down terrorists and avoiding IEDs and getting half his window to the world gouged by shrapnel. And still fucking up the operation and costing lives.

"But now," she continued, "I have zero credibility as an eyewitness. So the cops aren't telling me anything, they're not offering protection, and they're leaving me to find answers on my own."

"Which brings you to Vivi." Who *still* hadn't called.

"Well, like you said, she's covering the story. And if anyone knows how to get answers, it's Vivi."

"Don't these Innocence Mission people? They don't have investigators?" *Is one of them your boyfriend?*

"They have lawyers, mostly," she said. "And I've considered asking for help, but I'm just not sure I want anyone to know what I know. The cops are adamant about not telling anyone I witnessed the crime. So if I did, it might put someone I care about in danger. Believe me, I wasn't sure I should come to Vivi, but I was desperate for information and she's so connected."

"Why don't you just go underground until the police solve the crime? Will they let you leave?"

"No. I thought about going down to Florida to stay with my parents, but the police said I have to do some lineups." She shifted in her seat. "I can't tell you how much I don't want to do that again."

The cat's ears suddenly perked and he jumped from the sofa and mewed, swamping Zach with some measure of relief. "Vivi's home."

"Are you sure it's her?" She looked toward the hallway.

"Fat Tony wouldn't jump like that." He pushed up, walking around the coffee table to crouch in front of her.

"Look, relax. If it's not Vivi and someone else opens that front door, I'll kill them."

She stared at him, scrutinizing, and he forced himself to stay still. He'd endured worse. She had to get a good look at him sometime.

Slowly, she lifted her hand, her fingers warm as they neared his cheek, his scar. He could feel the heat of her palm getting closer, making his heart thud against his ribs. An inch from his skin. A centimeter.

"How did this happen?"

"Sheer stupidity and the mistaken belief that I am invincible."

"You're still alive."

Barely. This close to her and unable to do what every cell in his body wanted to do? He might as well be dead. "Yeah, pulse is on," he said. "Beats the alternative."

She laid her hand on his face, like satin on burning ember.

"Oh, my God!"

They both jumped at the sound of Vivi's voice. Zach stood, eyeing his twin sister's silhouette in the door.

"Samantha Fairchild!" Vivi exploded into the room, her skateboard banging to the floor as she launched toward Sam, arms wide. "Holy crap, it's good to see you. Why don't you answer your phone, woman? I've been trying to track you down."

"Well, I'm right here, looking for you. And your phone is here, by the way."

"I know, I left it, like a moron." She folded Sam into her arms and looked up at Zach, her eyes shining. "And look who you found." She winked at Zach.

He stepped back as they hugged, unconsciously

touching his face. His fingers traced the jagged hollow of the scar that ran from his cheekbone almost to his lip.

Sam was a different woman on the inside, and he was obviously different on the outside. Somehow, that changed everything... except the way he felt about her.

CHAPTER 6

Warm breath. Hot tongue. Sweet kiss.

Zach.

"Tony!" Sam rolled away from the cat bath, sliding off the sofa and pulling the comforter with her. She reached out to grab the cover, shaking off sleep but not the vivid dream.

"Sorry about that." Vivi padded into the living room in bare feet, her ebony hair shooting in twelve different directions, a wisp of a tank top hanging on narrow shoulders, boxer shorts rolled down to within an inch of her pelvic bone. "He's looking for morning love."

While Sam was obviously dreaming about it.

Swiping a hand through her spikes, Vivi slid into the club chair and folded her legs under her. "Did you sleep? I didn't sleep. Who could sleep?"

"Actually, for the first time in a week, I conked. Thanks for letting me stay."

"Pah!" She flicked her hand. "As if I'd let you go. Or Zach would have."

Sam didn't answer, letting the words hang in the air. Zach hadn't exactly insisted she stay. He'd been indifferent. It was Vivi who made the bed and fussed over her, dragging the conversation about the murder and the investigation late into the morning, ending up with more questions than answers.

The silence lasted a beat too long, and Vivi launched herself out of the chair. "Need caffeine, stat. You want some?"

"Sure, if you're making it."

While Vivi went into the kitchen, Sam headed into the hallway bathroom, her gaze drawn to a small leather bag open on the toilet tank, a razor and toothbrush angled out from the top. Unable to resist, she brushed her hand over the case, a shiver threatening at the intimacy of touching Zach's personal items. The razor tipped back in, revealing more of the contents. Toothpaste. Deodorant. Condoms.

She stared at the packets, a bolt of shimmering clear memory cracking through her. God, they'd gone through a lot of those things in three weeks.

Closing her eyes, she flipped the cold-water faucet and bent over the sink. The night they met, at a party right here in Vivi's apartment, he'd followed her into this bathroom when she'd gone to refresh her lipstick. She didn't need new lipstick, she recalled vividly. She just knew he'd follow. They'd been flirting, laughing, touching, brushing up against each other in a mating tango that had to culminate with a kiss.

She glanced at the wall next to the shower. That kiss had happened right there, and any lipstick she'd had on was toast. He'd dived right in, taking ownership of her mouth, unable to stop his hands from roaming up and down, his tongue from tangling with hers.

That kiss. That first endless, dizzying, warm, wet kiss that went on so long Vivi pounded on the door and yelled "get a room." They did. That spare room right down the hall, where they'd laughed and talked and touched and...

She turned back to the sink and splashed some more, cursing the little wobble in her knees.

Yes, that was the best sex she'd ever had and probably ever would have. Just remembering it had an effect on her. But the pain of never hearing from him again...no, thank you. That price was too, too high.

Water dribbled down her neck and into her T-shirt, chilling her skin. She popped up, sucking in a loud gasp when she saw Zach in the mirror behind her. Barechested, scowling, his hair a tousled black mess curling down to his shoulders, the black leather eye patch like a shield from eyebrow to cheekbone.

"Jeez. How about knocking?"

He yanked a towel from a rack and handed it to her. "You left the door open."

"I did not." She buried her face in the terry cloth, getting sensory overload from the smell of his soap in the towel.

"Sorry, but you did."

She handed the towel back to him, the tiny space and his proximity making her lungs ache for more air. "You still could have knocked."

"I didn't want to interrupt the DOP kit inspection."

Damn him. She gestured for him to move aside so she could leave. "I just wanted to borrow your toothpaste."

She gave him a completely fake, fast smile, then tried to shoot by, but he snagged the sleeve of her T-shirt.

"Where do you think you're going?"

As far away from the swirling purple tattoo above his heart as possible. That was new, too. "To the kitchen."

"And nowhere else."

She drew back. "Excuse me?"

"I'm serious, Sam. You don't leave this apartment alone."

"I'm not stupid, Zach." She yanked her sleeve from his fingertips.

"I'll take you home, or to work, wherever you need to go."

Him and his bag of condoms. "No thanks."

"I'm not asking for thanks. I'm not even asking permission. You can't go running around Boston alone."

She closed her eyes, the reality of that kicking her hard. She had no intention of running around Boston, but the fact was she needed some protection, or a really good hiding place. Or both. "Vivi and I will talk about it and figure something out. You don't have to be involved."

"I am involved." His expression was dark and serious, so different from the man she'd just been remembering. The man she'd made out with like a lovestruck teenager three years ago had so much fire and life, he was intense and sharp-witted and opinionated and brilliant. Had the injury changed him that much? Was he cold and serious on the inside now, too?

"You're staring," he said.

"I'm wondering."

He shook his head. "Don't bother. It's classified and I wouldn't talk about it even if it weren't."

"I didn't mean that. I'm wondering why you're so different from what you used to be."

He drew back, caught slightly off guard, then instantly copped the blank expression again. "We're both different," he said simply.

"I'm not different."

"Yes, you are. You're a Harvard lawyer with a mission and a new focus."

She laughed softly. "First of all, I haven't even started school yet, so, to be fair, I'm currently an unemployed waitress. Second, having a mission hasn't changed me. I have the same personality, the same character traits, the same..." *Hot, sweet, melting feeling inside when you're this close.* "I haven't changed. You have."

"How?"

"Your hair is long."

He shrugged. "Nice not to have to buzz every week."

"You have..." Her gaze dropped to the deep purple ink on his chest, the barbed wire on his bicep. "More tattoos."

"One for every tour of duty. Anything else?"

Did he want her to point it out? Fine. "You used to be much nicer."

A smile threatened. "Not really."

"Oh? That was an act? For sex?"

"Don't say that."

The truth hurt, didn't it? "You know what, Zach? I can do and say whatever I damn well please without a single word, comment, piece of advice, or even so much as a fucking *postcard* from you, which, by the way, I've managed to do really well *without* for three years."

His smile broadened to a teasing grin. "That postcard thing is really killing you, isn't it?"

"Ahem." Vivi tapped a spoon against a coffee mug. "Sorry to break up this cheery little reunion, but I've got an appointment soon. Sam, do you take milk and sugar in your coffee still?"

"Of course." Sam finally got by him, skewering him with one last look. "Why would I be any *different*?"

She walked out without seeing his response, and the bathroom door slammed behind her.

Vivi made an apologetic face. "I keep stepping in on you two at the wrong moment."

"There is no us two, and there is no right moment."

Vivi gave her a nudge toward the kitchen. "Come and talk to me."

Sam followed the aroma of coffee, settling into one of the two kitchen chairs with an exhale. "God, that guy gets to me."

Vivi chuckled as she poured milk into two mugs. "Always did, always will. You two are like fire and . . . fire."

Sam stabbed her fingers through her hair, pulling it all back as if she could just *yank* him out of her head. "Why am I even letting him get to me? He's just some guy I had a fling with."

"He's not just some guy." Vivi's voice tightened. "He's my twin brother. And as you know, we've been through some shit together in our lives, so I'm not going to sit here and bash him anymore than I did when we got orphaned in Italy and moved in with our American cousins and they would talk trash about the bad boy he was."

"I'm sorry, Vivi. I know you love him, and we both know that's the reason our friendship has dissolved over the past three years." Sam shook her head, regretting the decision to come here last night. "And, to be honest, if I had known he was here, I would never have called you."

"Well that's just sad." Vivi set a creamy, steamy cup in front of her with enough force to make a small coffee wave. "Because I've missed you."

Sam took the mug and closed her fingers around the ceramic, smiling at the woman across from her. They'd been good friends when she lived in this building. Different personalities, but they'd met in the elevator the day Sam moved in, and the connection was instant and real. They laughed a lot, killed plenty of bottles of wine, and loved to shop together. And then Vivi's twin brother was home from the war... and she threw a party for him. Sam's life changed the minute he opened that front door, a big, bad, sexy Army Ranger who called her Sammi.

No one had ever called her that before or since.

"I've missed you, too," she admitted, knowing that in her heart she was missing that man just as much. She took a sip to wash away that thought and leveled her gaze at her friend. "And I'm not going to lie and tell you've I've been too busy to call because you've never responded well to bullshit."

That got her a classic Vivi Angelino grin, baring an ever-so-slightly chipped front tooth and crinkling her espresso eyes. "Then let's avoid bullshit," she said. "Because there's enough crap flying in this apartment today."

"I'm sorry, Viv," she said, relieved to finally be saying these things. "It was easier just to avoid you than face the fact that you knew where he was and what he was doing... and why he didn't ever contact me."

"I really didn't know most of the time, because he was deep in some seriously classified crap over there. And I don't know why he never contacted you, because, I swear on my mother's grave, he never told me."

"He's ashamed to admit why he'd been with me in the first place; that's why he didn't tell you."

"What are you talking about?"

"Come on, Vivi, we both know what I was to him. Nothing more than an 'I could die tomorrow so I better fuck my brains out tonight' hookup."

Vivi cringed a little. "Way to underestimate yourself, Sam."

"Just calling it like I see it. It was intense, and believe me, we both enjoyed it. But it…" Meant so much more to her than it did to him. "He hurt me," she said simply. "And being around him reminds me of that. And being around you reminds me of that, too."

Vivi nodded. "I know. I knew it when you moved out of this building."

"Well, I had to move when I quit advertising. Somerville's cheaper." Still, she could have stayed in touch with Vivi, but it was so much better to let the Charles River come between them. They ran into each other a few times, had a couple of awkward calls, then in the past nine or ten months, nothing.

"I really do understand," Vivi said softly. "So you don't need to apologize anymore."

Sam turned the cup in her hands. "When did his injury happen?"

"About a year ago." Vivi shot a look at the hallway, then crossed her arms, bracing herself at the edge of the table. "He wouldn't *let* me tell you."

Sam bristled. "Why didn't you even tell me he was home and out of the Army?"

"Because you never asked about him the last few times I saw you."

"Pride will do that to a person, Vivi."

Vivi nodded. "And when I mentioned your name, he made me swear not to tell you."

"Why?"

"Pride will do that to a person, Sam."

The shot hit its mark. "I understand that you're loyal to him," she said. "It's always been the two of you against the world. I don't blame you a bit. It's just..." She waved a dismissive hand. "Never mind. It's ancient history and I really don't care."

Vivi sent a *yeah, right* eye-roll over the rim of her cup.

"I don't," Sam insisted. "I'm sorry he was hurt, but my scars are on the inside."

"Whoa. Deep."

"It wasn't just sex for me," she insisted softly, relieved to finally say it out loud to Vivi.

"I know." Vivi patted her hand. "It's the wicked curse of being female. Did you flip out when you saw him?"

"I held it together." She shrugged. "And, obviously, I have more on my mind at the moment than a broken heart."

Vivi leaned forward, a conspiratorial look making her eyes gleam. "Which is what we want to talk to you about."

For a moment, Sam said nothing, processing the "we." "What?"

One more time, Vivi looked out beyond Sam into the living room, presumably checking for Zach. "Let me give you some background first. We're starting a company."

"Who is we?"

"Zach and me. Well, he's not a zillion percent behind it yet, but I think he's just taking a little time to warm up to the idea."

"What kind of company?" she asked.

"A security firm that does personal protection and investigations. That'd be my department."

"Really? When did you decide to do this?"

"Well, I was down in New York on a story a few weeks ago, and I hooked up with one of my cousins. My great-uncle's wife's nephew." She threw out her hands in a classic Italian gesture. "Believe me, the entire country of Italy is related if you climb enough family trees. Anyway, this guy, John Christiano, works for this incredible organization that protects major league VIPs and investigates corporate espionage and does undercover work. Just amazing stuff, really."

"And that's what *you* want to do? Or what you want Zach to do?"

"Yes. To both. We'd obviously have to operate on a smaller scale, something a little less international, since we don't have corporate jets or oodles of cash and contacts at the CIA—well," she corrected. "We actually do have a contact at the CIA. And protection? Well, Zach's a brute. What more would it take?"

Funding. Office space. Clients. But Sam didn't want to burst Vivi's bubble. "Does he want to do that?" she asked instead.

"When we first talked about it, he got really, well I wouldn't say excited because not much excites him these days, but he did get kind of interested. In fact, he contacted our cousin, John, and actually went to New York and talked to him about working at his company. Evidently, this woman who runs the place has lots of former military and black ops types on her payroll."

"And?"

She shook her head. "She turned him down. The training and physical requirements..."

"He's been through Ranger training," she said, a rush of defense rising up in her. "He can do anything. He looks stronger than ever, actually."

"He has no depth perception. He has no left eye. She interviewed him and said no."

Sam's chest squeezed. "But still, he's so...capable." He was a lot of things that pissed her off and turned her on, but he was so damn competent at everything.

"Evidently not capable enough to suit this security goddess in New York. A sergeant, first class, too. A platoon sergeant with thirtysome guys depending on everything he did and said. This woman wouldn't even let him take a shot on the firing range—a freaking Army Ranger, Sam." Vivi's disgust was palpable.

Was *that* what had changed him so much? Sam doubted one lousy job interview could have had that much impact. "Surely he could still aim and fire. Don't you only use one eye to focus when you shoot anyway?"

"I know, right? I'm not even sure he would legally be allowed to own and operate a gun being half-blind, despite his military experience. My cousin Marc, who owns a weapons shop, said yes, but Zach hasn't even tried to get a license."

"What's he been doing since he got home?"

"Brooding." Vivi sounded good and disgusted with that. "He's just so dark and quiet. That's why I want to do this. If we owned our own company, we would make the rules. I mean, we wouldn't break laws, Zach would have to qualify to carry concealed, but nobody could say we couldn't hire him. He'd own the company with me."

"And you'd give up journalism?"

"About as fast as you gave up advertising."

"But I found my passion for the law." Thanks to Billy Shawkins and her unexpected courtroom wranglings. But reporting *was* Vivi's passion; chasing stories and writing about them was as much a part of her as vertical hair, a pierced nose, and her love of those electric guitars in her living room. "I can't imagine you doing anything else."

"Oh, I can. I can use my relentless curiosity for something that makes money and isn't as grueling. I mean, I like writing for the *Boston Bullet*, but, come on. It ain't the *New York Times*. And me?" She brushed her stiff mop-top, then tapped the diamond stud in her nose. "I ain't exactly *New York Times* material. So, I've been thinking about a career change, and then Zach showed up and all he wanted to do was trail me on stories and scare off my sources. This solution makes perfect sense to me."

It did have merit, Sam thought. "He's always been so protective of you."

"Exactly!" She tapped her knuckles on the table. "Ever since we were kids and had to move here and live with my cousins, he's been ready to kill anyone who looked sideways at me." She relaxed into a winsome smile. "My guardian Angelino. Don't you think that's a great name for the company? The Guardian Angelinos."

Sam laughed. "Yeah, it's cute. But is it what he really wants, or what you want him to want? 'Cause, God knows, I'm here to tell you that you can't make that man do anything he doesn't want to do."

She expected Vivi to grin, but her dark eyes grew serious and concerned. "I don't know what he wants, Sam, and, frankly, neither does he, although he won't admit it. All I know is that he had a really, really hard time over there." She leaned very close, her voice a whisper. "He won't talk about it to anyone, but it was bad."

"I gathered that," Sam said. "So this is probably a great idea for you. I hope it works out really well."

Vivi gave her a funny look, as if Sam had totally missed something, but the footsteps in the living room snagged their attention. Sam stayed facing Vivi, who beamed up at Zach as he walked in.

"Perfect timing," she said. "I'm just about to tell her our plan."

"You just told me your plans," Sam said, finally stealing a glance at him as he leaned against the counter, a white T-shirt damp and clinging to his muscles.

"Not all of them."

For a minute, nobody said a word. Then Zach shook his wet hair, adding a few more droplets on his shoulders. "Told you she'd hate the idea."

"What idea?" Sam asked, looking from one to the other. Zach looked pained; Vivi on the verge of excitement.

"The idea that you would be our first client," Vivi announced. "No charge, of course. Just for experience. I'll investigate, he'll protect."

Sam almost choked. *He'll protect?* Which meant twenty-four seven, round the clock, face-to-face with...She glanced up at Zach, who met her gaze with one that matched her miserable thoughts.

"You don't like this idea any more than I do," she said.

"I'm not all about Vivi's little company idea, no." But that wasn't it. He didn't want to be around her constantly. An old familiar ache tugged at her chest. Like when she'd open her email or the phone wouldn't ring or...

"No," Sam said, pushing up from the table to rinse out her cup. "Thank you, but *no*."

"Sam, a cold-blooded killer has your face on tape," Vivi said. "Don't be nuts."

Nuts? This idea was what was nuts. "I know that," she said calmly. "All the more reason to remember this isn't some game or an experiment for you two to start a new company. Lives are at stake." *Like mine.* "I just need to lay low and let the police do their job."

Vivi rolled her eyes. "You of all people know how well that goes. But yes, lay low. Just don't lay low alone and unprotected."

Zach said nothing, leaning against the counter, taking it in. Not exactly fighting to protect her, was he?

"I can't, Vivi," she said. "I just can't. There has to be a better way. A better..." *Protector.* "How about your cousin, John? Can I hire him?"

"If you have about fifty thousand dollars. We're free. Can't beat the price."

Oh, yeah? What was pride worth? "Well, I'm sure I can find an affordable bodyguard and not have to bother you two."

"It's not a bother!" Vivi stood. "Tell her it's not a bother, Zach."

But Zach, the son of a bitch, just stood perfectly still. "I can handle the job," he said tightly. "I proved that last night."

Handle it, yes? Hate it, too. "No. No." Sam was adamant. There had to be a better solution.

"Why the heck not?" Vivi asked.

Sam turned from the sink, her eyes flashing. Was Vivi dense? Couldn't she smell the tension in the room? "Vivi, did you not hear a word I just said to you?"

Her narrow shoulders drooped as Vivi backed down just a little. "Look," she said. "I know this is hard on both of you, with your history and all. But can't you rise above that and be smart about this, Sam?"

"Me? What about him?"

"I'm willing to do it."

"And clearly thrilled about it."

"He's not thrilled about it for reasons that have nothing to do with you, Sam," Vivi interjected, getting a harsh look from her brother. "He doesn't want to let you down."

Sam almost laughed at the irony. "Little late for that, isn't it?"

"She means, I don't want you to die."

The gravity of the statement, and his tone, silenced everything. Sam turned off the water spigot and finally met his gaze. "I don't want to die, either," she whispered.

"That guy could have killed you last night," he said.

"But Zach stopped him." Vivi gave a tight, but victorious, smile.

"I did what any man would do," he said modestly. "But, you know, Sam, I don't see any other ones around here looking for the job."

Ouch. "That's true," Sam said, swiping at a stray hair with the back of a wet hand. "I don't have anyone." Because the last guy she trusted crushed her heart and it never got whole again.

"Then it's decided. Zach will protect and I will investigate," Vivi announced, hands on her hips, light in her eyes. "Congratulations, Sam. You're the first client of the Guardian Angelinos."

Zach blew out a disgusted breath. "That is the stupidest name I ever heard, Vivi. You've got to think of something better."

Vivi pointed at him. "You're co-owner. You think of something better."

"I'm not *co* anything."

Vivi turned to the coffee pot, barely able to hide the triumph in her eyes. "Then let's get started. First thing, you go to Sudbury."

"Sudbury?" Zach and Sam said it at the same time.

"It's Sunday, kids. Rossi family dinner day."

Sam choked. "You're kidding, right?"

"I never kid about Sunday dinner."

"We're not going," Zach said gruffly. "I don't need to have my day ruined."

Vivi speared him with a look. "For one thing, they are your family, Zaccaria Angelino. For another, what are you going to do but sit in this apartment and fume at each other all day?"

Vivi had a point, Sam thought. She couldn't be trapped in here all day with him. "I wouldn't mind getting out to the suburbs today, if you think it's safe."

"It's safe," Zach said. "In fact, it's probably smart to get you out of here, since he saw you last night."

"Great," Vivi said before Zach could argue. "But I have to meet you there. I'm going to work out for a while, so I'll grab a ride out there with Nicki. Do you remember our cousins, Sam? Nicki's the shrink."

"I remember some of them." Sam turned back to the sink, still trying to come to terms with what she'd just agreed to. Had she agreed?

"Well, you should get a good dose of them today," Vivi said, setting an empty mug next to the coffee pot. "I think almost everyone's around, except Gabe, of course. And Zach, no matter what or when or where, Sam's our client and she can't be alone."

What was she getting herself into? Her most hated trait, the one that only emerged the day she found out she'd put the wrong man in jail, reared up to shake her down to the bones. She'd just made the wrong decision. A bad, wrong decision. "I don't think this is—"

Large hands landed on Sam's shoulders, surprising her with their strength and size. Warm breath and wet hair brushed her cheek. "Just accept it, Sammi."

Electricity shot up her spine.

"That's right," Vivi said brightly, holding a cup out to her brother. "The Guardian Angelinos have your back."

Before he took the coffee, he brushed his hand down her arm as if that could iron out the chillbumps that rose on Sam's skin.

Right at that moment, it wasn't her back she was worried about. It was her heart.

CHAPTER 7

Levon Czarnecki hummed the lyrics in his head, never on his lips. He only hummed one song, the one he was named for, despite its depressing, obscure, inane, impossible-to-understand message about the drudgery of life.

His mother had been a fool to pick that song for fertilization and conception. His life was anything but drudgery.

So he didn't use the name that titled the song, not professionally. When he did his job, he was just the Czar. And when he did his job right, he was a very rich Czar who lived for his solitude.

And there was no solitude to be found in Boston, a hellhole of tourists and pasty-faced Pilgrims living in the past. The delay on this job was really starting to piss him off. And when the Czar got pissed off, someone had to die.

He weaved expertly through throngs of tourists and

Sunday-happy locals who packed into Quincy Market.
Couples smashed together sharing ice cream. Families
trudging into Durgin Park for the pleasure of getting yelled
at by surly waitresses. Tourists—so goddamn many fucking tourists—cruising the bricks, buying souvenir junk
from street vendors, clapping mindlessly for dance crews
and mimes and a whole host of idiot street performers.

The crowd made him itch with the need to be alone
and apart, away from everyone but his music and his
land.

Did they know that? Is that why they'd picked this
meeting place? To put him at a disadvantage? Maybe they
thought he couldn't shoot them out in the open like this.
Maybe they thought he wouldn't show in such a public
place while Sterling's murder was still unsolved and on
everyone's brain.

Maybe they thought wrong.

He hated to be underestimated. But he really hated to
be owed money. And he really fucking hated having to
be where he'd just done a job. In and out, that's how he
worked.

He wanted to leave, today, fully reimbursed for the
damn fine clean job he'd done getting rid of their headache. Now they had to live up to their end of the bargain,
pay what he was owed for doing the job right and get
home. What the hell was the delay?

The tune with his name in it played in his head, loud
enough to drown out the nasty bass of a boom box and
the cheers of onlookers ogling break dancers.

He worked through the crowd, inwardly recoiling at
every person who brushed his body, imagining what he
could do to them if he got really mad. Breathing steadily,

he positioned himself at a vantage point that allowed almost a three-sixty view of the market. Scanning casually, he spotted his contact just as the man exited the parking garage. Short, stocky, wearing a Red Sox cap, carrying a plain black backpack. Could be him. They always sent someone different, but the whole lot of them kind of looked alike. Pale, beady-eyed, stout.

Levon waited for the signal, pretending to watch the black kids spinning on their heads to mind-numbing music, blending in with the crowd as he always did, no matter where he was.

Did they really think he was worried about being seen? Identified? Noticed?

Did they not know who they were dealing with? He wasn't one of their thuglike hit men. He was the Czar.

The man in the baseball cap cruised the market, twice passing the appointed spot, until he finally stopped right in front of the bronze statue sitting on one of the benches. He touched his cap, once . . . twice. The third time, he took it off, wiped sweat from his forehead, and put it on again. Then he repositioned his pack to the other arm, walked to the next bench, and sat right in the middle, tossing the pack next to him and spreading out his arms.

Bingo.

Levon waited a few more minutes, enduring the crappy music and dancing until the number ended and the crowd dispersed. He moved right along with them, curling around to the other side of the open-air market, the weight of his own black backpack, mostly from the ancient camera they made him bring today, dragging on his shoulders.

Time to move. He navigated the crowd until he was

out in the open, strolling and humming his song. He glanced at the statue as he passed. Red Auerbach, whoever that was. Ten more steps to his contact, then he stopped, reaching into his pocket for a cell phone that he put to his ear.

"Yeah. 'Sup?" Of course there was nothing but silence, because the phone hadn't rung or vibrated. "Oh, hey, how ya doin'?"

A quick glance at the bench and his contact slid over a foot, making room, but leaving the pack where it was. The Czar nodded thanks, then listened to dead air as he took the space, sliding his own pack off.

"Get out! You got tickets?" He held his pack right above the other one and looked again at his contact, who mumbled, "Sorry," and reached for his pack. As he did, lightning fast, the man's hands closed over the other straps and he switched the bags. Smooth as silk.

Levon gave him another nod, laid a casual, but possessive hand over the new bag, crossing his long legs, leaning back, and chuckling into the phone. "Hell, yeah, I want to go. Count me in." With his other hand, he pulled out a pack of Marlboros and put one in his mouth, then reached for a lighter.

The man next to him glared hard.

"What time you goin'?" he asked no one.

Next to him, his contact seized his bag. "Jesus, do you have to smoke out here?"

Levon ignored him, tucking the phone deeper into his neck and exhaling a cloud of gray. "Hell, yeah, man. I'll meet you there."

The contact shot to his feet, slung the backpack full of damning evidence on his shoulder, and marched off, practically knocking over a little girl clinging to her mother's hand.

What an asshole. No finesse.

He flicked the cigarette, ground it with a boot heel, and watched the man who'd taken his bag head across the open market toward the cluster of carts and vendors. Out of habit, he kept his eyes on the baseball cap. Out of caution, he kept the phone to his ear. Out of curiosity, he fingered the zipper on the bag, plucking it over the teeth a half inch. The backpack didn't feel that full, but then two thousand hundred-dollar bills really wasn't that much bulk.

Just as the zipper clicked over five teeth, enough for him to casually slip a finger inside, the baseball cap reached the other side of the market.

His fingers touched the spine of a book. A book? In his other hand, the phone vibrated. The cap got blocked by a crowd around a juggler and...someone was calling him. Something wasn't right.

He thumbed the Talk button, but didn't say a word.

"We're not paying you a dime until you finish the job."

"It's finished." Jesus, Sterling was dead. What the hell did they want, his heart on a platter? Shoulda asked for that.

"There was a witness. There was someone in the cellar watching you."

His blood simmered. "Get rid of him," he said. "I didn't get paid for two hits."

"I tried to arrange that, but it didn't work. And it's not a him. You'd know that if you watched the tape."

The tape? He had never even looked at it. He just took the prehistoric camera because they told him it had a tape in it, and brought it today because they wanted to destroy

the evidence themselves. He pulled the backpack zipper
further and glanced inside. Paperbacks. No money. Not
a fucking dime.

Fury catapulted him to his feet.

"Shit," he said sharply, his gaze darting over the
crowd. He caught a glimpse of the man carrying his black
pack, just as he rounded the back of a candy store, headed
across the back street toward the parking garage.

"Now you no longer have the tape; am I correct?"

He managed not to grunt in self-disgust. Was it possible he'd left a witness in the wine cellar? Fuck, anything
was possible.

"Yeah." His strides were long and purposeful, using
the phone as an excuse to look like a man who needed to
get somewhere. Because he did.

Levon knew exactly what was coming next. *You no
longer have the tape; you don't have the witness; you
can't get your money.*

"You didn't do the job until you get rid of the witness.
You should have watched that tape, Levon."

"Just gimme the name, I'll do the rest."

All he got was a snort of laughter. "For your prices,
you can find out the same way I did and take care of it
on your own. Get it done, and get paid. If not, you can go
fuck yourself."

Rage rolled through him like licking flames. "No
problem."

"Isn't it?"

Not if he got that camera back. "None at all." He tore
through the crowd now, slipping past the candy store,
jumping in front of a car, getting a blared horn in response.

"You there?" the voice on the other end asked.

"Of course."

He yanked open the door to the parking garage pedestrian entrance, coming face-to-face with a young couple who stopped, apologized, and backed off as he careened past.

"So when can we expect to hear some news from you?"

Levon didn't answer, taking the steps up to the next level two at a time, silently, listening. A door slammed, probably on the top level, based on the sound. Without missing a beat or a breath, he ran up the stairs, the phone still smashed to his ear.

"How long will it take?" There was impatience in the voice on the other end now.

About a minute. "Not too long." He closed his fingers over the rusted door handle and pulled it open without making a sound. Listened. Footsteps tapped around the other side, near an elevator.

He darted forward, moving the phone to his left ear so he could use his right hand to draw his S&W. Against the wall at the corner, he stopped, inching out to see his target pausing at a little Camry, pulling keys out of his pocket.

Jesus, couldn't they have sent a challenge?

He waited until the man clicked the lock and reached for the back door to throw the pack in; then he lunged, reaching his target before the man took his next breath, stabbing the silenced gun into the base of his skull and firing.

"How long will it take to get rid of the witness, Levon? Can you be specific?"

The man collapsed, his head thudding against the car on the way down.

Levon reholstered his weapon. "You want specific?" He grabbed the other bag, ripped open the back zipper, and pulled out the Ruger MKII he'd used to kill Sterling. That was the deal—turn over the tape, turn over the murder weapon, and get the money.

Fuck with the Czar and he'll fuck you right back. Aiming carefully, he pulled the trigger of the Ruger, firing into the hole he'd made with his own weapon. That oughta screw up ballistics.

"Yes. I want her dead."

He wiped every possible print from the handle of the Ruger and dropped it on the cement. Then he took both bags, but before he walked away, he reached into his pocket using the handkerchief to cover his fingers and found the business card. He tucked it right under the man's collar near the bullet hole. "Of course you want her dead," he said. *Her.* "That ought to be easy."

"Ought to be. For a professional like you."

He really didn't like that sarcasm.

"Oh, and you better come and get your man in the garage," he said quietly. "Because if someone else finds his body first, they'll also find Sterling's murder weapon, and your business card."

He pressed End and slipped into the shadows, taking the stairwell on the opposite side of the garage, down one level to the used SUV he'd bought for cash that morning. He threw both bags on the floor and rolled in with them, flattening his body on the floorboards while he waited.

In less than five minutes, tires squealed and an engine screamed up over the concrete, the rumble of a truck on a mission shaking the whole structure. They probably wouldn't take the time to search the place, but just in case, he stayed hidden for a long time, ignoring the vibration of his phone.

When it was dark, he took out a shaggy wig and fake beard, stuffed some filler into his cheeks to change the way he looked, and finally drove out of the garage, his plan formulating.

He'd find somewhere to rent an old-school VCR, then get a look at his next victim. A woman. As he knew so well, every woman had a weakness. He just had to find hers.

The biggest challenge of the day would be getting Sam safely out of Brookline. No, Zach corrected as he pulled his pristine 1968 Mercedes-Benz from its parking slot, the biggest challenge would be dealing with JP and not giving in to the urge to have knuckles meet face. But his immediate task was Sam.

Driving the tank out of the private spot he paid damn near half his combat pay to own in Brookline, he cruised down to Beacon Street, glancing at Vivi's building on the right and the supermarket and tree-lined hillside on the left.

Once more, he wondered exactly what would have happened to Sammi if he hadn't followed his gut—and her—out to the street. He almost hadn't. He almost let his stupid self-pity along with the constant threat of the boner he got around her stop him from following her outside.

Then she'd be dead right now. He was not the man for this job.

He whipped around and headed back up Tappan. Vivi's heart was in the right place, and it was a hell of a shame that Sam obviously believed he didn't want to breathe down her back day and night. Like he could even think of a place he'd rather breathe, but who wanted a one-eyed bodyguard with the scars to prove just how fallible he was?

And in this situation, fallible would be deadly.

He was only going to Sudbury today for one reason, but he wasn't about to tell Vivi and get her all worked up about her ridiculously named company. All he wanted to do was convince his cousin to take this gig for him. Marc Rossi was a master marksman, a former FBI agent, and, most important, impartial about Samantha Fairchild. He'd never make an impulsive move. He'd never make a stupid mistake. He'd never have his brain on the body he was supposed to guard.

Or maybe he would.

The thought lit a fire through him. Not that he was jealous of any of his cousins; he just didn't like the idea of another man near Sam.

If that was the case, then he should take the job.

Swearing out loud, he let the mental debate continue as he circled the block, checking out the two exits from the alley behind the building. Was that safer, or should he bring her right out front?

A man crossed the street, hood up, headphones hanging, looking at the building. Was he looking for Sam? A couple of joggers ran by, two men deep in conversation, glancing at the apartments. Were they trying to find her? A red SUV with tinted windows rolled past in the other direction, so slow he could easily be checking out the neighborhood.

Jesus, how the hell could he know? He picked up his phone and pressed the speed dial for Vivi. "Bring her down now, back exit, Beacon side."

Less than five minutes later, Sam was in the car and they were shooting off to the Mass Pike. She shifted in her seat, looking out the window, silent. This was gonna be a long ride if somebody didn't break down and talk.

"I remember this car," she finally said. "Didn't you rebuild this with your uncle?"

"Yeah. I bought it for two grand in high school, and my uncle thought it was maybe the only really smart thing I ever did. He helped me restore it." Which would be the one and only project he and his uncle Jim had undertaken completely without the help of JP, Marc, or Gabriel Rossi. Of course, of the four boys raised together, Zach was the only one who needed to be under the watchful eye of his uncle, the lawyer-turned-judge. So it might have been teenage prison in the garage with Uncle Jim, but the result was a beautiful twenty-five-year-old 300E in prime condition, and autobahn ready.

"And of course your uncle will be there today."

"Of course. And JP, my oldest cousin." He waited a beat, then, "He's a cop."

"Oh, it just keeps getting better, doesn't it?" She crossed her legs. She was still wearing the jeans she'd come over in but had added a loose cable knit sweater he assumed belonged to Vivi. "What does JP stand for?"

"Just Perfect." At her soft laugh, he added, "Don't believe me? Ask him. He'll tell you. Have you met him?"

"Yes, when I visited the Rossis with Vivi once. You were overseas, and it was a birthday party for your uncle."

Zach changed lanes, and five cars back, so did a dark red Expedition. Was that the same SUV he'd seen on

Vivi's street? His gut tightened as he divided his gaze from the road ahead to the one behind.

Oh, yeah. A very long ride.

"And who else is there in that giant family of yours?" Sam asked. "You better refresh my memory."

It wasn't technically *his* family, but he opted not to correct her. "JP's the oldest at thirty-eight, then Marc, then Gabe, who won't be there today." Because God only knew where Gabe was. Wherever, he was kicking ass and taking names, which was a shame because Gabe was the only one of his male cousins Zach truly trusted. Marc was okay in a pinch; JP was just a dickhead.

"Then the girls," she prompted.

"Yeah, agewise, Vivi and I are next in order, then Nicki and Chessie, the baby at twenty-five. Plus Aunt Fran, Uncle Jim, and, of course, my great-uncle Nino, who is Jim's dad and the Rossi kids' grandfather."

"But everyone calls him Uncle Nino, as I recall."

"Exac...shit." The Expedition was gaining a little.

"What's the matter?" she asked, turning to look toward traffic. "Is someone following us?"

"I'm just making sure no one is."

She let out a soft sigh, more of a shudder, really. "Listen, Zach, I don't like this any more than you do, you know."

"Don't worry, it'll all be over by this afternoon."

"It will?"

"This part of it." He made a gesture, indicating him and her.

"How?"

He'd made the decision while he waited for her to come down, and he stuck with it. Sam should be in on

the plan. There was no need to spring any more surprises on her, and it was obvious from her reaction in the
kitchen that she wouldn't mind a staffing change.

"My cousin Marc is former FBI, a weapons expert,
and since he owns his own gun shop, he has a couple
of managers to cover for him, so he'll have time. I've
decided he's tailor-made for the job of keeping an eye
on you."

He felt her gaze hot on him, but didn't turn. "You
decided that."

"Yes, I did." He watched the Expedition get behind
a truck, and he used the opportunity to gun the glorious
German-built engine of the 300 and put ten car lengths
between them; then he flew through the first toll with his
pass and lost him. For now, anyway.

"Is he in this security company, too?"

"The one that exists solely in my sister's imagination?"

"Didn't sound that way to me."

He shot her a look. "Not everything sounds the way it
is, especially when Vivi's putting spin on it. It's a stupid
idea."

"Actually, it's a good idea," she countered. "But a
stupid name."

He laughed. "So we agree on one thing."

"Okay, I'm fine with Marc if he wants to do it. I've
met him. I remember he was really…" She searched for
a word.

"Yeah, that's what all the ladies say."

"I thought he was married?"

"*Was*," Zach corrected. "Is now divorced. Which is
why he's no longer in the FBI."

"Really? How are the two related?"

He just shook his head a little. "Long story, and he can tell you if he wants, but, trust me, he'll be a better match for you."

"I don't need a match," she said softly. "I need to make sure I don't get killed."

There was the fucking Expedition again. He gunned it, and cut off another car, maneuvering to the exit.

"What are you doing?" she asked, tightening her grip on the armrest.

"My job. We're taking side roads." He completely lost the SUV, cutting down to Route 9 and meandering through Newton, then Wellesley.

As they traveled deeper into the suburbs of Boston, he relaxed, and Sam seemed to, as well. Or maybe she was just so relieved that he wasn't going to be her bodyguard that she seemed a little more at ease.

"You probably don't remember that I was at your house in Sudbury with you," she said.

Jesus. "I lost my eye, not my memory, Sam. Of course I remember that. Uncle Nino was the only person home and he made you pick basil from his herb garden and help him make his Genovese pesto."

"I've made it many times since then. He was very sweet to me."

"And old as the hills now. Over eighty. He'll be glad to see you again." Oh, hell, why had he just admitted that?

"I guess they're all going to wonder why I'm here. Including your cousin, the cop."

"They'll assume we're dating, except for Marc, because I'm going to bring him up to speed."

"Dating?"

"You have a better idea?"

"You want to lie?"

"You want all those people asking you about Joshua Sterling's murder, then casually mentioning to a friend that they met the witness—the witness only the murderer knows was in the room? Let them assume what they'll assume and I'll work out the details with Marc. He might even be able to score a safe house through the FBI."

She sighed. "How long will I have to live this way?"

The note in her voice made him want to reach out to comfort her, so he just grasped the wheel tighter. "Until they catch the son of a bitch. You said you're going to do lineups. Maybe you'll just see him and wham, it'll be over."

"I wish it were that easy," she said as he slowed at the Wedgewood blue colonial manor perched on a hill overlooking a mile-wide lake.

Instantly, his stomach matched his grip. "Home sweet home."

"I forgot how beautiful it is out here," she said. "So much space and a great yard for a family."

He rarely saw the Rossi house as beautiful. As a child, he had thought of it as just a place to live, far, far away from what he considered "home." *Their* house, not his. As an adult, it was still a place he didn't quite belong.

As he climbed out of the car, he checked out JP's oversized F150 that matched his ego and Marc's silver Corvette. Did he really want Sam cruising around with Marc in that piece of American-made crap? His Mercedes was a beast, and so much safer.

"Everybody here?" she asked, following his gaze.

"Everybody but—" The scream of an engine that

needed to be thrown into the next gear broke through the silence of Sudbury, pulling a startled gasp from Sam as a streak of cherry and chrome sailed into the driveway. "Chessie, who never met a speed limit she couldn't annihilate or a computer she couldn't hack."

He guided Sam to the front door, knowing who would answer it and what he would say to Zach. The question was, what would Uncle Nino say to Sam? Was Zach going to regret the honesty he'd shared with his great-uncle?

He reached up to the brass knocker with a stylized R.

"You knock at your own house?" Sam asked.

"I don't live here anymore." The gleaming Revolutionary War red door opened, filled by the human fireplug that was Nino, his barrel chest popping out of the top of a white apron that matched thinning silver hair, a mile-wide smile, and mirth-filled black eyes.

He extended his arms straight out, pulling both of them into his circle, his grasp tight and solid and strong.

"*Zaccaria,*" he whispered, pronouncing the name exactly as he'd heard it for the first ten years of his life, a name too feminine sounding for Americans, but so natural to his ear. He was Zaccaria long before he was Zach. Long before he became an orphan, shipped to America with his sister. "*Benvenuto a casa,*" Nino said. Always, always, welcome *to the home*. Nino'd tried so hard for this to be Zach's home.

"*Grazie, pro zio.*"

He eased back from the three-way hug as Nino took Sam's face in his big hands, denying her the chance to look at anyone or anything but him. Obviously, no reintroduction was necessary. Nino searched her face as though he were memorizing every angle and shape.

"Samantha." It sounded like a long sigh of relief.

Nino looked up and put a knotted, knuckly hand right on Zach's scar and held it there, one hand touching Zach, one touching Samantha, like he was joining them.

"I told you she'd be back," Uncle Nino said to him. "Didn't I tell you?"

"You told me."

Next to him, he felt Sam stiffen and Zach laughed. "He just wants you to make that pesto again, Sam."

"Jesus Christ, the swine must all be airborne at Logan." The loud, crass voice could only belong to one person. Before Zach was in the door, JP had started.

"JP Rossi!" Aunt Fran's voice carried back even in a hush. "I don't care how old you are, you don't speak that way in my house."

"Ma. I just heard Zach laughing. Which means pigs can fly."

Zach's fist curled, but Nino slid his calming hand from cheek to shoulder, adding a squeeze. "Come and drink wine."

Wine wouldn't help. Wanting to punch JP in the face was a sensation so familiar, it was not too different from breathing. The last time Zach's fist had made contact with that smartass mouth was about eighteen years ago, on Zach's thirteenth birthday.

The satisfaction had been worth being grounded for a week.

In the center hall, Sam paused on the way back to take in the jigsaw puzzle of portraits and family photos that rose along with the stairway, but Zach barely spared them a glance.

Of course, he made plenty of appearances on the family wall. His picture, and Vivi's, were right alongside the others at Christmas and on family vacations. She'd instantly blended into this family, never letting their unorthodox arrival color her relationships with them.

Unlike Zach, who never forgot it.

"Well, who do we have here?" JP's greeting sounded smarmy, buried, as always, in a Kennedy-quality Boston accent. Zach held back in the hall, not quite ready for the confrontation yet, letting Nino take Sam into the family room adjacent to the oversize kitchen, both forming a great room that had always been the heart of the house.

"This is Samantha Fairchild," Uncle Nino said. "Zach's friend."

"Hello, Samantha." Why did that prick always have to be here to ruin what could have been a passably pleasant way to spend the day? "Aren't you Vivi's friend?"

A prick with an excellent memory.

"I used to live in the same apartment building where Vivi lives," she said noncommittally. "And I was here once for your father's birthday."

"But that was quite a while ago. I've seen you since then; I'm certain of it."

Zach came up behind her, flanking her on the right. "Don't grill her, JP. The woman just walked in the door."

"I'm not grilling. I just am trying to figure out the timeline here." He smiled at Sam. "I guess it's just the police detective in me."

"You've seen her with me," Zach said. "Before my last tour, Sam and I went out."

"That's right. You're the ad agency girl."

"Well, I'm—"

"About to be the Harvard Law woman," Zach interjected. "Maybe you've heard of it?" Then he turned her right toward the kitchen and away from JP. "Come on, Sammi. It smells better in here."

"Oh, it certainly does." She took a long, slow inhale, her arm still firmly around his waist. All part of the charade, but he didn't mind. It had been a long, long time since a woman touched him like that.

A long time since *this* woman had touched him like that.

"It smells delicious, Mr. Rossi," she said.

"Uncle Nino," the older man corrected.

"I'm coming, Zach!" A woman's voice rose from the dining room, followed by the sound of silverware being abandoned on china.

"Aunt Fran," Zach whispered. "Brace for hug."

In a minute, she ambled around the corner from the dining room, her chubby arms outstretched. "It's been so many Sundays without you."

How many? Only Fran could count with two parts guilt and one part love. "Hey, Aunt Fran. I brought a friend to make up for it."

She pulled back, turning to Sam. "Oh, I remember you!"

"Sam Fairchild," Sam said, accepting Fran's embrace. "It's nice to be back here."

JP slipped out the French doors to the backyard, and Zach relaxed a little. "Where's Marc?" he asked, leaning against the granite-topped bar that surrounded the kitchen.

"Down fishing with Uncle Jim at the lake," Fran said. "Sam, can I get you something to drink? Tea or soda? Uncle Nino's wine?"

A female shriek answered from outside. "No, JP, don't you dare tell him! You don't have to be such a freaking cop all the time. Stop it!"

At Chessie's outburst, Zach exchanged a look with Nino, who glanced skyward. "I know," Zach mumbled. "He's really lookin' for it today."

"Well, don't give it to him, Zaccaria. That's what he wants."

The youngest Rossi marched in, hands plastered on her curvy hips, black hair wild over her shoulders, her crystalline blue eyes sparking with anger. "JP's a prick, you know that?"

"I know that," Zach said, approaching her, ready to get between Chessie and JP as he had a thousand times in his life.

"Francesca!" Aunt Fran knuckled the counter. "Not the girls in the family, too, talking like that."

"He is, Ma." She spat the words and stared daggers at JP as he cruised in, his face even more smug than it had been ten minutes earlier.

"Three weeks. She's had the stupid car three weeks and . . ." He punched his fist into his palm. "Bam."

"Fu—"

Zach stopped Chessie's F-bomb with a grip of her upper arm, giving JP a lethal stare. "Get off her case."

"Thank you, Zach," Chessie said, tilting her head onto his shoulder for a second before she headed through the family room toward the kitchen, to the person who really protected her. "I don't see any reason to upset Dad, do you, Ma? It's just a scratch."

Aunt Fran had Chessie in her arms in an instant. "I'll tell him, JP," Aunt Fran said, her look over her baby's shoulder fierce on her oldest son. "It's my job to break bad news to him, not yours."

JP shook his head and headed out. Behind Zach, the women's chatter rose. It was as good a time as any to go find Marc and do the handoff. "I'll be back," he said to Sam.

"Wait for me," Nino called from the stove, tapping a wooden spoon and gathering a dark red glass of wine. "I'll walk with you."

Zach glanced at Sam. "I'll be fine," she mouthed to him, waving him to the door. "Talk to Marc."

In other words, she was anxious to make the shift to a new protector. At least they both agreed it was a smart move. Not that he expected her to make a case to keep *him* as her bodyguard. It was obvious he made her skin crawl.

While he waited for Nino, he watched Fran and Chessie gather around Sam, circling her with warmth, generosity, and noise, like Rossis did. Sam laughed at something Aunt Fran said, and Chessie settled onto the next bar stool like she was all ready for girl talk.

Something inside him slipped a little, just looking at Sam in his family's kitchen, calm despite the chaos around her. She'd fit in, he realized with a start. Better than he ever had, ironically.

Nino shuffled over, his blue knit pullover already dotted with red sauce.

"*Grazie, ragazzino,*" he muttered as Zach held the

door. No one in the Rossi house spoke a word of Italian; they were as American as the Andersons on one side and the Thompsons on the other. But Uncle Nino knew plenty of words and phrases, and he used them only with Zach, hoping the younger man wouldn't lose the language. Even if it was just *ragazzino*, a nickname for a young boy.

Zach had lost the language anyway. He'd been a foreigner in this country, but lost all connections with the one he came from, leaving him firmly in no man's land between two homes.

Zach kept the old man's pace down the patio stairs, and that pace was slower than the last time he'd visited. The realization made his heart heavy.

"How ya feelin'?" Nino asked, looking directly at Zach's scar. He never beat around the proverbial bush, this old man. Right to the heart of the matter, every time.

"Fine."

"Still burning?"

He brushed his cheek. "Always, Nino. Like a hot poker."

"No relief?"

"Certain things relieve it." Sam's cheek and hair. Sam's skin. Sam's palm. Then why did the pain seem worse since Sam showed up? "What's on your mind?" Zach asked, hating the subject of his injury.

"Where's JP?" Nino asked.

"Probably taking pictures of Chessie's dented car so he can blackmail her."

Nino snorted. "He's just pissed off because you have a pretty girlfriend and he doesn't."

"She's not my girlfriend." Lying to Nino was pretty much out of the question, but telling him the truth wasn't an option either.

"But you managed to get her back." He gave a knowing smile. "I don't know what makes me happier. Seeing you with her again or the fact that you actually listened to me and took my advice."

"Don't get excited about either one. I didn't take your advice and I didn't get her back." He put his hand on Nino's mottled arm. "She dropped into my lap, and she's about to drop right out of it again."

"But she forgives you, right?"

"Doubtful."

Nino frowned. "If you think that little scratch on your face is gonna lose her, I'll have to give you a matching one on the right side."

"It's way more complicated than that."

His uncle turned and cupped Zach's face in his beefy fingers. "How many times I gotta tell you? If she loves you, she won't see your flaws."

"There's no love involved," he said. "And calling a scar of mutilated flesh where there once was an eye a 'flaw' is like..." He just shook his head out of the grip, not even able to think of an analogy. "Forget it, Nino."

"That's all it is," Nino insisted. "A flaw. So what? I got big ears and hands the size of dinner plates. You think that kept your great-aunt Monica from jumping my ugly bones? And that woman, she could jump with the best."

"I think big extremities are generally a plus." Zach was losing his patience, wanting to get Marc alone, who was deep in conversation with Uncle Jim. "Is this what you wanted to talk about?"

"One of the things. What did I tell you when you got back from that war?" It was always "that war" with Nino. "What did I tell you before you left?"

"I don't remember," he lied. "You plied me with homemade wine and I said things I didn't mean."

"Ehh!" Nino waved a hand in Italian disdain. "You said the truth and we both know it."

"Come on, Nino. I was drunk, about to deploy, and deep into it with the sexiest woman I'd met in forever. Don't hold me to what I said that night. Everything changed in Iraq." Why had he confessed so much to Nino that night? He wasn't in love with Sam. It had been... good, satisfying sex. That's all. She knew it; he knew it. Nino lived in dreamland thinking it was more.

"Oh, it's more than that," Nino said, confirming Zach's suspicions. "I can tell by the way she looks at you."

"Then your vision's worse than mine." He hesitated a beat, the impact of how it would feel to lie to this man hitting him hard. He'd trust Nino with his life, and Sam's. Still, he'd promised her that no one in the family would know. "It's just temporary."

"What is it with you and the backing off?" Nino's voice was surprisingly strong, his face reddened with emotion. "You love a woman, you tell her. No, not Zaccaria. He loves a woman, he ignores her." He slugged some wine, scowling over the thick-rimmed glass. "Now she's giving you a second chance and you're wallowing in self-pity like a chickenshit."

He knew better than to argue. "What else is on your mind, Nino?"

They were still out of earshot of Uncle Jim and Marc, but Nino lowered his voice anyway. "It's about Gabriel."

"Have you heard from him?"

"He might be back in the country soon." Like Zach, Gabe trusted Uncle Nino with information no one else could have.

"Oh, man. That's great." He could use a shot of his favorite cousin. "When?"

"You know Gabriel. Everything in gray, nothing black, nothing white. But he's still not able to come up for air, if you know what I mean."

He meant Gabe was still dark, still working for a very shadowy division of the CIA, as he had been for almost as long as Zach had been in the Army. In September 2001, they'd each had their own way of reacting to what happened in the world. Zach had dropped out of college and joined the Army; Gabe had parlayed a low-level position in the State Department into a job as a spook.

"You mean even when he's on U.S. soil, no one can see him or know what he's doing."

"Exactly," Nino confirmed. "So he won't be able to come home, and he has to have a nice, safe place to live." Nino reached into his pocket and pulled out a key. "He asked me to do him a favor and rent something safe and clean."

Meaning CIA-approved.

"It's in Jamaica Plain," Nino said. "And since you two are so close and he trusts you, I thought maybe you could head on over there and, you know, mop it up a bit." In other words, sweep for bugs. "Then you could stay there, instead of on your sister's office floor."

His temporary state of living drove Nino crazy, but

it wasn't the living arrangement for Zach that suddenly made him smile. "It's totally safe?"

"Gabe had to get his higher-ups to do the usual wrangling, but the address doesn't show up on any GPS systems, and the owners don't really exist, if you know what I mean."

Nino didn't realize it, but he was handing him a safe house for Sam. "And no one cares if I stay there... or if anyone visits?"

"Visits? I'd be very careful with that. But I wouldn't give you this key if I thought it was a problem, Zaccaria." He put a single key in Zach's palm. "And if your friend Sam is truly trustworthy and you don't tell her much in the way of details, then you may have company."

"What about Marc?" He'd have to know why Zach had this hideaway house.

"Just you, Zaccaria."

Another reason not to give Marc the job.

"Hey!" The bark came from out of the woods, so sharp, Zach pivoted in one second, his hands fisted, his body poised for attack.

JP came walking out from between the trees, a cell phone to his ear.

"Now what?" Zach muttered, dropping his hands but not the urge to use them.

"Is it possible there's something you're not telling us about your girlfriend?" JP kept walking, purpose powering a cocky stride. "Is there?" he demanded.

JP came to a stop and punched his phone, sliding it into his pocket. "Because that was a friend of mine in Boston PD," he said. "You'll never guess what he told me."

"You ran a background check on her?" Nino asked.

JP looked hard at Zach. "We gotta talk, man."

Instead of slamming JP's face, he slipped his hand into his pocket and dropped the key into it. "I already know everything you're about to tell me."

"Not everything."

CHAPTER 8

Taylor Sly had money, and a lot of it. Vivi glanced at the ostentatious gold sign hanging outside the brand-new brick monster on Dartmouth Street, imagining the kind of woman who would frequent a private health club like Equinox. No woman Vivi would hang with.

Climbing the stairs, she was greeted by a receptionist with wild blond hair and bony shoulders, seated at a see-through acrylic desk that, oddly, distorted her perfect body and made her look chubby.

That had to be some kind of criminal offense at Equinox, where health was considered a mind-set, not a lifestyle. It said so on the door. Whatever it was, membership was steep.

"Welcome to Equinox," she said, a porcelain-perfect smile wavering as her gaze drifted from Vivi's head to her toes, the receptionist's lip practically curling as she eyed Vivi's black and white checked Vans. "How can I help you?"

"I have an appointment with Jagger Musenda."

The woman didn't respond, but touched a flat-panel screen in front of her, then pressed a headset so small Vivi hadn't seen it under her hair.

"Jagger, your twelve o'clock is here." She nodded to Vivi. "Have a seat."

"Can I look inside?" Vivi asked, jutting her chin to the glass doors that led to the gym.

"Jagger'll be here in just a few minutes. He'll give you a tour."

Taylor Sly's personal training session was going to end at noon, after which, if she was the creature of habit Vivi's quick research had shown her to be, she'd shower, blow dry, make up, and leave Equinox at about the same time Vivi did. If Vivi timed her tour and bogus interview of a new trainer perfectly, they'd be walking out at approximately the same time, introduced casually by the trainer. Giving Vivi access to the elusive, impossible-to-reach Taylor Sly, the woman Teddy the oversexed waiter had mentioned last night.

Taylor had been dining at Paupiette's the night of the murder; Vivi had confirmed that with Sam, although Vivi hadn't mentioned that she planned to track the woman down this morning.

As far as Vivi could tell from the stories that had run, Taylor hadn't spoken to a single journalist. The available police records—which were sketchy at best—showed Taylor had two separate police interviews this past week, about the standard amount for every patron and employee in the restaurant that night.

The owner of an elite modeling agency and a former model herself, Taylor probably wouldn't grant an interview to some investigative website. So Vivi had decided to get creative, an approach she expected would be the hallmark of the Guardian Angelinos.

Thinking about her company, she stood at the window, looking down at the mid-Sunday bustle of Back Bay, her body humming with excitement as the idea moved from concept to execution.

The Guardian Angelinos just needed one good success to get started. And now they had a client who needed protection and a crime that needed to be cracked. If she and Zach did this right, the company had a shot. Every dream had to start somewhere, right?

So whatever she got out of Taylor—if anything— wasn't going to be turned into yet another anonymous quote for the *Boston Bullet*. No, it was going in File Number One for the Guardian Angelinos.

"Viviana Angelino?" A man's voice pulled her from the thoughts. "I'm Jagger Musenda."

She'd had a blurred mental image of a man with such an unusual name, but no matter what she'd conjured up, it wouldn't have been this...big, black, or beautiful.

"They sent you from Central Casting, I'm guessing," she said, coming forward with her hand extended. He took it, engulfed hers, and grinned.

"You look like you already work out, Viviana," he said, holding the glass door for her. "Although we recommend cross trainers over skate shoes."

"It's Vivi, and I do work out. Just thinking about a switch." From the Y, where nobody gives a shit about lifestyles. "I wanted to check this place out and talk to a trainer. Maybe some of your clients." Like Taylor Sly.

"No problem. Let's start with the personal training

area, then we'll do the weights, the cycling and Pilates center, the yoga rooms, the wifi hotspot and café, and, of course, the private spa." He glanced down at her. "Your current club have a spa?"

"Not exactly."

He started his spiel, asking enough questions to force her to pay attention to him, but she was still able to check out every treadmill and elliptical for her target. Taylor Sly was nowhere in sight.

"You may be aware that there are four distinct styles of training," he said, guiding her to a mirror. He dwarfed her in size and breadth, a magnificent human from his perfectly shaped shaved head right down to his size fourteens. "The first one is—"

"Whatever you do," she said, holding his gaze in the mirror. "Is what I want to do."

He grinned. "I do everything, including fourteen hours a week of modern dance. You sure you want to go there?"

Fascinated, she turned. "I used to do ballet, but it bored the crap out of me."

"I bet it would. I hold a black belt in Shaolin Kung Fu. You'd like that."

She let out a low whistle. "Damn. I'm impressed." And getting further away from her goal here, she reminded herself. "So tell me about your clients. Who are you training today? Seems like you'd be slow on a Sunday."

"I have a few clients that insist on Sundays, and, frankly, for what we charge, they can come in any day of the week." He put an authoritative hand on her shoulder, forcing her to turn with just the pressure of his thumb. "As I was saying—"

The door to the training room opened behind them, but the mirror didn't give Vivi a view of who it was.

"Hey, Jagger, did I leave my lifting gloves in here?" a woman asked.

"I didn't see them, Ms. Sly."

Bingo. Vivi stepped away from the mirror to get a look at her. "Oh, hey. Hi."

The woman, already backing away from the door, hesitated, a baseball cap pulled so low over her face, Vivi couldn't see anything but large reflective sunglasses, high cheekbones, and a wide glossy mouth. "Hello."

Damn, she was leaving. "Are you a client of Jagger's?" Vivi stepped closer to the door. "I'd love to talk to you about the program."

She just pointed a French-tipped nail at Jagger. "He's the man, and that is all you need to know if you're looking for a trainer."

"How long have you been training with him?" Vivi got closer, adding her friendliest smile. "I really wanted to talk to some of his long-standing clients to get a reference. Can I talk to you privately for a minute?"

Very slowly, Taylor eased the sunglasses down her nose, revealing blue-green eyes fringed with dark lashes and dramatic dark brows. Eyes that had sold a lot of tubes of mascara back in the seventies, when Taylor Sly graced the pages of *Glamour* and *Cosmo*. They had some crow's feet now, but were still stunning.

"It's not a good time, Miss..."

"Angelino. When would be a good time?"

The eyes scrutinized again, slipping over Vivi's face with purpose and intent. "Not now." She pulled away and let the door close.

Vivi immediately reached for the knob, but a huge black hand closed over hers. Tight.

"She said it's not a good time."

She wrenched out of his grasp. "I really want to talk to a client of yours and she's right here."

"I can get you a list of references," he said, guiding her back to the mirror. "Don't bother that woman."

Vivi swore mentally as the window of opportunity slammed shut. As Jagger continued the four disciplines of personal training, Vivi ran through all her other options to get to Taylor Sly. Slim and none—at least, if she went through the standard channels and requested an appointment or interview.

Vivi loathed *standard* channels.

By the time Jagger had taken her through the weight room, Vivi was itching to get out and hook up with her cousin, Nicki, to drive out to Sudbury. God knew how Zach was torturing poor Sam by now.

"Thanks, Jagger," she said, pointing to the glass doors of the lobby. "I'm going to pass on the spa today; this place is going to be out of my price range."

He gave her a long, curious look, following her out. "Then why did you come in?"

She liked him, and that was a fact. Not only was he physical perfection, he was very cool and had a nice, easy sense of humor. And most of all, she liked to keep her lies to a minimum because she really did believe that St. Peter was counting and one too many would send her the wrong way when all was said and done.

"I wanted to talk to Taylor Sly."

Surprising her, a smile pulled at his lips. "You should have just said so."

She gave him an apologetic look. "Sorry to take up your time."

He reached into his back pocket and pulled out a pair of fingerless leather gloves. "Unless I'm wrong, and I rarely am, she's in a limo in front of Starbucks, less than a block from here, while her driver gets her an iced organic chai tea. Every Sunday, Tuesday, and Thursday, like clockwork at 12:40 PM. Wave these in the window, and you might be able to talk to her."

Vivi drew back, unable to stop a smile. "Dude. I like the way you work."

"She liked your look, I could tell. Maybe you have a shot. Did you bring your portfolio?"

She realized what was happening; Jagger thought she wanted modeling representation. Which was, actually, a brilliant way to get a few minutes with the elusive Ms. Sly.

"No, but I just want an appointment. Thank you so much," she said, taking the gloves. "You rock."

He gave her a little hitch of his chin in good-bye, and she headed out to find the limo in front of Starbucks.

It was there, exactly as he'd said, double parked. She tapped on the back window, peering into blackness, not even sure anyone was in the car. No one responded, so she waved the gloves.

"I got these for you, Ms. Sly."

Instantly, the window came down and Taylor Sly leaned forward. The sunglasses and hat were gone, revealing a beautiful woman about forty-five years old. "Thank you, Ms. Angelino."

She didn't reach for the gloves, so Vivi leaned a little closer. "You think we could talk?"

"I think so, yes. Call my assistant, Anthea, for an appointment tomorrow."

Yes. "I'll do that, thank you. Don't you want your gloves?"

"They're not mine." Taylor sat back, out of sight, and the window rolled up. At the same instant, the limo pulled away, inches from Vivi's toes. She jumped up on the curb, staring at the back end as it joined the traffic...holding the gloves.

She stuffed them into her jacket and looked back at the limo, lost in traffic now.

Zach barely spoke through dinner, making Sam feel the need to keep up with the chatter at the table, which now included Vivi and Nicki, the psychologist who was second to last among the five Rossi siblings.

Marc and Vivi carried most of the conversation. Like the rest of the family, Marc was dark-haired, dark-eyed, strong-featured, and strong-minded. Sam liked him immediately, much more than the more daunting oldest Rossi, JP. As soon as she'd met Marc, Sam was comfortable with the idea of him being her bodyguard, even though Zach had yet to mention it.

Marc was friendly to her, even a little flirtatious, which seemed to make Zach even quieter. Nicki was more like JP, a watcher, not a talker, and all of them seemed deferential to their father and Uncle Nino, which, in Sam's mind, made them a typical Italian patriarchal household, with Aunt Fran the loving, affectionate, forgiving mother of them all.

Except something told Sam there was a lot more going

on in this family than standard dynamics; she just hadn't figured them all out yet. The looks that passed between JP and Zach were dark, but neither said a word to the other. Chessie chattered and Nicki opined, Uncle Jim made the occasional dry remark, and Vivi was like a live wire that kept them all electrified.

As soon as the meal ended, Zach folded his napkin, thanked his uncle, and pushed his chair back. "Guests get cleanup passes," he said. "I'll play you a game of Eight Ball, Sammi."

The nickname caught her off guard, as did the suggestion. Had he even talked to Marc yet? Maybe that was his plan—the pass-off over billiards. Because there was certainly no discussion of her situation at the table, and she hadn't seen him talk privately to Marc at all, just Ninq and Vivi, when she arrived. Now, Marc was in the kitchen with Vivi and Chessie.

In the flurry of activity, people leaving, cleaning, finishing the discussion, Sam followed Zach to a finished basement set up with a wide-screen TV, a bar, and a gorgeous rosewood pool table. The size and well-used comfort of the room suggested this was as much a gathering place for the Rossis as the kitchen, but for the moment, the family had left them alone.

Wordlessly, Zach took down a pool cue and chalk, then racked the balls.

"I think you forgot to mention something to Marc," she said, leaning against the wall to watch him.

"I didn't forget."

"When are you going to ask him?"

He looked up from the opposite side of the table, the Tiffany-style light casting a gold and red glow on his face, the eye patch looking more menacing than usual. "I don't like his car."

She choked a soft laugh. "Seriously?"

"I thought I'd talk to him about driving something safer."

"When?"

"You want to break?"

"I want an answer. When?"

"I'll break." He came around, lined up the cue, and scattered the balls, knocking one in. "That was the fourteen. I'm stripes."

"Zach. You changed your mind, didn't you?"

He didn't answer for a moment, studying the pattern of balls on the table. But something told her he wasn't thinking about his next shot. "I just don't see any real benefit to bringing someone else into this."

"You saw plenty of benefit on the way out here. What changed?"

He glanced at her. "Would you hate it that much if I decided to stick around and protect you?"

Part of her would. The part with the job of guarding her heart and using common sense. Other parts—like every female hormone in her body—didn't seem to mind being around him at all. Longed for more, in fact.

She dug for the heart-guarding, common-sense-wielding part, taking her own pool cue from the stand on the wall. "What about the safe house?"

"I got one. We'll leave here and go there."

Her jaw unhinged. "How did you do that?"

"I have connections." He lined up a shot of the ten ball in the corner pocket.

"Good ones." JP's voice just beat Zach's shot, making

him hit too hard, miss the shot, and send the cue ball into the pocket.

Slowly, he straightened and turned as his cousin entered the game room. "Private party, JP. See ya."

"Connections in the police department," JP said to Sam, his midnight eyes boring through her. "Can't beat those when you're escorting an eyewitness around town."

Sam tightened her hand around the pool cue. "So you know."

"You didn't tell her yet?" he asked Zach.

"Tell me what?" She looked from one to the other.

"Nothing you don't already know, Sam, believe me."

But she didn't believe him, leveling her gaze on JP, a solid bear of a man with a thick neck, short hair. He wasn't quite as handsome as the rest of the family, more rugged and tough looking, imposing in a different way than Zach and Marc. For a second, she wondered about the missing Gabe, who was barely spoken of, but dragged her attention back to the conversation.

"Why don't you fill me in, JP, so I can decide if I already know it or not."

"You want to tell her or should I?" JP asked Zach.

"JP thinks he found some kind of mysterious notation in your police file, Sam." Zach took another shot, apparently forgetting that the rules of the game made it her shot. "He claims someone has put you on a secret list of witnesses notated with something called the Triple I."

Sam felt the blood drain from her head a little. Obviously JP knew everything about the situation...and more. "The Triple I?" she asked. "What does that mean?"

"When there's a witness of…" JP tilted his head toward Sam, with a mix of apology and accusation. "Questionable credibility—"

"There's nothing questionable about her credibility," Zach ground out, turning from the table to glare at his cousin.

"—*perceived* questionable credibility, they might get put on a TI list, with the goal of loading that person's file with anything that will impeach, intimidate, or prove incentive to lie when the case comes to court."

Sam let the words roll around her head. *Impeach, intimidate, or prove incentive to lie.* Lovely.

"Zach's right," she said. "I do already know this. Not as some formal notation in my file, obviously, but I've known for a long time that I have enemies in the Boston PD."

"So you can leave now, JP," Zach said.

"Wait." Sam took a step toward him. "I have a question for you. Just how 'intimidating' can this intimidation be? Because, to be honest, all you've made me want to do is fight back."

Zach shot her a look over his pool cue. "Don't even think about it, Sam. Are you forgetting that a cruiser passed you just seconds before some clown jumped you last night? You think that was a coincidence?"

Her heart skipped at the thought. "Oh. I never made that connection."

"I did," Zach said, his focus back on JP. "I've never been all that impressed with Boston's finest. Who in the PD benefits when a witness for the prosecution is discredited, by the way?"

"In this case?" JP notched his brow. "Friends of

officers who've lost their jobs because of this witness's testimony."

"It wasn't my testimony that got me enemies," Sam said, vaguely aware that Zach was coming closer to her to line up his next shot. But it felt like a move of solidarity and protection as he closed the space between them.

"It was her work to exonerate a wrongfully accused and incarcerated man that got officers fired," Zach said. "And if this 'Triple I' bullshit really does exist somewhere other than your imagination, the cops who put it together should be fired."

"Most of them have been," JP replied coolly. "And for God's sake, Zach, I'm just the messenger. Don't shoot me. Your principal could be caught in friendly fire."

"She won't be." In front of Sam, he leaned forward to line up another shot.

"Because you're protecting her? With no gun and one—"

Zach smacked the cue ball, slamming a striped ball into the pocket with a thud. "Yes. I am."

"Listen to me, Zach. I want to help you."

"Mmm." The sound was rich with doubt as Zach walked away, rounding the table and chalking the end of the stick. "I've been on the receiving end of your help a few times in the past. No thanks."

"I know Quentin O'Hara," JP said.

At the name of the lead detective on the Sterling case, Sam stepped closer to the table, and JP. "You do?"

"Frankly, I think he's a damn good cop," JP continued, turning to her. "Have you dealt much with him?"

"A little," she said, thinking about the police detective who'd been her main contact since she'd witnessed the murder. "He took my statement the day after the murder and brought me in to the South End station three times last week to review it. He went in and out of the room while I looked at pictures of possible suspects and…" She tried to remember how much she'd seen of him on her last trip to the station. "He might have been there when I met with a sketch artist, but I think that was his partner, Detective Larkin. There were too many cops around for me to be certain."

"And you're nervous when you're there," JP said sympathetically. "Understandable. I don't know Larkin, but I know O'Hara. He's kind of a hardass, I'll give you that, but a straight shooter. So, just to be on the safe side, I'll do some very, very quiet digging around."

For a moment, Zach didn't answer, still sizing up his cousin as though trying to decide where to land a punch. Then he nodded once, which felt, to Sam, like a huge concession.

"In the meantime," JP added, pointing an assertive finger at Sam but looking at Zach, "get her somewhere safe and keep her under constant surveillance. The guy who did this was a professional; almost no one on this case disputes that. We got a trained killer on our hands, and if he needs to get rid of a witness to finish the job, he will. In Sam's case, it's just easier for him if the cops are looking the other way, making it even more dangerous for her."

"Thanks for the advice," Zach said, his tone flat enough that Sam couldn't tell if it was sarcastic or not.

JP headed out, then paused at the door, looking at Sam. "Let me ask you a question, Sam. *Could* you ID the killer in a lineup?"

Wasn't that the million-dollar question? "I'm not sure," she said honestly. "I've made a mistake in the past."

"We all have. At some point, you just have to move on." He gave her a tight smile. "Let me know if you need anything. You, too, Zach."

Zach gave a noncommittal grunt as he missed an easy shot. With a shrug, he put the cue stick back and walked over. "You can get the three in the corner, if you use a little English."

"Zach, aren't you at all concerned about this notation thing he's talking about?"

"I take everything JP says with a boulder of salt." He put his hands on her shoulders and inched her closer. "Lean over."

The order, delivered in her ear with just enough force to ruffle her hair, sent chills down her body. From behind, he engulfed her, wrapping his arms around her to hold the cue stick with her, leaning her forward so her backside nestled into his crotch.

"Now aim the cue at that cushion, see? Halfway between the pockets. It should bounce right off and hit the three into the side."

She couldn't even find the three ball. The sea of green felt before her practically disappeared at the heat of his body making full contact with hers.

"Zach…"

"Just take the shot, Sam."

"You're not going to ask Marc, are you?"

She felt him exhale, more warm breath on her cheek. "I can't."

The little hitch in his voice tore her heart. "You can't or you won't?"

"Both. I can't trust anyone else to do the job as thoroughly as it needs to be done. And...I won't...tempt you or us to do anything. You have my word."

She let out a soft laugh. "What exactly do you think you're doing right now?" Tempting the hell out of her.

"I'm playing pool." He pulled the stick back and whacked it, totally controlling the shot while she did nothing. "We're going to have to do something to pass the time."

The way he said "something" make her insides roll like the cue ball over the felt as it hit the cushion; then the three clunked right into the pocket.

He didn't let her go.

She tried to straighten. "Well, we're not going to do this."

"Play pool?"

"Play full body contact."

He eased up, but didn't let go. "I want to be the one to keep you safe, Sammi." His voice was low and soft and intimate. "Me. Not Marc. Not anyone else." It sounded like the admission pained him.

"But this isn't safe," she said, turning her face enough so that their cheeks brushed. "This..." Was going to hurt so much when it was over. Didn't he realize that? "Scares me."

Very slowly, he stepped back, breaking all contact. "I knew I scared you."

He meant his eye, his scar. She meant something else completely. "You've already hurt me once, Zach," she whispered as she turned to face him.

"This is different."

Different? It didn't feel different. Her blood was on

fire. Her pulse was jumping. Her skin was electrified. Her hands were aching to touch him. And her mouth? Hot for a kiss. It wasn't any different from the last time they were together, only this time, she knew the cost of all that lovely sensuality.

"I just don't know if this is a good idea for us to be... isolated." *Weak.* She sounded as weak as she felt.

"You prefer Marc, then?" His voice was gruff, his brow drawn in a dark frown. "With perfect vision, a master shot, and no messy history to muddy the waters?"

Yes, yes, a thousand times yes. "No." Oh, God. "I just don't want to get hurt again."

"The whole purpose is to ensure that you *don't* get hurt."

Was he playing games or did he really not get it? She'd been devastated by his disappearance. "Then tell me what happened," she said, surprising herself with the request. "I have to know or else I can't trust you again."

He touched his scar, shaking his head. "Can't. It's classified."

"Not your injury. Mine. Here." She touched her heart. "Why did you walk out and then... nothing? Why did you do that to me, Zach?"

Pain darkened his face. "It's not important."

"It is to me," she shot back. "I can't go hole up with you in some safe house without knowing, Zach. I have to know."

"You already know; you just don't realize it."

She closed her eyes with a soft exhale. "Things need to be said, Zach, and I want you to say them." It was the only way she could survive.

"Nothing needs to be said." He put his hands on

her face, holding her cheeks, his fingers warm and strong and so big on her. "Can't we just forget that ever happened?"

Was he crazy? Forget those nights? That passion? The most amazing days and nights of her life? Forget them? "No," she whispered.

"Please, Sam, we can just...start over." He inched her closer, torture all over his face, agony for how bad he wanted to kiss her. She could see it, because he looked like she felt. Wanting, wanting it so much.

"Start ov—"

He stopped her words with a kiss, covering her mouth, his lips like a brand, burning, shocking.

She pulled back. "How can we start over?" she asked, her voice shaky and raspy from the impact of the kiss. "We never finished."

"Yes, we did." He stepped back, fast and hard, leaving her cold and achy. "Not neatly, maybe, but we did."

"Zach, ple—"

He cut her off with a wave, clearly angry with his lack of control. "Look, I'm...I won't do that again. I won't," he promised. "I won't kiss you again, Sam."

As he walked out of the room, she just stared at the doorway, aching from her mouth straight down to every other body part that had just been teased by his touch.

"I hope not," she said. But deep inside, she knew that was a lie.

CHAPTER 9

He waited in the bushes for fifteen minutes, watching the couple stare at Fox News in their living room, a little Yorkie asleep on the sofa next to the old lady. Then Levon glanced at the upstairs apartment and felt relatively certain it was empty. Relatively.

Because who'd stay home waiting for a killer to drop by and do his thing? Understandable that Miss Samantha Fairchild would hide. Giving him plenty of time to do some research. Because the more he knew about a victim, the easier it was to do his job and not leave a shred of evidence.

And that was why he was the Czar.

He considered his options. That dog had to pee sometime, so one of the old folks would probably come out to the front, leaving the door to the building open. Levon might be able to slip in, run up the stairs, and break into the upstairs apartment. But that was a little riskier than he liked.

His best bet was the back, he decided after circling. It would take some climbing, but he could get up there. Still, he waited until the dog jumped off the sofa and the man stood, complaining.

At that moment, he hustled around the back, eyed the balcony, and tried to figure out how to get up there.

Which he did in very little time, clearing the back window just as the light in that bathroom came on. He had to hang for a few seconds while Mama relieved herself; then she left the room, and he took the chance of making some noise, using the drainpipe and pulling himself up to Samantha Fairchild's back door.

It wasn't chain locked; another sign she wasn't home. He picked the lock in less than three minutes, leaving no outward signs that anything other than a key had done the job, opening the door carefully in case there was an alarm that would require him to jump and run.

Silence.

He slipped inside and glanced around, moving stealthily to the front door, also unchained. And, oh, that was cute. She kept a plant by the door so if anyone came in and knocked it over, she'd see spilled dirt.

So, she was scared. And on guard. That would make it more difficult, but not impossible. Finding Ms. Fairchild had been laughably easy; killing her would be simple, too. He preferred not to do it in her home, although he certainly would if that was the most expedient way. But the Czar's MO was always to do his work in the most crowded place. Like a busy restaurant on a Saturday night, where there were so many, many possible suspects.

And, preferably, no witness. Sadly, this one had complicated his life and job, so she had to die. But first, he needed some information about his victim.

He stood in the living room, letting his eyes adjust, taking it in. He examined the bookcase, always a good way to learn a little about a person. Her tastes ran to legal thrillers—probably where she learned the plant trick—and romance. Some family pictures, Mom and Dad, two much older brothers. No family of her own.

Oh, and look at that. A whole shelf of law books. *Surviving Justice...Wrongly Convicted...When Justice Goes Wrong...True Stories of False Confessions*. There must have been twenty books on the same subject.

Levon looked around, ignoring the simple, cozy furnishings, and headed toward the hallway to the bedroom. One room was a quasi-office, guest, storage thing with...more books about the legal system. On the bulletin board, front and center, a letter from Harvard Law School.

Dear Ms. Fairchild...congratulations, you have been accepted...

How nice for her.

Next to the acceptance letter, a yellowed newspaper clipping with a picture of a black guy flanked by a woman and a man. He skimmed the caption. William Shawkins, freed after ten years in prison...his attorney, Joseph Wahl...his accuser, Samantha Fairchild.

His *accuser*?

A few hairs on his neck rose and a smile broke across his face. So she was no rookie in the witness business. That painted everything in a very different color now, didn't it? He took a long, hard look at Shawkins, who hugged Samantha, beaming at her. That required a little more research.

He left the office, stepped into the hall, and was headed toward the bedroom when the front door at the bottom of the stairs opened and the dog started barking, loud.

Not a chance that Yorkie could smell him up here, so someone must have arrived. He heard voices, one female and too young to belong to the lady downstairs.

He touched the gun in his pocket, silenced and ready. Christ, he hated to do a job like this. No matter how careful he was, he'd leave evidence. A hair, a footprint, something. There were so many better ways.

Still, opportunity might be knocking, and the faster he could be done, the sooner he could be paid.

He headed back out to the kitchen. He could wait on the balcony, maybe jump her when she was in the shower. Assuming she was alone. Of course, she could have a man with her.

Then... oh, hell. What was one more dead? Maybe he could make it look like a murder-suicide. He'd done that once, in that job in Phoenix. Worked real well.

The dog was quiet now, but that didn't guarantee anything. He opened the back door and slipped out onto the little wooden deck, closing the door without making a sound.

Zach had reluctantly agreed to go to Sam's apartment for some clothes and sundries, as long as she wore the Cleopatra wig and they were in and out in a minute, dragging out the process by passing her house once, then snaking through the streets, taking a backward route and ultimately parking across the street behind the house.

The wig gave her a headache, and so did his relative

silence the whole trip. They'd only said what was necessary; no discussion of the family, no replay of the day's events, nothing intimate or warm. Which was probably the real cause of her headache.

She took him through the opening in the fence and showed him the balcony where she'd jumped. He gave her a nod that said he was impressed, but, as with the entire ride from Sudbury to Vivi's and during the whole process of his gathering some necessities before they came here, he barely said a word.

It was as if he didn't trust himself to say anything. The kiss, his unwillingness to trade out the job to Marc, the whole day and evening just hung over them like a dark, ominous cloud.

More reason to hate the idea of being trapped in a safe house in Jamaica Plain for God knows how long, Sam thought as they came around the front. As she unlocked the front door that led to her stairs, the Brodys' door popped open and Sam jumped back with a soft gasp.

Zach instantly moved to block Sam.

"Who are you?" Mrs. Brody demanded. Behind her, Nutmeg yapped so loud Sam practically had to yell.

"It's me, Mrs. Brody." Sam inched out and pulled off the wig.

The other woman's eyes flew wide as they darted from Sam to Zach, finally settling on her, but not until she'd taken a few more uncertain looks at Zach. "What are you doing?"

"Costume party," Sam said quickly. "And I'm going to be away for a few days, so can you get my mail?"

"Of course." She couldn't stop her gaze from moving

to Zach, who nudged Sam up the stairs, pressing against her to force her up faster.

"Thanks, Mrs. B.," she called over her shoulder. "We're kind of in a hurry."

"What's he supposed to be? A monster?"

Every muscle in his body tensed against her as he hesitated imperceptibly in his step. Sam just reached down and grabbed his hand, pulling him. "Come on. Let's go."

"Wait, Sam, I have your mail." Mrs. Brody reached inside and produced a fat bunch of envelopes, magazines, and catalogs. Sam hadn't gone out for mail for days, and her bills and the Victoria's Secret catalog were the last thing on her mind.

She gathered the handful of mail and stuffed it under her arm, heading upstairs.

At the top of the steps, she unlocked the door, the keys shaking just a tiny bit in her hand. "If I open the door very, very slowly, the plant won't tip over. If it already is, then..." Then someone had been in her apartment. But that's not why she was shaking.

Mrs. Brody's words echoed in the empty stairwell. *A monster.*

"I'll go in first," he said, inching her aside.

He didn't have a gun, but his body was taut enough with unreleased tension that if anyone was hiding inside, Sam had a feeling Zach would kill him with his bare hands.

He opened the door very slowly, dragging the plant across the wood floor, not spilling any dirt. So at least no one had come in this way. Still, Sam waited by the door as he went in and looked around.

"There's no one here," Zach said when he returned. "Come in and get what you need fast."

She slipped by him, scanning the living room and dining area, pausing to drop the mail on the kitchen counter, breathing out a soft sigh at the sight of her modest apartment. Home was comforting again, even though it had been so scary for a week. Now she had Zach, and felt secure.

But she wanted to move fast, regardless of how nice it was to be home. She headed to her bedroom, mentally listing what she'd need, opening the closet to grab an overnight bag and start packing.

In less than ten minutes, she had clothes, basic cosmetics, shoes, and her laptop packed up and ready to go. Zach hadn't even walked into the room to check on her. Slipping the bag over her shoulder, she took a quick look around her room, longing for a safety net that had somehow been yanked from her.

He was gone when she walked back in the living room. "Zach?" Her heart dipped as she spun around and saw the kitchen door wide open. "Are you out there?"

He didn't answer and she tensed, listening. She startled when his head popped around from outside; he was on the balcony. "This door was unlocked."

"No, it wasn't. I'm sure of that, Zach. I turned the..." *Had* she? Good God, would she ever trust her memory for details again? Just like a witness to swear under oath she'd locked the door when she left. Of course she had. She'd left a plant by the front, so she wouldn't have slipped out and jumped the balcony without locking the door.

Would she have?

"I was pretty upset and scared," she admitted. "Maybe I forgot to lock it."

"Or maybe someone picked their way in."

Another dip of her heart. She looked around, everything exactly as she'd left it. Wouldn't she sense if someone had been there?

"Let's go," he said, pulling the door closed and locking it carefully. He brushed by her, moving toward the living room. "You want your mail?"

"I guess." She yanked open one of the drawers where she kept plastic supermarket bags. As she grabbed one, she thought she heard a noise on the back patio, loud enough to make her freeze in the act of stuffing the mail into the bag. She looked hard at the door, half expecting it to be kicked open.

"What's the matter?" Zach asked, coming back into the kitchen.

"I heard something out there."

He frowned, looking and listening. "I was just out there."

"An animal, maybe?" Her heart and head throbbed in syncopation now. "Let's just get out of here, Zach. It feels spooky."

"Let me look. Step back." He unlocked the door and opened it slowly, his shoulders taut, a hand fisted, his boot placed to make a swift kick. He jumped outside hard enough to scare anyone or anything, then looked from side to side. For a second, he disappeared from her sight as he walked to the side where she'd jumped. Then he came back in, shaking his head.

"Nothing. Let's go."

She nodded and followed him to the front door. Going

this way eliminated her clever plant scheme, but it didn't matter. She wasn't coming back here until this whole thing was over.

Downstairs, they passed the Brodys' door without incident, but her landlady's comment still pressed on Sam's heart as they rounded the house and walked toward the backyard to leave through the fence, the way they had come.

"Listen, Zach, I'm really sorry about my neighbor." She didn't mean to have pity in her voice, but it came out. His jaw clenched in response. "I'm sure she really just thought you were dressed for a costume party, too."

"Whatever, Sam. Let's just go."

The tone in his voice made her shoulders slump as she hustled to keep up with him. "You don't think I look at you that way, do you?"

"I really don't think about it," he said, stepping it up. "I want to get out of here fast. Let's go."

She grabbed his arm. "Zach, wait a second. Talk to me."

"Not now, Sam." He gave her a little nudge forward. "Get to the fence."

"God damn you," she muttered, walking toward the fence ahead of him. "How can you be brooding over some inane comment from my landlady?"

"I'm not brooding."

She slowed her step and turned to force the issue. "You're not a monster." She reached up and put both her hands on his face, feeling the muscles tense under her touch. "You're not."

He just stared at her.

"You're *not*," she repeated, frustrated that he wouldn't answer.

"Are you finished yet?"

"No." She yanked him closer, covering her lips with his, kissing him with all the fury and fear that raged in her.

He...didn't respond. Nothing. No kiss, no tongue, no movement, nothing.

Cold inside, she slowly inched back, still holding his face in her hands. She stared at him for three, four, five interminable seconds.

"Now I'm finished," she whispered. Brokenhearted, mortified, furious, and finished.

"I thought we agreed no more of that."

"I was making a point."

"So was I."

Fury fired through her veins. "All right. Fine. Let's go." She marched to the fence, lifting the boards that created an opening, sensing he wasn't right behind her. She climbed through, then stepped aside, holding the fence slat up for him. But he was still in the yard, ten feet behind.

"Be that way." She let the boards snap back down into place, then started into the alley.

"Sam, wait."

She ignored the order, just as an engine screamed, lights blinding her as a car whipped into the alley a few houses away.

She turned, caught in the glare, frozen as the lights got brighter and the growling engine louder.

"Sam!" Zach leaped across the alley, slamming into her, throwing her down to the ground just as the car bore down on them. He rolled her out of the way, stones stabbing her back as Zach got them both out of the path of the speeding car.

A scream of terror caught in her throat as the crack of a gunshot split her eardrums. Another shot popped as the car passed and a third before it disappeared down the other end of the alley.

For one breathless second, they didn't move. Then Zach leaped, grabbing her by the arm and pulling her with him. "Move it!"

The wig tumbled off as they ran, tearing between houses, the wind whistling in her ears as they made their way to his car. He hesitated at the street, checking out both directions, but there was no sign of the dark vehicle that had almost run them down or the driver who had shot at them.

"Let's go." He pulled her toward his big gold car, yanking the back door open and shoving her in. "Lie down," he ordered, climbing in to drive.

"Is he following us?"

He floored it so hard, her whole body slammed against the backseat. "Just stay on the floor, Sam, and don't get up until I tell you."

From the shadows of the next yard, the Czar prayed as hard as he'd ever prayed before. And his prayers were answered. The footsteps picked up, a car engine started—a good German one, too, judging from the sound of it—and tires squealed as it took off.

He couldn't see from where he hid, but all that told him that the bastards had missed their shot.

The fuckers were trying to kill his witness so they didn't have to pay him. Levon didn't like that. He didn't like that one bit. He'd get her long before they did.

Disgust rolled through him at the amateur effort. Firing like a bunch of gangsters in the alleyway. How graceless was that? He could do this so much more creatively. And now, he had a nice little piece of bait that they were far too stupid to use.

CHAPTER 10

Zach flipped his pillow, adding a little punch, pressing his scarred face against the cool cotton, aching for relief. Even six months after the last surgery, the lingering sensation of prickly spears of pain never really went away.

Except when something cool and soft and dry touched it.

The pillow gave him a split second of relief; then the fire-hot needles burned again. All of him burned, actually. He slept in boxers, the sheets thrown off the completely inadequate twin bed, the windows of the second-floor bedroom wide open. Still, sweat tingled his skin, making him imagine the pleasure of a third icy shower in the lone bathroom across the hall.

Outside, the night was silent, the blue-collar town of Jamaica Plain relatively quiet at three-something in the morning. The occasional car, a dog. No real threats.

Yet.

He'd done a fine job of assuring Sam they were safe, telling her just enough about his cousin Gabe to make sure she believed that if this house was safe enough to meet his standards, it was safe enough for them. He'd combed every inch of the house, checked the usual places and the unusual, and felt certain it was clean, especially knowing that if Gabe's people had found it, they'd probably swept it thoroughly too.

And he was absolutely certain no one had followed them from Somerville.

Wasn't he?

Fuck. Why did he keep questioning his capabilities? Maybe because while he was standing in her yard behaving like a miserable dick and feeling sorry for himself, she had marched right into the line of fire. Would Marc have let that happen?

No, he wouldn't have.

And yet, Zach had stubbornly refused to give up a job he didn't want in the first place.

Why?

Swearing softly, he turned again. Burn. Press. Soothe. Burn again.

Why did he refuse to leave Sam under someone else's watchful eye—*eyes*? Why had he ever let her go in the first place? He'd done such a great job of convincing himself it was the right thing to do that when he looked into her deep blue eyes...all he could do was wonder what the hell he was thinking when he made that sweeping, lasting, selfish decision.

But when he looked into the mirror, he knew it was the right thing to do, selfish or not.

He heard a noise upstairs, and he propped up on his

elbows, listening. Her soft sigh, maybe. A shudder after crying?

A memory punched, shockingly clear. He could see his own hand twisting the shower faucet in Sam's apartment in predawn darkness. He hadn't turned on a light in the bathroom, didn't want to wake her. But he could hear her strangled sobs, muffled into the pillow. He knew he should march out to that bedroom, take her in his arms, tell her.

But he couldn't. Instead, he'd flipped the cold water on, and just stood in the prickly, painful spray until he knew she'd stopped crying. Until his own silent tears were washed away. Until he could go get dressed, and leave for Kuwait, and pretend he hadn't heard her.

Just like he was doing tonight.

He listened again, but the house was quiet. He'd left the door to his tiny bedroom open, so he could hear anything. Pretty easy since the three-story walk-up couldn't be much more than twelve or thirteen hundred square feet total, with three rooms for living, eating, and cooking on the first floor, this one and a bathroom on the second, and Sam's room alone at the top.

Still shaken and finally done trying to get him to talk, she'd headed upstairs when they arrived, and remained there all evening and into the night.

Which should be a relief to him, but just felt like…*punishment*.

He'd heard her taking a shower while he sat in the dark downstairs and ate cold leftovers and nursed a beer he'd snagged from Vivi's place. She went back to her third-floor room after her shower, while he made the rounds and checked every door and window again, finally going to bed. If she moved, even paced her bedroom floor, he'd hear her, since every other floorboard in this hundred-year-old house squeaked. He welcomed any sound, if only to block out the memory of her voice still in his head.

You're not a monster. You're not.

And then, that kiss. So different from the one he'd given her. His was desperate, a plea for a second chance he didn't deserve. Hers was...tender.

The thing was, every kiss with Sam was different. He remembered that, from the first one. He draped his arm over his face and drifted back. Vivi's bathroom. That party. Sam's sexy laugh, her I-dare-you-to-follow-me look. And, Christ, he had. Like a hound dog on a scent trail.

He'd knocked on the bathroom door, pushing it in, just like he had this morning. She'd put lipstick on her bottom lip, glossy, wet, making that sweet swell of flesh even more edible. In five seconds, that gloss was gone. In five minutes, so was her top. In five hours, he was inside her for the third time that night.

His balls throbbed at the memory, and he flipped over again, hating this new annoyance on his body. He smashed the unwanted erection against the bed with a soft groan.

If only she'd come downstairs and they could...

No, she deserved more than sex, even if it was great sex. She deserved more than his vague answers to her questions, even if it really was all he could offer. And she deserved more than him, even if he wanted her with a need so intense, it hurt.

He bit the pillow to stave off growling in frustration,

to keep from grinding his wood into the mattress and howling for her. Anything to stop himself from throwing off the sheets and climbing those stairs and telling her what he needed.

Something told him he could convince her, too. The chemistry was still sizzling between them, a slow simmer that one touch would spark into more. Maybe he should go up there. Maybe it could be "just sex" again, couldn't it? Just another round of wild, fast, furious fucking. He could satisfy her need for talking with five minutes of meaningless conversation and five hours of what they both wanted and needed.

What *he* needed, anyway.

Who was he kidding? He needed so much more than that with Sam. He took a deep, slow breath and pressed his burning cheek on the pillow, torn by what he wanted and what he knew he should do. Was she this ripped apart?

Upstairs, a bare foot hit the top step.

He reached to the nightstand, grabbed his patch, and looped it over his head, positioning the protective flap between his brow and cheekbone, the elastic so tight the piece flattened the scar tissue of knotted skin where his eye used to be.

Sam moved slowly, as if she were trying to avoid making noise, but she failed. His hearing was too good, and he could count which stair she was on. Then she paused just outside his open door, no doubt listening for the sound of his sleep.

Or planning to come in...

After a second, she went into the bathroom, and light spilled from under the door. He came up on his elbows, listening to the toilet flush, water flow from the faucet, a soft sigh as he imagined her rinsing her face, drying it.

He pictured her pouring water on his face, soothing his fiery pain. That would be bliss. Then laying her cheek against his. More bliss. Then laying her body against his...way past bliss.

She turned the light out before she opened the door, obviously not wanting to wake him. After a moment, she continued down, her feet brushing softly over the stairs.

He sat up, ready to follow.

He listened to her movements in the kitchen, getting up and walking to the hall to make sure she didn't turn on a light or open a door. Was she safe alone down there?

Probably safer than if he went marching down with a boner sticking through his boxers. She was hungry, no doubt. The sounds drifting upstairs confirmed that, a soft tap of a plate on the counter, the roll of a drawer, the screech of an old oven door.

He could monitor her movements from here, and let her eat in peace. She deserved that.

"Oh! My God!"

He bolted into the hallway, pausing for a fraction of a second to balance on the two handrails and vault down the whole staircase in one long leap. Landing on the balls of his feet, hands splayed for attack, body taut with aggression, he lunged around the corner to the kitchen where she squatted on a chair, a look of horror on her face as she stared at the ground.

"We have visitors," she said in a shaky voice, sleep-mussed hair casting shadows over her face. "Maybe a whole family of them."

"Jesus." He lowered his hands and flexed the fingers he'd just stiffened, ready to kill.

"I'm sorry I woke you. A mouse just ran over my foot and scared the crap out of me."

He scanned the linoleum, where a gray mouse cowered on the floor, shaking. "He's more scared of you."

"I know, I know." She let out an embarrassed laugh. "And I feel like a complete cliché jumping on a chair."

He bent over, hands open. The mouse scurried left, following the warped boards under the cabinets. "There are more?"

"One under the sink, one...I don't know."

He crouched, blocking the mouse's escape with one hand and waiting for the perfect instant to..."Got him." He clipped the tail, snagging him.

"Oh!" She backed up on the chair as he stood, dangling it. "Ew. Don't kill it, Zach."

He looked over the mouse at her. "No? That's how you get rid of them, you know."

"Can you take him outside?" She flicked her fingers. "Then maybe you can find the other two and send them all out together."

He smiled at her. "I had no idea you were such an animal rights activist."

"I'm just...compassionate. But get that thing out of here, will you?"

"Don't move."

"Fat chance."

He unlocked a back door to a small stone patio and a postage-stamp-sized backyard, tossing the offender on the grass. He took a second to peer out at what wasn't exactly the most high-security yard they could have, while the adrenaline finished running its course, along with the southbound blood that had had him so erect a minute ago.

When he walked back in, Sam still had her feet up on the chair, her gaze locked downward.

"He's under the sink. I heard him scurrying around."

Zach opened the cupboard door and saw the mouse immediately, hiding in a corner, then running to the other side, away from the light. It took a minute of wrangling, but he managed to get that one, too, and deposited him with his brother.

"The last one is in the cabinets somewhere. Or escaped to their little mouse hideout."

"We'll listen for him." At the sink, he washed his hands, using a half-empty bottle of dishwashing soap left by the previous tenant. "I'll get mousetraps tomorrow."

"And kill them?"

"Unless you want to give them all names and turn them into pets, that's the usual course of action."

She made a face. "I have leftovers in the oven, but...I'm not really hungry now."

"You have to be. You haven't eaten since this afternoon, and, don't worry. There are no mice cooking in the oven." He popped open the door, the smell of red sauce and Uncle Nino's sausage wafting out. "No wonder the entire rodent population of Jamaica Plain showed up. You gotta eat this, Sam."

"No, I can't. I lost my appetite. I'll just put it back in the fridge."

"I'll do it." He grabbed the edge of the foil dish, gingerly holding it with two hands, setting it up on the gas burners of the stove. Behind him, he heard Sam leave the kitchen.

He ignored the punch of disappointment and put the food back on a shelf in the empty refrigerator, grabbing a cold Sam Adams when he did. He popped the top, took a gulp, and headed back to his miserable bed.

"That beer looks good, though." She was curled into a corner of a sofa, her arms wrapped around her legs, her whole body folded protectively around a throw pillow.

"Take this one." He walked over and gave it to her. She took the bottle with one hand and his arm with the other.

"Stay with me." She looked up at him, and even in the dark he saw her eyes were red-rimmed and a little swollen. "We can share it."

Everything human in him just wanted to hold her like she held that pillow, the fear and sadness in her voice squeezing his gut. He didn't move.

They'd shared quite a few beers together, always from the same bottle.

"I won't make you talk," she said, the soft plea still in her voice. "I just really don't want to be alone."

"'Kay."

He sat next to her, on her left, of course, so she got the better half of his profile. Still, he was close enough to feel her warmth and smell the citrus in her hair. Close enough to hear her swallow a deep drink of beer, and his whole body ached to taste the suds of Sam Adams on her lips.

True to her promise, she didn't speak. She took three long sips of beer, then offered it again. He took it, closing his mouth hungrily over the place where hers had just been.

She remained quiet, but he felt her sideways glance. He left about an inch of beer at the bottom and gave her a chance to finish it. She shook her head, so he downed the rest, the cold liquid barely squeezing through his tight throat.

He reached forward to put the bottle on the coffee table, staying in that position for a moment. Like he was about to get up. He should, of course. He should go back to bed.

Or he should scoop her in his arms, carry her up the stairs...and leave her the hell alone.

He stayed paralyzed in that position.

She sat just as still, waiting, barely breathing the thick, crackling air between them. He should go. He should go. He should—

She put a hand on his shoulder, guiding him to sit back. "You used to like to talk," she said.

He chuckled. "I knew you couldn't just sit here in silence."

"It's just that you've changed so much."

"We established that this morning. Long hair, more ink, big face slash, few words."

"That's not the only way you've changed."

He refused to look at her, knowing it would all just get deep if he did. "War changes people, Sammi."

"How did it change you?"

"You have to ask?"

"Did it change you on the inside, too?"

Was it war that had changed him? "I think that I was like this all along, and war just brought out the worst in me."

"Like what?"

He just shook his head. This was deep enough. "I'll talk, Sammi. About something else."

Her frustrated sigh was soft, but he heard it. "How about your family?"

Okay, he could do that. "You just spent the day with them, what could you possibly want to know?"

"I meant your family in Italy."

"Oh, you mean my *real* family." He said it before he realized it was out.

"The Rossis aren't your real family?"

"They get the job done," he said vaguely. "And the family in Italy, sorry, I don't know them. Left at ten, as you know, and there's nothing those Italians love more than holding a grudge. So I doubt I'll ever see any of them again."

"But there were other relatives you could have lived with when your mother died, right? You have cousins in Italy, don't you? Why didn't you go to them?"

"For one thing, there was a feud. In Italy, there's always a feud. It's a national tradition."

She laughed softly. "What was it about?"

Something stupid, but then all feuds were like that. "I think you know my father died in the 1980 earthquake."

"I did know that," she said, turning a little to face him, getting a little closer without realizing it. Her scent wafted, making him want to lean over and taste the lemons that smelled so good in her hair.

"Vivi told me that the only reason you and she and your mother lived was that you weren't at the church that night when your father was killed. That always gave me chills."

"Yep, and that's what started the feud, since that was the first Communion of one of my father's nephews, and he'd been pressured by his sister to go even though my mother couldn't. Vivi and I were not even one. My mother never forgave anyone on that side of the family, cut all ties, and moved away from Naples. That's really not that unusual over there."

"Cutting all ties? Moving away without leaving word? It seems so rash."

"It is, but she was a stubborn woman." He gave her a sideways glance, acknowledging the dig. "When she found out she had cancer," he continued, "she wrote a will that would ensure that no matter how hard they fought, the Angelino family would not get us."

"And she didn't have any family?"

"Her own parents were too old to raise us, and the only family she had was the Rossis, who were cousins on her side, and had grown up in America after Nino, who is her uncle, had emigrated here as a teenager. She contacted him, and he lived with Jim and Fran and their family, so they made the arrangements for us to move in with them."

"And they seem like they were happy about it."

He shot her a "get real" look. "Fran, maybe."

"Not your uncle Jim?"

"It got sprung on him at the last minute, so he couldn't say no or find some legal loophole to avoid being responsible for two more kids when he already had five. And, in case you didn't pick up this subtlety, he's been pissed off about it ever since."

"Actually, I didn't pick that up at all. I thought he treated you and Vivi just fine."

"Nobody had issues with Vivi," he said, hearing the bitterness in his voice. "She was adorable."

"You can be adorable."

He laughed at that.

"Did the Angelinos in Italy fight for you?" she asked.

Not a bit. No one fought for them, not during the months they were wards of the country, not after they moved to America. And the Rossis wondered why he arrived with a chip the size of the Mediterranean Sea on his little shoulders. "My mother's will was ironclad."

She was quiet for a moment, considering that. "It must have been hard to lose your mother so young."

"Yeah," he said, attempting a casual "what can you do" tone that he must have missed, because she gave him a doubtful look. "Of course it was," he admitted. "I was ten. I had Vivi to worry about. We were alone and..." She'd *promised*.

An ancient hurt curled through his chest.

Sarò sempre al tuo fianco, Zaccaria. He could still hear her voice, remember the thin hands, her disease-ravaged body.

I'll always be by your side. And that foolish little Italian boy took her literally. He thought she'd never leave him. Of course, now he knew she meant that...metaphorically. But he'd believed her.

"It was rough," he said, clearing his throat and his mind. "Especially in the beginning when the only person who spoke any Italian was Uncle Nino."

"What did Nino say to you in Italian when we got there this afternoon?"

He smiled. "*Benvenuto a casa.* It means welcome home."

"It sounded more, I don't know, personal."

"It is," he admitted. "It's kind of a code between us. Those are the first words he ever said to me, when Vivi and I arrived in the United States. Not just welcome, welcome *home*. He wanted me to feel like it was home, even though it wasn't."

"Why not?" she asked, obviously frustrated with him. "They seem like a very loving family. What makes you think they didn't want you? I never heard Vivi say that, not once. And nothing in the dynamics I saw today suggest you aren't considered part of that family. Why do you feel like an outsider when they don't treat you like one?"

She didn't have to see it if he felt it. That made it real enough for him. "Vivi acclimated better than I did," he said in response, avoiding the question he didn't want to answer. "In case you haven't noticed, she's more Rossi than Angelino."

"Oh, I noticed. I also noticed that you and JP are at each other's throats. Has it always been that way?"

"Pretty much from day one."

"Did he resent the new arrivals?"

"Who knows what goes on in that screwed-up head of JP's? Ask Nicki, she's the shrink. I imagine he had a party the night he heard I was injured..." He shook his head, a slow smile forming. "This is right where you wanted me to go, wasn't it?"

"I thought talking about your family might open you up."

He laughed softly. "You'll make a helluva lawyer, Sam."

She dropped her head back, laughing a little, too. "I hope so. Have to get through law school first."

He just looked at her, at that white, sweet column of exposed throat, at the thick lashes that brushed her delicate cheekbones, at the palest of freckles on her clear skin, at the strands of long, sandy blond hair tucked behind her ear. Just her exposed ear was so much of a turn-on, his erection threatened the thin cotton boxers he wore. Just her *ear*.

Imagine what her whole naked body could do to him.

He didn't have to imagine; he could remember.

"So, did I talk enough for you?"

She shrugged. "I thought we were just getting started."

He blew out a soft breath, getting just an inch closer, hoping she didn't notice. "We didn't talk that much, Sam. I mean back then. We did other things." Other things like he wanted to do right now.

"You're right. But we also talked. Before, during, and after making love," she said bluntly. "Then we'd eat, share a beer, and go at it again."

He got a little harder, but didn't move away. Couldn't move away.

"You're not going to kiss me, remember?" There was a little challenge in her voice, along with a little warning. "So don't think I don't notice you getting closer."

He laughed a little at getting caught. "I'm not going to kiss you." He just looked at her, memories washing over him. "You know, you're always asking if I remember things. Do you—"

She put her hands over his lips. "Yes. Don't."

"You don't know what I was going to say." Christ, even her hands smelled sweet.

"Yes, I do."

"What?"

"If I remember..." She half laughed, half sighed. "That little magic trick you used to do."

He laughed, too, mostly because that was precisely what he'd been thinking about. "That was no trick," he said, leaning in as she took her hand away from his mouth. "That was unparalleled skill."

"Now you sound like the cocky guy I fell in..." She coughed softly, checking herself. "You sound like you again. And, yes, Zach, that was some mad sex skill you had, yes it was."

"*Is*." Closer, but not touching.

"Don't."

"Have to."

"Zach."

He breathed on her cheek. "Sammi."

"Oh." She was losing it, fighting and losing it. That made his gut tighten, low and hot in his balls.

It made him want to...talk. And not about his family. "The image of you on that bed, that night, touching yourself while I whispered in your ear...like this..."

She shuddered.

"That got me through war, Sam. That sustained me from one end of Iraq to the other."

"Then why—"

"Sammi." He quieted her with another soft breath. "Shhh. Listen to me. I'm talking."

She tensed, her knuckles whitening on the pillow in her lap, her lips parted, her breath coming a little faster. "This isn't talk, Zach. It's verbal sex."

"You like that." The ear beckoned, like a magnet pulling his whole body toward hers, his lips to that sweet lobe and precious curl of skin.

"Yes, I do," she admitted on a sigh of defeat.

"You're wet, aren't you?"

"Oh." The word came out in a soft rush. She tried to shake her head, but it ended up a nod.

"Touch yourself." He blew the words into her ear and could swear he could see the tiny blond hairs stand on end. She gripped the pillow tighter on her lap.

"Pretend it's me."

She struggled to swallow. "I don't want to."

"No?" He tugged the pillow fringe, and she let go of the barrier, exposing her legs, the T-shirt so high on her thighs he could see the shadow between her legs. His mouth went dry.

"I'll tell you what to do."

She kept her head back, eyes closed, the sweet flesh of her throat pulsing, proof that her blood was rushing as hard and fast and hot as his.

"Let me tell you, Sammi." He dropped the pillow and it hit the floor with a soft thud as he got so close he could almost feel the silky strands of her hair on his lips. But he didn't touch. "Open your legs."

She tried to breathe in, but the air got caught, and sounded like a soft gasp. Slowly, she relaxed, her legs widening with another soft sigh of surrender.

"Pull your T-shirt all the way up your legs. All the way."

She released another shuddery breath, finally turning to face him, her lashes fluttering open. "You're really going to do this, aren't you?"

"No, baby, you are. I'm just going to…talk you through it." He smiled and inched closer. "And watch you come."

Her eyes were dark with confusion. "What about you?"

"I'll get what I want."

"I won't—"

"I know you won't, Sammi. That's not what I want."

She frowned at him.

"Shhh. Touch. Touch right between your legs. Where it's hot and wet. Think about my tongue." He pictured her the way she'd been that night, naked on the bed, her hair everywhere, her legs spread, her eyes locked on his while he told her what to do.

Just like that night, she didn't look away, but slid her hand where he told her, her whole body vibrating a little, tension palpable, every breath ragged, their gazes locked.

Blood slammed into his already hard shaft as she touched herself with one hand and lifted the T-shirt with the other, dragging the material over her nipple.

Jesus. At the sight of her budded rosy tip, his mouth actually ached to taste it. He leaned down, but stopped himself, digging for control he didn't even dream he had.

"Tell me, Zach," she whispered, her own control long gone.

"Wet your finger."

She did, slowly, torturing him as she slid it into her mouth and he imagined it was his cock.

"Slide it inside you."

She put her hand between her legs, her hips rising a little, a soft moan in her chest.

"All the way."

"Ohhh."

"Rub your clit. Like I did, Sammi." Her eyes squeezed at the sensation, her lip caught between her teeth, her hips rocking as she pleasured herself.

He let his gaze drag down her face, to the breast she'd exposed and fingered with her other hand. His balls burned hot and tight, his own climax perilously close as he watched her start to fall over the edge.

"Think about my mouth on you, Sammi. My tongue inside you. Sucking, licking, loving you." He got so close her hair brushed his nose and patch. "Come for me, sweetheart. Come."

Her back bowed as she let out a low, stuttering moan, a soft flush rising on her skin. He had to fist his hands into the sofa to keep from touching her, taking her, finishing this fantasy inside her.

"Zach...oh, my God, I want...you." She rolled her head from side to side, her back still arched as she rocked her hips.

Blood thrummed him into a stiff, aching column, his throat desert dry, his pulse like a bass drum in his ears.

"Put your fingers in, Sam. All the way. Stroke it slow, slow, slow. Feel how wet you are, how ready, imagine how hard I am. Imagine I'm sliding in, deeper, filling you, all the way, honey. I'm all the way."

Her hips thrust softly, her head back, her mouth open, her whole body quivering with response.

"Now, come, sweet Sammi. Come."

She was lost, gone, completely under his spell.

"Let go," he whispered in her ear. "Just let go."

She cried out softly, then bit her lip and thrust her hips forward, holding them still for one long, extended moment of exquisite pleasure; then she shivered and rocked again, groaning, moaning, then quieting as the orgasm subsided.

"Zach."

"Shhh." He let his lips touch her ears, his hands balled in tight fists, his heart clobbering his chest. His cock had long ago burst through the opening of his shorts, the tip soaked with moisture and the beginning of his own orgasm.

But that wasn't what he wanted in return. Not even close.

Slowly, her breathing steadied. Her hands reappeared, and she opened her eyes to look at him.

"When you talk, Zach Angelino, it's a beautiful, beautiful thing."

He leaned closer and put his mouth over hers, just enough to brush her lips. "When you come, Sam Fairchild, it's the most beautiful, beautiful thing."

She flicked his lips with her tongue. "It's your turn."

"Yes, it is." He stood, not caring that his erection led the way. "Come with me."

Wordlessly, she followed, holding his hand up the stairs, not pausing at his room.

"Don't you need to get something from your bag?" she asked when they passed the bathroom.

"No, we don't need those tonight. Not for what I have in mind."

"What exactly do you have in mind?"

Bliss.

And it was better if they didn't have protection close by. Then he wouldn't break his promise to her, and to himself. He walked her to the bed and drew back the comforter, gesturing for her to climb in. She fingered the T-shirt she wore with a questioning look in her eyes.

"Keep it on."

She looked a little surprised, but slipped into the bed, sliding over to the side to make room for him.

"Turn over," he said.

She followed his instructions, facing the other side, and he rolled in behind her, lining their lengths, nestling her into his body.

"What are you doing, Zach?" she asked, her voice still a little unsteady.

"Shhh." He nudged her face back to the pillow away from him. "I want to sleep with you. Just . . . sleep."

She shimmied her backside against his very hard cock. "Doesn't feel like sleep."

"It will when you're asleep. Aren't you tired, sweetheart?"

"Infinitely so."

He kissed her hair, and inhaled the fragrance. "Then sleep, Sammi."

He put his head on her pillow, cool against his scar, his face in her gloriously thick hair. Wordlessly, he curled his arm around her waist, betting everything he had that he could do this.

Right at that moment, she *was* everything he had.

"This is all?"

"Not quite. I need to trust you not to turn around."

For a moment, she didn't say anything; then she just nodded, taking one of his hands around her waist, curling her fingers into his and placing their joined fists right over her heart.

The way they'd always slept together.

He counted the beats, listened to her breath, and waited until her body relaxed into sleep. When he was sure, he unlatched their hands and reached up to slide off his protective patch.

Finally, the moment of pure heaven. He laid his face

against her hair and let the softness soothe his burning scar, the ecstasy of it almost making him want to cry out. It felt so good. So, so sweet and comforting and good.

She could turn at any second. She could turn and wake and see everything that he had to hide from her. And how bad would that be?

Bad.

But for the rest of this night, he finally, finally had no pain, none at all.

CHAPTER 11

When Sam came down the steps after showering and dressing the next morning, Zach was on his cell phone, a serious look on his face as he listened to the caller.

Somehow she just knew that the sexy, sweet intimacy they'd shared last night had disappeared with the sun. It made her ache all over again, the way she had a few minutes ago, when she'd awakened, and he was gone.

He put the phone against his neck and mouthed, "There's coffee if you want it."

She got a cup, avoided the temptation to peek through the blinds he'd closed drum-tight, and did a quick scan for more critters or evidence of them. Giving him privacy for what seemed like a serious conversation, she stayed in the kitchen, sipping coffee, trying to remember the last time she'd slept so soundly.

It would be so easy to fall back under Zach's spell. Could she possibly give him her body and not her heart?

She was rationalizing, of course. Making excuses for...the inevitable. One more night and—

"We have to go."

He stood in the doorway, as dark and dangerous as he was last night when he whispered in her ear and made her lose every shred of control. He wore a black T-shirt, the thorny edges of his tattoo poking out from the sleeve, faded jeans, black boots that looked tailor-made to kick some ass.

"Where? Why?"

"Vivi's, and I don't know why."

"Is she okay? Is it safe to leave?"

"I can get us in and out safely, yes. She needs me and I'm not leaving you alone."

"What's the matter with her?"

He lifted a shoulder. "She needs me." As though that required no explanation.

They were back in Brookline in less than twenty minutes, parked in a spot behind the building she didn't even know existed when she lived there, in the back and up the stairs in a matter of minutes.

Just as Zach lifted his hand to knock on 414, voices rose from inside, followed by a female laugh and a man's deep tone. He froze, inching back.

"Who is that?" Sam asked.

"Chessie. Marc." He stood still for a moment, listening to a slower, older voice, the words impossible to make out, but Sam recognized the speaker.

."And Uncle Nino," she said. "What are they all doing here?"

"I don't know," he said gruffly, rapping hard. Instantly the apartment went quiet.

"Feels like a surprise party," Sam suggested.

"Or a fucking intervention."

Vivi opened the door, holding Fat Tony in her arms. "Hey," she said, lifting up on bare toes to kiss Zach's cheek and usher Sam in with her free hand. "Come on in."

"Why is everyone here?" he asked.

"It's a staff meeting."

"What?"

As they came around the end of the hall to the living room, several familiar faces came into view. Uncle Nino sitting at the table in the dining area, an unfinished jigsaw puzzle in front of him. Chessie and Marc sat side by side on the sofa, a newspaper open on the coffee table, a laptop perched on Chessie's knees.

"Welcome to the first meeting of the Guardian Angelinos," Vivi announced, her eyes bright with excitement. "I told them everything," she said to Zach and Sam. "The murder, the witness, the whole deal. And most important, I told them about our company and they're all in, Zach. All three of them."

He puffed out a disgusted breath. "Christ, Vivi, you told me there was some kind of emergency."

"There is," Chessie said. "The Internet just went down."

"I'm serious." Fury vibrated off him as he looked from one to the other, his gaze settling on Marc. "Don't you have a business to run?"

"I have staff, and this is more important."

"And more interesting," Chessie said.

From his seat by the window, Nino cleared his throat and snapped a puzzle piece in place. "Hear them out, *ragazzino*. In my opinion, this is urgent."

Zach crossed his arms and shifted his attention to Vivi. "What's urgent?"

"What's going on is a major turn in the case," she said.

"We have a case?"

"Yes, we do." She looked at Chessie. "Is the Net back up yet? I want to show the story to them."

"Hang on, I'm working on it."

Sam slid into the space next to Chessie, sharing a quick smile and looking over her shoulder at the computer.

"Do it fast," Vivi said. "I want Sam and Zach to understand why I brought you all in for the first company meeting."

"Vivi, there is no company other than what exists in your imagination," Zach said, obviously fighting for patience. "I'm going to keep an eye on Sam and kill anyone who comes near her until someone is arrested for the murder of Joshua Sterling. You are going to be on your unstoppable quest for information to help us get there. Beyond that, there is no...*company*. Even the name is so ridiculous I can't say it."

"The Guardian Angelinos?" Chessie lifted her hands from the keyboard long enough to do a little double air punch. "I love it. Can I do the logo, too? I'm a hell of a hacker, but I'm really working on my graphic skills."

"A logo is awesome, Chess." Vivi beamed. "Thank you."

"You'll need an office," Nino said, eyeballing his puzzle. "I bet your uncle could be persuaded to do something with that high-priced real estate he's been sitting on in Back Bay since he retired."

"Uncle Jim's old law offices!" Vivi practically shrieked. "How sweet would that be?"

"You need a company car," Marc said. "I have a client who owns a Ford dealer—"

"Hold it." Zach held up his hands, color rising in his face. "There's no logo, no offices, no company car. And no…Guardian Angelinos." It obviously pained him to say the words. "And there's no—"

"Internet!" Chessie exclaimed. "I got it. Come here and read this, Zach."

But Sam was already reading, the familiar logo of the *Boston Bullet* at the top of the story. Her gaze dropped to the picture of Teddy Brindell, and her heart stopped.

"He works at Paupiette's," she said.

Chessie angled the computer screen so Zach could see, too. "Not anymore," Zach said quietly, putting a hand on Sam's arm. "Did you know him very well?"

Man Brutally Slain in South Dorchester.

The headline swam before her as she automatically reached up and took the hand Zach was offering. "Oh, this is horrible."

"It gets worse," Vivi said, all the enthusiasm gone from her voice now. "And, honestly, this is why I called everyone together, Zach. This really is a big case, and we really do need more than just you and me to attack it."

"How does it get worse?" Sam asked. How could it?

"I spoke with Teddy Brindell the night he was killed. I mean, like minutes before he was killed, if that report is accurate. The last two words he said to me were Taylor Sly."

"Taylor Sly?" Marc leaned forward. "Boston's most secret madame?"

"I thought she was a former model," Sam said. "Who owns a modeling agency."

"The FBI thinks that's a cover, but we were never able to crack her."

"She was in the restaurant the night of the murder," Sam said. "I saw Joshua Sterling talking to her when I went to get the wine."

"What did this Brindell guy tell you about her?" Zach asked Vivi.

"Nothing. He just said her name like she was the key to the whole murder. And now he's dead." For a moment, the room went silent as the facts gelled.

"Did anyone hear him say that? See you talking to him?" he asked.

"I don't know. It was late, outside of the Colonnade, near the cab stand. I don't remember anyone being around, but I wasn't really focused on anyone but Teddy. I was on my board. I skated back to the restaurant to see if anyone else was coming out, then got a cab home."

"What cab company did Teddy use?" Chessie asked, already clicking onto a search engine. "Metro? Boston?"

"Checker," Vivi said. "I'm positive."

"I'll find out what Checker drivers were at the Colonnade that night."

"The police will do that," Zach said.

"And you think they'll be telling us what they find out?" Marc shot back. "The fact is, whoever killed Brindell..."

"Could want Sam, too." Zach squeezed her hand. "Because maybe that camera didn't get your picture. Maybe the killer is systematically taking out every single person who worked there that night."

Sam's whole body went icy. "No," she said softly, shaking her head.

"I have an appointment with Taylor Sly later today," Vivi said. "She thinks I could be a model. I think she could be a lead. If Sterling talked to her that night, then she might know why someone wanted him killed. No one at all seems to be able to come up with a motive."

"A model, huh?" Chessie looked dubious. "Maybe she wants to turn you into a prostitute."

"Whatever she wants," Zach said, "I don't think you should go alone. Marc?"

He nodded. "I'm already planning to go."

"In the meantime, I'm going to do some digging around on her and this Brindell guy," Chessie said. "I've already found out he lived in Chestnut Hill."

"That was in the article," Zach said.

"And had sixty-eight dollars in his checking account." She gave him a smug smile. "That was so not in the article."

"Do you remember anything about him and this Taylor Sly that night?" Vivi asked Sam. "Did he wait on her? Talk to her?"

Sam frowned, remembering the scene. "She was sitting at table nine, by the back wall, with a man who I'm pretty sure I've seen her with before. They were my table, drinking...a Cakebread chardonnay and they had salmon...I think. Teddy had the front section that night, so..." She closed her eyes, picturing the scene at the restaurant before she'd gone down for the wine. Joshua Sterling crossed the dining room, she'd seen that when Keegan walked in, and reached out to greet Taylor Sly.

"And Joshua definitely talked to her. I saw that, and I told the police I saw that."

"When you saw that," Vivi prodded, "was Teddy in the kitchen?"

Was he? Was he one of the servers helping with the wine for the upstairs party? Damn, this was the problem. Memory was so selective.

"I don't remember," she said honestly. "I was never that friendly with him, and I avoided him, mostly." Her gaze dropped back to the computer screen where Chessie had brought up the article again. "The police say his murder was a gang slaying, so that's not anything like the professional who killed Sterling."

"What the police say and what the police have are not always the same thing," Zach said. "Who knows that better than you?"

Sam's phone beeped with an incoming call, and she slipped it out of her bag.

"Speaking of the police…" She read the ID, the possibility of what this meant tightening a band across her chest. "It's Detective Larkin, one of the leads on the case."

She stood to answer it, walking into the hallway while the others talked in hushed tones behind her.

"Hello, Detective."

"Sam, why aren't you at home?"

Her heart flipped. "Because I don't want to get killed like Teddy Brindell."

"You saw that, huh?"

"Do you think it's related?" she asked, imagining the slightly rumpled detective, balding, blue-eyed, so much softer than his counterpart, O'Hara.

"We have to consider every possibility," he said, "but

this was clearly a gang-related incident in a very tough neighborhood."

"What about the shooting in my neighborhood last night?" she asked. "Was that gang-related?"

For a moment, he was silent. "Sam, there was no shooting in Somerville last night."

Like hell there wasn't. "What do you need, Detective?"

"We're ready to do a lineup."

Oh, God. How long had she been dreading those words? "No more pictures?"

"Not this time. We've got the real thing, Sam, and that's critical in a case like this. Frankly, I think we're going to get lucky."

Not if she picked the wrong guy. Again.

"Can you be here in half an hour? Or would you like someone to come and get you?"

His tone was gentle, and she was so glad this wasn't his partner, who'd be barking at her by now. "I can be there and I have a ride," she said, looking up as Zach stepped into the hallway. "We have to go to the South End police station. For a lineup."

He nodded, his look just sympathetic enough that it squeezed her heart a little. He understood just how hard this was going to be.

"Oh, and, Sam?" Larkin said. "You remember that you are not to speak of this case to anyone, right?"

"Right."

"Then who are you talking to?" Now there was a sharp edge in his voice.

She wet her lips and scanned her brain for an answer. "My bodyguard," she finally said. "I had to hire a professional, Detective." *Since the police won't do the job of protecting me.*

"All right, but please. You are operating under a gag. The utmost confidentiality is critical in this case."

"I understand." In the next room, the conversation rose, breaking the very rule she was promising to keep. She stepped farther away and cupped the phone. "I'll see you soon, Detective." She hung up and looked at Zach. "It's official. You're a professional bodyguard."

"So it seems." He lifted his T-shirt to reveal a cool, sleek pistol. "Marc hooked me up with hardware."

Behind him, Uncle Nino came out into the hallway, his gaze on Zach. "Listen to me." His voice was soft, but rich with the tone of an order. "This is a good thing. It keeps the family together, using skills God gave all of you. I want you to do this, *ragazzino.*" He put his hands on Zach's face. "You need this."

"I don't need anything, Nino," he said, backing away from the old man's touch. "But Sam needs help, so I'm doing what I have to do. Beyond that, I don't want anything to do with this family...business."

Nino shook his head and shifted his attention to Sam. "Talk sense into him, Samantha. And I'll have some dinner ready for you two tonight. It's the least I can do for..." He gave a wide grin. "The Guardian Angelinos. What else do you need at that house?"

"Mousetraps." They both said it at the same time.

Nino chuckled. "And here I thought our little company was trying to trap a rat."

How did she end up back in this room?

Okay, not the same *room*, but the same situation. This

was a different precinct, different cops, but once again, Sam found herself facing a police lineup. Once again, she held a man's future in her hands.

Last week, when they brought her in, she'd only had to look at pictures on a computer, and Detective Larkin even said that was just about the only way identification was done these days. But, for some reason, they were doing a lineup.

Maybe it was a psychological test. Maybe they wanted her to crack.

The computer IDs were so much less personal, and a total waste of time, since none of the photos looked remotely like the man she had seen in the wine cellar.

But this, this was personal. A man, not a picture, who had a life, a heart, a family, hopes and dreams, and maybe even a job he wanted to keep. Or he could be a professional killer who deserved the worst punishment the legal system could muster.

How could she be sure?

The easiest thing, the chickenshit obvious thing to do, was to just say "None of them are the man who shot Joshua Sterling."

But she couldn't be sure. What if one of them had? What if she *thought* one of them had, and she was wrong?

She'd read so much about eyewitnesses in the years that she'd worked to help get Billy cleared. Through the Innocence Mission, she'd become an expert on the reliability—or not—of an eyewitness. She'd gone from being a woman whose worst personal trait was never believing she could be wrong to being one who second-guessed far too many things.

So many elements affected what witnesses thought they saw, including what was told to them afterward, how traumatizing the event they witnessed was. Something as mundane as a chemical change in the brain caused by what someone ate that day could impair and affect memory.

Not what they *saw*. What they *remembered*. Two very different things.

And every day that slipped by since Joshua Sterling was killed, she remembered less.

"Are you ready, Ms. Fairchild?" Detective Larkin was still in his good-cop mode, using a gentle voice on Sam.

But Quentin O'Hara was also in the room, and his very presence made her nervous. Detective O'Hara was tall, imposing, classic black Irish, with blue eyes and jet-black hair. He rarely smiled, and when he did, the expression was rich with double, triple, quadruple meaning. She didn't know what he was thinking, and everything about him put her on edge.

Especially now, as he stood hawklike in the back of the room. There were a few other investigators, and a woman named Dr. Irene Gettleberg, who Sam strongly suspected was a psychologist.

Were they trying to break her? Trip her up?

Intimidate, impeach, and provide incentive to lie?

Sam took a deep breath and nodded to Detective Larkin. "I'm ready," she said, staring at the glass, knowing what happened next. The lights on the other side came up quickly, glaring down on six men who stood against a wall with long black lines marking their height.

They looked straight ahead, cocky, worried, bored, and maybe...guilty.

They all had dark hair, but two she could knock out

immediately. The killer's hair was short, and those two couldn't have grown that much hair in a week.

Unless the killer wore a wig.

She swallowed, but that just moved the lump from her throat to her chest.

"Start on the left," Detective Larkin said, coming close to her. "Take your time and look at every detail of their faces. You said the man seemed tall. That one on the left is over six feet. Is that tall to you?"

"Detective, don't make suggestions." Dr. Gettleberg's admonition was firm. "This needs to hold up in court."

Especially since a sharp defense attorney would rip Sam's testimony into tiny shreds and sprinkle it like confetti over the jury. Wouldn't that be a fun day in court?

"I need each one of them to turn to their right," Sam said, sliding her gaze over their faces. "I only saw his profile."

After a minute, they did, although Sam didn't hear the instruction being given.

The two with the long hair, both tall, had smooth skin. Could someone fake those pockmarks she'd seen? A really good makeup artist, like a movie-quality artist, yes. But the bulb in the wine cellar had caught the shadow of the blemished skin, and the shape had been like a three-quarter crescent moon. She was certain of that.

She eliminated one and three, and turned her attention to the four other men. The second one was a little short. Although, she'd been crouching behind the wine racks, and maybe that distorted her perception of height. The fourth and fifth men definitely had big enough noses and short enough hair, and one had a bit of a beard covering what might be pockmarked cheeks.

Could she ask for him to shave?

"A front view again?" Detective Larkin asked.

"No, wait." She squinted at the man with the beard. There was something slouchy and thin about him. The killer hadn't been husky, but he'd been...elegant. He wore a dark jacket and looked as if he could have been any of the patrons of Paupiette's. This guy was too...sloppy.

But maybe that was an act. A professional killer—and assassin—surely had some performance skills. Had the man who killed Sterling been adopting that posture as part of an act? Had he worn fake hair, fake blemishes?

Doubt chewed at her insides. She blew out a breath and closed her eyes, trying to clean the visual slate. What else had she seen of him that night?

His hands.

"You need to think, Sam," Detective Larkin said, an edge of impatience in his voice. "Try to remember."

"Please," Sam whispered. "I'm trying."

She eyed them all again. If she picked the one who was a plant to make her look like a fool, some people in that room might be very happy.

"She's *trying*," O'Hara said from the back. "She better do more than try."

She ignored him and thought about the hand that held that gun. He'd hidden it under his jacket, right hand on the gun, back against the wall, left cheek facing her. When he pulled the gun out, did she see a ring? A mole? A mark?

Or was she looking at Sterling at that very moment? His shocked face, the way his eyes burst open when he'd been shot?

Her gaze landed on the sixth man. As tall as the first, with the right kind of hair, and rough skin. Had that skin just looked pockmarked in the shadows of the cellar? Had his nose been that flat at the top? Weren't his ears a little bigger?

He could be the man. He could be. That, right there, could be the very man who put a bullet in Joshua Sterling...or it might not.

The last thing she wanted was to even cast a shadow on the wrong man. Look what she'd done to Billy Shawkins. A fine sheen of perspiration tingled on her neck and down her spine.

She'd put the wrong man in prison once before.

"I don't see him."

Somehow, she knew from the moment she'd walked into the police station that would be her response. She'd never accuse another man, ever. That killer who had her face on tape should rest easy; he had the best witness possible. An uncertain one.

"You're sure?" Larkin sounded devastated.

That was just the problem. She wasn't sure of anything. "I can't positively identify any of these men."

Which meant she wasn't any closer to safety, security, or a normal life.

Behind her, O'Hara yanked the door open, not even sparing her a word. Dr. Gettleberg looked hard at her, then made a note on a clipboard.

"You don't have a suspect, do you?" Sam asked.

Larkin didn't answer.

"This was a test of me, wasn't it?"

"That's not true," Larkin answered.

"I don't believe you."

"You should believe me. And you will when you step outside. We have more restaurant employees and Paupiette's patrons coming in today to look at the very same lineup, to see if they remember any of these men as patrons that night. You, of course, are first, as the eyewitness."

"Really? Are those people here now?" Suddenly, she wanted to see some coworkers—alive and safe. "Because, Detective Larkin, if the person who killed Sterling also killed Teddy Brindell because he knows there's a witness, don't you think everyone who worked there should be warned?"

He gave her a patronizing pat. "Mr. Brindell's death is unrelated, Sam. He had collected a lot of cash, and he was rolled, plain and simple. Looking for any other connection, well, you just aren't going to find one. Believe me, we've thought through every angle."

"But just in case, don't you think the other employees should know—"

"Please..." He leaned in to underscore the next sentence. "No one knows you witnessed the murder. We have to keep it that way."

Well, *someone* knew.

"All of these employees think you found Sterling's body. Don't let the truth out or we lose all our leverage."

She wasn't entirely sure she followed that reasoning, but he indicated for her to go out and down a corridor, ending the conversation. Rene's was the first familiar face she saw, and despite her general dislike of the sommelier, a wave of comfort rolled over her. They were all in this together.

"Rene," she called, aware of the sharp look from Detective Larkin.

"Hello, Sam." He reached out for her, uncharacteristically warm, but it felt perfectly normal. They hugged quickly and pulled back. "Did you hear about Teddy?" he asked immediately.

She nodded. "So sad."

"Were you..." He put his hand up to shade his eyes and mime "looking" at the lineup.

"Let's go." O'Hara appeared out of nowhere, giving Rene a nudge. "Detective Larkin will walk you out, Ms. Fairchild. And remember..." He pointed a finger at her face. "We want to know where you are. All the time. I mean every single minute."

"He's exaggerating," Larkin said, guiding her away, speaking very softly. "But don't lose touch. And do not tell anyone that you're a witness, Sam. No one. Not even someone you think you trust. Because, right now, you can't trust anybody."

"But he knows," she said.

"Who knows?"

"The man who did it and has the tape."

"Maybe." He shrugged. "We still don't know if that tape worked or if he even looked at it. He might have thrown it in the river to get rid of what might be incriminating evidence."

"Just catch him," she said. "So I can sleep again."

"That's what we intend to do."

As the elevator doors opened to the main floor, she scanned the people and cops milling about, looking for Zach. Her gaze falling on the metal detectors. Had he gotten in by leaving the weapon in the car? Or was he still outside where she'd left him?

The need to see him hit her hard, surprising her with

its impact. Not just because she felt safe with him, but because she *needed* to see him. It made no sense, but nothing about Zach Angelino did.

"Sam? Is that you?"

She turned at the sound of a man's voice, skimming the crowd for someone tall, dark, and dangerous, but landing on medium, pale, and pleasant. It took a second to place him, and longer to remember his name. But she did, just as he reached her, with his hands outstretched.

"How are you, Larry?"

The fact that she remembered the name of the man she'd chatted with at the bar just moments before her life took its latest turn surprised her. And it made his smile even wider. "I didn't think I'd see you again. I heard you quit after the incident."

"I did," she admitted. "It was just too..."

"I know." He squeezed her hands and inched closer. "I can't believe there's a lineup. It's so old-school. I feel like I'm in an episode of *Hill Street Blues*."

She didn't laugh, unable to share just how horrible the situation was for her. "Yeah, I know," she said weakly.

"No, you don't," he replied. "You probably don't even know what *Hill Street Blues* is; you're that much younger than I am. But I'm going to ask anyway. Could we have a cup of coffee later? I should be done with the lineup in a little while, and..." His voice trailed off, no doubt reading her expression.

"I can't, Larry. I have to go, so maybe another time."

"Can there be another time?" he asked, his expression serious. "I'd really like to take you out, if you're free. Are you?"

Her smile was tight. Was she free, or had she already

been captured by Zach Angelino? Would she ever give any man a chance, even a nice, boring guy like this? *Especially* a nice, boring guy like this. "Not exactly, no. I mean—"

"I'm not married," he assured her. "I make a good living, I have no serious baggage, and…wait for it now…I can cook."

She laughed, surprised by the wit she hadn't even noticed when they met that night in Paupiette's bar. "That's quite a résumé, but as long as this is going on…" She waved around as though the entire police station encompassed *this*. "I'm just kind of preoccupied."

"How are you preoccupied? I thought you quit."

Larkin's warning rang in her ear. "It's just got me in a funny place, you know?"

"I know." He gave her wistful smile. "Maybe you'll change your mind."

"Maybe," she said, without much promise.

With an awkward good-bye, he headed away. She went in the opposite direction and spotted Zach on the other side of the lobby, his uneven gaze targeted on her. Just the sight of him—the long black hair, the leather patch, the badass T-shirt, the unshaven stubble—sent a thrill from her heart to her toes.

Larry didn't stand a chance against him. No man did.

Zach approached her slowly, with determination in his step and a half smile that almost killed her.

"So who's the guy with the rug?"

She laughed softly. "Really? That was a toupee?" Poor Larry, he really was older than she thought.

"A good one, but, yeah. You give him your number?"

"You sound jealous."

He put his arm around her. "He was drooling."

"You were watching?"

"That's my job."

He guided her toward the door, a strong arm protectively on her back, his *job* being the only reason she let herself be this close to him. Because she had to remember the lesson of the lineup room: Her judgment sucked.

CHAPTER 12

Well, if you and your FBI buddies are right, then prostitution pays."

Vivi paused at the icy expanse of white marble floor in the Clarendon, the whole complex so new she could practically smell the sawdust of the last few condos being loaded with luxury.

"We're right, and it does," Marc replied.

"Then why didn't you nail her?"

"She's got friends in high places, that's why. What I'd love to know is what you think she's going to tell you that she hasn't told the cops." Marc gave her a sideways glance. "Especially dressed like that."

She purposely clicked her stacked heels on the marble, smiling smugly as she smoothed her hands over skin-tight, body-hugging pencil jeans and a T-shirt that barely covered her midriff.

"This is black tie for me, baby," she said, grinning up at him. "Plus, I'm here for a modeling gig. Those chicks don't wear business suits. No need to give Ms. Sly any reason to change her mind about me and my cover girl potential." She hesitated near the bank of elevators, looking around and seeing no one who was a candidate for Anthea, Ms. Taylor Sly's personal assistant at the modeling agency called On The Sly.

"Let's sit down," she said, indicating a white leather bench. "We can't get up there on our own."

"I could."

"I'm sure you could." As they sat, she gave his leg a sisterly squeeze. "That's why you're going to make such a fabulous Guardian Angelino."

Marc's dark eyes were serious. "I won't lie to you, Vivi. I love the idea. I miss the game in a big way."

"Ever think about going back to the FBI?"

He just shook his head. "Too many burned bridges. Too much crappy history."

"You might have to do undercover assignments again if you work for us."

"Not one that would compromise my relationship with my wife," he said.

"Ah, you say that as if there might be another someday."

"One can hope. But, seriously, I like the company concept, Vivi. I think you have the brains and nerve to pull this off."

"And I have the brother and cousins. I'm not cocky enough to think I could do this job alone. I need Zach, I need you, I need Chessie. Hell, I need Uncle Nino to cook for me."

"You might even need JP."

She held up a hand. "Not if it costs me Zach. You saw those two yesterday. Some things never change."

Marc shook his head. "I think JP's trying, I do. He can be an arrogant asshole; I'm the first to admit that. He thinks he knows everything and has to control stuff. And, God knows, when Zach was going through his wild phase—"

"Which was basically from eleven until he joined the military," she interjected.

"Yeah, JP had enough of him. But, damn, we're adults now. I want Zach to see the benefits of family. Even if he doesn't think the Rossis are his."

Vivi leaned back, her eyes on the elevator doors, her brain on her wounded, scarred brother. "Maybe Sam'll help him."

"Maybe," Marc said. "If she's a miracle worker."

The doors opened and both of them stared at the nine-foot-tall drink of chocolate milk with stick-straight ebony hair and a tight white miniskirt that ended well above midthigh. She sauntered out, golden eyes on Marc.

"I'm going to bet my Eric Clapton–autographed Fender that's Anthea," Vivi whispered out of the side of her mouth.

"Yep. Gold standard call girl," Marc replied.

"Ms. Angelino?" The woman glided over to them, her gaze staying on Marc, giving a slow appraisal. "I'm Anthea Newcomb, Ms. Sly's assistant." She smiled slowly at Marc. "She only mentioned one candidate. But do you have your book with you, sir? I'm sure she'd be interested in you."

"I'm sure she would, too," he said with a playful smile. "But I'm not in her business."

"He's with me," Vivi said. "I promise he doesn't bite."

"Well, I do," he admitted. "But only if you ask."

In the elevator, Anthea threw Marc a few more lusty glances, and totally ignored Vivi. Good thing she really didn't want a modeling job; she'd have been crushed.

"So how long have you worked for On The Sly?" Vivi asked.

"I'm employee number one," Anthea said in a rich voice. "So, a long time."

The doors opened to the twenty-seventh-floor lobby, a miniature version of the one below. A concierge sat behind a desk, surrounded by soft uplighting and more gleaming marble.

Anthea nodded to him as they passed, heading down a wide hall to a set of beautifully carved mahogany doors. She used a handheld device to punch in some numbers and the doors unlocked with a soft click.

She opened them both at the same time, as though presenting Marc and Vivi to royalty. The front entrance was a massive circle, almost exclusively decorated in blinding white and cream except for a round center table with a floral arrangement half the size of the Public Garden. A few rooms jutted off at odd angles, but Anthea walked them to the right, to another bright, white living room with two full walls of glass looking out over Boston.

"Have a seat, sir. Ms. Angelino, come with me."

They shared one quick look, Marc quirking his brow in something like a warning; then Vivi followed Anthea back through the entryway to another suite of rooms. Everything was so bright and light and white, it was like the home of an angel. And huge. She had no doubt this was two condos turned into one, and had to be at least six or seven thousand square feet.

Running a modeling agency would surely pay well, but not *this* well. Ms. Sly definitely had another source of income. At another set of double doors, painted white, Anthea reached forward, opened them, and stepped back.

"This is Ms. Sly's office," she said. "Where's your book, Ms. Angelino?"

"I didn't bring one." Vivi ignored the surprised response, turning her attention to the floor-to-ceiling view of downtown Boston, looking all the way out to the Citgo sign.

This sitting area was no standard office. It had long sofas, cocktail tables, a bar, a view. But no desk. No phone. No file cabinets or portfolios or *Cosmo* covers on the wall. And no Taylor Sly.

"You're a reporter."

Vivi pivoted at the sound of the voice behind her. "Yes, I am."

Taylor Sly was like an exotic flower—pretty no matter where you put her, but in her element, surrounded by her natural environment, she was positively stunning, aged to perfection. "Well, you're certainly no model."

Vivi gave her a tight smile.

"Why didn't you tell me you were a reporter?"

"I didn't think you'd talk to me." Vivi reached into her pocket and produced a brand-new pair of workout gloves. "But I did bring these."

"Thank you." She took them and dropped them on a coffee table with indifference, her attention so riveted on Vivi that it was a little disconcerting. "Vivi Angelino."

She said the name as if she knew it.

"That's me."

Smiling a little, she took a few steps, circling, but not predatory. Scrutinizing.

"Just so we're clear, I'm not here to get a modeling gig. I lied to get the meeting with you."

Taylor paused, light dancing in eyes so blue-green they bordered on turquoise. "I like that," she replied.

"You do?"

The smile broke wide, revealing perfect teeth. "I lied to get my first job," she admitted. "Said I was sixteen. I was barely thirteen. I got it. Cover of *Seventeen*."

Vivi's eyes widened. "I guess the rest is history."

"I guess it is." She waved to a chair. "Sit down and tell me what was so important you lied to me to get in here."

Vivi sat and Taylor took a chair directly across from her, silk pants rustling as she sat, a soft cinnamon scent all around her. Her face, backlit from the sun pouring in the windows, was a work of art. Almond-shaped eyes, prominent cheekbones, luscious lips.

No wonder the woman sold a billion dollars' worth of products and started her own modeling agency. Could she also be a madame? It seemed preposterous, but Vivi knew enough about people that she realized anything was possible. And Marc had been a helluva good FBI agent. If he said Taylor was running a prostitution ring, then she probably was.

"I'm not here as a reporter. I'm working as a private investigator." The words felt oddly comfortable on Vivi's tongue.

One perfectly arched brow notched north. "I assume this is about the Joshua Sterling murder?"

"Yes. My company is investigating it."

"Do you have a card?"

Shit. "Actually, we're new. We're brand-new. We're called the Guardian Angelinos, and I'm the vice president in charge of investigations."

The other woman seemed intrigued. "You're starting your own company. I love that. I'm so supportive of women-owned businesses."

"I'm a co-owner, with my brother," Vivi added. "He's in charge of security and personal protection."

"Excellent." A sneaky smile broke across her face, her remarkable eyes dancing. "I'm all for using men for their brawn while we provide the brains."

"He has brains, too," she said defensively. "But my background is in investigation."

"For the *Boston Bullet*," Taylor said. At Vivi's look, she added, "I did some homework before our meeting. You would, too, as any smart businesswoman would." She settled in a little closer. "How can I help you, Vivi? Your business is just starting and you probably need a break."

"We sure do." Vivi relaxed, liking her more every second.

"You're trying to solve Sterling's murder."

Vivi tilted her head. "I'm not trying to do the Boston PD's job, Ms. Sly."

"Taylor."

"Taylor. I'm trying to help a client who is peripherally involved in the case."

Her expression grew serious. "A suspect?"

"No."

"A witness?"

"Just someone with a very strong interest in the case being solved."

Taylor nodded, understanding that Vivi wasn't going to give her more. "You know I was in the restaurant that night."

"Yes, and I know you spoke with Mr. Sterling. How well did you know him?"

Something flickered in her eyes. "I knew him very well."

"Then, my sympathies on the loss of...a friend?" She left it as a question, and Taylor didn't answer. "Or was he a business associate?" Like one of her top johns?

"He was my lover."

Vivi just stared at her, stunned speechless.

"And, yes, the police know this already. I've been interviewed extensively. I'm not going to hide the truth. We were in love, and he was planning to leave his wife for me."

Vivi must have looked as gobsmacked as she felt. "And they know that, too?"

Taylor nodded once, a daring look in her eyes. "And they've cleared that little bitch."

They'd cleared Sterling's wife? A woman scorned? "Is it possible they're just saying that while they amass evidence?" Vivi asked.

"What's possible..." She shook her head, stopping herself from saying more.

"Taylor, please. Tell me. I can help."

"Maybe you can," she said, considering that. "Maybe a rogue investigator is just what this case needs because those fucking cops—excuse my language, but they are bastards. They don't want to touch Devyn Sterling because she's a Hewitt and they're next to God in this town."

Vivi knew that to be true. "Well, I don't have any

problems bringing down Hewitts or God, so tell me how I can help."

"Well, frankly, I'm sorry to say this, but I don't think she did it. I mean, obviously she didn't do it. She was right in the middle of the dining room when it happened. But I don't think she paid for the assassination either."

"She certainly had a motive if you and her husband..."

"She doesn't have the stomach for it," Taylor continued. "But she has the genes."

"The Hewitt genes?"

A slow smile threatened. "Darling, if I could tell you what I know, not only would you have the investigative scoop of the decade, also your little company would be turning business away."

Tease. "How can I get you to tell me?"

Taylor just shook her head slowly, as if it could never happen. "I'm tempted, though, to help out a woman and take that—"

"Hey! Stop!" They both spun at the sound of Anthea's outburst, but two men bolted into the room. "I'm sorry, Ms. Sly..." Anthea said on a sigh.

Taylor's warmth disappeared, replaced by ice and fury. "I'm in the middle of an interview, Detective O'Hara. What do you need?"

Of course, Vivi thought. He was the lead detective on the case. She'd never been close enough at a press conference to get a good look. Nor had she ever seen the other cop with him.

"This is a search warrant," O'Hara said. "And we're about to use it." His dark blue eyes sliced Taylor with malice and accusation.

"Get out, Detective O'Hara. I've given you all the statements I intend to without a lawyer present." Taylor looked dismissively to the other man, sliding her hands into the pockets of her trousers in a gesture that seemed oddly masculine and wrong on someone so completely feminine. "Where is Detective Larkin?"

"Doing lineups," O'Hara said. "And not here to protect you."

Taylor shook her head. "No, you may not search."

"Then you're under arrest for obstruction of justice." O'Hara's lips curled. "It's a start, Sly."

She glanced at Vivi. "Fine. You win. You can search. Give me one minute to say good-bye to my newest model."

O'Hara finally looked at Vivi and nodded. "Don't count on too much work in the future, miss."

Vivi said nothing, but let Taylor guide her to the door. There, Taylor turned to Vivi and gave her a close and unexpected hug. So unexpected that it was momentarily awkward as they both went the same way, then Taylor quickly moved her head and placed her mouth near Vivi's ear.

"Finn MacCauley," she whispered. Then she pulled away and gave her a long, meaningful look. "I predict great success for you in this new endeavor," she said. "Take every opportunity that comes your way."

Vivi nodded, the words rolling around in her head as she let Anthea take her the rest of the way out, meeting Marc at the door, where two more detectives and two uniformed police officers waited.

"That was timely," he said, walking out with Vivi. "Is she a suspect?"

Vivi waited until they were in the elevator, and even then she looked around for closed-circuit security cameras. "Yes," she whispered. "I think she is."

As the doors opened, they stepped out, then onto the street, the information she had nearly erupting from her mouth as she told him everything.

"His lover? And they're not after the wife?"

"Precisely," Vivi said, navigating the cobblestone with her heels. "But, Marc, that isn't the most important thing she said. You're not going to believe the name she whispered to me when I left."

He looked at her, waiting.

"Finn MacCauley."

His eyes popped. "The Irish mob gangster?"

"You know another Finn MacCauley?"

Marc shook his head in disbelief. "Vivi, that guy gets blamed for every murder in the city of Boston. He hasn't come up for air in, like, twenty-five years, and I tend to think that's because the rumor that he was whacked by his lieutenants and buried in the Central Artery during the Big Dig is true."

"Isn't he still on an FBI Most Wanted list?"

"He is, but only because they haven't found his corpse. In ten years, he'll be in his nineties and presumed dead."

Vivi shrugged. "I think she was a very credible source."

"Yeah, a madame running a prostitution ring who is openly admitting to an affair with the deceased and clearly the number-one suspect of the lead detective. She's majorly credible."

Vivi shot him a look. "I liked her."

"Rule number one of investigations, little cousin. Liking someone doesn't mean they're honest."

She considered that. "What's rule number two?"

"When someone hands you a lead to a killer, you know, like whispers their name in your ear?" He put his arm around her and guided her toward the Starbucks on the corner. "They're usually trying to put the blame on someone other than themselves."

CHAPTER 13

Sam spent the rest of the morning and early afternoon up in her room. Zach didn't really know exactly what she was doing, but it was clear she didn't want it to involve him. So, he stayed on the first floor, waiting for Nino to arrive. He had a long conversation with Vivi about her visit to Taylor Sly, and even the news that the police seemed to be that much closer to finding the person who hired the killer—since obviously Taylor Sly didn't pull the trigger herself—didn't make Sam very talkative or sociable when he went upstairs to tell her.

Zach imagined the ordeal of the lineup had been tough on her, and while he killed time in the afternoon, he'd used her laptop to read up on the history of Billy Shawkins's exoneration case, the Innocence Mission, and the extracurricular activities of one of their volunteers. One of their brilliant, beautiful, amazing volunteers.

All that did was ratchet up his respect for her, and remind Zach that a woman like Sammi needed her equal in life, a man as physically attractive as she was, as tremendously successful as he had no doubt she'd be, and more emotionally committed than he could ever be.

Not a shell who never really fit in anywhere, who had spent the better part of the last twenty years as the center of no one's life, and who would go through the rest of his life laden with guilt for mistakes he shouldn't have made.

She deserved a whole man, inside and out. He must have looked as miserable as that thought made him feel, because when he let Uncle Nino in and helped him with the grocery bags he carried, he got a loud tsk and shake of the head.

"What?" Zach asked.

"You're miserable, *ragazzino*."

"I'm hungry. What're you making?"

Nino pulled a salami out of a plastic bag and stuck it in his hand. "Dinner's later. Eat this now. Where's your girlfriend?"

"Principal," he said.

Nino looked over his shoulder. "What?"

"She's not my girlfriend; she's my principal, which is the technical term for the person being protected by a bodyguard."

"Principal my ass. She's your girlfriend, or oughta be."

Zach smiled, settling in at the kitchen table to slice some salami and reggiano cheese while his great-uncle cooked, an activity so familiar, he didn't even have to look at Nino. He knew what he was chopping by the sound of his knife and the smell of the room. Sage.

But the déjà vu was deeper, conjuring up an older memory. Naples. His mother. Little handpainted blue tiles on a backsplash and a dog they'd taken in as a stray and named Aldo. Which meant the old one.

God, he hadn't thought about Aldo in a long time. When he'd been taken away, Vivi cried so hard she threw up, and Zach had to clean her. He was still mad about Aldo when they got to the States and couldn't get a dog because Chessie was allergic to them.

"Did she find the killer in that lineup?" Nino asked, yanking him out of his unwanted memory.

"No, she's pretty gun-shy about the whole thing." He told Nino a sketchy version of the Billy Shawkins story. But his mind went back to Aldo. And that blue and white kitchen.

"Wonder what my mother would think of Sam?" he said, barely aware he had spoken out loud. But the clunk of Nino's knife on a cutting board assured him he had.

"Your mother was an excellent judge of character. Headstrong as hell."

"You didn't really know her," Zach replied.

"I met her a few times, and she's my blood, so that makes her like me and I know me. A good judge of character."

Zach took a bite of the hard cheese, the taste and smell like home. It made the memories even more poignant. "She must have been," he said. "Because she loved the hell out of me."

Nino turned, his dark eyes soft. "You have pain in your voice."

"I have reggiano in my mouth," he said, chewing at the same time. "No pain."

"She didn't love you."

Zach froze midchew, and scowled. "Like hell she didn't."

"It went way past love, especially with you. She doted on you. The sun rose and set on you. You were her reason for breathing, working, waking, sleeping. She thought—"

Zach held up his salami-cutting knife. "I get the picture."

"Do you?" Nino asked. "Do you, Zaccaria? Because I don't think you've ever forgiven her for dying and leaving you without a personal fan club."

He stared at the old man. "You been talking to Nicki? This is very deep shrink stuff that has no basis in reality."

Nino just shook his head the way he did when words in any language failed him. "You can't have yourself a girlfriend if you don't love yourself. It's just that simple."

Zach put the salami next to the cheese and stood up and headed to the door. "Thanks for the snack, Nino. I'm going to check on—"

Sammi was standing in the living room, cell phone in hand, three feet away. Fuck. How much of that bull crap had she heard?

"We have to go somewhere," she said.

"The police station again?"

"Revere. I have to see Billy."

He gave her a questioning look, and she lifted the phone as if it held the explanation, but all he could read was Suffolk County Department of Parole.

"It's from Adam Bonner, his parole officer. He says that he's having some issues with Billy's work attendance, and he thinks I should talk to him."

"In person? Can't you call him?"

She gave her head a little shake, her eyes sad. "I want

to see him, Zach. I need to see him. Obviously, I have to talk to him if he's skipping work, which is so not like him. But, I don't know, after today? This?" She jiggled the phone. "Was like a message from beyond. I really need to see him. I'd really rather go alone, but I know you'd never let me."

"You got that right." Anyway, it beat staying here and being psychoanalyzed by his great-uncle.

Nino promised he could let himself out and that the place would be secure, so they left through the back alley where Zach kept his car parked. Despite the afternoon traffic, he navigated the winding roads in the warehouse district of Revere easily, constantly on the watch for anyone following right up until they crossed a set of railroad tracks to the parking lot of a mammoth, windowless building bearing the sign North Side Paints.

"He usually comes out that side door over there," Sam said, pointing to a set of double metal doors near a half-empty parking lot.

"You come here a lot?" he asked.

"When I can. He doesn't have a car and has to take, like, three buses and the train to get home, so sometimes on my days off, I pick him up when his shift is over." She glanced at the clock in the dash. "Which is in a few minutes."

He parked where they could watch the entrance, scanning the area as he did.

"I saw a paint factory burn up in Pakistan a few years ago," he said, studying the building. "Brutal fire and explosion. Of course, it was deliberately set, but the smell was unforgettable."

"I didn't know you were in Pakistan."

Of course she didn't. Because he had cut off all contact long before Pakistan.

"What did you do there?"

"I blew up that paint factory, among other things."

She gasped softly. "*You* set the fire?"

"Not by myself." He tapped the steering wheel, taking in the height and depth of this factory, mentally figuring how they'd have handled it. "But it was clean, I'll say that. No one got hurt."

"No one at all?"

"Well, none of the good guys." He cocked his head. "Which I was."

"Still are," she said softly. "Even if you blow up paint factories."

"Past tense. I'm not blowing shit up anymore."

"But you're still one of the good guys." She gave him a teasing smile. "You're one of the Guardian Angelinos."

He snorted softly. "You and my sister."

"Me and your sister what?" He heard the laughing tease in her voice and stole a glance. Her eyes were glinting like sapphires.

"You feel better already, don't you, Sam?"

"I always feel better when I get here." She waved toward the building.

"Yeah, nothing like a paint factory to put you in a great mood."

She laughed again. "I know I'm going to see Billy. And that just makes me happy."

A spark of jealousy flared, surprising him with its strength. "You like him that much?"

"I love him," she said, throwing propane on his sparks.

"Seriously?"

"Seriously. How can I not? I basically destroyed the man's life, stole his days and nights, and put him in a prison for ten years, and now that he's out, he calls me buttercup."

"Buttercup?" He practically choked on the fumes of jealousy now. "You?"

She punched him softly. "You don't have to sound so stunned that a man would call me a pet name."

"I'm not. I called you plenty."

"But not for the same reason."

God, he hoped not. "What's his reason?"

She nodded toward the factory. "Let him tell you."

At the doors, a group of men exited, all wearing charcoal jumpsuits, carrying masks and lunchboxes, deep in conversation. Of the six or seven of them, some big, some old, some black, some white, one who apparently called Sam Fairchild *buttercup*. Zach had seen pictures when he did his Internet research, but couldn't pick him out from this distance.

"Can I go get him? He won't know your car."

One more glance around, using the sixth sense he'd honed on hundreds of patrols. "Yeah, but I'll go with you."

The tiniest flicker of panic flashed in her eyes. "No, he won't know who you are."

Was she that ashamed of how he looked? The scar burned just from the rise of blood to his face. "I'm sure he saw worse than me in prison."

"I just wanted to...talk to him first. Tell him...who you are." She actually seemed a little panicked.

"I'll introduce myself." He flipped open his door and

stood, watching over the roof as she did the same, her expression wary as she came around the car.

The men looked up at the sound and Sam waved. "Hey, Billy."

A few of the men said something, laughed, and then one broke away from the group, beaming at her. One of the black men, slight in build, with threads of gray in close-cropped hair. As Billy got closer, Zach could make out a gold tooth in the front of his mouth, and some deep black pigmentation marks on milk chocolate skin.

A very distinctive-looking man who would be hard to mistake for another, he thought as Sam approached him.

Billy's attention shifted from her to Zach, and he slowed his step noticeably. He didn't care, except that Sam saw the faltering step, too. He hated when people reacted to his wound that way.

"Hey, Billy, surprise."

"Well, look at you!" Billy reached for Sam and gave her a gentle hug. "This is a gift from God, I tell you. I can't wait to get home, and I just didn't want to ride those stinky buses." He turned to Zach and stepped back, taking him in.

"Billy, this is—"

"I know who it is."

He did? Sam said nothing, her smile tight.

"I recognize him."

Zach felt his jaw go slack. "You do?"

"Don't remember the fella's name," he said, stroking a nonexistent beard.

"Zach," Sam supplied quietly. "His name is Zach."

"That's right." Billy pointed to him. "Angel or Angelo or—"

"Angelino." Zach reached out a hand. "I'm afraid I don't remember meeting you, Billy."

They shook and Billy revealed his gold tooth, with a crucifix carved in it. "We've never met, but Samantha here told me all about you."

She did? An unfamiliar jolt slid through Zach, something that might be described as . . . a thrill.

"Billy," she said softly, a warning in her tone. What was she warning him about? Something not to say? Some secret they'd shared? About him?

"Well, you did tell me all about him. Why lie, buttercup? Can't lie when Jesus is watching. And He is watching." He put a hand holding a gas mask on her back and one with a soft-sided lunchbox on Zach's, inching them toward the car. "We've had a lotta long talks these past few years, and my friend Samantha told me all about the boy who went to war and forgot about her. What got you? Shrapnel? IED?"

It was Zach's turn to hesitate on the next step. "I didn't forget about her."

"No? Then what the hell happened to you? Other than a run-in with an ambitious explosive? No eye under there? That's a heck of a scar."

Zach peered right over Billy's head at Sam, who, son of a bitch, looked miserable. No damn wonder she wanted to "warn" Billy who he was meeting. She wanted to tell him not to talk.

But Zach wanted him to talk. Wanted to know everything Sam had said about him.

"That's correct, sir, no eye," he replied. "I'm sorry but the mission was classified."

"Oh, classified." Billy drew the word out to many

syllables, making a playful mocking face to Sam. "Is the reason you never called Miss Samantha Fairchild classi- fied, too?"

"No," he said simply. "That was just...stupid."

"Yes, it was, son," Billy said. "Damn stupid. This your car? That thing's almost as old as I am."

"Not quite," Zach said. "But it makes as much noise."

Billy chuckled, and didn't shut up from Revere to Roxbury, but, thank Christ, he stopped talking about all of Zach's shortcomings. Especially once Sam brought up the subject of his work attendance.

Billy turned from the front passenger seat, where she'd insisted he sit, to glare at her. "Adam Bonner is and always has been a man who lives to make trouble."

"On the contrary, Billy, he wants to help you. He helped you get this job and if you're not showing up—"

"I had one sick day, Sam, and I was really sick. Diar- rhea like you ain't never seen. I'm sorry, honey, don't make the face. It's the truth; you can ask Alicia. She was there, holding my hand through the whole thing."

"That's true love," Sam said. "But Adam made your work absences seem more chronic, Billy. Are you sure everything's okay?"

"I was just promoted to varnish batch loader, butter- cup! Would they do that if they thought I had a problem showing up for work? Do you know how important that job is on the line?"

"No, but I believe you. I just wondered if everything's okay."

"More than okay," he assured her. "'Specially now that I know you got your main squeeze back."

Zach spared a glance in the rearview mirror to get her reaction to that, but her attention was still on Billy. "You sure? Did you pop the question to Alicia yet?"

He sighed heavily. "I'm...thinking about it."

"Billy," she admonished. "She's a wonderful woman. Don't let her go. Don't pass up the opportunity of a lifetime. You'll never find another one like her. Ask her tonight?"

He smiled. "She's down in Natchez seeing her mama right now, but she'll be back in a week or so. Anyway, I'm just waiting on the Good Lord to give me a sign. I just haven't seen it yet."

"Well, don't wait for her to pack up and move out as your sign, Billy. It'll be too late to get her back." Sam sat back, still scowling at him. "And go to work every single day. Even if you have to drink Pepto-Bismol."

He laughed at her and pointed toward the next intersection. "Turn right here, son, and head on up the hill to the last little house on the right. That's my home." He lit up with pride. "That I would never be living in, with my Alicia and my brand-new Barcalounger, if it weren't for this young lady right here."

"Billy." Sam leaned forward and put her hand on his shoulder. "You know how I feel when you say that."

"You feel like you screwed up my life more than you helped it. Let go, Sam. Do me a favor and go be the best damn attorney in Boston. There you go, drop me off here. Thank you, Zaccaria."

She'd told him his full name, too? "No problem."

Billy unlatched his seatbelt and climbed out slowly, blowing a kiss to Sam. "If I do marry her, you'll be my best man, right?"

Sam laughed, opening her door to get into the front seat. "Of course. That's why I want you to pop the question."

"Then I just might." He motioned Zach. "Walk me to the door, young man."

Zach hesitated a second, but the neighborhood seemed very quiet and empty, and he'd watched every possible car on the way. They hadn't been followed. He got out and came around to the side to walk with Billy.

"You listen to me, and you listen good," Billy said, his voice low and stern. "That one there…" He pointed over his shoulder. "Is the real keeper. Be good to her. Promise me."

Zach wet his lips and swallowed. "She's in good hands, I assure you."

Billy leaned closer, putting a bony hand on Zach's arm, narrowing ebony eyes and staring right into Zach's good one. "You better promise me because I'm not afraid to be back on the inside. So believe me when I say if you hurt her again, I really will kill you."

Zach said nothing, facing down a man half his weight and size, and, oddly, feeling a little intimidated. He shook it off. "I understand that." But no promises.

Billy wasn't having it. "It's your business if you don't want to marry her, son. God knows I understand the weight of that decision. But here's what I'm asking, and I want your word of honor sworn on the graves of whatever men died by your side the day you lost that eye."

His gut clenched. "There were five of them," he said solemnly. "What do you want me to swear to?"

"Tell her why."

"Why."

"You know what I mean. Tell that woman why you walked away and left her behind."

"Billy, it was…" How could he tell this old man it was "just sex"? He wouldn't do anything to damage his impression of Sammi, and this guy would never understand.

"On the souls of the men who died beside you," Billy said. "All five. You tell her. And you tell her tonight."

Billy's eyes bored a hole in him. "I swear," Zach whispered.

"There's a shortcut right past that driveway," Billy said, looking satisfied as he pointed in the other direction. "Road's a little ragged, hill's a little steep, but it'll take you back down to Tremont a lot faster than turning around. Very, very few people know the shortcut. But tell Sam not to attempt it alone; it's too steep for her."

His affection for Sam was evident with every word and the look in his eyes when he waved one more time to her. "I love that girl, you know?"

"I know."

"Do you?"

Zach just looked at him, the question not clear. Did he know or did he love her? "Yes," he answered, and that seemed to work.

"God bless you both," Billy said quietly, then headed into the one-story clapboard house.

Zach watched him go inside, then returned to the car, slipping behind the wheel without looking at Sam. What had he just promised?

"See why I love him?" she asked.

"I see that it's mutual."

"I'm so lucky he's forgiven me. More than forgiven

me, if that's possible. He's...well, he's a changed man, too."

Zach just nodded as he pulled out, studying the route Billy had suggested and the sign at the end of the street that said "Dead End."

"Where are you going?" Sam asked.

"He said it's a shortcut."

"Really? I didn't know that."

"He doesn't want you to. Not safe enough."

"He's very protective."

"I could tell."

She laughed softly, pulling her seatbelt as though it constricted her. "I just texted Adam back to find out what's the deal with one day off. Billy wouldn't lie." She gave him a long look. "Are you okay?"

Was he? "Yeah. Fine."

"You know, I tried to head that off at the pass. I didn't..." She took a breath and let it out very slowly. "I didn't really want you to know I talked about you that much."

"Yeah, I figured that out." He found the shortcut and followed it down a long, steep hill, surprised that it led right into Tremont, silent while the last hour of conversation—mostly the last few minutes—replayed in his head.

Sam said nothing, facing her window.

The silence was so thick it hurt. He broke it. "Sam, it's been three years...and..."

He could practically feel her stiffen in anticipation. Where did he start? How did he say this?

He had to. After all, he'd just sworn on the souls of five men.

"Yes?" she prompted when he didn't continue.

"Why aren't you seeing someone by now?"

"Well..." She laughed softly. "I almost had a date this afternoon with a nice lawyer, but you had to go and ruin it by telling me he had a wig on."

He couldn't smile. It mattered too much. "Sam, did you...did you really think you were in love with me?"

A soft flush colored her cheeks. "Come on, drive home. I'm dying to see what Uncle Nino cooked."

"Sam."

She let out a slow, soft sigh. "I told you that morning you left, Zach. I loved you."

For one crazy second, he had that sense of déjà vu again. The blue tiles. The food smells. Aldo.

"I always think love...is going to end," he admitted. "So maybe I just made sure it happened sooner rather than later."

She just stared at him. "You know, as explanations go, that was crap."

Yeah, it was. But at least he didn't have to worry about those five souls he'd just sworn on. He'd kept his promise.

CHAPTER 14

When the gold 300E pulled up to Shawkins's house, the Czar smiled to himself in congratulations. Damn, he was good. He had had a hunch that she'd go tracking him down at work after he sent that text, and he was right about the guy he'd seen her with at the police station. Muscle. Muscle in an old-school Mercedes.

And here she was, bringing Billy Shawkins home exactly as he hoped she would.

Of course, he hoped she'd get out of the car, go inside for coffee, and let him climb in the back to wait and blow both her and her bodyguard's brains out when she returned. And make it look like Bad Billy had done the deed. Who'd believe that ex-con anyway? It would have been an open and shut case. Of course, Shawkins had been harboring hatred for years and finally lost it—that bitch put him in prison for ten years for a crime he didn't commit.

It would have been nice and easy. But Levon's life was just never that easy.

However, this new wrinkle was tempting his trigger finger. If that big ugly guy with the patch stood out there and shot the shit with the ex-con any longer, Levon could fire from where he sat, a few driveways away. Bang. One to Samantha's brain while she climbed out of the back-seat and got into the front.

But he couldn't take a chance with that guy. No doubt he was carrying, and his posture screamed military even if his hair didn't. Definitely military, with the war wound to prove it.

Levon smiled, the thought reminding him of his favorite song. *Levon wears his war wound like a . . .*

Levon stopped humming when the old man started toward the house, watching as Beauty and the Beast talked, then backed out. Should he just shoot now? Body-guard would have to tend her, and Levon could get away. But, still, it was sloppy. And she might not die.

Anyway, that approach was kind of sophomoric. The same kind of shit they were attempting with that bogus drive-by in Somerville last night. He had to do this the right way, and that meant he had to be a little patient and a lot creative.

They'd go right by him now, back the way they came. Then he'd pull out, just like any other person leaving their driveway, and keep a good long distance to follow.

It was time to find out where Samantha Fairchild was spending her nights.

But, son of a bitch, the Mercedes went the other direction. That was a dead end. He waited for them to turn around, but the gold sedan disappeared around the corner, and he lost sight of it completely.

God damn it, there *was* a way out back there. Not on

any GPS, and he'd checked three. He gunned it out of the driveway, past Billy's house, cruising to the top of a hill that was paved but hadn't seen an asphalt truck in a long time. It was a steep pitch, too, probably a bear in the winter. Halfway down, he cold see the Mercedes.

If they saw him, he could be marked. This was a little-known street, obviously some back route she knew about from being a regular visitor. He started down the hill, committed now. He drove closer, wanting to follow, but not be seen.

The Mercedes's brake lights flashed, and Levon considered backing up, but that would also put him on their radar. He just needed to go very slowly, let them get ahead, and then follow carefully.

But the Mercedes had stopped.

Levon let the truck drift a few more feet.

The Mercedes still didn't move. And worse, Levon was in their view now. He tried to slow down, stay back, but it was too late.

Patch peered in his rearview, and Samantha turned around, only to have the driver push her deeper down in the seat for cover.

Oh, fuck it all. His pulse quickened and his palms sweated on the steering wheel. A rarity for the Czar; but then, so was stupidity.

Would she recognize him? Thank God he didn't wear a wig today, and she'd never seen his natural, reddish hair. He had makeup on, colored lenses, and jowl changers. And without the elevator heels he'd worn to kill Sterling, he was barely five-ten.

Should he keep going, back up, or stay put?

Or fire two shots and hope that wasn't bulletproof glass?

Or throw it in reverse and peel backward? But if he did that, then Samantha would know without a doubt that he had marked her. He looked in his own rearview mirror and gauged the hill. Backing all the way up could rip the transmission from this piece of crap. That ancient Mercedes could fly up backward and upside down.

Why the hell had that guy stopped, anyway?

Because he was smart. And probably armed. He wanted to force Levon out of the car, or around them, or something. To get a shot at him. He could see the driver unlocking his seatbelt. Was he coming after him? Could Levon take them both, right now, right here?

Ugly, ugly. Yes, he could do the job, but the likelihood of leaving evidence was incalculable. Along with the likelihood of getting killed. He had to get out.

He threw the gear into reverse and slammed on the gas, jolting forward as the truck jerked and got traction on the potholed asphalt, tires squealing as he catapulted backward, the engine screaming, the weight fighting gravity, a feat for a good piece of machinery. A miracle for this.

The Mercedes rolled into action, doing exactly what he was doing, only better and faster. Son of a *bitch*.

He floored it and the truck fishtailed wildly, forcing him to fight with the wheel to stay on the road and go faster, farther. The Mercedes was five feet from him now, screaming, too, but in a much more powerful and controlled way.

Killing that son of a bitch would be fun. But he couldn't risk his whole career for the fun of it.

Finally he crested the top of the hill, whipping in a

tight circle to face the road, then smashing the gear back into drive. He slammed on the accelerator just as the Mercedes reached the top, turned on a dime, and cut him off, screeching to a stop.

Levon had to jam the brakes to keep from hitting him.

Now he was trapped, and there was only one thing to do.

"I'll get him out of the car," Zach said as he dragged the slide of the pistol Marc had given him and it clicked with a loud, satisfying finality. "You don't move, Sam, until I have him completely under control. Then you get a look at him."

She looked over his shoulder, inhaling a calming breath. The ride up the hill straight at what could be a killer had left her whole insides watery. "He's doing something. Getting a gun, maybe? Be careful, Zach."

He barely nodded, throwing open the door. He climbed out, aiming his pistol with two hands, as mean and menacing as anything she'd ever seen. He took long, slow strides toward the truck.

He left his door open, so she could hear, but the truck's windows were up and tinted, making it difficult to see the outline of the driver through the Mercedes's back window. It could just be some idiot following them. Could be one of Billy's neighbors they'd spooked by stopping on the hill. Could be some guy in a hurry who got pissed off that the car in front of him had stopped on the shortcut and decided to back up.

Or it could be the man who killed Joshua Sterling, hunting her down.

The man finally rolled down his window. Sam held her breath in anticipation of a shot, but he held up empty hands. "What the hell, dude?" he yelled at Zach.

"Get out of the car."

"Show me your fucking badge, then I'll get out."

"You're lookin' at it. Get out." Every step Zach took was predatory, intense, focused. If the guy driving the truck was just…no one…then he was probably saying his last prayers right this minute. Because Zach looked every bit the killer.

"Hey, just take my wallet, man. Just take the cards and I got about sixty bucks. Please. I need the truck. Please."

"Get out and put your hands on the car."

He opened the door, wearing a collared pullover with a Sears logo and dark pants, a tool belt hanging.

"Take that off and drop it on the ground." Zach said, nodding to the belt.

He unlatched his tool belt and released it to the ground; then he shot both hands up in the air again.

"Where's your wallet?" Zach asked.

"In my back pocket," he replied, starting to lower his right hand.

"Turn around," Zach said. "And stay that way."

The man did as ordered, giving Sam the first direct look at his face. Her heart dropped a little as nothing about him looked even vaguely familiar. He was certainly not the short-haired, pockmarked, six-foot murderer she had seen in the wine cellar.

"What are you doing in Roxbury, Mr. Martin?" Zach asked, the wallet flipped open. "It's a long way from Brockton."

"I'm trying to find an address for a washer repair.

That's what I do. I work for Sears." He glanced over his shoulder at Zach. "And everyone pays me in checks, man, so I don't have a lot of cash."

"What address are you looking for?"

"I think it's, um, 329 Hale Street. But there's no such number. I saw your car go down that hill and that ain't even on my GPS, so I followed."

"Step aside and put both hands on the hood."

He did, and Zach held the gun on him, while he reached into the car and looked like he was unplugging a GPS. Sam squinted at the face, kind of jowly. Hair over his collar. Definitely not as tall as she remembered. Or was he?

Oh, God. It was like the lineup all over again.

With one hand on the pistol and one on the GPS unit, Zach pressed a few buttons. He threw it back in the car and notched his chin toward the man. "Hands on the hood. Spread your legs."

He got a vile look, but the man flattened his hands on the hood of the truck and widened his stance, allowing Zach to pat him down.

Zach took a step back and gave a nod to Sam. "Come on out and take a look."

"A look at what?" the man asked. "Are you two some kind of perverts or something?"

Sam ignored the comment, walking closer.

"The GPS has home programmed as the same address that's on his license," Zach said. "Do you recognize him?"

The man narrowed blue eyes at her. "Who the fuck are you? Why would you recognize me?"

"Turn your head," she said.

The man just stared at her. "Fuck you."

"Turn," Zach ordered, raising the gun to the man's head.

He gave her a profile and Sam looked closer. No pockmarks. No bump. And no one's hair could grow that much in a week.

Unless he'd been in disguise that night.

"Can you face me again, please?"

He did, his expression softening. "Who you looking for, lady? Why are you staring at me?"

She'd only heard the killer say two words...*I'm in*...but this man's voice was completely different. At least, she thought so.

The all-too-familiar twist of second-, third-, and fourth-guessing curled low in her belly.

"No." She shook her head and then looked at the man who held the gun. "It's not him."

"You're absolutely positive?"

She wasn't absolutely positive of anything, except they'd just stopped a Sears repairman whose only crime was getting lost. She hoped.

"That's not him," she repeated, walking back to the car. She slowed her step, took one more look, and offered an apologetic shrug. "Sorry, sir. Really."

Zach flipped him his wallet, and the man fumbled and missed. By the time he was standing up from getting the wallet and his tools, they were already halfway down the street.

Sam watched him in the side view mirror, shaking his head as he got back into the truck.

"Sometimes," she finally said, "I don't think I'll ever trust my judgment again."

"Then you'll have a hard time in the courtroom, Sammi. Not to mention everywhere else in your life."

"Don't I know it."

"You're going to have to trust your instincts again at some point. Even if they're wrong, like mine just were." He put his hand on hers, as if it were the most natural thing in the world. And, oddly, it was. Sam didn't move; instead she just enjoyed the warmth and strength in that hand that had just held a pistol, ready to kill for her if he had to.

"I know," she agreed.

"Otherwise," he continued, "you'll never make a decision you won't second-guess. You'll never believe in yourself."

Exactly right. "That's my biggest fear."

"Then fight it and don't let one mistake haunt you for the rest of your life. That's just the suckiest way to live."

"Sounds like the voice of experience, Zach."

He just gave a noncommittal shrug.

"I know I shouldn't second-guess every decision," she said. "I mean, stopping that guy, that was the right thing to do."

"Damn straight it was. If that had been the guy who killed Sterling and is after you, then—"

"*Might* be after me," she corrected. "We have no proof."

"So you think that car that almost mowed you down behind your apartment and shot twice at us was just another random drive-by on a normal night in Somerville?"

She closed her eyes on a sigh, not bothering to argue. "But that wasn't the man," she said. "Although, you know, what if he was wearing makeup that night? He could be a master of disguises for all I know. He could be anywhere. Him." She pointed at a man getting into a parked car. "Him." Another one walking on the side of the road, a cell phone to his ear. "Or her." A blue SUV driven by a young woman.

Zach squeezed her hand. "You know what you need, Sammi?"

An unholy tendril of sexual longing curled through her at the tone and the question. That's what she needed, all right. Another hands-free orgasm. "What?"

"Some of Nino's homemade wine. I asked him to leave it."

"While you were talking about your mother?"

He lifted his hand. "I knew you were eavesdropping."

"Listening as I walked into the room is not eaves-dropping. Anyway, I wonder what she'd have thought of me, too."

"My mother? If I like you, she'd like you."

"Do you like me?" she asked, a smile tugging.

He just threw her a sideways look. "What do you think?"

She didn't answer as he parked in the spot behind the house and led her through the back door, their system for entering kind of normal now. He cased the first floor, and when he was certain it was clear, guided her past the kitchen. Then he searched the second and third floors.

While she waited, she inhaled the smell of something delicious Nino had cooked for them and eyed the carafe of red wine on the counter. God bless the man, she did need some of that.

Next to it was the plastic shopping bag full of the mail she'd brought home last night. She'd never even looked at it. Opening it, she tugged out the catalogs and bills, and one slightly oversized envelope with a typed address. No return address, but it was postmarked Boston.

Her heart jumped. Could it be? She tore it quickly, so desperately needing good news. Normal news. News that would make her certain of her future, her law degree, her dream.

Zach walked in. "Everything's clear."

"God, I hope this is what I think it is," she said, the edge of the envelope still sealed shut.

"What's that?

"Scholarship approval. I applied for about twenty of them, but haven't heard—ow!" She snapped her hand back, automatically sucking on the paper cut. "Shit, that hurt."

"Here, let me."

"It's okay," she said, sucking some more, then letting blood dribble on the envelope. "Like Harvard isn't going to get enough of my blood." She laughed.

He got the envelope open and blew into the slit to widen it, then handed it back to her. "I'll let you do the honors, Counselor."

She gave him a smile and reached in, the smile fading. "It's only one page. I smell a rejection." Ignoring the trail of blood she left on it, she opened the trifolded letter and stared.

And then the rest of her blood turned to ice.

"Here's a paper towel for the blood, Sam."

His words garbled, drowned out by the exaggerated thumping of her heart as she stared at the picture.

At her face. Her expression of fear. Like looking in a mirror. Except it was a picture...caught on tape...and at the bottom, red marker the same color as her fresh blood.

Until we meet again.

She looked up at him, the paper fluttering to the floor from her shaking hands. "It's from him."

"Jesus." He reached for the paper but she dropped it, letting it float to the counter.

"Don't touch it. It could have evidence. Don't..." Her gaze shifted to the look on her face in the picture. "I can't pretend he doesn't know me, Zach. And he wants me. He wants me *dead*."

Using the paper towel, he lifted one minuscule corner of the paper, which had been printed in black and white from a laser printer.

"How did he get that off a video camera?" she asked.

"I suppose there are a lot of ways. Copying it onto a computer, freezing the frame." With his other hand, he grabbed a clean towel and spread it on the table, gingerly laying the paper faceup.

"That must have been the moment I saw it happen. The very second. I was..." She frowned and shook her head. "See how faulty the memory is? I thought the camera was looking down more, you know, like it would have gotten the top of my head. That's like the killer himself took the picture."

He dropped into the seat across from her, studying the picture. "Unless this guy is a complete idiot, this makes no sense."

"Why?"

"Why warn you that he knows?"

"To scare me." She rubbed her arms, chills still blossoming. "Which he's done magnificently."

"To what end?"

"To let me know he knows my name, where I live. That I can't hide from him." She hated that her voice cracked.

"Exactly," he said, reaching a reassuring hand over to her. "Which would only put you on high alert. In deeper hiding. Unwilling to take any risk that would expose you to him."

She nodded, frowning at the picture, still not imagining that was the angle that the video would have gotten. "So why send it?"

"Maybe he didn't."

A fresh set of goose bumps danced up her arms. "Then who did?"

"That's what we have to figure out." He angled his head to look at the picture again. "Except you said he had the video camera with him. I suppose he could have given the tape to someone else. Like the person who hired him to kill Sterling. Maybe someone who wants you to stay hidden."

She swallowed hard as realization hit. "I guess I should call Detective O'Hara."

"Not so fast." He nodded to the picture. "Let's give that to Marc tomorrow. He has some really good connections at FBI evidence labs, and we should learn as much as we can from it before we hand it over. Nothing's going to happen tonight. I'll fill Marc and Vivi in tomorrow; then we'll decide what to do."

She pushed back from the table. "I'm afraid I lost my appetite again."

"Go take a bath," he suggested. "And here, take some

wine." He got up and got her a glass. "And let me know if you want company."

She smiled, for the first time since she'd opened the envelope. "You'll just talk me into...things." She took the glass. "And I need to be alone."

An hour later, the wine had done its trick, and the bath had just about finished her off when a thought occurred to her.

If Zach was right, and whoever sent the picture wanted her to stay hidden, was it possible that person didn't want the killer to find her? Why not? She had to ask Zach his opinion.

Climbing out of the lukewarm water, she toweled off, ran a brush through her damp hair, and stepped into the sleep pants and tank top she'd taken into the bathroom. Slipping into a pair of flip-flops, she opened the door and froze, sucking in a surprised breath.

A light flickered downstairs, and the notes of soft music drifted up with the aroma of food. She tiptoed down the stairs and peeked around the corner to the candlelit table, where two juice glasses of wine and a basket of bread waited.

Zach came around the corner from the kitchen with two steaming bowls of pasta. "I was just going to call you for Nino's linguine and clam sauce. Don't tell me you're not hungry."

She hesitated on the bottom step, fighting a smile. "This is a nice surprise."

"I'm full of surprises, Sammi."

She tingled at the endearment and the way he held his hand out to her. She took it, almost melting at how gentle his touch was.

"You feel better?" he asked.

"I do. I will." She let him lead her to the table. "I had to ask you something, but..." She just shook her head as he pulled out the chair with the same flair Keegan might with his best customer. "I forgot what it was."

"Who would want you to stay in hiding?" He took the chair on the corner, next to her. For the first time in days, he was on her right, his scar and patch easily visible, and highlighted by the candlelight.

"That's exactly the question I just asked myself," she replied. "We must have been thinking the same thing at the same time."

"I thought about that an hour ago," he said. "The rest of the time I was thinking about you."

She laughed self-consciously. "What are you up to, Zach?"

"Having dinner. Is that a crime? Although, I imagine someone who works at a four-star restaurant thinks this is." He handed her a paper towel. "No cloth napkins or fine crystal tonight."

"Three star. This'll work." She put it on her lap and reached for the glass. "Not sure I can take another of these." Or all of this... *romance*. "But cheers."

He lifted his glass to hers. "Here's to long conversations, Sam." He touched her glass with his. "The first of many."

She didn't drink. "Conversations? That means you want to..."

"Talk." He took a drink. "Specifically, I want to tell you what happened to me."

An inexplicable lump formed in her throat. "How you got your injury?"

"How I made the stupidest decision in my life, which I will no doubt live to regret forever."

So it *was* the voice of experience she'd heard in the car. "And that's how you got hurt?"

"No," he said, putting down the glass and closing his hand over hers. "It's how you did."

CHAPTER 15

I won't lie and tell you I knew I loved you when I got on that plane to Kuwait."

Her eyes, even lit by the candles, showed he'd made a direct hit.

"But I think I did by the time I landed."

She lifted her fork, then set it down again. "That must have been some flight."

"It was long," he acknowledged. "I spent the whole twenty-some hours next to my lieutenant, Scott Pillius. We'd done previous tours together, in Baghdad, a thousand foot patrols, a hundred near misses, a couple dozen good men and women lost. We were like brothers by then, and getting on that plane, knowing we were in it together?" He shook his head. "Well, we weren't going back to patrol neighborhoods and train Iraqi soldiers, like I told you we were."

She finally took a sip of wine. "You lied about what you were going to do?"

"I didn't tell you the truth. In the military, there's a fine distinction between the two."

"So what were you going to do, you and Lieutenant Pillius?"

Just the way she said his buddy's name, the sweet way it came off her lips, hurt a little. Scott would have loved her.

"Supporting Delta ops and Navy SEALs on terrorist hunts. Cleaning al-Qaeda scum from caves and safe houses. I was the platoon sergeant, in charge of four squads, about thirty-five soldiers, taking them into the inner cordon, weeding out suicide bombers, and women and children—who were sometimes one and the same— just some general housekeeping before the Deltas and SEALs swooped in to get who they came after."

He took his own drink, Nino's potent wine burning his throat as much as the confession he'd practiced while she'd bathed. She listened intently, her blue eyes trained on him, her body still but for that vein pulsing in her neck.

"Anyway, Scott and I, we talked all the way over. Nobody had any illusions that it was going to be easy. So, maybe to stay sane, we talked about how we'd spent our free time before deployment."

A soft flush of color rose in her cheeks. "You told him how we spent those three weeks?"

"It wasn't quite three weeks," he corrected her, deliberately not answering the question. "It was only nineteen days."

She closed her eyes. "You counted."

"Every one."

She put her fingers to her lips as though she were shocked by that, or just speechless.

"Didn't you?" he asked. "Didn't you count every day and every night?"

"To be honest, I counted the ones after you left, not while you were there."

He sighed, shaking his head, so damn sorry for that. "Well, I counted the ones we had, because..." *Because they mattered so much.*

"So what happened on the plane?"

"Well, first, let me tell you that I heard you crying when I got out of the shower that morning."

Her eyes filled. "I didn't want you to leave."

"You know, Sammi, for the first time since I'd joined the Army back in 2001, I didn't want to leave. I loved the Army. It was the real family I never had, one that I'd chosen, not...chosen by fate and a mother who was trying to make a point." He waved a hand, knowing their food was getting cold, but also knowing that neither of them cared. "But that time, I didn't want to go back to war. I didn't want to leave you."

She blinked, a tear snaking down her cheek, as painful to him as if it were a trickle of blood. "And when I said I loved you?"

He swallowed. "I just didn't know how to say it back. I didn't know for sure yet. I didn't want to just say it because we'd had great sex and I was leaving for war. It seemed so...cliché."

"There's a reason for clichés," she said softly. "Because they're...real."

"I didn't say it because I was scared to," he finally said.

"I was scared, too," she said. "But I said it. And I planned to keep saying it. I thought I'd send perfume-

scented love letters or be on the phone with weepy, emotional calls. But they never happened." Her voice cracked,
but she swallowed a sob. "So then I thought maybe I'd
say it again when you swept me into your arms at some
kind of patriotic homecoming where we both ran to
each other with flags waving and bands playing. I never
dreamed I'd never hear from you again."

Her tears rolled now, and his heart cracked with every
whispered, pain-filled word she said.

"There were no bands when I came home," he said
softly.

She wiped her face, digging for composure. "So what
happened on that plane?"

He blew out a long, slow breath. "Scott told me that
his wife was pregnant with twins. Which, of course,
being one, I thought was pretty cool. They knew it was
a boy and a girl, and before he left, they bought a house
in Columbus, where the seventy-fifth was stationed. His
plan..." He laughed softly just thinking about Scottie
and the way his eyes danced when he'd made his admission. "Was to finish this tour, get out, and be a stay-at-
home dad. Milly, his wife, was an accountant making
good money, and they'd decided he was going to be Mr.
Mom."

She smiled. "That doesn't sound like an Army
Ranger."

"I know," he agreed, thinking of his buddy beaming
over a diaper change. "He was so excited about it. He
just wanted to cook and do laundry and go to the park,
and raise those babies right up to college. He wanted the
whole nine yards, a life with... a wife."

"And you..."

"I realized I kind of wanted the same thing. With you."

Her throat made a soft sound, a mewl of pain, and it cut him like a dagger to the heart.

"I told Scottie that, well, I might have found my girl. My wife. My life."

She just stared at him, her eyes pools of tears. "Zach."

"He was killed two days after we got there."

"Oh, no." She blinked, and the tears fell. "What a horrible shame."

"They're all a horrible shame, Sammi." He heard the hitch in his voice, too. "Every single senseless death is a travesty. And every single soldier leaves behind someone. A wife, a mother, a child. Every one of them leaves a wake of pain and misery for the person they love."

"So you changed your mind." He heard the defeat in her tone, saw it in her eyes. "No love, no life, no wife...no one gets hurt if you die."

He shrugged. "I decided the day he died my odds sucked, and that if I wrote to you or called you or kept this...this...going, you'd end up folding the flag at my funeral. I thought you deserved a chance to move on to something a little more stable. I thought if I just let you go, you'd naturally find someone else."

He let his words fall on the table, final and precise.

"You thought wrong." She shoved the cold food to the side and leaned on the table. "And you could have asked me what I thought about being that wife, living that life. Didn't I get a say?"

"I knew what you'd say, Sam. You'd say you'd wait. You'd pray. You'd build a relationship with my family and have my picture next to your bed and live for emails that hardly ever came and phone calls that came even less. Then you'd have to face the man at the door with the inevitable news."

She slammed her hand on the table and pushed her chair back, anger coming off her in waves. "Well, you were *wrong*, Zach. It wasn't inevitable. There was no man and no funeral. And, damn it, I *lived* for those emails and phone calls anyway." Her voice cracked. "I waited for that…that…that fucking postcard that never came."

"I'm sorry." Hollow, hollow words.

"No, you're not." Her tears were dry now, but her fury fresh. "How long have you been home, Zach? A year? And you had to have come home at least once or twice before that, right?"

"Twice."

"Oooh!" She punched her fist in the air as if she could hit him. "And you couldn't call? Even when you were alive and healthy and fine?"

He didn't even wince. "I was home for a few weeks and didn't even see everyone in my family on those leaves."

"And when you came home for the last time?"

"I was injured." He said it simply, as though that explained everything.

"And your point is, what? That I wouldn't be interested in a man with one eye?"

He stood slowly. "This conversation wasn't supposed to be about my injury."

"Oh, no?" She held her hands up as if she had to stop everything. "Well, sorry, but we just can't avoid it anymore."

"I don't even think about it, Sam." He scooped up the dishes, hardly touched.

"You fucking liar."

He clunked the plates back to the table. "I am *not* a liar," he said. "I just told you the truth. From my heart, all that talking you wanted, I gave it to you. And now you want to pin me to the wall and give me shit about my *eye*?"

"It's the elephant in the room, Zach. You try to act like it's not there, but it is. Like you are normal, but you're not. Like you don't want pity, but when someone calls you a monster you—"

"I do not." He ground out the word. "I do not want pity."

"Then what do you want?"

Us. Love. Forever. Sight. Wholeness. You. Nothing Zaccaria Angelino could ever have.

"What do you want?" she asked again, more softly, defeat in her voice.

He went with the easiest. "You."

"I want you, too, Zaccaria." She whispered his name and held out her arms. "I want you so much."

But he couldn't move into those arms. "You deserve better." And that, he knew, was the real reason he couldn't write that fucking postcard. Even when he was whole.

So she closed the space between them, taking that one step that he couldn't. And his heart folded in half with love for her.

"Zach." She cupped his face like she had in her apartment, her warm, dry palm closing over his scar. "I don't want better."

He just looked at her.

"I want you," she said. "Just like you are. *You.*" She grazed the scar, threatening to slide her finger under the patch. He tried not to flinch. "I want that man who left me crying. The man who talked all night and made me laugh and drove me crazy. I want that man, no matter how he looks. Because that man, that man you used to be and that man I know you still are, that man looks..." She lifted the patch, inched it over his forehead, slid it off his head. "Exactly the way he's supposed to look."

She traced her fingers over the sewn flesh, the bumps of skin where an eye used to open and close, the burn incendiary now. He couldn't speak, couldn't utter a word that was in his heart. Couldn't say what he was feeling because he'd sound like an idiot.

But Sam didn't notice, because she was still touching him.

"That man who made decisions on a plane and then unmade them without consulting me...that man is still the most beautiful man I've ever known."

He gritted his teeth. "Now I know you're lying."

"I am not lying, Zach." She inched up on her toes and kissed his good cheek. Then his scarred cheek. Then his mouth. Heat coiled up inside him, his body betraying his brain, his need so much bigger than his pride. "I want to make love to you," she whispered. "And then I want to talk all night long."

"At least you've got it in the right order." He wrapped his arms around her waist and pulled her into him, closing his mouth over hers, folding her against him, devouring her lips and tongue. He could almost feel her melting, softening, angling her tender woman's body against his hard man's need.

He bent over and scooped her up, buckling her knees
in one arm and draping her shoulder over the other, then
bringing her face up to his to continue the kiss. She
wrapped her arms around his neck, arching up to him.

The kiss didn't end until he had her halfway up the
stairs, where he kicked open the bathroom door, inhaling
the lemony smell lingering from her bath as he leaned
over to stuff his hand in his hygiene kit.

"We're gonna need these tonight."

She kind of smiled and sighed and nestled into his
arms to let him get what he needed. "Just bring the whole
box."

He did, all the way up to her bedroom, where he
laid her on the bed. She stretched like a cat and practically purred, spreading her arms and bowing her back in
invitation.

He started with the tank top, easing it over her head
slowly like a striptease, revealing inch after inch of luscious skin, the soft curves of her breasts, the budded ber-
ries of her nipples.

His mouth watered for a taste.

She dipped her head out of the top and shimmied it
over her arms, half naked under him.

"Oh, my God, Sam. Oh, my God." He stared at her
breasts and tenderly touched one, circling the baby-soft
skin, lowering his head to kiss the other. Her fingers
threaded his hair, guiding his head to her nipple, a soft,
gentle moan from her throat as he suckled her.

He finally released the skin from between his lips, sitting up again to rip off his own T-shirt. Her gaze dropped
over his chest, lingering on the tattoo, then lower to
where his erection made an obvious bulge in his jeans.

"Nice gun." She grinned, indicating the holster and weapon he still wore.

"You like that?" He took it off, then unsnapped the jeans, lowering the zipper.

She looked hungrily at his cock, the uncircumcised head already pulsing through the foreskin. But it was the jagged, dagger tattoo that ran up his hip, alongside the length of his erection, that stole her attention. The tour in Pakistan.

She closed her hand over his shaft, sliding the skin up and down over the head, waves of pleasure and bliss rolling with each touch. "Oh, this is beautiful."

She'd always been complimentary. Loved the fact that he wasn't circumcised, swore it increased her pleasure.

"When we were together," he said, slipping his fingers into the elastic of her sleep pants. "You'd never been with an uncircumcised man. And since?"

She looked up at him, the playfulness in her eyes gone. "I haven't been with anyone since you left."

His fingers stilled. "No one?"

She shook her head.

"What were you waiting for?"

She closed her hand over his wrists and guided his fingers deep into her pants, over a soft mound, between her legs where sticky sweet moisture already dampened the tiny tuft of silk.

"I was waiting for you." She raised her hips to give his hands full access. "Even though you didn't want me to, I waited and worried and wondered." Each word was like a blow to his gut, each inch of her flesh on his fingers sending jolts of need through him.

"I prayed and watched the news and had my fantasies

that you would come back." The hits were to his heart now as he curled his fingers against the tender skin between her thighs. Emotion warred with excitement, pain punched pleasure.

She pushed her pants down, over her knees, and spread her legs so he could see what he was touching, all he'd been missing. She lifted her hips, to show him the sweet, wet, pink skin of her womanhood as she looked right into his face, his scar, his darkness.

"I know you didn't want me to, but I waited for you anyway, Zach."

He tried to speak but nothing came out of his mouth, and his throat was so tight, he knew all he was good for was a sob.

He pulled her up to him so they were kneeling face-to-face-and this time he took her face in his hands and kissed her. He kissed her as gently as he could, trying to use his mouth against hers to say all the words she deserved to hear. Appreciation. Adoration. Affection. Love.

The kiss grew hotter, their mouths hungrier, their hands desperate to touch everything they'd missed. They stripped each other, falling back on the bed, sheathing his engorged erection, rolling and caressing, stroking and kissing. She tasted like lemon and butter, and smelled like sex and soap, enthralling every sense and cell in his body.

"All right, Sammi. Now." He straddled her, inching her knees up as their gazes locked. As he entered her, she closed her eyes and bit her lower lip, nodding with permission to complete this. He probed farther, sliding his shaft into her body, hissing in air as her tight flesh enclosed him and magnetically, magically pulled him in.

"Thank you for waiting for me," he whispered, fully hilted.

"Thank you for coming home."

His pulse exploded in his ears, almost drowning out her strangled breaths, her soft whimpers, her whispered cries of his name. Lost, bursting, and seconds from detonating, he held completely still, fighting every impulse to rock against her, remembering exactly how she liked to come.

She ground against his pelvic bone, her jaw loose, her eyes closed, her face pink with pleasure. Digging for control, he stayed still while she moved beneath him, a sob escaping between her moans, then a long groan of ecstasy as she reached her climax.

Almost instantly she began a different, steady rocking, taking him in and out, pulling his orgasm from deep inside. Fire licked at his balls, need squeezed low in his back, tension twisted up his shaft until he couldn't take it anymore.

White light blinded him, her hair tangled in his hands, her scent making his nostrils flare as he let go, hammering against her, spilling all he had over and over and over again, his own grunts distant and deafened by pleasure.

He fell on her, strangled for air, dripping with sweat, helpless and shameless and lost.

His face smashed against hers, his scars pressed against her creamy complexion, their joining skin soaked.

She inched far enough away to be able to see him, looking directly into his mutilated, scarred, stitched-up hole of an excuse for an eye.

Her finger traced the bumps again. "I'm getting used to you touching it," he whispered.

"Zach." Her voice was full of wonder and disbelief. "You're crying."

He smiled. "The bastards didn't get my tear ducts."

"Why did you decide to tell me? What happened?"

He snuggled her closer, inhaled her sweet smell, kissed her cheek. "I made a promise to someone." He kissed her again. "I swore on—"

He shot straight up and slammed a hand over her mouth, the tiny crack of something in the distance...in the kitchen...stealing all his attention.

"Fuck."

He grabbed the gun and vaulted off the bed, landing silent on bare feet.

A distinctive double snap of a pistol slide being racked echoed up the stairs.

"Oh, my God," she whispered. "Someone's in the house."

Footsteps on the hard wood of the living room. The soft music went silent.

He pointed to the other side of the bed and mouthed, "Hide!" and she rolled over, soundlessly slipping to the floor.

A boot hit the bottom stair.

Zach focused on the bedroom door, spinning through what-if scenarios for the best line of attack, every sense alive, just as if he were on a sweep mission, clearing out bombs, ready for the worst at any second.

But then he had two eyes for visual cognition. Now he had to rely on four other senses, and gut. For some reason, some stupid, inane reason, his gut wasn't on fire.

Why not?

Had he lost his touch? His famous ability to detect any

anomaly in the area? Had Sammi's sweet, sweet body turned his mind to Jell-O?

Not that he needed to *detect* an *anomaly*. Because some motherfucker was coming upstairs with a racked pistol, and that bastard would die before anyone else did.

How would a professional attack? This was a hit man, an assassin. He'd come around slowly. But he sure as fuck wasn't quiet. Why not? He was on the landing outside the second-floor bedroom now.

Staying in the shadows, Zach moved silently, grateful his nakedness meant he could be completely silent, and his vision was strong since he'd made himself used to dim light.

He crouched and dove to the other side of the door, getting in position, using the door as cover. When the prick took one step into the room, he was dead.

He was coming up now, three steps away. Zach didn't dare take the chance of moving, of leaping into the hall and firing away. He could be hit first if he made so much as a single sound. He had to have the element of surprise on his side.

Although the intruder had seen the candles, the dinner, the signs of life. He knew they were up there. He turned the damn music off to *warn* them.

One more step.

He heard his breath now, slow and steady. A killer with no fear, no guilt, no compunction.

There was only one problem with killing him. Then they'd never know who hired this fucker, and someone out there might still be after Sam. So he had to get a name out of him before he blew his brains out.

He was on the top step now. Zach glanced at the bed, to make sure Sam stayed hidden on the other side of it, against the wall. There was no sign of her. Good girl. She wouldn't want to see this.

A boot hit the hall and Zach braced to attack.

A man's foot stepped over the threshold, giving Zach a view of a steel-toed boot. A military man.

Something unearthly sent a shiver up his spine, tingling at the base of his neck. Some people didn't deserve to wear even the lowliest part of a uniform.

Just as the man entered the room, Zach lifted his bare foot and smashed the door right into the guy's back, leaping forward to attack as he stumbled, seizing him from behind.

The other guy elbowed him soundly right in the gut, spinning to take him down, but Zach slammed him in the side of the head with the pistol, got a knee in his groin, and pulled him to the floor.

A grunted "*fuck*" was all he heard, as a mighty arm took a swing at Zach's face, smashing his nose hard enough for him to feel it crack. Zach managed to get on top, a hand to his throat, but the other guy flipped him hard, knocking his head against the door. Zach kicked at his hand, and was rewarded with the satisfying sound of the other man's gun sailing across the floor.

Zach lifted his weapon, but got a boot in the stomach, throwing him sideways to the floor. The other guy took the top, pulling back to slam a fist just as Zach managed to turn the gun toward him, his finger on the trigger. One press, one touch, and this dude was DOA.

Suddenly he was blinded by light as the room exploded in brightness. Sam had turned on the light.

"I have his gun. I can kill him."

Caught off guard, the man jerked toward Sam's voice,

off guard enough for Zach to flip him and wrestle him to the floor.

"Don't shoot yet," he yelled to her. "He's gotta tell us who..." He blinked at fiery eyes leveled at him. They looked up in shock, horror, and then disbelief. "...sent him." He finished, blood draining from his head, dripping from his nose, splashing on the face below him.

"Jesus Christ almighty." He wiped the blood off his face. "God damn it, man."

"I have a straight shot, Zach." Sam's voice wavered, but not much.

"Don't shoot him," he managed to say, inching back, the realization of how close he had come to killing this man exploding like an IED in his brain.

"Why not?"

Despite the blood dropping from Zach's nose all over his face, Gabe managed a slow, shameless grin. "'Cause I'm his motherfucking cousin. And, dawg, can I just say that you are one ugly sonofabitch?"

CHAPTER 16

Billy's knees hurt, but he folded them on the hard wood anyway and closed his hands in prayer, leaning against his bed where his Bible lay open to Psalms.

"Hello, Jesus. It's me, Mr. Shawkins."

If Alicia were here and not down in Mississippi visting her mama, she'd laugh at that. She loved to remind Billy that Jesus would just call him Billy. But there were so many praying people named Billy, plus Jesus respected him too much to use his first name.

Jesus loved him, of that he had no doubt.

"I saw my friend Samantha Fairchild today." He looked up, making contact with the rough plaster of the ceiling, imagining the clouds where his God lived. "She told me to get a sign that I should marry Miz Beckerman. Whatdya think, Jesus? Could you send me one?"

The slightest ping of metal against metal echoed softly down the hall.

That made Billy smile. Alicia's kitty probably bumped something, but he'd take it as a sign anyway.

"Think I should surprise her, Jesus, or let her pick out her own ring? I've got two thousand dollars, as you know, right there in that drawer. She and I could go together and get whatever she..." Billy closed his mouth, certain he'd heard another sound.

What did that darn cat get into now? The little furball came with Alicia; he'd accepted that. But still, it was a troublemaker.

"Course, she's a traditional kind of lady, and she might want—"

The soft sound halted him again. Was that the cat mewing? Or...was that the back door, waiting for the oil he'd promised Alicia he'd put in the hinges?

He froze in his prayer position, slowly laying his hands on the green chenille bedspread and very, very quietly pushing himself to a stand, aware that all the little hairs on the back of his neck were up the way they used to be at Walpole when bad trouble was brewing among the inmates.

When someone was about to get hurt, or worse.

His hands felt regrettably empty as he stood. In another life, another time, he'd be armed. No one should live in Roxbury unarmed. A man ought to have the right to protect himself.

But ex-cons didn't have no such rights, no matter how exonerated they might be. Plus, Alicia hated guns.

Was that a footstep? Was someone in the kitchen?

He glanced to the closed window, which was near enough to the ground for him to climb out. There was no other way out of the house without passing the kitchen.

The hall was dim, lit only by a night-light stuck into a socket 'cause Alicia said the cat hated the dark. And because of that, he'd left a lamp on in the living room, and the stove light in the kitchen.

A foot scuffed linoleum. What could someone steal? His two thousand dollars, his TV, his Barcalounger. Let him have it, the miserable crack addict. He wasn't gonna die for his stuff, and they'd be caught soon enough. They'd find out what happens on the other side.

Without making a sound, he inched around the bed, considering his options. The window would stick, the closet door would squeak, the bed was too low to hide under.

He peeked down the hall again, seeing no one, but hearing the side door that led to the garage open, recognizing its own distinctive cry for WD-40. How much time did he have? He didn't have anything of value in the garage, but then, he didn't have much of value anywhere.

Except in that dresser drawer. His stomach turned at the thought of that hard-earned money burned up on crack or meth.

Hands shaking, he eased open the bottom drawer and slipped his hand past all his nicely folded undershorts to find the envelope. He took one more look at the window, swollen from last week's rain and glued like day-old pigment in the color grinder. Maybe he should try anyway. As he moved the curtain, he heard a tool hit the garage floor, the sound seemingly deafening.

Fear crawled up his skin, and he squeezed the cash. Somebody might kill for this much. If he ran out the kitchen right now, he could land smack into someone holding a hammer, a wrench, a gun.

Clutching the money, he darted into the hall, stopping at the basement door and opening it as quietly as possible, then slipping into the blackness, closing the door soundlessly behind him.

On the top step, he hesitated, mildew and dust tickling his nose. He knew every hiding place down here. In the corner behind the stationary tub, in the storage area in back of the stairs. But the furnace and water heater made the best spot. Too skinny for most men, but he'd squeezed in there just a few weeks ago when the water pump was leaking.

Perfect. He moved with purpose now, determined to outwit the little prick, Jesus on his shoulder guiding him. At the bottom of the stairs, he turned left, reaching out his hands like a blind man to feel his way, bare feet on the cold cement, his eyes trained on the flickering blue light at the bottom of the furnace. It wasn't running, of course, but the pilot light was steady.

Over his head, he heard footsteps, heavier than before, probably comfortable in the knowledge that nobody was home. He reached the water heater, shimmying his body between the warm metal of the heater and the cool of the unused furnace. If this had happened in January, he'd have burned himself just touching it.

But it was July, and Jesus was on his side. He had to suck in his stomach and turn sideways, but he maneuvered into the slot, still clutching his two grand.

If this wasn't a sign, then what was it? Once this punk was gone, he was calling Alicia down in Natchez, telling her to come home and marry him. He had his—

The basement door opened and light doused the area. Billy crunched his teeth together to keep from sucking in a surprised breath. He hadn't counted on the light. He could be seen, but if he was perfectly still, a thief would never even look at the furnace.

He peered through the slot he'd just entered, unable to move an inch without risking making a sound.

He couldn't see the stairs from this angle, but heard footsteps.

As the man came around the two-by-fours nailed together to make a wall between the water heater and the laundry area, Billy backed deeper into his spot, saying the Lord's Prayer so fast the words ran together in his head.

The intruder came closer.

Billy held his breath and closed his eyes, thanking Jesus for his dark pajamas and black skin. Tonight, right now, he wanted to be a shadow.

"Hello, Mr. Shawkins."

Billy's eyes popped open, gasping as the man stood inches from him, just outside the opening.

"I got money," Billy said, slowly raising the envelope. "That's all I got. Take it and leave."

"No, no, Mr. Shawkins." He sounded disappointed and a little disgusted as he raised a pistol to his face. "I don't want your money."

"What do you want?"

He grinned. "The same thing you do. Revenge on Samantha Fairchild."

Billy frowned. Samantha? "No, I don't. I've made my peace with her. I don't want to hurt her."

"Oh, I'm not gonna hurt her. You are."

No, he was not. "Well, I don't know where she is. She was here today, but she left. I swear to God, I swear on the Bible, I swear on the name of Jesus in Heaven, I don't know where she is."

The man sighed, a baseball cap pulled so low it was impossible to see his hair or eyes, just a sharp jaw and tiny teeth. "Well, then we're just gonna have to get her back here, aren't we?"

"I don't know how."

He inched the pistol farther into the slot. "You better figure it out, Mr. Shawkins. 'Cause I'm not leaving this house without a dead body behind me. It's gonna be you or it's gonna be her. I'd say...she owes you."

Sam had finally fallen asleep to the sound of the men's deep voices, lulling her into a secure slumber. No one was going to get her with those two on the watch. But when she woke, Zach had a muscular arm wrapped around her waist and once again, he slept with his cheek resting on her hair.

She didn't move, no matter how much she wanted to, knowing instinctively that the position gave him so much comfort and relief that even slipping out of bed to go to the bathroom would hurt him.

She closed her eyes and listened to him breathe, letting the sheer wonder of being in his arms float over her. The heat of their entwined legs. The pressure of his hips against her backside. Zach Angelino, back in her bed. Back in her heart.

Oh, Sammi. Big mistake.

Or was it?

She pushed away the worry and wallowed in the bliss.

She heard a noise in the kitchen downstairs, and she

pictured Gabriel Rossi, the intruder she and Zach had
damn near killed. A little shorter than Zach, but no less
muscular, Gabe moved like an animal, laughed from his
heart, and swore like the devil's best friend.

And like the whole Rossi-Angelino family tree, Gabe
was gorgeous. His hair was buzzed so short it revealed
a beautifully shaped skull and highlighted wolflike blue
eyes under slashes of black brow. His neck was thicker
than Zach's, his jaw less defined, his smile so fast and
easy it was infectious.

He never said what he was doing, why he was there,
or how long he'd stay, at least not while Sam was awake.
She picked up enough of his nonverbals to know it was
better not to ask.

Water ran in the sink, and she heard the back door
open and close. She tensed a little, ready to get up.

"He's not leaving," Zach whispered into her hair.
"And neither are you."

"He's our guest. We should make him coffee."

He snorted softly, releasing her hand to explore her
body. "You were asleep when I came in." His erection
stiffened against her backside as a dish dinged on the sink
in the kitchen, the sound floating up the stairs and making
guilt outweigh desire.

She slid her hair out from underneath him, earning a
soft grunt of disappointment. Turning, she smiled at him,
pleased that he'd never put his patch back on. He could
wear it in public, but for her, he didn't need to hide.

"I'm going to the bathroom; then I'm going to see if
he needs anything."

"Oh, he needs something," Zach said. "But you can't
give it to him."

"Meaning?"

"He's going on a mission in the next day or so. What he needs is good luck, great timing, and eyes in the back of his head. Fortunately, he has two out of three."

She slipped out of bed and grabbed her sleep pants, stepping into them and straightening her tank top.

"So he'll only be here for a day or two?"

"If that. He might leave this morning after..." His voice trailed off.

"After what?"

He grinned and rolled over, reaching for his patch. "Go get some coffee and I'll tell you what my spook cousin and I cooked up while you were sleeping. I'll be down in a few minutes."

Still curious what he had in mind when she got downstairs, she glanced around the living room. The only sign that someone had slept there was an afghan she'd never seen before neatly folded over the back of the sofa. Their dinner dishes were cleaned, too.

The kitchen was spotless, too, except for a backpack and a roll of something that might be a sleeping bag tied under it. Coffee brewed on the machine, a single cup washed and rinsed on a dishtowel that had been folded with military precision. She tiptoed to the door and inched the blinds to reveal a heavily overcast morning.

Gabe was on the grass doing one-handed push-ups. Fast. Without a break. His white T-shirt was drenched in sweat, camo pants low on his hips.

She couldn't help watching.

After what had to be over a hundred one-armed pumps, he bounded to his feet, cracked his neck left to right, and looked toward the threatening skies. He closed his eyes, made the sign of the cross, and marched toward the door. A religious man with Satan's swearing skills?

"Morning, Sam," he said as she opened the door for him, not at all surprised to see her. "Did you count? I lost track at one seventy-five."

"I lost track at twenty-something. Do you do that every day?"

He plucked at the sweat-drenched shirt and grinned at the sucking sound it made as it separated from his skin. "Hell, yeah. Five A.M., rain or shine. Romeo still asleep?"

She laughed softly. "He's on his way down. I understand you two are cooking something up."

"Just a felony. We figure we know a good soon-to-be lawyer."

A felony? "Three years until I get my degree, and probably another to pass the bar." She poured a cup of coffee, then added some milk. "So you better not get caught, or get a real lawyer."

As she put the milk carton back in the fridge, he grabbed her arm. "I never get caught." His gaze dropped to the milk, where it turned to pure lust. "That fucker looks like the Holy Grail to me. Can I have it?"

"Of course." She gave the bottle to him. "Help yourself."

"Zach's right about you." He twisted off the plastic cap, flipped it into the trash without looking, and put the bottle to his mouth to gulp.

Her stomach did a somersault imagining exactly what Zach had said that was "right" about her. But she refused to ask, instead giving him a wry smile as he wiped his mouth like a twelve-year-old who knew he had broken the rules and didn't really care.

"What's funny?"

"Your mother let you do that?"

He chuckled. "Lemme tell you something, Sam. My ma's got two weaknesses, I'm happy to say. Me and Chessie. Ever notice how we're the only Rossis with blue eyes?" He winked one of them, the thick lashes brushing together. "Frannie had a secret lover; that's my opinion. Chess and me? We're not Judge Jimmy's kids. You can tell by looking at us."

For a minute, she thought he was serious; then he laughed and nudged her. "The whole family's batshit crazy, don't you think? Throw in the two orphans from Italy—one a daredevil, the other just *the* devil, and I don't have to tell you who's which—and we had a helluva household. I miss them all."

She regarded him, considering what he'd add to the chaos, insults, and love that went zinging around "Frannie's" table. "I bet your mother'd do anything to see you, Gabe. Even keep a secret."

He held up a hand, like "don't go there." "Honey, I'm not afraid of Ma spilling the beans. It's somebody trailing me to her that worries me. I got freaks who want me dead."

"Welcome to my world," she said drily, taking her cup to the table. "Maybe you need some help from the Guardian Angelinos?"

"Oh, please, Vivi's smoking crack again."

"You don't like the idea?"

"Hell, yeah. I love the idea, but the name sucks donkey nads, if you know what I mean."

She laughed. "So, whatever you call the business, do you think her idea can work?"

"*Her* idea? Oh, that's rich. Okay, I'll let her take credit, but I'm the one who put her in touch with our second or third or whatever cousin down in New York. I've worked on a case with that Christiano dude, and he's a bad emeffer. Plus he cooks like freakin' Nino. But, yeah, Vivi and Zach could do what his company does." He stopped for a dramatic pause and grinned. "If they had about a million bucks."

"They need an investor, then."

"Slightly." He tossed the empty milk container in the trash. "Aren't you client number one?"

"Yep, and I'm pro bono for them, so no million bucks for this job."

"There could be paying clients, though. I sure as shit know a few. And something has to feed my boy Zach's need for controlled adventure now that he's not on first approach. And, trust me, he can be in charge of recruiting. That son of a bitch has saved so many Delta and SEAL asses, you can't imagine how many favors he's owed. You have no idea what that animal did over there."

"No," she agreed. "I don't. He doesn't talk much about it."

"He's just bitter."

"About his injury?"

"About having to leave." Gabe sat in one of the chairs, knuckling the Formica top to make his point. "That man would never have left the military if they didn't squeeze him out."

"They squeezed him out?"

He shrugged. "Desk duty. Same difference to a guy like

him. And don't listen to that BS that says you can't be a
Ranger with impaired vision. He maybe can't do some of
the shit he did before, but he can still sniff out trouble in a
safe house and clean out a room of terrorist asswipes and get
mission-critical information out of a battle situation with the
one eye he has closed tight. But Uncle Sam didn't think so.
And neither did Christiano's ass-kicking chick boss."

"Could you possibly clean up your language in front
of a lady?" Zach marched into the kitchen, barechested,
the fly on his faded jeans unbuttoned, the tattoos and
some scars on full display, except for his eye, which was
covered by the leather patch. The one visible was narrowed in fury.

"Here's Happy, dwarf number seven." Gabe stood and
yanked his shirt off, revealing a few tattoos eerily similar
to Zach's and just as many muscles. At the sink, he threw
the shirt in, flipping cold water on it and dousing it in
some dish soap. "So, Sam, you ready for a little action?
We'll need you on the job."

"What's it entail?"

Zach stabbed his hands through wet hair, taking the
other seat to stare at the photo of her that still lay on the
table. "Gabe's a digital-imaging expert," he said. "Did
he tell you what he noticed about the picture, or was he
too busy reviewing the shrapnel holes in my résumé?"

"I love it when you whine," Gabe said with a chuckle,
leaning against the sink, abandoning his efforts at laundry.

"What about the picture?" Sam asked.

He shifted his cool blue gaze to her. "Here's what I
see in that picture, Sam. First of all, that's from a high-
res, expensive digital camera; you can tell by the way the
light curves over your face. Even a really top-quality film

camera, which it doesn't sound like the one your hit man took, would not have the change in density between the light and dark that's on there. See?"

She squinted at the picture and certainly did not see, but nodded, accepting his expertise.

He gave the shirt a squeeze and shake, then smoothed it over the rim of the sink. "You said the camera was above you, right? Pointed down at, what, about a forty-five-degree angle?"

"Yes, maybe ten or twelve feet off the floor."

"Then there was another camera in the room. A much better CCTV, with a feed somewhere. More than just Harry the Hit Man has your picture, sweetheart. Hate to break it to you."

Her jaw dropped as she processed that.

"My guess is if we find out who that is," Zach said, "we find out who arranged to have Sterling killed."

"Bingo," Gabe said. "And, you know, the hit man doesn't get his money until all the witnesses are taken out. If he can't take you out, whoever hired him to do the job doesn't have to pay. Or, if they do the job themselves, they can pay him less. This is an old trick, usually complicated by one other little fact."

Zach leaned forward. "The assassin has to prove he killed you to get his money. Unless they get you first."

Inside, her whole being grew cold. "Are you saying there are two people after me? The person who hired the assassin *and* the assassin?"

Zach nodded. "It's possible. I'd like to know exactly where that other camera feeds and who knows they're in there. Gabe might be able to get us that information if we can get the chip from the camera."

"Knowing your height and the angle of that picture, I think we could find the camera. I'm kinda good at stuff like that." Gabe added a cocky smile. "Shit, I'm good at everything."

"That's the felony?" she asked.

"Simple restaurant break-in," Gabe said. "No biggie. If I can get the chip out of a hidden CCTV, I know someone who can find out where it was programmed to be sent. We'd know where it's going, and we might know—assuming it's not legit and installed by the restaurant owner—who monitored the hit and maybe who paid for it."

"Right now, it's the only lead we have and maybe one the police don't have," Zach said. "I think it's worth a shot to get whatever information we can."

Sam agreed. "But the police have scoured that cellar. It was a crime scene. Do you mean to tell me they haven't found a hidden camera and therefore don't know who has the feed? They would confiscate that as evidence."

"Hey, maybe they did," Gabe said. "Maybe the fucking cops sent this picture to you."

She and Zach shared a look, both thinking of what JP had found in her file. *Intimidate. Impeach. Provide incentive to lie.*

But would someone actually destroy evidence of a murder to get her?

"It's a long shot," she said.

"My favorite kind," Gabe replied. "Whatdya say, cuz? You up for an adventure?"

Gabe and Zach grinned at each other like bad boys about to vandalize the playground.

"I really hate to ruin your fun," Sam said. "But I

have a key and I know the alarm code. We can just walk in."

"Keys to the wine cellar?" Zach asked.

"I know where one is hidden. Anyway, there's never a guarantee that the restaurant's empty. Chef comes in during the wee hours, so does the maître d' and the sommelier. Plus, there's a cleaning crew. It's just unlikely to walk in and find no one. But I still like the idea, and think we should do it."

"Look, if there's no subterfuge, I'm out." Gabe laughed at Sam's stunned look. "Kidding, hon. But, seriously, if you don't need me, then I'd be much happier if you two handled this and I could maintain a zero profile. If you tell me your exact height to the quarter inch, I'll show Zach a formula that'll help figure where the camera is or damn near. Then you two get the chip, which will take a few minutes and some tools that I'll give you, and meet me afterward. I'll take it from there."

"Five foot five and three quarters, barefoot," she said. "Are we going to call Detective O'Hara and tell him someone sent me this picture?"

Zach looked at her as if she was nuts. "No."

"Yeah, you're right. I'll go get ready to leave. The earlier we're there, the less chance of people in the kitchen." As she walked past Zach, he dragged a finger over her knuckles and gave her a secret smile.

"No second-guessing now, Sammi."

"I promise." She left and crossed the living room, on the way to the stairway, when she noticed her flip-flops, discarded under the dining table, lost when he'd scooped her up and Rhett Butlered her to bed.

Her smile widening, she sidestepped and reached under the table to get the shoes.

"See, what'd I tell you?" Zach asked, his voice soft and conspiratorial, but loud enough for her to hear.

She froze as her fingers curled around the straps. Eavesdropping was never a smart move, but when it was the man she once loved talking about her...how could she resist?

"Oh, you're right," Gabe said. "You better run like hell."

"I will, as soon as this whole business is over."

Her smile faltered and disappeared as she quietly picked up the shoes and tiptoed up the stairs. No need to second-guess—now she knew exactly what she was in for.

Again.

CHAPTER 17

I hate you. I hate you with the strength of a thousand suns," Vivi snarled at her phone, comfortable that her boss had hung up and didn't hear her exclamations of disgust. The very last thing she wanted to do was chase down a story about a mugging on the Emerson campus. Seriously, this was investigative reporting?

"I have a murder to investigate, dude," she said to the phone as she tossed the device on the coffee table in her living room. "I hate you, Tom Swift."

Well, Swyff, but her editor at the *Bullet* wasn't always too swift, so he'd earned the nickname. The phone dinged again, this time a text.

Get on the interview, Vivi. You haven't filed a story in days.

God, he was relentless. She typed in *bite me...* then deleted. Probably not a great time to get fired. She still needed income, plus the *Boston Bullet* connections could provide a steady stream of potential clients for the Guardian Angelinos.

I'll head over to Emerson and track the victim down.

She stabbed Send and swore softly. Some people were just not made to have a boss, she thought as she grabbed a light hoodie. It wasn't cold, but the skies were threatening, which meant take the T, and carry the board.

Where the hell had she put her Charlie Pass? She checked all the usual places, finding nothing, frustration mounting, then stuck her hands in the jacket pockets.

No Charlie Pass, but she pulled out a tiny jump drive. Was this hers? She flipped it around, certain she'd never seen it before.

Curiosity outweighed the need to get over to Emerson. Instead, she powered up her laptop and stuck the drive in the USB port, trying to remember if she'd ever seen the device before. Maybe she'd picked it up at the *Bullet* office last time she was in?

There were three documents in a file called FM. One was a jpeg; the other two were Word docs. She tried the image first, opening up to a scan of a newspaper article. The *Boston Globe*, she thought, but old. Very old. In a typeface she hadn't seen on anything but microfiche, probably from the late 1970s.

The headline had been cut off, but as soon as she started reading, she knew what the FM stood for.

Once again, alleged Irish mob leader Finley MacCauley eluded arrest…

A fine chill made the hairs on the back of her head do a little happy dance, the way they always did when she was on to something. She minimized the image and clicked on the first unnamed document. Across the top, the words CONFIDENTIAL/DRAFT in huge oversized caps. Her gaze slid down to the opening paragraph...

The Brahmin crowd is about to be hit with a bomb... proof that Boston socialite and wife of columnist Joshua Sterling, Devyn Hewitt Sterling, is in fact the illegitimate daughter of notorious fugitive Finley Mac-Cauley, who has been missing and, some think, dead. Adopted in a secret legal exchange that left no record of her birth mother's name...

Joshua's wife was the daughter of Finn MacCauley? The very name Taylor Sly had whispered to her yesterday afternoon?

That's where she got the jump drive! When Taylor hugged her, she slipped it in Vivi's pocket... making sure it didn't turn up in the police search. But why didn't she want it in the hands of the police? Had Joshua given this to Taylor? Why? Because his wife was connected to Finn?

Had Devyn Sterling arranged to have him killed before he took this public? Why would he do that to her? For the same reason he'd have an affair with Taylor Sly. He was scum. But not even scum deserved to die.

Her phone beeped with a call, and she just knew who it was. A look at the ID confirmed it.

"I'll go this afternoon, Tom," she said before her boss could bark at her.

"I'll put someone else on the story," he said, disgust in his voice.

"No, please, I'll do it. I promise. This afternoon."

"It'll be on the *Boston Globe* website by then, Vivi. You're losing your edge, kid."

She bristled at the nickname and the comment. "I'll go

now, Tom. Then I need the afternoon to work on something else."

"Vivi, do the interview and get your ass in here by eleven for a staff meeting. You miss, you're done. Is that clear?"

"Crystal."

She hung up, her brain still on Taylor Sly. If she broke this story, he wouldn't fire her. Forget that! If she cracked this murder, the Guardian Angelinos would be launched as a force to be reckoned with.

Didn't that big, bad trainer say Taylor worked out on Sundays and Tuesdays? If she couldn't get into Equinox to talk to her, then that creature of habit would be in a limo outside Starbucks in less than two hours.

And Vivi would be in a freaking staff meeting.

But the Angelinos were a team, and there was no reason to miss this opportunity. She had Marc on the phone in a matter of seconds.

"You seriously want to work for the Guardian Angelinos?" she asked.

"You know I do."

"I have your first assignment."

If information was power, then Sam should be a superhero. She knew that this interlude with Zach was temporary, that he was going to "run for the hills" when this "assignment" was over. So all she had to do was get through this ordeal alive, and without giving up her heart to a man who'd already put a bayonet through it.

But driving through a dreary Boston morning on the way to break into Paupiette's and steal evidence, neither one of those outcomes seemed guaranteed. She was in grave danger…physically and emotionally. How could she stop either one? She couldn't hide forever from a killer who wanted her dead, especially if there was more than one person. And she couldn't help feeling whole and happy when she made love to Zach Angelino.

It *wasn't* just sex. Not then, and not now.

"You're awfully quiet," Zach said as they navigated the South End traffic and pedestrians.

"Mmm. Lot on my brain."

"I'm surprised you're not asking more about Gabe."

Gabe? Like she had room in this worryfest for him. "CIA?"

"Something like that. I don't even know the exact organization. All I know is the pay is through the roof, the perks are off the charts, and the life expectancy is about thirty-five."

"How old is he?"

"Thirty-three, but don't worry. He's invincible, or at least I like to think so."

"You're closer to him than your other cousins; I can tell."

"Closest in age, and mind-set, yeah. He was a little bit of a troublemaker, too, when I was growing up. So it wasn't unusual for the two of us to be in the doghouse at the same time. JP was just perfect, naturally, and Marc was too damn wily to get into trouble. Gabe's a risk-taker and I was a risk…maker. So we have more in common than you might imagine."

"And he never sees the family."

"Very rarely. But he'll get out of that dark world eventually."

"And then he can be a Guardian Angelino."

Zach snorted softly. "Right." He turned into the alley behind the restaurant. "Is that the back basement door?"

"Yes, but we'll go in the side, into the kitchen. And that's the maître d's car. Even though the restaurant's closed on Tuesday, I'm not surprised he's here. Keegan's a workaholic." She took a deep breath and corralled her inner calm. This was going to take some acting skills. "Let's go. I'll occupy Keegan; you go to the wine vault."

"Wait." He put his hand on hers and leaned over the console to kiss her. She froze, letting his lips touch hers, then backed away.

A little smile tugged at his mouth. "Just trust your judgment, Sammi. Especially where I'm concerned."

"I am," she said coolly, reaching for the door, but he closed his hand over her arm, stopping her.

"No, you're not. You're second-guessing. Just trust your instincts because they're good."

So was her hearing.

Saying nothing, she stepped out of the car, took a slow, steadying breath, and let Zach drop a casual arm around her as they walked up to the side door. They appeared very much like boyfriend and girlfriend, running an errand together.

The door was locked, but her key still worked. In a moment, they were inside the dimly lit, sparkling clean kitchen of Paupiette's. The stoves were all off, the ovens cool, the stations shiny, the floor waxed.

The alarm pad on the wall behind the kitchen door didn't even blink.

"Hello?" Sam called, to no response.

The went farther inside, and Sam pointed to the large swinging door that led to the cellars. "Wine vault's down there, about ten feet to the right of the stairs. But the key is down that hall," she said, indicating the throughway that separated the kitchen from the dining room. She'd already told him which wineglass shelf was used to hide the spare vault key.

As they crossed the kitchen, she glanced toward the chef's office, the door closed, and no light on underneath.

"Call him again," Zach said. "We're not alone in here."

"Keegan? Are you here?"

The door from the dining room slapped open, hitting the wall and making Sam jump two inches in the air.

Keegan Kennedy breezed in, then froze at the sight of Zach, taking a half step backward before his gaze moved to Sam and his expression relaxed into a welcoming smile.

"Samantha! I knew you'd be back." He reached out both arms. "I've missed you."

She returned the hug, and added an extra squeeze. They'd all been affected by the tragedy, but Keegan was the de facto "leader" of the restaurant, and she imagined he was hurting more than the rest of the staff.

"Hey, Keegan, it's good to see you, too," she told him. "I'm just here to get my check. And this is Zach Angelino."

They shook hands and exchanged a quick greeting. "I have your check, Sam, in the office. Come with me."

They had a plan for what to do if someone was in the kitchen, and Zach stuck with it. "I'm going to use the facilities," he said, heading toward the dining room.

"Not there," Keegan said. "Use the employee's bathroom in the back."

"Oh, don't you dare make him use that bathroom," Sam said quickly. "You have to see the one in the dining room." She gave him a nudge in that direction. "It's gorgeous, as bathrooms go. It was in *Boston Magazine*. Go have a look while I talk to Keegan."

"It's closed," Keegan said. "Come this way. The employees' bathroom is over there, on the other side of the break room."

Sam opened her mouth to argue, but picked up Zach's silent message as he followed the chef. Something like...*Don't argue, just go with the flow*.

She did, following Keegan to the chef's office, where Keegan had a desk as well. Zach disappeared toward the small room they called "the lounge" even though no one ever lounged there very much. Sam gave him a look over her shoulder, but he just ambled on toward the bathroom as if nothing were amiss.

"So," she said as they reached the chef's office door. "How have things been, Keegan?" Her job would be to keep him talking for as long as it took Zach to get to the wine vault, find the camera, and remove the chip.

"Fine." Keegan opened the door to his office, a long, narrow room with one desk facing the wall, and a few shelves and cabinets. On the empty wall was a huge bulletin board that was usually stocked with menus, printouts from websites, pictures from magazines, quotes from chefs.

Now it was covered with newspaper articles about Joshua Sterling's death.

She recoiled at the sight. "Why do you have all that up there?"

"A man was killed in this restaurant, Sam. It's news." He sat behind the desk, unlocking the top drawer.

She took the chair next to his desk, the one usually reserved for employees getting chewed out for huge mistakes. She'd never been in that particular hot seat with him or the chef, as she always stayed out of controversy and just did her job...until the night Sterling was murdered.

Her gaze shifted to the wall, landing on the silver-haired victim, in a picture with his wife. Sam had avoided reading a lot of the press coverage, and hadn't seen that story. Devyn Sterling was even prettier in real life than she was in that picture, but there was definitely something distant and cool about her. Not the kind of woman she'd imagine a gregarious man like Joshua would marry.

"You should have listened to Rene that night."

Keegan's comment pulled her back to the moment, and confused her. Everyone knew she found the body that night, but no one knew she actually witnessed the murder. Only the police had that information, and, in fact, only a few of the main investigators on the case were supposed to know. But the way Keegan sounded, she wondered just how much he knew.

"Don't think I haven't thought that a million times," she admitted, keeping her answer purposefully vague. "Although someone had to find the body."

"It would have been better if it had been Rene."

"What would have been better?" A deep male voice startled her with the question, coming from the kitchen.

Keegan gave her an amused look. "No need to be skittish, Sam. It's just Rene." He ripped the check out of the book. "Here. We're in here, Rene. Look who's come to see us."

Rene opened the door wider and gave Sam a brief nod

with no smile of greeting. No warmth like he'd shown her at the police station. "You're not going to work here anymore, are you?" he asked.

"Great to see you, too," she said drily. They'd never liked each other, and apparently the tragedy of having a murder in the wine cellar and another server killed in a gangland slaying wasn't going to change that.

"Rene, why are you here?" Keegan asked. "You get one day off. Take it."

"I need a bottle of wine I left in the cellar last night that I promised to a customer." He held up his key and Sam's heart dropped a little.

"Before you do, Rene," she said, standing and giving him a warm, if completely fake, smile. "I'd like to talk to you. Privately."

"Anything you have to say to me you can say in front of Keegan."

As long as it took five more minutes, she'd tell them her life story. "I just wanted to say I was sorry...about that night." She had no idea where this was going, but prayed it would take a long time to get there. "It was crazy, you know? Do you remember? What was going through your head that night?"

Rene narrowed brown eyes at her. "Nothing, Sam. Nothing was going through my head." He pivoted and headed out.

"Wait, Rene. Please, I want to talk to you." She threw a look over her shoulder at Keegan as she followed Rene. "Thanks," she said, waving the check. "But I really want to talk to him."

He was up in an instant, a surprisingly strong hand on her arm. "Let it go, Sam."

"I... I can't." *He'll run right into Zach.* "We've always had a contentious relationship, and now that... someone has died, you know, I have a whole different perspective..." She heard the cellar door whoosh open and his footsteps on the stairs. Shit. "I just want to talk to him."

"No, Sam, he's really struggling. He's had a horrible time with this. I think he's this close to quitting, and I can't afford to hire someone else. If you talk to him, he might just break down."

"Sam?" She turned at the sharp sound of Zach's voice. "Is there a problem here?" He took three long steps into the office and gave a fierce look at the much smaller maître d'. "Get your hand off her."

Keegan let go, clearly aware of the reshifting of power. "Just leave Rene alone, Sam."

She would now. "All set?" she asked Zach.

"You have your check?" he asked.

When she nodded, Zach looked at Keegan. "Nice meeting you, Mr. Kennedy." He put a strong arm on her shoulder and led her out.

"Zach," she whispered as they crossed the kitchen. "What—"

"Outside."

She kept pace with him, silent until they were in the car. Then she couldn't contain her questions. "Did you get it? Did he see you? Do you know how—"

He put a single finger over her mouth. "I got it."

She fell back against the headrest. "Really?"

"Really."

Wow, he was good.

He had his phone out and speed-dialed. "Hey, it's me,"

he said quietly. "Where and when?" He listened briefly, then ended the call without responding.

"Gabe?" she asked when he hung up.

"He's way the hell out in western Mass, so it looks like we're taking a drive."

"I don't mind. I have no desire to hole up in that house and jump at every sound I hear."

He gave her a sexy, sideways glance. "Holing up in that house alone doesn't sound so bad."

She stiffened, and knew that he noticed. "We can't just do...*that* all day."

"We can't? I seem to recall—"

She held her hand out, halting him. "Don't. Just...don't."

"Yeah, I thought so," he said on an exaggerated exhale.

"You thought what so?"

"When you left the kitchen, you stopped in the living room, right? Did something before you went upstairs. Overheard a conversation, which, as we already established, is not eavesdropping."

She managed not to let her chin hit her chest. He had told her he had amazing auditory skills, so it was entirely possible that he knew she was still in hearing distance of the conversation. "Maybe. What difference does it make, Zach? Information is power, so I'm feeling...strong."

"Good information is power. Bad information can screw up your whole day."

"Don't try and worm out of this, Zach. I know what I heard you say to your cousin. 'When this is over, I'm going to run like hell.'"

"Yep, that's what I said." He started to put the car

in drive, then stopped, turning to her. "We were talking about Vivi and the Guardian Angelinos. That's who I want to run like hell from."

She opened her mouth to argue, then shut it. Damn if she didn't want to believe him with every fiber of her being.

He cupped her jaw in his hands, leaning close. "Samantha Fairchild. Please stop doubting me and stop doubting yourself. Some things you don't have to second-guess. You don't have to think twice, not about me."

Her whole body ached, truly ached, to believe him. It would be so easy; it would be so wonderfully easy and good. But... "I just don't want to hurt that way ever again."

"I won't let you." He leaned in and brushed her lips with his. "I swear I won't."

When he released her, she closed her eyes and gave up the fight with a sigh of resignation. "Okay. But I still don't want to go back to Jamaica Plain if we don't have to."

"We don't have to," he said, pulling out of the alley parking lot. "I have a great idea. All you have to do is relax and be pleasantly surprised."

She shook her head, the adrenaline from the trip to Paupiette's starting to fade. "I still can't believe you managed to pull that off and not run smack into Rene when he came down the stairs."

"I didn't go back up the stairs; I went through the back alley entrance. It's really easy and fast to get back up that way."

"That was lucky."

"And brilliant."

She smiled, thinking about the route he took. "You

know, it's possible that killer did just that and was back in the restaurant eating dinner or drinking while I was in the basement screaming for help."

"More than possible," he agreed. "Easy."

So maybe that man she saw pull the trigger was right there in the restaurant all along. Maybe he was some-one…she knew.

CHAPTER 18

The handoff took place at a gas station in Framingham, in a light, misty rain, without either man acknowledging the other. Zach put gas in the Mercedes, leaning casually against the pump as a dark blue Porsche, almost as old as the car he was driving, pulled up and waited his turn. Zach never even looked, but let the chip he'd stolen, and had wrapped in a tissue, rest on the top of the pump. As he drove away, he sneaked a peek at the driver of the Porsche, recognizing Gabe under that baseball cap and behind the shades, seeing him slip the tissue into his palm.

Zach never looked again as he pulled out onto the Mass Pike.

"I thought you were going to give the chip to Gabe?" Sam asked, surprised. "You said we were meeting him in Framingham."

"I just did," he said. "And that's just how good a spook he is."

She looked suitably stunned. "And you," she added.

"Why all the way out here? Why not do that secret exchange right in Boston? Or can't you tell me because it's classified information?"

"Yeah, top secret." Zach remembered the dark clouds in Gabe's eyes when they'd talked about the family, joked about Gabe's mother missing him. "Honestly? My guess is he wanted to drive past the house in Sudbury."

"Drive past it?"

"Just to see it. He misses them, too." More than the son of a bitch would ever admit. "Did you want to see him again? Verify my story? Get proof I really was referring to Vivi's company when I said I'd run like hell?"

"I believe you."

He made a little air pump with his fist. "Yes. Progress."

She laughed, already more relaxed. And with each mile away from Boston, she seemed to unwind more. Until her phone buzzed with a text.

"Oh, no," she said, reading it. "I don't know what your surprise is, Zach, but we have to go back to Boston. Billy needs me."

"Can it wait?"

She read the text again, shaking her head. "He says it's important. But my real worry is that if he's texting now, then he didn't go to work. And after what his parole officer wrote to me, it looks like maybe he has some explaining to do."

"I have some explaining to do, too," he said, reaching over to try to take the phone. "I'm taking priority today."

She laughed, keeping the phone out of reach. "Who gave you priority?"

"Honestly? Billy did. Tell him I'm explaining something to you and he'll understand."

"He will? What did you two talk about yesterday?"

"Now, that's classified." Speaking of classified information, what he wanted to tell her was just that. But he ached to tell her anyway. "Look, he's had you all this time, worrying about him, loving him..." He swallowed, surprised at how truly envious he was at that. "Now I want you."

Her eyes were moist as she looked at him, but her pretty lips were easing into a smile. "How do you do this to me?"

He grinned. "You never could say no to me."

"Sadly, that's true. All right, Zach, you win. I'll tell him I'll come over later. Where are we going?"

"I'll give you a hint. We've been there before."

She frowned. "We have? We didn't go very many places."

"Does a green Army blanket ring a bell?"

"Wachusett Reservoir." Her face lit up. "That was a great day, wasn't it?"

The joy in her voice kicked his gut a little. "Sex in the sunshine, yes, it was."

"I can't believe we did that. By the spillway? Remember?"

"I want to go where we have a nice memory, Sam." The waterway was nestled in the middle of Massachusetts, surrounded by forests and country roads, and almost no houses. The day they'd spent up there had been burned in his memory, and was another that kept him sane when war raged around him. "And I'd like to make a new one."

Her expression softened. "Okay, let me just call Billy."

"Tell him you're with Zaccaria." He shot her a look. "By the way, I can't believe you told him my Italian name."

"Why wouldn't I? I told him all about you."

"No doubt he heard all about the postcard that never came."

"The *fucking* postcard," she corrected. "Of course he did. Oh, I have to leave a message." She held up a finger and talked into her phone. "Hey, Billy, it's Sam, returning your call. I'm on my way—"

He put a hand on her leg and squeezed, shaking his head in warning. "Don't give away your location," he whispered.

"On my way…out. I'm with Zach, so we'll be over later." At Zach's warm look, she added, "Much later. Gimme a call and let me know what's up. You know I can talk if you need me, Billy. Bye."

Behind him, a semi hauled ass, and Zach eased over to the right lane, and the truck did the same. Just pass, Zach mentally ordered the driver, checking out the dark green and silver grille that took up his whole rearview mirror, the Peterbilt logo practically in his backseat. Swearing softly, Zach went back into the left lane, picked up speed, and headed to the 495 exit to take it north up to rural Massachusetts.

The truck did the same. A little pissed, Zach weaved through some traffic, flying past another eighteen-wheeler spitting waterspray.

"What's going on?" Sam asked, glancing to the back.

"Just testing someone who's driving erratically. That's always the first thing you look for when on patrol.

Anyone acting inconsistent, anything even slightly out of the norm."

She instantly seemed more on guard, the lightness of a few minutes ago disappearing with a perceived threat. "How do you decide what's out of the norm?"

"Listen to my gut instinct." He swerved into the other lane, taking a small opening between cars, then back again, flooring it. The semi stayed with him, and Zach caught the name of Hanrahan Produce on the side. He'd have to tell Uncle Nino never to buy their stuff.

He played a few more games of lane changing, but couldn't lose the truck.

"Zach, are we being followed?"

"I don't think so, but there's a jerk behind the wheel of that semi, and I think he wants to fool around." He put a reassuring hand on her leg. "Don't worry. We'll lose him on 495. This sucker's built for the autobahn at a hundred and twenty in the snow." He got onto the interstate exchange and put the Mercedes through its paces, leaving Hanrahan Produce in the dust.

Her phone buzzed again. Picking it up, she let out a frustrated grunt. "Why doesn't he just call?"

Assuming the question was rhetorical, Zach stayed focused on the road, checking the rearview periodically for a familiar semi.

"He wants to know where I am," she said after reading the message.

"Why?"

"I don't know. He just says 'where are you and when can you get here? Need you.' Oh, Zach." She put her hand on his arm. "He wouldn't say that if it wasn't important."

Shit. "We can go back."

"It's just that this is so unusual. Wait, I have an idea." She punched in another number. "Hey, Vivi. Where are you?" She listened for a second, and Zach could hear the cadence of his sister's voice in the phone, but not the words. Then Sam said, "Well, I wanted to ask you to do me a favor, but it doesn't sound like you have time." Another beat. "Zach and I are..." She looked up at him. "Taking a long ride and getting reacquainted."

That made him smile, and if he knew his sister, she was grinning from ear to ear, too. She always loved the idea of them together.

She was always smart that way.

"All I need for you to do is run over to Billy Shawkins's house and check on him. Oh?" Sam gave Zach a hopeful look. "That's not too far from Roxbury; could you do it on the way to your meeting? Perfect."

After listening to Vivi, Sam asked, "Oh, what did you find out? All right, well, we have more to tell you, too. But you're right, not on the phone. Maybe Zach and I can come over to your apartment tonight."

Sam disconnected with Vivi and turned to him. "She said she has news. Major-break-in-the-case news, but didn't want to say it over the phone."

"Smart." He gave her hand a squeeze. "You're sure about Billy? 'Cause we can go back if you want, especially if Vivi has news."

She shook her head, threading his fingers. "I'm sure, and everything else can wait. But I will say, Vivi sounded very excited."

"Because she thinks if she cracks this case, she's going to put her little company in business." He knew how his sister ticked.

"But that won't matter to you," Sam added pointedly. "Because you're going to run."

He thought about that for a while. "You know, Sam, it's not that I hate the concept," he finally said. "I just want to do it right. Like my cousin's company. Jesus, you should see his operation. Technology up the wazoo, a war room, private planes—that's plural."

"What's the name?"

"The Bullet Catchers."

She shrugged. "Eh, I like the Guardian Angelinos better."

"Whatever you call it, an operation like that needs a lot of cash, an office, staff, computers. I don't want some rinky-dink security operation run out of a basement."

"Yeah." She squeezed his hand. "Now how about the truth, Zach?"

"That's the truth."

"You don't trust yourself." Her words hit so hard he had no response. "You think because this lady who runs this big, fat, rich security company with plural planes and a war room turned you down, you're not good enough."

"No," he countered. "I think that the fact that I have impaired vision, no license to carry concealed, and a sketchy war record means I'm not good enough." The truth, bitter pill that it was, tasted foreign on his tongue and lodged in his throat.

"You're doing a damn good job of keeping me alive."

"I'd do that no matter..." He glanced into the rearview mirror and muttered a soft curse, peering into the rain to be sure of what he saw.

"The truck's back," she said, whipping around.

"Listen to me," Zach said, calmly putting his hand on

her shoulder. "Just stay low in your seat, but stay facing forward. If he's following us, I don't want him to know we know."

She did exactly what he ordered, her gaze locked on the right-side mirror. "He's catching up with us."

"I see that." He reached under the seat and got the Glock 19 Marc had given him, setting it right next to him on the console panel. "You have GPS on your phone?"

"Yep. Want me to find an alternate route?"

"Tell me what happens at the next exit, which is in..." He squinted through the rain, catching the sign just as they passed and the one oversized Mercedes wiper wiped the windshield clean. "Two miles."

She started clicking away, while he steadily increased to eighty, eight-five, ninety.

Like God was against them, the rain suddenly intensified just as a different truck blew up on their right, damn near matching Zach's speed and spewing blinding, relentless rooster tails of rainwater from every tire as it passed. The Mercedes swerved, hydroplaning over the shoulder for a fraction of a second, then back on the road.

"Central Street is the next exit," he told her.

"Got it. It looks either rural or residential. Two lanes, very slow. You could lose a semi out there; the road is windy. He could never keep up. Then we're going due west to the reservoir."

He whipped onto the exit, tapping the brakes to slow just enough to not fishtail. At the bottom of the exit, he still didn't see the truck pulling off.

"Look right for me," he ordered, not willing to trust his peripheral vision.

"Clear."

He powered through a red light, spraying water and earning a soft intake of Sam's breath through clenched teeth as they careened across two lanes to the other side, to the entrance of a small shopping area. He pulled in to hide in the lot and watch if the semi followed them.

"How the hell did he find us?" Zach asked, pounding the steering wheel. "It just doesn't make sense. It's like we're tracked."

She gave him a look of horror. "What?"

"Gimme your phone."

She handed it to him, tentatively. "No one's touched my phone, Zach. No one."

He opened up the back, moved the SIM card, checked it thoroughly. Nothing. Still, his gut burned.

"Let's go," he said, giving it back to her. "We'll need the GPS on the back roads. You can navigate."

"You want to go back to Boston?"

He considered it. "I don't want to get back on the highway yet. Let's be sure we don't have a tail, then decide what to do. He could still just be some dickhead with a bad sense of humor."

"Or somebody following Gabe who saw you leave the chip."

But Zach didn't think so, on either count. "Go through your purse, Sam. Every inch of it. Tear apart the lining, anything in it, too. Just look for a tracking device."

She did, while they made it into the forests and the winding roads near the reservoir, barely seeing another car, and he started to relax. They circled part of the massive body of water, not really able to see as the rain picked up.

The truck and the rain had wrecked his plans; now he

just wanted to get the hell out of harm's way. And something told him that Peterbilt was going in the direction of harm's way.

He saw the truck in the rearview just as Sam shrieked. "Oh, my God, Zach. I found it!"

But it was too late. The Peterbilt was hauling ass, right for them. "Hang on, honey."

She clasped the seat and armrest as he kicked it up to ninety. The car screamed and hydroplaned again, but he managed to get a grip of the road.

The truck made a vicious and stupid veer around a curve, and Zach half expected it to tip over, but it didn't, gaining on them. With purpose.

Gritting his teeth, he floored it. "He's big and he's slow, so I'm going to lose him, but you take the gun, and get ready to shoot at him if we have to. I need both hands to make sure we don't lose control."

She racked the slide. "If only there was a shoulder or side road, you could pull over and he'd fly right by."

"That's my plan." The Mercedes screamed and ate up another corner that would have to slow the semi down.

The fucking truck made exactly the same move.

Ahead, more soup, but no cars. He was kissing a hundred now, the wiper practically useless as they approached a quarter-mile-wide section of the reservoir.

The road was built up to the meet the bridge, with a wide shoulder on either side over the water. They had to get off this road, but a U-turn was virtually impossible except for that shoulder, so he only had one choice.

"Hang on, I'm gonna pull over; then we'll U and get out of here. He can't maneuver that fast. There's nowhere for him to turn after the bridge."

He jerked the wheel to the right, slamming on the brakes so they screeched toward the edge of the hill, the water about ten feet below a rock embankment. The semi came screaming right behind them, showing no sign of slowing.

"Gimme the gun." He reached for it, just as he looked into the rearview mirror and saw the truck swerve to the right. *Fuck*. Twenty tons of steel going eighty miles an hour bearing right down on them.

She turned, her hands covering her mouth. "Oh, my God!" She looked at him with horror in her eyes. "Zach!"

He threw his arms over her to brace for the impact, knowing the only place they could go was sailing into the water.

Her scream was muffled in his shoulder just as the Peterbilt logo smashed into the back, throwing the whole car forward, flipping it ass over front, upside down and airborne for one time-suspended second, then hammering the water roof-first with a brain-cracking jolt.

Vivi wanted to blow off the staff meeting to track down Taylor Sly, but she knew Marc had that handled, and Sam's request to check on Billy worked better time- and travel-wise, so she caught the Orange Line to Ruggles and headed to Roxbury.

At the Ruggles Avenue stop, she threw her board on the pavement, popped some headphones in even though nothing was playing, and kicked off toward Tremont. She might look like an uninterested skater lost in music, but she was anything but. Instead, she eyed the two men on the corner, checked each car cruising by, gauged the group of students headed up toward Northeastern.

Gentrification had left its redbrick fingerprint on most of Boston, but this section of Roxbury was still pretty rough.

Uphill, she trudged, grateful the worst of the morning rain seemed to be over. The skies were still slate gray and thick with the possibility of rain, but this was Boston, and sunshine was rare, even in July.

She checked the address on her phone again; then, when the road leveled out, she skated down the middle. Billy Shawkins lived in an iffy neighborhood. Not exactly a meth haven, but still not a fabulous place for a woman alone. She scoped the houses, nodded to a few neutral if not friendly faces, and popped the board up when she reached the address Sam had texted to her.

This house looked just a tad more loved than the others. The clapboard had been painted a nice forest green, the lawn was freshly mowed, and the few bushes near the house were neatly trimmed. Not exactly lush landscaping, but no rusting washing machine in the driveway, like the house next door.

Mail had been delivered, along with a *Boston Globe*, but not yet picked up.

She tried the doorbell, which didn't sound like it worked, then knocked, rubbing the toe of her black-and-white-checked shoe along the weathered welcome mat. She knocked again, harder.

"C'mon, Billy boy. Sam won't rest until I tell her I talked to you." Sighing, she headed around the house, standing on her tiptoes to peer into the empty garage on the way, then to the backyard to see if there was any sign of him there.

"Can I help you?"

She startled at the voice, a middle-aged blond man who looked wicked sophisticated for the proud owner of a rusty washer in the driveway.

"I'm looking for Mr. Shawkins."

"He's at work."

"Well, if you don't mind, I'm just going to check out the backyard, because a friend of mine says he didn't go to work today and I want to make sure he's okay."

"I saw him leave."

She shrugged and held up a friendly hand. "I'm not trying to rob the place, honestly. Just checking for him."

She continued to the back, and when she got to the tiny deck that had been obviously built by hand, she turned to look through the shrubs to give one more "I'm not a criminal" wave to the neighbor, but he was gone.

Just as she lifted her hand to pound on the back door, she stopped, staring at the latch. The door wasn't completely closed. Probably not the most brilliant move in Roxbury, but she tapped anyway.

"Billy! Mr. Shawkins, are you in there?"

Silence.

She nudged the door farther, her body tensing. "Billy? It's Vivi Angelino, Sam's friend."

Still silent. She dropped the board on the deck and reached deep into the pocket of her cargo pants to pull out the little pistol Marc had given her while he was passing out weapons like they were business cards at their first meeting, a few fingers of anticipation and nerves walking up her spine.

Should she go in? Should she flip the safety and aim the gun? The role of PI and crimesolver still felt a little strange to her. But this was like a test run. Billy had nothing to do with the Sterling murder, right? Maybe he was hurt, or sick, or maybe something serious had happened, like a heart attack. Maybe that's why he wanted Sam to come over, but he didn't want to alarm her with the details.

She called him one more time, then pushed the door open and stepped inside a tiny mudroom, with a few jackets on hooks, a closet. The door on her left probably led to the garage, and beyond that was a tiny kitchen, made nighttime dim with drawn blinds, smelling faintly of last night's chicken, but pristine and orderly.

"Billy?" she called, loud enough to be heard throughout the small house.

Still quiet. The gun felt heavy in her hand, like maybe she'd watched one too many reruns of *Spenser for Hire* on the WB. Through the kitchen, she headed past a miniature dining room with a table for four covered in a lace tablecloth. Billy mustn't live alone. Cheap silk flowers in the living room confirmed that a woman's touch was in this house.

She checked out the darkened hallway. One of the doors must be the basement; the others led to two bedrooms and a hallway bath. That was it. That was the whole house.

One more call out, then she headed down the hall. One bedroom was full of boxes and junk, clearly a storage area. The other had room for nothing but a dresser and double bed, which was turned down neatly, as if someone was about to climb in. A book lay open on the spread—no, not a book. *The* book.

Billy had been reading his Bible when he called Sam? Didn't seem like an emergency, that's for sure. The bathroom was empty, a dry but used towel hung neatly by the tub.

Unless he was in the basement, Billy was definitely not home. Maybe he'd straightened up and decided to go to work after all. Or maybe he was on a bender and wandered out, leaving the back door open.

A bender after Bible-reading.

Something was definitely weird about this situation.

At the basement door, she turned the handle and called again, tapping for the wall switch, but couldn't find one.

No way she was going down there. She didn't love Sam *that* much. Hell, she didn't love anybody that much. Just as she took a step back, she heard a sound. A scratch? A...tap against metal.

God *damn* it. "Hello? Billy, are you down there?" Please don't be down there. She *so* didn't want to go down there.

Anther tap, definitely something or someone was alive down there. Chills went zinging up her spine, her heart ramming her ribs. "Billy?"

She stood stone still, everything in her being rebelling against what she knew she should do. What a good Guardian—

"Help me." The words were barely a whisper of air.

"Billy? Oh, my God." He must have fallen down the stairs. She took a few steps down, reaching for the wall, searching for a light switch. "Billy? Are you down here?"

The power of the punch in her back stole her breath, knocking her forward with so much force that she flew off the stair and hung in the air before landing and rolling and crashing to a stop.

The basement door above her slammed with a thud

louder than her cry of outrage and pain, followed by footsteps down the stairs.

Pain shot from her knees to her brain, white-hot electrical jolts of agony stealing her breath and ability to think.

"You're not Samantha."

The voice was over her, low and menacing, and really pissed off.

She spread her empty hand, the gun tossed in the fall. *Nice work, Spenser.*

"No, I'm not." She tried to stand up, but a powerful hand clasped her shoulder and pushed.

"I want Samantha."

Jesus God, what was going on here? This wasn't Billy Shawkins!

"What do you want?" She used every available cell in her body to sound unafraid and ready to fight.

"I want Samantha. Give me your phone."

No fucking way, dude. "I don't have—" The barrel of a gun pressed on her temple.

"Five. Four. Three. Two—"

"Here." She handed him the BlackBerry. "But she's not around today."

The only answer was footsteps up the stairs. She stared in the direction of the sound, desperate to at least get a silhouette when he opened the door, then ready to pounce on every inch of the place to get her weapon.

For a moment, she heard and saw nothing, waiting for the even the briefest glimpse of her captor. Then he opened the door a crack, enough for her to see him bend over.

"You dropped your pistol."

As he slipped through the door, she bit back a yowl of frustration. Stupid, *stupid*.

"You two be good down there, now." The door latched and locked behind him. She tried to stand, half certain something had to be broken.

You two? She reached out, night blind. "Is someone down here?"

The only sound was the tiniest tap, tap, tap, like a Morse code of death.

CHAPTER 19

The vicious snap of Sam's neck was louder than the splash of the car hitting the water, then rolling over.

For one interminable second, she heard nothing, saw black, and couldn't breathe. There was just nothing.

Oh, God, *dead*.

"Sam!" Zach's voice was sharp and right in her ear. She forced herself to open her eyes and suck in air. The seatbelt strangled and jammed against her hips as the car bobbed, floating momentarily.

"I'm okay," she said. "I'm alive." *Thank you, God.* "Are we..."

"Listen to me and do exactly what I say, when I say it. I can't get the power window to work and can't open a door until we balance the pressure. We're going to sink in about thirty seconds."

Sink. Thirty seconds. Nothing was making sense, but she fought for calm and control. "Can we get out?"

"Absolutely. Keep your right hand on the door handle; that'll keep you oriented, but don't try to open it."

"'Kay." She grabbed the door handle with one hand and pulled at the chest belt that choked her with the other. "I can't breathe."

"Not yet. Don't unhook yet. As soon as the water gets in the car and takes us down, we'll open a door and swim out. We have about three minutes, okay?"

"What about him? The truck?"

"He could be waiting for us. My weapon should work wet or dry, but it's all we have. I didn't see much cover, unless we can swim out under the bridge. You can swim, right?"

"Yes, but what if—"

"There's no time, Sam. Just do as I say." He turned the pistol toward the back window and shot once, twice, and again, each explosion deafening in the vacuum of the closed car.

Instantly water started pouring in through the window, and they started to sink fast.

"The door probably won't open until the car's almost full and we've balanced pressure. When I say, take a deep breath and hold it. I'm going to take your belt off and mine; then you're going to fall into the water while I open the door. Take my hand and we'll swim."

"Don't I need both hands to swim?"

"Make it work. The water will be pure murk, so don't let go." He reached over to her seatbelt latch, his face inches from hers, his scar so close she could see the blood pulsing violently in the shredded skin.

"Zach." The word hardly came out.

"Just be calm. Don't panic, Sam. Don't."

"I'm not," she lied. "But if we die when we come up…"

He shook his head. No time for forgiveness, confessions, or admissions of anything. "Do what I say and don't let go of my left hand. I'll be firing with my right if I have to."

He unlatched the belt, holding her as best as he could as her body started to fall toward the water rushing in. As she slipped, he leaned forward and put his lips on hers. A fraction of a second, and she was nearly submerged.

"Take a breath, I'm opening the door!"

She sucked in air, her heart hammering as she wildly searched for his hand. He grabbed hers, then used all his strength to open the door, still bracing himself in his seatbelt.

The door must have opened because water rushed in, much harder than she even imagined, the shocking pressure smashing her back to her door. With a bone-crushing grip on her hand, Zach somehow yanked her through the water, pulling her out the door as they both kicked furiously.

Outside the car, the mud was too thick to let in much light. How deep were they? She had no idea, but continued to kick in the direction Zach took her, using her right arm to push through the water.

It would have been much easier with two hands, but it was so black and she was so dizzy, she'd have lost him and never found him. He knew that. Trusting him completely, she kept kicking through the murky water, her lungs starting to fill and ache.

Already numb from cold and unable to hold her breath one more second, she released a little air, seeing the bubbles in front of her face going in the same direction they were. Up. Five more long kicks and she saw daylight shimmering on the surface.

But what was on the other side? A truck driver with a rifle?

They popped through the surface, and she instantly opened her mouth and sucked in air, but got a mouthful of rainwater. She spat it, blocked her mouth with her free hand, sucked again; then he shoved her right under again and started pulling.

He must know where they were going, or saw a threat above. She held on, kicking against the fifty-pound weight of her soaked jeans, both of her loafers ripped off by the water, numb to the bone already.

Back up for air and she gasped it quickly, expecting to be pushed down again, but shocked to feel the muck of the bottom under her feet. It was shallow enough to stand. When she did, she realized they were in a muddy swamp at the pond's edge, about a hundred feet from where they'd gone over. The bridge and road looked completely desolate.

She spun around, and Zach did the same.

"Is he gone?"

"Just stay low, in the weeds." He continued to turn three-sixty, searching what was nothing but swamp, forest, pond, bridge, and empty road for what looked like miles. His patch was gone, the rain flattening his hair and pouring over his face.

Her teeth started chattering as her veins turned to ice and her stomach rolled with nausea. He grabbed her, pulling her into him.

"You're freezing." He squeezed her as if he could transfer warmth to her, but he was just as cold.

The impact of what they'd just survived hit her, along with a hammerblow of reality. They were miles from anywhere, with a lunatic truck driver who could be lurking around any corner. They had no phones. No GPS. No bag, no car, no hope.

And they'd been followed here. Who'd put that device in her purse? Someone had slipped it way deep in a side pocket, buried under a packet of gum and some ancient store receipts.

Right now, it didn't matter who'd tracked them. Just that they got out of here alive. Reliving the horror of the car suspended in midair, tears stung her eyes and she fought them with whatever strength she had. The last thing an Army Ranger wanted to see was tears.

"Just let me think, Sam," he said, his voice calming.

"There was a farm or a house about a half a mile back," she suggested. "Could we get help?"

"Possibly."

"What else can we do?" Her voice cracked and she worked to maintain composure.

He didn't answer, still circling and scanning. "We have to stay off the road, under cover. We need to get to the woods." He spoke with so much assurance that she almost melted in relief. "We can follow the tree line along the road, and get back to that house. I'm sure whoever lives there will be all warm and welcoming when I knock on their door."

"I can knock on the door." She certainly wouldn't let him in if she lived alone in a rural area. "Then I'll call…the police?"

They shared a look.

"The police had their hands all over your bag when

you went through the metal detector yesterday," he said. "As much as I hate to think JP was right about that note in your file, I'm not inclined to go to them first for assistance."

"You're right," she agreed. "Vivi?"

"Yeah. Vivi or Marc. If we can get an approximate location, one of them can find us. We're less than two hours from Boston, so it won't be that long."

He pulled her deeper into the sludge where it eventually hardened to terra firma, and they were able to scramble toward the road, which was deserted, but curved about half a mile away, and a car—or semi—could come at them any second.

Keeping them low, he looked left, then right, his gun still drawn. They'd be fully exposed running across the road and into the woods.

"You ready?" He glanced down at her sodden body, her bare feet. He had one sneaker on, one foot in a waterlogged sock.

She swallowed and nodded. "Let's do it."

"As fast as you can run, right into those woods." He took her hand and yanked her with him, rain drenching as tiny rocks and pebbles stabbed at the bottoms of her feet.

She didn't dare stop, keeping up with him as he practically dragged her, the rain blinding, her head throbbing with the expectation of a bullet hitting her at any second. They reached the grass and she stumbled, but he pulled her up so hard her arm almost dislocated.

Ten more feet and something jammed into her foot, making her buckle, but she ignored the pain and refused to look down. The line of trees was twenty feet away, a thick green veil of safety. He didn't stop when they got there, dragging her deep into the darkness of the branches, a thick coating of pine and mulch and sticks underfoot, the rain blocked by the umbrella of tree limbs that he tried to swipe out of the way but snapped in her face. In the winter you could see right through this forest, but the New England summer was lush enough to provide cover.

Finally, he slowed, tumbling to the ground and pulling her down with him, wrapping his arms around her as they both fought for air.

Light-headed, breathless, and still shaking, she fell against him. Her feet were bleeding, a sharp stick poking out of one arch. She yanked it out without telling him, watching blood spurt.

"The farm, if that's what it was, was due west from here," he said. "That way."

"But the building I saw was on the other side of the road," she said. "That's north of the road after it curved. We should follow the road."

"That's exactly what they'd expect us to do." He pulled her up. "We'll head through these woods, and we'll find that farm."

Forty agonizing minutes later, there was a break in the trees. Five or six times during the trudge, the ground had just given way and become a mucky swamp of tall grass and a foot of water. A dozen times another sharp twig or stone jabbed her brutalized feet, but she refused to give in to the pain.

At the sight of daylight through the trees, Sam almost did cry out, in relief.

In the clearing was an older, colonial-style house

tucked onto a large pie-shaped lot. Trees blocked the view of the road, except for where they broke and a long gravel driveway led to the front.

"I didn't see this house," Sam said. "What I saw was on the other side of the road, about a quarter mile or so farther down the road."

"My guess is that's a barn or utility building, probably part of this parcel of land. But we need a house, with a phone. You need to tell whoever lives there that your car went over the bridge and you need to use the phone. Tell them your husband is out on the road trying to flag down help."

She nodded and headed off to the house, as pain shot like firebrands up her legs.

There was no answer when she rang the bell, shifting from foot to foot to take the weight off the injury. Frustrated, she pressed four times quickly, hearing the desperate chimes in the house, leaving muck and blood to soak into a ragged brush mat.

She maneuvered to a window, peeking in, seeing rooms but no people. She limped to other windows, around the house, tried a utility room door, knocking first, then jiggling the handle.

As she was rounding the back, Zach came jogging to her. "There's definitely a pole barn about half a mile on the other side of the road."

"No one's home here," she told him.

"Perfect. Let's make some calls, get some provisions, and head for cover across the road."

Not breaking in wasn't even discussed. He circled the perimeter once, with Sam on his heels.

"I want the least-used entrance," he said. "And inside,

we shouldn't leave any trace. The last thing we want is for someone to come home and call the cops, with helicopters circling over us."

He located an entrance to a walk-out basement, so common all over New England, and proved that water didn't ruin a pistol. With one shot, he neatly blew off a lock, then headed in, his outstretched hand holding her back until he'd looked around.

"Let me make sure we're alone." In less than a minute, he returned. "Everything we need's down here in the basement. There's a utility room over there, with a refrigerator full of bottled water. There's a guest room right past it. Steal a blanket or towel or whatever you need to get warm and dry; just don't leave any obvious signs that we've been here. I'll use this." He held up a cordless phone.

He was already punching buttons as she gingerly trotted past a Soloflex exercise bench and a rack of free weights.

She didn't hear anything he said, just moved to the guest room, grateful the tile floor continued in here since it would be easier to clean up her trail of blood. Quickly, she surveyed what she could carry and what they'd need. She eased a pillow out of its case and stuffed the homemade bag with a blanket, towels, and liquid soap to clean wounds. The dresser drawers were empty, dammit.

"Hurry up, Sam."

She closed the drawer with her hip, then hit the refrigerator for bottles of water. There was no food, except a box of energy bars, so she dug in and took four, then used one of the towels to wipe the water and blood she'd left on the floor, backing out toward the door.

Zach was reciting their route into the phone, and somehow she just knew he was leaving a message and not in conversation. Fortunately, Vivi checked her voicemail obsessively, far more often than Marc. So if they only had time for one call, that was the one to make.

She froze at the sound of an engine, a car in the driveway. They looked at each other for a split second, which was about all they had to tear across the backyard and get into the woods.

"Run!" he ordered.

She did, not even looking back, throwing herself into the thickest of the trees and rolling to the ground with her stuffed pillowcase. Seconds later, Zach followed, just as they heard a car door slam.

He pushed her down, covering her with his body, keeping them both deep in the trees while footsteps crunched over gravel. Sam didn't dare speak, her heart thumping while she waited and wondered.

"He's inside. Through the utility room, not the basement." Zach helped her up, taking the sack of provisions. "All right, let's go. Through these woods, same direction, to that pole barn."

"If we can get across the road without getting shot."

"Yep." He put his arm around her. "Big if."

Marc's plan called for perfect timing, which he usually had. As an FBI agent, he'd been gifted with the ability to track down a target and interrogate, often able to get answers and information when no one else could. He missed that aspect of his job. He missed every aspect of his job, and the possibility of doing the same kind of work within the loose and comfortable confines of family had captured his interest since the first time Vivi mentioned it.

He was in, all in. Starting with getting to Taylor Sly.

He waited in the shadows of the overhang of the parking garage across Dartmouth Street, facing the entrance to the redbrick brownstone that housed the Equinox health club. Vivi thought he should corner her when the limo took her to Starbucks. He had a better idea.

The stretch was ten minutes early to pick her up after her workout, exactly as Marc expected a good, regular driver to be, especially in a drizzle just heavy enough to snarl downtown Boston traffic. The doorman flagged the limo into the no-parking zone in front of the building.

A quarter mile away, a large delivery truck turned off Columbus to head up Dartmouth, providing the perfect cover. He timed his exit from the parking garage to just beat the truck, walking in front of it directly to the limo.

The driver got out, and before he could lock the doors, Marc snagged the streetside door and slipped into the back of the limo. The doors clicked with the lock, and he congratulated himself.

Sliding across the leather to the darkest corner of the car, he waited for Taylor Sly, watching the entrance to the building. She came out right on time, hair pulled into a ponytail and sunglasses on, despite the weather. She wore a loose workout jacket and tight jeans, a phone to her ear as she followed the driver.

Marc stayed way back and quiet, watching her slip into the back of limo. The driver closed the door before she even realized she wasn't alone, a slight startle her only reaction.

She slid her glasses down and eyed him. "You're Vivi's friend."

"Cousin, actually. Marc Rossi. I'd like to talk to you, Ms. Sly."

"There are more conventional means."

"Never was a fan of convention."

The door popped open, and a nice-looking Baby Eagle Beretta preceded the not-so-nice-looking face of the limo driver.

"It's all right, Devane," Taylor said, waving him off. "This man isn't going to hurt me."

Devane narrowed mean eyes at Marc. "How did you get in here?"

"Trust me, it wasn't easy." No need to get the guy fired. "And I'll get out by the time you stop at Starbucks."

He got a very dubious look in return, but a smile threatened on Taylor's face as she dismissed the driver. "If this is any sign of how you and your cousin plan to run the business, I'm impressed."

"You must have been to give her that choice piece of evidence in a murder trial. Why?"

"Because I don't trust the cops," she said simply. "They'd hide it; she'll do something with it. Is that why you're here? She read the files?"

"What exactly does Joshua Sterling's widow's connection to a fugitive have to do with the murder?"

"If you have to ask, then I'm not that impressed after all."

"You think Finn MacCauley ordered the hit?"

She tilted her head. "Again, if you have to ask, I'm not that impressed."

"And why don't you trust the cops?"

"This is Boston, my friend. Enough said." She leaned forward. "Look, I have no reason to advertise my relationship with Josh. I don't need to squash his wife because, to be perfectly honest, I did that often enough when the man was alive. But he was going to reveal her relationship to Finn because it would have gotten him notoriety beyond belief. And, trust me, that's what made Josh tick."

"Why would Finn care enough to order a hit, especially since there are a lot of people who think the man is dead?"

"He is not dead." She crossed her arms. "And don't ask how I know because I won't tell you."

"You didn't answer my question."

"I assume that Finn would care because anything that brings attention to him is going to fan the FBI flames to go after him again. He's an old man, living in seclusion, and probably wants to die that way."

"So he'd have his own daughter's husband killed?"

She snorted softly. "This is Finn MacCauley we're talking about. He kills with no compunction."

He did, Marc agreed. But thirty years had passed without incident. All of a sudden Finn MacCauley rises from the dead to have his illegitimate daughter's husband taken out?

"So your boyfriend was ready to sell his wife down the river, huh?" Marc leaned back, aware that they were minutes from Starbucks and that she would no doubt end the interview there. "Nice guy."

"He had his strong points."

"You're lucky he didn't sell you down the river."

She lifted a shoulder. "Not the way I fuck."

Lovely. "You know where to find Finn?" Because if the guy was alive, and the Guardian Angelinos brought him in, they'd be made.

"No," she said simply. "But he's the one who paid for the kill, and there's not a cop in Boston you can trust with that information."

"So take this to the FBI."

She smiled. "You know they don't like me either, don't you, Mr. Rossi?" The limo came to a stop. "Get out now."

"I'm not done asking questions."

"But I'm done answering." The door opened, and the Beretta was back. "It's time to leave, Mr. Rossi."

He pushed forward toward the door, keeping his gaze on her instead of the gun. "Thanks for the lead."

"Any time." She leaned closer to him. "Hope it helps the cause."

Whose cause? he wanted to ask. Instead, he climbed out, nodded to Devane, and walked away, the rain stronger now. He shouldered deeper into his jacket and continued through the pedestrian traffic, considering what he'd just learned, and what it could mean to the Guardian Angelinos.

Stepping under a building overhang, he called Vivi, but got voicemail, and then tried Zach, with the same results. He turned the corner and headed toward the public library, anxious to get on a computer and read the docs he'd gotten from Vivi. In the library, he could also do some research on one of Boston's most notorious criminals, the leader of an Irish mob that terrorized the city in the 1970s and disappeared underground in the early eighties.

He spent about an hour in a computer carrel in the stacks, searching and sending some links to his own email. He dug up plenty of information about Devyn Sterling, too, born Devyn Hewitt, evidently adopted by a truly blue-blooded Boston family, if the papers Vivi had were to be believed. And if Taylor Sly was to be believed.

Who had the best motive to kill Joshua Sterling? An old man who'd found peace in seclusion? A scorned wife? Or his mistress? Or had they all missed someone else completely?

As he got up to leave, he glanced through the shelves, above books, catching the movement of someone a few stacks away. He walked toward the open reading area, and so did the other person. He abruptly turned and pivoted around a stack behind him, purposely moving quickly.

Every instinct he had told him he was being watched.

He headed toward the massive reading room, then to the stairs and then the exit, the whole time hearing footsteps behind him. Not just watched, but followed.

He darted down the wide marble stairs, as close to a full run as he could in the building, slipping out the Dartmouth Street door and crossing Copley Square. He tried to stay with groups moving toward Trinity Church, the massive landmark on the other side of the square.

To his left, he noticed a guy talking on a phone, seeming uninterested, but his gaze followed Marc. Looking over his shoulder again, he saw a man hustling out of the library, a hood over his head, his focus locked on Marc. A group of tourists separated them momentarily, and he

used the opportunity to bolt to the church, taking the five
stone steps up to the portico in two huge strides, joining
a tour group escaping the rain.

Inside, the light was luminous and eerily red from the
murals and stained glass, the rows of wooden pews pep-
pered with bowed heads, some voices echoing up to what
the architect no doubt thought of as Heaven.

There were columns and a wide aisle circling the wor-
ship area, but mostly the church was a vast open space.
He glanced back to the entrance, not seeing the hooded
runner. He stayed with the tour group of about twenty
people following each other with pamphlets open, reading and looking up, taking pictures. He moved with them
until he could slip into a far pew, which he did just as the
hooded man arrived at the back of the church.

He moved swiftly down the pew, stepping around an
old lady in prayer, then diving into the shadows of the
side aisle, spying a Bride's Room.

No one was getting married on a Tuesday morning.
He could trap him in here, and get some answers.

He shouldered the door and it opened, leading to a
large, empty dressing room decorated with silk and peach
sofas and chairs and a dozen full-length mirrors. He
moved to the back, down to a bathroom area with toilets
and another wall of vanities and stools, just as the door
opened and a shoe scraped on the marble.

He popped into the stall, which was enclosed floor to
ceiling and protected by a carved mahogany door, which
he closed but didn't bolt, not wanting to risk making
noise. A man's footsteps moved through the dressing
area. Getting closer.

Marc drew his Ruger slowly.

"Excuse me, sir, can I help you?" The woman's indignant voice echoed through the empty dressing room.

"I'm on the tour," the man replied.

"This is a private room, not part of the tour. You need to leave."

At the sound of a fist hitting flesh, Marc vaulted out, just in time to see a uniformed woman stumble backward with a cry of shock. The hooded man whipped around, and Marc threw a round kick, thudding a boot into his stomach. The man's face turned red as he stumbled backward.

Marc raised the gun and the woman shrieked. The other man used the distraction to grab the door and bolt.

"Help me!" the woman pleaded, blood pouring from her nose.

"I'll get help," Marc promised, shooting out the door and back into the church, scanning for the hooded jacket.

Gone, or hiding.

There were multiple exits along the sides and any number of hiding places.

He bit back a curse, holstering his gun and starting a careful walk, peering into every face in every pew. Outside, a fresh downpour obliterated the crowds.

The man was gone.

Marc had information, and the real trick was knowing what to do with it. He knew, but Zach would hate it. Too bad.

JP answered on the first ring. "We need your help."

"Who's we?"

"The Guardian Angelinos."

CHAPTER 20

"Jesus Christ, Sam. Why didn't you tell me your foot was hurt this badly?" Zach gently rubbed the towel over the gash, assessing how bad it was.

"Would it have made a difference? We still had to do what we had to do."

"Wouldn't you make a damn fine soldier," he mused, giving her a quick smile.

"No thanks. How bad is it?"

"Pretty bad, swollen as hell." He held the foot up and got a good look underneath. "You hit a vein, so let me get the worst of the dirt out of the cuts. As soon as we get on the road with Vivi, we'll stop and get some antiseptic and bandages. In the meantime, no weight on this."

"What if we have to run?"

"We'll cross that bridge...when we're knocked off it."

"Very funny."

The shelter they'd found was more a storage facility

than a working barn. The front half, the part visible from the road, was open under an awning of steel. Behind it, where they were, was probably the original barn, built from wood two-by-fours, the only light from two slots in the walls where sections of wood had fallen away.

"We're not going anywhere," he assured her. "But it could take Vivi some time to get a car and get out here. Two hours, maybe three. If I had had time, I'da called Marc, too."

"What if the guy who owns the house comes over here?"

"Unlikely that anyone with a finished basement and workout equipment spends a lot of time in a filthy pole barn." He placed the other clean towel in front of her, creating a clean spot for her foot by covering the dirt and weeds that had grown up through the cracks in the floorboards.

"You think the cops are following me, Zach? Trying to run me off the road?"

"I think we have to consider every possibility, and that's one of them."

"How about the possibility that it was an accident?"

"Don't be naïve."

She didn't want to be naïve, but, God, she didn't want to believe she was the target for multiple killers, some of whom were law enforcement. "Some of those truckers are surfing the Internet and texting while they drive. Maybe..." She just let her voice and the impossible thought fade. She closed her eyes, her pulse still pumping harder than normal. All the rationalization in the world didn't change the cold, hard truth. "He knows where I am."

"Not at this moment," he said calmly.

"We can't go back to the safe house in Jamaica Plain."

"I put that on the message to Vivi, too, to make sure she lets Nino know." He got the blanket out of the bag and smoothed it out for her. "Just relax. There's nothing we can do right now but wait."

She leaned back and automatically reached for him, drawing him to her. "Zach, how long can I live like this? What the hell am I going to do? I can't spend the rest of my life in hiding."

"I know," he said, lying down next to her. "Don't panic."

"Is that was this is? Panic?" She held out her hand to show how it was shaking. "I can practically feel adrenaline rushing through me."

"It's like a hot, black ball in your stomach, huh?"

"Spoken like a man who's had a few brushes with death."

"A few. One really bad one. The one I wanted to tell you about at the reservoir today."

"You did?"

"That was my plan, to tell you everything." The deep emotion in his voice caught her by surprise. She skimmed her fingers along the scars, loving that he never flinched anymore, but gave her access to that tender place.

"Then tell me now," she whispered. When he started to shake his head, she made her touch firmer. "Tell me."

"I got torn up by some grenade shrapnel. Didn't wear my eye protection so I could see better, and now I can't see shit. And I...just made a bad decision."

Something in his voice said there was more. "By not wearing eye protection?"

"By leaving my position. Rule number one and I broke it."

"Why?"

He snorted softly. "The million-dollar question, huh? Because I had to make a call to collapse the outer cordon when I heard the SEALs on the inner cordon taking huge fire. There was no air support like there was supposed to be, so I made the call to take my men and pull them in closer to help the boys in the inner ring."

He might as well have been speaking Latin, but Sam didn't need to understand the terminology. She heard the pain and regret and remorse. "I'm sure you made the best decision you could have made under the circumstances."

"That's not how the Army saw it. I left my position, and the enemy exploited that move, so I lost a man in my platoon and four from another. Oh, and my eye, so I actually got a better end of my decision than those guys did." He drew in a slow, pained breath, turning away. "I live with that decision every day."

"I bet you saved more lives than you lost over there."

He lifted a shoulder.

"You saved mine today." She curled one long strand of his hair around her finger and gently tugged his head toward her. "Here's what I think you should do. Let go of that mistake and get on with your life."

His lips curled in a smile. "I could give you the same advice."

"I have gotten on with my life," she said quickly. "Changed it entirely, as a matter of fact. The only vestige of my bad experience is my lack of trust in my own decisions. And you're already helping me get over that."

"What about your bad experience with me?" he asked.

"What about it?"

He just looked at her, then took a deep breath and on a sigh, said, "Samantha Fairchild, I want to ask you a very important question."

The proposal-like tone of the question made her heart stutter. And the way he turned toward her, curling his arms to pull her closer to him, sent a sharp wave of heat through her body. Whatever he asked, she was in no shape to say no. "Yes?"

"Would you forgive me for what I did?"

She heard the sincerity in his voice, and the plea. "On one condition."

"I say it in a postcard?"

She smiled at that, ridiculously happy that they already had new inside jokes. "It's harder than that, Zach."

"What is your condition?"

"That you forgive yourself."

"For not calling or writing? For not giving us a chance?"

"For making that mistake. For losing those men, and your eye."

His expression grew serious. "I may never do that. Every time I look in the mirror, I think of them. I don't see me; I see my mistakes. And I don't see a man who's good enough for you."

She leaned up on one elbow, propelled by how wrong that was. "Zach? You aren't a man who cares about what he looks like. And, by the way, you still look pretty damn good to me; I'm used to you like this. I don't see your face or your scar or your missing eye. I see you. A man who is smart and protective and kind and resourceful. I see you exactly how I saw you the day you left for Kuwait. And you know how I felt then."

"You loved me." He spoke softly, treating the words as though they were so fragile that just saying them might break them.

"Yes, I thought I did," she replied.

"You thought you did?"

"Heartache has a way of changing history," she admitted. "By the time I accepted that I'd never hear from you again, I'd convinced myself I never loved you at all. It was just great sex."

"It was great sex." He leaned close, his lips brushing hers. "You know what else it was?"

She shook her head, gripping his arm with her fingers, waiting with her breath held.

"It was the first and last time I really believed I belonged somewhere."

"With me?"

"With you, in you, next to you. I never felt like that, at least not on U.S. soil. When I was with you, I was…home."

Something in her cracked, an emotional jolt so real, she felt in her body. "Zach…"

He kissed her, a slow, deep, wet, warm, endless kiss that made her tingle and float and forget everything but his mouth on hers. Home. She was *home* to him.

She closed her eyes and opened her mouth, taking his tongue as he cupped her face in both hands, then dragged them down the front of her T-shirt, the wet cotton clinging to her body. Yanking the shirt up, he stripped it off, both of them already breathing heavily.

He reached behind her and unhooked her bra with a flick of his fingers, but the wet material stuck to her. He looked down, and she could feel her nipples hardening under his scrutiny.

Slipping a finger under one strap, he peeled the garment off her like tape, revealing her breasts, wet and speckled with dirt. He removed a tiny twig sealed to her flesh, then thumbed one nipple, staring at it, a low groan of appreciation in his throat.

But he just circled the peak, budding it as he lifted it and lowered his head to suckle her. He licked, sucked, kissed, and sent a thousand electrical impulses down her body, between her legs.

She plucked at his shirt, pulling it up, trying to get it off. He wouldn't relinquish her breast, so she gave up and dropped her hand to his jeans, fumbling with the snap.

He did it for her, finally breaking the contact, long enough to fight the wet pants and get them off, and then undressed her without hurting her foot.

When they were both naked, he leaned her back so he could stare at her, burning her with scrutiny somehow more intense, despite his debility. "When I was at war," he whispered, "you kept me alive."

She tried to swallow, but couldn't. "How?"

"There were so many nights, Sam." He closed one hand over her breast, then stroked all the way down. "So many nights with explosions like thunder in the distance, and all I could think about was this. You. Us. The way we used to be together. The way we might never...be again."

"Why did you think that?"

"Because the explosions weren't thunder in the distance," he said, lowering his body to hers. "They were real and they were close. I never thought I'd come back. And even if I did, I've never felt..."

"What?" she urged.

"Good enough for the home that you offered with your heart and your body."

She put one hand on his cheek, skimming the other down his chest to close it over his erection. "You are more than good enough," she assured him. "More."

He leaned in and kissed her as his finger curled into the wet, slick flesh between her legs. She opened her mouth so he could dip his tongue in and out with the same rhythm as his finger.

Automatically she spread her legs as he kissed his way down, sucking sweat from her skin, nibbling at her belly button. He skimmed her skin, dragging his hands over her hips, inching his thumbs together right between her legs.

He glanced to their discarded, wet clothes. "If my wallet didn't make it—" He reached to his jeans, pulling out a soggy billfold and a condom from inside. "We're in luck."

Her body still hummed and rocked, ready for him, aching for him. He sheathed himself and straddled her, looking down from above, his face darker than ever, his expression fierce as he lined up his body to penetrate hers.

He entered her, balancing his weight on his hands, holding her gaze, inching deeper with agonizing caution.

She felt her lids shutter as she rose up to take him in, reaching her hands to his neck and pulling him closer to her, the need for all of him overwhelming.

"Come here," she managed to whisper, her brain faltering at the bliss of each inch as he filled her. "Come to me."

He lowered himself and she kissed his mouth, his cheek, his scar, his missing eye. He let her, moving with abandon now, lost in the sensations that ricocheted between their bodies. Another climax took hold, twisting through her, as painful as it was pleasurable, too much to take. She gripped his shoulders and gave in to it, barely relaxing when another wave hit, taking her again as he ground into her.

Her response seemed to send him over the edge; his moans grew lower and longer and more helpless until his body shuddered with his own release, his head back, his mouth slack, his control shredded.

"Zaccaria," she whispered. *"Benvenuto a casa."* Welcome home.

"Grazie, amore mio." He breathed the words into her ear. *"Sarò sempre al tuo fianco."*

Chills danced down her spine at the romantic, foreign words. "What did you say?"

"Shhh." He rested against her, breathless, his heart beating so hard and steady it felt like her own.

Vivi waited long enough to be able to make out shadows in the basement, a room that looked as if it was divided by stairs and unenhanced by any natural light.

"Billy?" she whispered harshly. "Are you down here?"

A muffled moan came from somewhere to her left. She tried to stand, but pain rocketed up her leg from her ankle. Twisted. *Shit.* She could get up and put some weight on it, but it was going to throb like a mother for a while.

"Where are you?"

Another soft grunt. Ignoring the pain, she used the

banister to pull herself up, reaching out to feel her way toward the sound. She hit a wall directly in front of her, trying to picture the room. She inched left, touching nothing but air.

"Where? I can't see a thing."

The grunt was weaker this time. Jesus, what had the guy done to him? And why?

She limped to the sound, hearing the soft rumble of a water heater. Her hand hit metal, then stabbed into space next to it, slapping warm skin. She jerked back with a little cry.

"Is that you?"

"Mmmm."

Carefully she reached in again, into what appeared to be about an eight-inch space between an ancient oil furnace and an even older water heater. She touched wiry short hair, and bony shoulder, a stubbly face with a cloth stuck in his mouth and a fat roll of duct tape around it.

"Can you breathe?"

"Mmmm." That was a yes, she thought, feeling under his nostrils for air as she worked to rip the tape and ungag him.

"How did you get inside there? Never mind," she said, knowing he was easily sixty or so. "Save your strength. I'll get you out."

But how? She ran her hands up and down the two units, one of which got hotter as she went lower, no doubt near a pilot flame. She couldn't see the light until she got almost to the ground, then saw the small blue flicker of a flame.

"Can you slide out?"

He slumped a little, his strength clearly sapped. Oh,

Lord. Every gas furnace gives off carbon monoxide, and in this tiny enclosed space, he was surely inhaling fumes that were otherwise dispersed safely into the basement air and into vents one would assume were built into the walls or floors.

Again, she stabbed her hand in between the units and tried to pry her fingers between him and the warm metal trying to figure out how to slide him out. When he was alert and upright, Billy could have squeezed in and out of this space. But slumped and sleepy and near death? Impossible.

Could she blow out the pilot light? Would that stop the fumes?

She knelt again, squinting into the dusty vents, finding the steady blue flame. She blew as hard as possible, flickering the flame but not even coming close to extinguishing it.

"Is there a safety switch somewhere?" she asked. "Don't most units like this have to have some kind of off switch?"

"I do' know," he murmured.

The sound of the latch upstairs made her freeze. Her captor was coming back. Slowly, Vivi shifted in front of the heater, bracing her back, ready to kick the guy in the nuts the minute she sensed he was close. The door hinges squeaked and a trickle of light shone on rough wooden stairs.

When he closed the door behind him, Vivi held her breath, not moving a muscle. He probably wanted the element of surprise as much as she did, and that's why he was keeping it dark. Without making a sound, she slipped her hand into the opening between the two units and closed her fingers in a reassuring squeeze of Billy's narrow shoulder.

Then footsteps down the steps, the distinctive stench of gasoline arriving before he did.

Her stomach rolled. What was he planning?

She inched away from the furnace, silently slipping into a corner.

His feet hit each step with slow, deadly deliberation, kicking her heart rate up so high, she swore he'd be able to hear it.

She tensed her good leg and lifted it in preparation for a swift kick, forced to lean on the twisted ankle without releasing so much as a grunt of pain.

He walked to the furnace, then back to where she was. "We got a problem," he said, his voice so close she knew he was right in front of her.

"Hell, yeah we do." She shot her foot forward, hitting something hard. A gun. For a split second, she just closed her eyes, waiting for the shot, but he snagged her foot and flipped her down, then blinded her with the beam of white light in the face.

"Don't fuck with me."

She blinked into the industrial-strength flashlight, unable to see even the shadow of the man holding it. "What the hell do you want from me? And this guy is dying from carbon monoxide fumes—do you know that?"

He whacked the side of her head with the flashlight. "Let's go."

Pain exploded through her head, but she managed to push herself up, the light still blinding her. "Look, I don't know what you want with her or me, but why are you letting this guy die?"

"Now."

Where? But she knew better than to ask. "Him, too?"

"Just us, and if he tries, he dies." He stepped back, still blinding her with the light. "Because right up there—" He flipped the light to the top of the furnace for one second and she automatically followed it. Then it was back in her face. "Is a container of gasoline. If our friend Billy so much as vibrates that furnace, or someone comes down here and tries to free him, that container will fall, and in a matter of seconds, the entire place will be blown to bits. Did you hear that, Billy?"

Billy didn't even grunt, but the man grabbed her shirt and pulled her up, pushing her toward the steps. A gun jabbed her back. "Go." He pushed her toward the stairs. "I kill for a living, my dear, so don't even think about trying to outsmart me."

She had been thinking about just that, but she'd wait and bide her time. He needed her for something; that much was clear. As long as he did, she was alive.

But once he didn't...

"Billy?" she called over her back. "You're gonna be okay, dude." Not that she believed that for a minute. "Billy?"

Silence.

CHAPTER 21

Billy." Sam's eyes popped open, pulled out of a fitful sleep.

"Actually, the name's Zach." He was dressed, pacing the tiny structure.

"I forgot about Billy. I wonder if Vivi made it over there."

"I'm more concerned about her getting here. It's been almost three hours." He kneeled in front of her. "I need to do some recon. Would you be okay if I left for a few minutes?"

No. "Of course." She glanced at her foot, swollen and throbbing. "If I went with you, I'd slow you down. What are you going to do?"

"Just check out our options." He kissed her forehead and tipped her chin up to his face. "I'll be back."

After he left, she managed to pull her still-wet clothes on, then tore the pillowcase into strips to cover her foot. Then she waited in agony for him to come back. When he did, he seemed more determined than ever to get out of the pole barn.

"Our friend is still home," he reported. "And he kindly left his garage door open with two vehicles in it. We're going to borrow one." He indicated her foot. "Can you put any weight on that?"

"Some. A little." Not much. "I'll do what I have to." She stood, barely able to control a yelp of pain.

Zach had an arm under her in a split second. "Let's get you to the road, and you can wait under cover while I get a car."

Every step was sheer hell, but she made it by using him as a crutch. They limped through the woods, which seemed even more shadowy now, although the rain had stopped. At the road's edge, he guided her into a thicket of pines, easing her to the ground, making sure she was hidden.

"I don't like this," he muttered.

"I'll be fine, Zach."

He shook his head, his body tense as he glanced around, but they obviously had no other options. She couldn't make it all the way back to that house. At the rate she was moving, they'd be easy targets for a long time. "I should watch for Vivi anyway, in case she shows."

"All right, but listen to me, Sam. Stay under cover, okay? Don't stand up, don't walk up to the road, don't come and find me. I'll be back." He started to leave, then took one step closer and crouched to get face-to-face with her. *"Sarò sempre al tuo fianco."*

"You have to tell me what that means."

"When I get back." He placed one more kiss on her forehead and left, his footsteps soundless over the bed of rain-soaked leaves, gone before she took her next breath.

Sarò sempre al tuo fianco. The words kept her calm as she planted her gaze ahead at the bit of road she could see, staying still, trying to hear every sound. It was completely silent; not even a leaf moved.

Come back to me, Zach.

The achy longing of waiting for him was a familiar sensation, but this time her heart felt different. This time, she was sure of him.

She tried to count, to figure the minutes, wishing she had a watch. She got to sixty at least five times before the anxiety that hummed through her started to turn sour. It would take him that long just to get back to the house, wouldn't it? Maybe the owner was outside. Maybe he had to negotiate for a car.

He could, he *would* do what had to be done. Maybe he had managed to get into the house and call Vivi again.

She counted to sixty another seven times, or it seemed like that. Her skin crawled with the discomfort of partially dry clothes and the remnants of river water. And worry. *Come on, Zach.*

She got up on her knees, keeping the weight off her foot, and looked down the road, dying for a glimpse of him. From the opposite direction, she heard an engine scream. She backed deeper into the bushes just as a silver SUV came careening toward her.

The vehicle slowed as if the driver were looking for something, forcing Sam deeper into her hiding place, watching it roll by close enough to see into the open driver's window. At the sight of spiky black hair and a familiar face, Sam jumped out into the road, relief and joy numbing the fireworks of pain in her foot as she waved wildly.

Vivi hit the brakes and met Sam's gaze, her expression unreadable as Sam closed the space, hobbling toward the SUV.

"Get in the back," Vivi said, her voice bizarrely strained, her eyes narrowed and fierce.

Was she mad she had to come out here? Did she not understand the severity of the situation? Sam grabbed the back door handle as Vivi calmly closed her window, the dark glass blocking her from view.

"Vivi!" Whipping the door open, Sam threw herself in. "You can't bel—"

She saw the gun first, pointed directly at her, and then the man who pointed it at her.

"Larry?" The word croaked out.

"Do what he says, Sam. He kills for a living."

Larry the *lawyer*?

"Excellent advice." He steadied the gun, pointing it right at Sam's head. "One misstep from either of you and Sam is dead."

"Wha...why..." Words just stuck in Sam's throat as her fingers closed around the door handle. Could she jump?

"Hit the accelerator hard," he ordered. "Make a U-turn and get on the highway. Now!"

"No!" Sam cried, looking over Vivi's shoulder in Zach's direction. He *had* to at least see what kind of car she was in.

But Larry reached over and slammed his hand around her neck, yanking her down and stabbing the barrel of the gun into her temple.

"I swear to fucking God she's dead if you don't drive."

Sam wanted to scream, but the hard, cold steel pierced her temple, vibrating with fury and fear. She smelled sweat and grease and gasoline, her insides turning to water with terror. All he had to do was flick his finger.

Vivi hit the gas and made the U-turn.

"Faster!"

The vehicle lurched forward, the engine loud. Maybe Zach heard that. Maybe he would follow. Or maybe she was never going to get out of this car alive.

The high-pitched wail of an engine cut through the silence of the woods, stopping Zach stone cold still in the middle of searching the open garage for a key to either car.

He waited, listening. Had Vivi come? Had she picked up Sam and they were—

Going in the wrong direction. The engine gunned again, louder and faster, and most definitely headed away from him.

What the hell? He had few options. Break, enter, and hold the guy at gunpoint for his keys? That would take the least amount of time and explanation. From the other side of the basement door, twenty-year-old rock and roll blared from tinny speakers and a man grunted as he worked out.

Zach drew his weapon and silently turned the knob of the door, remembering the layout of the basement. If the guy was on his Soloflex, he'd be facing the other way.

He peeked around the corner. An older man sat shirtless on the bench doing reps, his back to Zach. Taking one step inside, Zach saw exactly what he needed on a table ten feet away. Keys and a phone.

Waiting until the man started the next set, Zach soundlessly entered and tiptoed to the keys, closing his fingers around them so they didn't jangle. He slipped the phone in his pocket and backed out before the old guy stopped at eight reps.

If he started either of the cars, the owner would be on the phone with the cops in seconds. He glanced at the keys and cars, picking an older Lexus sedan over the other, more muscular SUV.

In it, he turned on the ignition without starting the car, able to then slip the gear into neutral. Hopping out, he pushed the car out of the garage and as far down the drive as he could before jumping back in, turning on the engine, and thanking the Japanese for building a machine so quiet that the owner couldn't hear it over the music, or the crunch of gravel.

On the road, he drove straight back to the copse of trees where he'd left Sam and swore mightily. She was gone.

Why would she leave? Did she go back to the barn? Why? If she was with Vivi, why not get him?

Fresh tire marks on the asphalt—marks that he knew were not there before—pulled another heartfelt curse from his throat. The sickening reality that he didn't want to face engulfed him as he laid on the accelerator and tried to think.

How long did he have until he got pulled over for driving a stolen car? Following the gut that kept him alive a hundred times before, he jammed on the gas, got it up to damn near ninety, and still managed to dial the phone he'd just stolen.

Marc's answer was tentative. "Yes?"

"I need your help."

"Where the hell have you been?" Marc demanded. "I've been trying to reach you—"

"Sam's in trouble. Someone has her." God *damn* it, how could he have left her?

"The Irish mob," Marc shot back. "Or the Boston PD. And not to take her in for another lineup."

"Exactly what I'm thinking. What do you know?"

"I had an unusual meeting with Taylor Sly today."

"The model prostitute?" Zach got the entrance for 495 and made an instant decision, heading back toward Boston.

Traffic was pretty light on this outer band highway, so he threaded the few cars while listening to Marc tell him about documents that he'd been given that indicated Devyn Sterling was the illegitimate daughter of mobster Finn MacCauley.

Nothing that told him who had Sam.

"What are you doing with that jump drive?" Zach asked.

"I talked to an agent at the Boston FBI office. Straight shooter, good guy. Except he did the only thing a straight shooter could do."

Zach knew what he was going to say. "Contacted the lead investigator on the Sterling murder."

"He had to, Zach. It's hard evidence connecting a victim to a known killer, and possibly provides a motive for Sterling's murder."

"Is Finn MacCauley even alive?" Zach asked.

"Don't know. But if he is, he might still wield some power. And he is still on the FBI's Most Wanted list."

"Fuck this fugitive," Zach growled. "I only care about one thing at the moment." He rolled up on a silver Highlander, who tapped his brakes. *Idiot.* He zipped around, not able to see the driver behind blackened glass. Anyone with untinted windows was getting a searching glare from him. "I can't find her alone."

"Isn't Vivi with you?" Marc asked.

Worry flared at the question. "No, I left her a message hours ago."

"Shit, Zach. She's missing, too. Okay, I have an idea."

"It better be good."

"Does Sam have a cell phone with her? I can get JP to triangulate both their phones and get locations."

"Her phone's waterlogged. And how the hell did JP get involved?"

"By birth," Marc said brusquely. "He's family. How'd her phone get waterlogged?"

"When we were forced off a bridge by a produce truck."

"Jesus."

"Listen, call everyone Vivi knows and find out whose car she borrowed. If she didn't, then she can't be far because she's looking for me. And then get to Billy Shawkins's house in Roxbury. Hale Street. Sam sent Vivi there today right before my car ended up in the bottom of a reservoir."

"Got it. So, what the hell are you driving?"

"A nice Lexus I stole." Behind him, about a mile away, the flashing lights of a cop car. "But Massachusetts's finest is on my ass." God *damn* it.

"How close are they?"

"Oh, he has me now." He briefly considered trying to outrun the cop, but decided against it, slamming on the brakes and whipping to the shoulder. "He's about to hit the jackpot. No license, no registration, no eyepatch. Just a gun I'm not allowed to carry and a car I stole."

"I'll see if I can get help from JP on the other line."

"What can he do?"

"You'd be surprised if you'd just give him a chance. Don't hang up, and stall the cop."

He put the phone on speaker and tossed it on the passenger seat as he grabbed the Glock. When you only have one thing to live for and it's gone, you can fuck the rules. Which was what he was about to do. He racked the slide and watched the cop get out.

The cop started to walk to the Lexus; then his partner got out and called to him. The cop signaled for Zach to stay, and returned to his car.

Zach watched, the weapon ready, his heart still hammering while he waited. And waited. And waited a good goddamn twenty minutes. Every car that passed physically hurt.

Hurry it up, JP. Finally, the cop jogged back to the car.

"Mr. Angelino?" he asked.

"Yeah."

"We're going to escort you into Boston."

"Thanks." Zach kept the gun low as another cruiser flew by going west, made a sudden U-turn, and screamed in front of them.

"Let's go. Stay between us."

Zach pulled out as Marc's voice came back on the speaker. "You okay?" he asked.

"Have a police escort. Eating crow."

"Yeah, but there's one catch," Marc said. "They're escorting you to the Southie police station."

"What? Why?"

"Just be glad you're not in cuffs in the back of one of those cruisers, man. I'll meet you there."

"Check Shawkins's house," he demanded.

"They're sending somebody, but they want me to tell them everything Vivi told me. They're looking for her and for Sam, Zach."

Zach could do nothing but drive, trapped by the cruisers, at least headed in the right direction. He hoped.

CHAPTER 22

Sam just kept her eyes closed and didn't move. She tried to figure out where they were going based on general direction without being able to see the road, but after several police cars had zoomed by, sirens on, Larry forced Vivi off the highway onto side streets. Still flat on his lap with a gun jammed in her temple, Sam lost her sense of direction.

And she really lost that growing sense of confidence that had been building for the last few days. How could she have talked to this man—the night of the killing and again in the police station—and not realized he was the man who shot Joshua Sterling?

She tried to look but he held her firm with the barrel of his gun.

How had he done it that night? Had he talked to her—*flirted* with her—at the bar, changed his hair and clothes, and slipped into the wine cellar to assassinate a local columnist? The door to the back alley had been left open, she recalled, giving him access to the wine cellar after he left the bar, exactly the route Zach had followed that morning.

And Zach had pointed out that "Larry" wore a toupee, and makeup could cover the blemishes she'd seen on his face. But who hired him?

Full-body fear wiped away the questions. What did it matter? Whoever Larry the lawyer really was, he had a gun to her head, and he was taking them both...somewhere.

"We're going back to Roxbury," he said to Vivi. "So take this exit."

Back to Roxbury? To Billy? She managed to move her head a centimeter, but he just jabbed the gun harder.

"Billy," she whispered. "Is he—"

"Not a word," he said, a little sound of crazy in his voice that scared her as much as the gun. "Not a single word."

She defied him. "Why are you doing this? I couldn't identify you. I'm no threat to you."

"You're a plant and you have to be eliminated, and I have a plan to do that."

A plant? "I don't know what you're talking about."

"Sam," Vivi said, her voice oddly calm, "I got some of this out of him already. He thinks you were purposely placed to witness Sterling's murder so the hit man can't get his money."

"No, that's not true," Sam said, attempting to look up at him, but her head butted into the gun. "I was there by accident."

"Doesn't matter. You saw."

"I didn't see...you." Could that help her? "I could never identify you," she repeated. "Even now, I haven't really seen you."

He choked softly. "As long as you're alive, you are an impediment to my income. A Harvard girl like you should understand that."

She didn't. She didn't understand anything. Just that she was about to die, she'd never see Zach again, and she'd somehow dragged Vivi and Billy into her mess. She had nothing to lose, though. She would fight for her life. And theirs. As soon as there was a moment he didn't have her a millimeter from death.

"Take the back route," he ordered. "The way we left."

"Is Billy okay?"

"No," Vivi said, disgust in her voice. "He's breathing carbon monoxide and sitting next to a bucket of gasoline on top of a furnace with a pilot light."

Sam's heart turned over and shattered. She'd done this to Billy. She'd somehow led him to Billy, who he thought could be bait, but he got Vivi instead.

"Turn here, or I shoot her." His voice was flat.

"Why don't you?" Vivi challenged, taking Sam's breath away with shock. "Seriously, dude, if you want her dead, you got her. What the hell are you waiting for?"

Sam tried to quell the gut-level response to tell Vivi to stop; she knew Vivi too well. Getting information was Vivi's gift, and Sam waited silently to see if this tactic would work. If they got out of this alive, they had to know who the real enemy was.

If.

"I like to do things right," he said in answer to Vivi's question.

"Then shoot us both and be done with it. Why are you making a side trip to Roxbury?"

"To send a message, to avoid evidence, and to do this the right way."

"A message to who?" Vivi asked.

He was silent, but she felt his body grow taut, and so did Sam's. *Don't get too mad, Larry.* Not enough to pull that trigger. "I just don't like to be fucked with."

"Yeah, well, who does?" Vivi was so amazingly calm, just carrying on a conversation like they weren't hostages, like they were just three friends driving through Boston.

"They should have done the job themselves if they didn't want to pay," he finally said.

"Who's they?" Vivi asked.

"They couldn't do it right, not a job of this level," he said, clearly more to himself than to them. "They're morons, trying to run you off a road and shoot you down in the street. Sloppy, unprofessional morons. At least they're smart enough to call in a professional, but then they piss on me in their typical small-minded, cheating way. I'm going to get my proof, I'm going to get my money, and I'm going to put a few of those bastards in jail for blowing up a house."

Sam almost moaned. "Billy's house?"

"So they will not fuck with the Czar again. Okay, park the car right here on this hill, facing as it is now." He laughed an evil laugh. "I know a secret way out."

The hill by Billy's house. Oh, Lord, he was the Sears repairman. She and Zach had had him and let him go. She looked at him, and didn't recognize him.

The agony of that stabbed as hard as the gun.

"Put the emergency brake on and leave the keys," he ordered. "And, trust me, if you do one single thing that I don't like, this woman is dead."

Sam felt the car stop; then Vivi turned the engine off. "Who are they?" she asked quietly.

"The fucking Boston cops, of course." He looked down at Sam. "Which is why I know you're their plant. Who better to use as a witness than someone they'd all love to see dead anyway?"

The first person Zach saw when he entered the South End police station was JP, who leaned against a wall, Styrofoam cup of coffee in his hand, deep in conversation with another detective.

Marc came up beside him and put a hand on his shoulder. "O'Hara wants to talk to us."

JP looked away from his conversation and caught Zach's gaze, nodding once in greeting. Zach returned the nod and walked off with Marc.

"Any word at all?" Zach asked. "Did you go to Shawkins's house? Has Vivi called?"

"Negative to all. They sent a cruiser to Shawkins's place and he's not home. The house is empty."

"Did they search?"

"No warrant," Marc said. "But I spoke with the officer who went over there, and they did a pretty thorough walk-around. He's not home and no one is inside. And we'll get a court order for a search warrant tomorrow."

"I don't need a fucking search warrant," Zach practically spat. "Aren't you worried about Vivi?" And Sam. *Where was Sam?*

"Hell, yes, I am. Her boss said she missed a staff meeting, which isn't that unusual. But she's not answering her phone, and JP found out she hasn't used it all day since I left her in town this morning. They don't have a location on it yet."

They exchanged a look as the two detectives came around the corner, jackets off, guns on display. Ron Larkin's tie was askew, but O'Hara was as smooth as if he'd just walked into the office.

"Gentlemen," O'Hara said, extending a hand. "We'd like to review some facts with you."

"Here's the only facts you need to know, Detective." Zach got right into his face, not caring he was covered in dried mud, not caring his scars were on full display, and sure as shit not caring that he hadn't been asked. "Samantha Fairchild was abducted about an hour ago, shortly after an eighteen-wheeler tracked her to the middle of the state and attempted to kill both of us. It is your job to find her, and if you won't, I will. And I don't care what fucking laws I have to break or whose fucking neck I have to snap to do it."

"One more word and you'll be arrested for threatening an officer."

Zach's fists curled, but Marc got hold of him. "Hear him out, Zach, and get some more information. Where the hell are you going to go? They might have some clues."

His blood boiled, his whole being anxious to bolt and go...somewhere. Anywhere but here. O'Hara opened the door to an office and led them in. But the other detective, Larkin, held back and put a hand on Zach's arm.

"Listen, I'm kind of alone in the way I feel, but I really like your Sam, and think she's getting the shaft. One of the cops who lost his job because of her happened to be O'Hara's friend. So, you're not going to get anywhere by pissing him off. But I want to help her. Do you have any idea at all where she might be? I'll send somebody out."

"Detective!" O'Hara's voice was sharp. "Close the door, and I'll handle this alone."

Larkin gave his partner a quick look, and a half-assed shrug to Zach, then left, slamming the door. Inside, O'Hara was at a table, clicking a laptop and firing questions at Marc.

"Did Ms. Sly say why she gave these computer files to your cousin and not the police?"

"She said she didn't trust the police," Marc replied.

Zach stayed standing, considering what would happen if he went after Larkin and took the help he offered.

"Did she say if there were any other copies?"

"For Chrissake, Detective, what difference does it make?" Zach exclaimed. "What's on it tells you that the old guy who used to run the Irish mob is the father of the victim's wife. Where the hell is *she* in all this?"

"Under surveillance."

Behind his eyes—the good and the bad—tiny red spots of anger exploded. "You have her under your watch, but not Sam Fairchild?"

"*Surveillance*, Mr. Angelino, not police protection. Because we consider her a person of interest, if not a suspect. Not a witness who has a record of making the wrong call."

Zach's fist formed just as the door opened and a woman demanded their attention. "We have a homicide report that you'll be interested in, Detective O'Hara."

And then his fist relaxed, his body suddenly numb, the surge of adrenaline that had just riled him turning to hot ice in his chest, strangling and suffocating.

A homicide report.

Sam. God, no, not Sam.

"What is it?" O'Hara asked, walking out to talk to her.

Zach inched toward the door, listening, catching bits of the woman's words.

"Vic is a female...one of the Charlestown...shot in the head. Vehicle owned by..." The rest of the words slipped away, like Zach's whole world.

His world, his heart, his life. Gone. Not Sam. Please, God, not after he just found her again.

And, holy hell, not Vivi.

He stood behind a chair, his fingers digging into the leather, his jaw clenched tight enough to break his teeth.

O'Hara stepped back in, calm and cool. He pointed to Zach and Marc, using two fingers. "You stay here until I get back. Detective Larkin will lock this room, and no one goes near that laptop." He started to leave, but Zach snagged his sleeve, whipping it around.

"Who is it?"

"We don't have a positive ID."

Zach's blood reached the boiling point as he fisted the shirt and his nostrils flared. "Who?"

O'Hara just stared hard at him, then jerked his arm free. "It appears that Taylor Sly is dead, Mr. Angelino. So that little jump drive right there, that truly is the key to at least one murder and maybe more."

Relief washed through him. Taylor Sly, not Samantha Fairchild.

Still, he wanted to go to the Charlestown wharf to see this female victim and verify the cop's statement. He let go and nodded once, grateful for the information. Marc waved him out into the hall.

"I heard," Marc said softly. "The victim is Sly."

"Maybe."

JP marched toward them. "C'mere," he said, taking them to a far corner in the hallway. "I have to talk to you."

They stood close together, the three of them in front of the large window that looked out over the parking lot. Over his shoulder, Zach watched as Larkin went back into the office that was supposed to be locked.

"I have someone tracing the location of Vivi's phone," JP said softly. "Not supposed to, but at this point, I've cracked the rules pretty bad." He looked hard at Zach. "No word on Sam?"

"No." Zach's gaze moved to the parking lot, falling on a man who crossed with purpose in his gait. He looked familiar...Keegan Kennedy. The maître d' of Paupiette's. What was he doing here? He was on the phone, then snapped it closed, walking to a compact car in the parking lot.

Over JP's shoulder, Detective Larkin stepped out of the room they'd just been in, ending a call at the same time. And Zach's gut flared like the Fourth of July over the Charles River.

"C'mon," he said to Marc. "Let's go."

"Where?" JP asked.

"Just..." Zach looked at him, then notched his head to include JP as well. "You, too."

They got into an elevator and beat Larkin downstairs, slipping out through the side door and into JP's big 150 truck.

"Pull around and see where he goes," Zach said, after telling them who Keegan Kennedy was. Kennedy zipped a little white Prius around to the other side of the building, and Larkin walked out and around the front of the car. And got in.

"Would you look at that," Marc said. "Interesting bedfellows."

"Follow them," Zach told JP. "Maybe they're going to Charlestown."

But in two turns, it was apparent they weren't going to Charlestown at all, and Zach had to make a decision. He went with his gut. "Stay with them, JP. I want to know where they're headed together, and why."

Without arguing, JP drove down Mass Ave, staying well behind the Prius, but not losing it, until it turned onto St. Botolph Street.

"Paupiette's," Zach said.

"So the question isn't why is Kennedy going with Larkin to work, but why is Larkin going with Kennedy to work?" Marc asked.

"Not to work," Zach corrected. "The restaurant is closed on Tuesdays."

The three-story brownstone on the corner was definitely dark and deserted. Marc drove down the street, slowing at the alley just as Keegan and Larkin turned the corner, toward the kitchen entrance that Zach couldn't see from this position.

"I know how to get into the basement," Zach said. "And I happened to leave it unlocked when I left here this morning."

Marc looked at him. "You're full of surprises today."

"Let's do it," JP agreed.

Marc parked a short distance away, and they slipped into the alley and down the three steps to the basement entrance, and walked right in.

The hallway was as dark as it had been this morning, soundless but for footsteps above. The three of them, weapons drawn, pressed against the wall, stayed in the shadows, and moved toward the stairs, communicating silently with gestures and looks.

Voices floated down from the kitchen, muffled by the door at the top of the stairs and distance, but strong and deep enough for Zach to pick up the cadence of a conversation among at least three or four men.

JP and Marc took either side of the bottom of the steps, and Zach, still shoeless, silently climbed the stairs.

"Gentlemen, we have a lot to celebrate," a man said. Was that Keegan Kennedy? He wasn't sure, inching closer to the door to listen. "First of all, Joshua Sterling is dead, so we have succeeded in our first and most important mission."

"Hear, hear!" Glasses clinked, along with the rumble of male laughter and some unintelligible conversation.

"More important, our leader is presumed dead, and that works perfectly into our plans, leaving us with all of the profits and none of the pain." That voice was Detective Larkin, without a doubt.

Behind Zach, JP took a few steps closer and nudged him. "Their leader is presumed dead?" JP asked in a soft, soundless whisper, his eyes lit like a hunter on the kill. "You know who that is?"

Finn MacCauley. No wonder JP looked excited. If a criminal as notorious as Finn MacCauley were brought in, it would make JP's career. He'd be a local hero. Not to mention he could bust one of the lead detectives on Sterling's murder as an accomplice.

Zach returned his focus to the voices behind the door.

Let JP get glory and fame; it didn't matter at all. The only thing that mattered was finding Sam, and if he didn't hear something that resembled an answer soon, he was out of there.

"She'll be here any minute," one of the men said, giving Zach a little zing at the pronoun. *Who'd* be there any minute?

"And this has to be done right, gentlemen," Keegan Kennedy said. "Exactly as planned. She has to die, quickly and neatly. And then all evidence needs to be disposed of, except that which points to our friend Levon Czarnecki."

The three men shared a look. Who the hell was Levon Czarnecki?

"That guy's a nutcase," Larkin said. "You know that, don't you?"

Another man laughed. "A nutcase who's a fucking chameleon. Anyway, the work was done by Hanrahan, so Czarnecki can take us to court."

That got a big laugh, but Zach frowned at the name. Hanrahan. Hanrahan Produce...the truck that drove them off the bridge.

"The whole thing was messy," another man, a new voice, much older. "Not the way it was done in the old days."

"Fuck the old days," another said. "Things are different now, old man."

Zach could read JP's thoughts as clearly as if he were saying them out loud. If that was Finn MacCauley, he was getting a piece of him.

Downstairs, the alley door slammed.

"She's here," one of the men said. "Get ready. She walks in, and Keegan fires from right there."

On the steps, the three men shared another look as footsteps tapped down the hall. One person's footsteps. At the bottom, Marc stepped forward, seeing who it was.

"I wouldn't go up there if I were you, Ms. Sly."

Ms. Sly?

Our leader is presumed dead.

A woman stepped into view, stopped at the sight of Marc's gun, but lifted her chin, undaunted. "You know they'll kill you," she said. "All I have to do is make one noise."

"Then you're their leader?"

She tilted her head and gave a long sigh. "Why are you doing this?"

"Why am I?" Marc snorted softly. "You're the one about to get gunned down by...whoever those men are."

"Those men work for me," she said. "And you're sorely mistaken if you think they'd hurt me. I'm the brains behind an operation they've been trying, and failing, to start for years. Who else would be smart enough to pin Joshua Sterling's murder on Finn MacCauley? And you could have run with that, and you and your cousin could be big heroes."

"Move it," Marc said, waving his gun back down the hall.

"Don't be as stupid as Sterling. Look what I had happen to him." She glanced up the steps, seeing JP and Zach but not reacting to their presence. "Come on, you're Italian. We're just an Irish version of your mafia. One hand washes the other. I've given you the lead of a lifetime; now, you take it and I'll forget we ever saw each other."

Zach came down a few stairs, stepping close enough for her to get a good look at him. Her eyes widened. "You were supposed to be killed today."

"So were you." He got right in her face, using his monstrous scar to its full potential.

She smiled. "One of my ladies had to be sacrificed. And, of course, I have connections everywhere, so my death will be confirmed. But yours?"

Zach shut her up by lifting his gun, so close to pulling the trigger it wasn't funny. "Where is she?"

"I thought she was at the bottom of some lake in western Massachusetts." She inched back, the first scent of fear on her. "If not, I have no idea. I suppose he got her somehow."

Who was *he*? And how did he get Sam in a car?

"Zach." Behind him, JP held out his phone for Zach to read.

V. Angelino's phone location: Roxbury.

Sam wouldn't get into a car with a stranger, but she'd get in with Vivi. They were both in Roxbury...with a professional killer.

"I'm out." Zach got past them all, but JP came after him.

"Don't," JP said. "We're going to need you."

"Sam needs me."

"Hey!" The door at the top slammed open. All three men reacted by backing out of view, leaving the woman standing at the bottom of the steps.

"We have a problem, Keegan," she said calmly.

"Yes, we do." A shot punctuated that, hitting her right in the heart.

The pounding of feet on the way down the stairs was

all they had to hear. The three of them bolted down the hall, in a full run, throwing the door open and getting out just before shots hit the metal behind them. They ran left, Marc leading them into the door of a small complex of offices, shooting up a narrow wooden stairway to the second floor.

All three flattened against a wall, hearing footsteps running on the sidewalk below, and a shout, but no one entered the building. Still, it was only a matter of time.

JP was already on the phone for backup.

"This building goes through to the alley," Marc said. "Back downstairs, the opposite door."

"Let's go," Zach said.

"No way." JP grabbed his arm. "Do you know who that is? Do you—"

"Yes, I know. He's yours. And Larkin. And Kennedy. Take the whole damn mob and eat them for lunch and your next promotion. But I'm going to get Sam and Vivi."

"You don't know for sure that they're out there," JP damn near growled. "We need you. We need firepower. We need three good men until backup gets here. Don't you dare leave, Zach. You have no idea where she is."

But he did. In his gut, he did.

It was like god damn déjà vu all over again. He was ready to leave his men on a hunch, ready to abandon his position on gut, ready to take a risk that had a huge downside.

But if he didn't, and he lost the only two women he ever loved, one he was born with and one he intended to die with...what kind of man was he?

"You can't go," JP insisted, fury on his face. "You

don't know where she is, where you're going, what you'll find. We need you here until backup comes. You'd just get shot trying to be a hero anyway."

Someone ran back up the street.

"They're circling us," Marc said.

The window was closing, and Zach had to get out or live with the consequences.

CHAPTER 23

Sam and Vivi, both one trigger pull from death, shared a silent look, but didn't dare speak as their captor led them into Billy's house. Inside, Sam braced for the worst, Vivi's words still burning in her brain.

He's breathing carbon monoxide and sitting next to a bucket of gasoline on top of a furnace with a pilot light.

What would she find? Billy, hurt. Billy, bound and gagged. Billy, near death. How many times was she going to be the cause of this man's misery?

Larry pushed her down the hall of the house, to the basement door, ordering Vivi to open it. When she did, the air that floated out smelled like gasoline, roiling her stomach and terrorizing her heart.

"Billy?" Sam called, not caring what the man who held a gun to her back would say.

No answer.

"I swear to God, if you hurt him—" The gun poked her rib.

"I would hope you'd have so much sympathy for me, Samantha. But then you wouldn't recognize me as the man you saw in the wine cellar that night, would you?"

She shook her head.

"Of course not. But how ironic that we talked at the bar, then you were the one they sent." He pushed her down the steps, behind Vivi.

"Nobody sent me," Sam said.

"I have to say, you were an inspired choice. The cops wouldn't protect, you and no one would believe you anyway."

A soft moan came from somewhere in a darkened corner to the far left. Billy was alive! Instinctively, Sam moved toward him, only to get an arm wrapped around her neck, cracking it backward.

"Move," he said, pushing her closer to Vivi. "You, get over there. Sit on that crate."

Vivi did as she was told, moving slowly, no doubt buying time and thinking of how to get them out of this, thinking exactly what Sam was. As long as they were alive, they had a chance. There were two of them against one of him. All he had was a gun.

If one of them could get that weapon...they'd be saved.

But he held his gun tight, obviously an expert with it.

Sam peered into the darkness, at the two metal appliances in the corner. "Billy?"

He moaned again. He was in there, wedged in a tiny space but alive. She squinted, barely able to make out a hunched-over form in the shadows.

"Please," she said, looking at her captor. "Please let me say good-bye to him."

"Oh, for Chrissake, shut up. You think he's your friend? He hates you for what you did to him."

Billy grunted, but something kicked Sam's gut.

Hate kicked her. Vengeance. The need for blood. This son of a bitch *Larry's* blood. The sensation rocked her, so fresh and real and...deadly.

Wait till she told Zach how that felt.

With that thought, another sensation rocked her. Just as potent, just as bone-deep, just as real as the hate she felt for the man about to kill her.

She had too much to live for. Way too much. She would live to love Zach Angelino. She would. Nothing and no one would stop her.

Her gaze collided with Vivi's, whose midnight-black eyes burned with the same passion. They were connected, like sparks arcing between them, like an invisible rope tying them together.

"In front of her." He pushed Sam down hard, slamming her knees on the concrete floor, pain almost doubling her.

He knelt next to her and, with the hand not holding the gun, reached into his pocket and pulled out a phone. Vivi's BlackBerry, Sam knew, recognizing an Airwalk sticker across the back.

"One last call?" Vivi said sarcastically.

He just smiled and held it to her, pressing a button. "One last video. Say your name."

She clamped her mouth shut.

"Say your fucking name."

She just lifted one brow and stared him down.

He shoved the gun into Sam's gut so hard she gasped, closing her eyes and waiting for the shot.

"Vivi Angelino!"

"Thank you. Where do you live?" At her hesitation, he leaned closer to Sam. "You really want her to die, don't you?"

"Brookline."

"Where do your parents live?"

Vivi's eyes grew wide with dismay. "They're dead."

"Brothers? Sisters?"

She stole a glance at Sam, who nodded, the wordless communication clear: *This guy was going to die.* "A brother."

"The people who get this video," he said, "will make sure everyone in your family dies a slow and ugly death if you don't do this right. Now hold the camera." He handed it to her.

Could she use the phone as a weapon somehow? She gave Vivi a hard look, trying to communicate that thought, but Vivi took the device gingerly, one eye on the gun in Sam's side.

"Turn it around," he said slowly, as if he was talking to a child. "Be sure you have Sam and me in the picture together. Got it? Okay. Now, watch me, Sam."

He reached up and slowly pulled off his blond wig, short black hair in a net underneath. He slid off his glasses, then took his hand and dug his fingernails into his face, scraping off something that looked like a gelatinous mask.

As it slid down, the pockmarks she remembered so well appeared.

"Now tell me, Sam, am I the man you saw kill Joshua Sterling?" He was looking right into her eyes.

She looked away, refusing to meet his gaze, catching

Vivi surreptitiously pressing buttons on her phone in her peripheral vision.

"No," Sam said, looking at him to be sure to keep his attention off Vivi, who was probably dialing 911. But would the cops come to her rescue?

"No?"

"His eyes were not brown."

One of those brown eyes narrowed at her in anger, and she shot a quick glance to Vivi.

Out of the corner of her eye, she saw Vivi hit one more button; then she kicked, fast and hard, knocking the gun away from Sam's body. He jerked it back, but Sam pulled back and slammed her fist right under his nose as Vivi landed one in the groin.

He fell backward as they both rose to pounce, the gun unsteady in his hands, his face distorted with pain. The crack of a shot was so loud it sounded like an explosion, the noise ripping through Sam's head as Vivi grunted and froze midkick.

Sam spun to her, catching her expression of horror as she clutched her stomach and blood started spurting through her fingers.

"Vivi!"

"Stop!" He had his balance now, on his feet, the gun still in his hand.

Sam folded next to Vivi, seeing the blood drain from her face as fast as it poured through her hands. "She's dying!"

"And so are you."

They were trapped. Marc hid at the top of the front steps as someone climbed up. JP and Zach silently moved down the opposite hall to the back stairs.

As they lost sight of Marc, a gunshot echoed.

One of the office doors flew open, and a woman screamed in terror, but Marc yelled, "Get back, get down! Police!"

Zach went ahead of JP down the back stairs, staying flat against the wall, his gun drawn. He heard movement outside the door in the alley, hiding in case it opened toward him, bracing for his shot.

He looked up the stairs to JP, who hid on the landing, and nodded, ready to take down whoever was about to come in.

But no one did.

Zach and JP looked at each other, waiting. Everything was silent until the soft vibration from JP's phone.

"Get it," Zach whispered. It could be information. It could be...

"Vivi," JP said, looking at the phone. "It's from Vivi. It's a picture. He's got them both—"

"Gimme your keys!" Zach demanded.

"Don't, Zach."

"JP, come on," he pleaded. "She's all that ever mattered to me. Come *on*."

JP opened his mouth to argue, then stopped, reaching into his pocket and tossing them to Zach, who grabbed the handle of the door and yanked it open, whipping left and right, ready to kill. The alley was empty, so he ran toward the truck, jogging by a Dumpster.

A shot whizzed by his head, and he ducked and rolled, taking cover behind the Dumpster, waiting for the next shot.

It didn't come.

But the familiar snap and slide of a pistol racked behind him. "Drop it."

Fuck. He didn't drop the gun, but stood slowly, holding his weapon tight, but easing his hands out to either side.

"Drop the gun and put your hands on the Dumpster, Mr. Angelino." Detective Larkin's perfected police procedure voice. As if he hadn't just been running a meeting with a bunch of thugs and mobsters. "You're under arrest." He heard the man come one step closer, right behind him.

Zach looked over the Dumpster down the alley, just as JP stepped out of the door. Directly across from JP, something moved. Keegan stepped out, gun pointed at JP, who was watching Zach.

Zach twisted his wrist, aimed the gun at Keegan, and fired, knocking him down. Just as he did, he caught the message in JP's eye, then ducked behind the Dumpster, so JP's shot whizzed over his head and hit Larkin in the shoulder, downing him.

As if they'd been working together their whole life.

Without even looking at his cousin, Zach leaped over the body toward JP's truck as sirens screamed everywhere, cruisers flying toward the restaurant.

In seconds, he tore out of St. Botolph Street, screaming toward Roxbury, running every light, ignoring the cops, ignoring everything but the one thing that mattered. Saving Sam and Vivi.

CHAPTER 24

Sam wrapped Vivi in her arms, the metallic smell of blood mixed with the gunshot making her dizzy. Vivi's eyes fluttered and she closed them, unable to speak.

"Put her down and finish this!" Larry's wig and glasses were gone to reveal crazed eyes, his makeup gel hanging off half his face. The man who called himself the Czar looked like a monster.

She refused to let go of Vivi, refused to lay her on the hard cement. If she did, then she'd just lunge after the man and get her own bullet in the stomach. But she wouldn't make his video. At least he wouldn't get the proof he wanted.

Seizing Vivi's phone from the floor, he stabbed at buttons, then held it up to his face. What had she done before she kicked? Made a call?

"This is me, assholes." Then he turned the camera, backing closer to the furnace and heater. "This is her. Did you see me kill Joshua Sterling?" he demanded.

She just stared at the camera.

"Did you?"

"No."

"You fucking bitch!" He waved the camera again. "Then die anyway." He turned the phone back to his face. "This is the gun I'm about to use. Watch me."

He raised the gun and she dove away, the shot ricocheting off the floor, then pinging loudly as it hit the metal furnace. He backed deeper into the shadows, standing right below the gasoline container he'd put on top.

"I don't care if it's recorded or not." He lifted the gun, aimed it directly at her. "They'll have to know I—"

"Billy!" she screamed, and Larry turned just as Billy reached up and knocked the open bucket right onto the madman's head, raining gasoline all over him.

He shrieked and Sam pounced on him, ripping the gun from his hands as he writhed in pain and covered his eyes.

"Run, Sam," Billy grunted. "Run."

Larry thrashed and waved his hand, blinded but charging at Sam. She took one step back, her feet hitting Vivi, then lifted the gun and aimed it right at the bastard's heart. She fired once, the recoil almost knocking her over. He growled in fury and attacked again as she fired another shot, her whole body reverberating from the explosive jolt.

He stumbled to the floor, facedown in a pool of gasoline that streamed in the direction of the pilot light.

"Get out!" Billy said.

Vivi moaned softly.

"I can't." Sam dropped to her knees, abandoning the gun. "I can't leave you two." She glanced at the liquid as it curled and meandered on a gentle slope toward the light that would ignite the fuel and explode the furnace and probably the whole house.

She had minutes, maybe less. And two half-dead people she loved very much.

"Sam..." Vivi's voice was weak and broken.

"Sam..." Billy's was the same. "Save her. She's young. Please."

She scooped her arms under Vivi and tried to deadlift her, the pain in her wounded foot like a hot iron. She barely got Vivi up, stumbling toward the steps, grunting with the effort and already slipping on the blood-slickened cement floor.

"Come on, Vivi, you can do this. You can."

But Vivi hung in her arms. There was no way Sam could carry her up the stairs. Instead, she dug her hands under Vivi's arms and dragged her. At the bottom of the stairs, she turned around and took one last look at Billy.

"Go," he moaned from his trap. "Hurry, Sam."

"Oh, Billy. I'm so sorry. I'm so sorry for everything."

"Sam, go."

With every ounce of strength she had, she hoisted Vivi's body up one stair, then another, then another. Maybe she could do this. Maybe she could get Vivi up, then come back...

Halfway up the stairs, she took one more look at the gasoline. The stream was less than a foot from the pilot light. She had a minute, if that.

With a loud, low growl of effort, fueled by surging adrenaline, she reached the top stair just as a loud bang shook the house.

For one brutal second, she thought the furnace had exploded.

But there was no light, no fire, and not nearly enough noise. So what was that sound? A gunshot? In the house?

"Sammi!"

Relief made her dizzy. "Zach! In the basement!" She fell against the door as it whipped open, dropping right into his arms.

"She's shot," she said, trying to hand Vivi over to her brother. "Get her out! Get her out!"

"Jesus." He scooped his sister up effortlessly, turning to take her into the hall.

"No, get her out! The place is about to explode!"

"Then go!" He reached for Sam's sleeve, trying to get all three of them out, but she shook her head.

"Billy's down there, Zach. He's trapped behind the furnace. There's gas everywhere and a pilot light."

He shoved Vivi back in her arms. "Run the hell out of here. Now!"

"You can't," she said, stumbling back, holding on to Vivi. "There's not enough time. There's—"

"Go!" He pushed her toward the kitchen, hard. "I'll get him. Get out of here!"

Clinging to Vivi with superhuman strength, she ran to the open door, barely able to get them both through. Outside she faltered and almost dropped her, then clung tighter, running as far as she possibly could, finally falling on grass and gently letting Vivi to the ground.

She turned back to the house, vaguely aware of sirens cutting through the night like screams, getting louder with each passing second. She crawled around Vivi to hold her and still see the house, cradling her head, lifting her up to slow the flow of blood where a bullet had gone into her stomach.

"Hang on, Vivi. Help's coming." She stared at the back door, willing Zach to appear, praying, begging, tears streaming down her face and onto Vivi. "Come on, Zach!" she sobbed, barely aware that she'd taken Vivi's hand and squeezed it.

The ground rumbled as a burst of white and orange mushroomed from the house, the crash deafening as windows, wood, and flames fanned twenty feet in the air.

The scream stayed in Sam's throat as she threw herself over Vivi's body to protect her, fire and sparks spitting all around them. She finally lifted her head, smacked by heat and smoke, her eyes burning so much she couldn't trust what she saw.

Where was he? Where? *Oh, God, please don't take him.*

There was a shadow at first, black against black, then the silhouette of a man, framed in fire, head down, back hunched, a body limp in his arms like an overgrown baby. He ran through the flames, sparks landing in his hair, glass crashing around him. Debris rolled from the house in waves, but Zach never stumbled.

He tore across the grass and collapsed in front of her, easing Billy to the ground next to Vivi.

Smoke and dirt smeared his face, his hair singed, his chest heaving with the effort of every breath.

"He's alive."

"So is Vivi."

"And..." He reached over the two bodies between them and she did the same, falling to each other. "So are you, Sam."

"I knew you'd come for me," she whispered, the words trapped in her strangled throat, drowned out by a cruiser wailing to the scene and an officer hollering orders for fire and EMTs. "I knew you would."

"Always, Sam, always." He closed his hand over her face and let his forehead drop against hers. "I'll always be at your side." The words sounded awkward, even foreign.

Sarò sempre al tuo fianco.

Now she understood what that meant.

The worst part wasn't when JP and Marc arrived, accompanied by Detective O'Hara and a few more cops, marching down the lime-green corridor of Mass General emergency center like a full platoon. The questioning actually got Zach's mind off what was happening in the OR where trauma surgeons were working to remove a bullet from his sister's body and keep her alive.

He didn't flinch when Chessie and Nicki got there, tearful and clingy, bearing clean clothes and shoes for Sam and him. And one of his leather patches, not that he'd even missed it all these hours. A little while later, Aunt Fran and Uncle Jim came in together, launching an assembly line of family hugs.

But when Uncle Nino shuffled in, his signature pilled Polo shirt obviously hastily pulled on over pajama bottoms, his thin hair uncombed, his lined face set in an expression of pure misery, Zach almost lost it.

Sam instantly sensed his response, reaching over to slip her hand into his. "She's going to be fine," she whispered for the twentieth time, as if saying it made it so.

Nino came right to him, taking his face in his hands and looking up through watery eyes. "We can't live without her, *ragazzino*."

"We won't." He said it, even though he didn't believe it. He'd seen her in the ambulance, white from the loss of blood, near death.

His father. His mother. Not his sister, too.

Uncle Nino turned to Sam, reaching for her the same way, then folding her into a full embrace. "You saved her life."

Not yet she didn't. Zach enclosed them both in his arms, proof that he wasn't immune to the family penchant for hugging. "She was amazing."

Sam smiled up at him, her face still dirty and tear-stained, but her eyes clear blue, and filled with affection and gratitude.

"And the other guy?" Nino asked. "Your friend? Where is he?"

"Billy's been treated, and some of his friends from work came to take him for the night, and his girlfriend is on her way back to take care of him. He's going to be fine, but they're going to run some tests over the next few weeks."

Nino nodded and tossed a thumb toward JP, where he stood in a cluster of cops, O'Hara in the middle. "What about him?"

"JP's good," Zach said.

"Good?" Nino's eyes bulged at Sam. "Did he say good? That's like calling him a saint from this one."

"He was..." Zach shook his head. "In the right place at the right time, and he saved my ass." He thought of the moment his cousin tossed him the keys. Maybe JP had a heart, after all.

"After you saved mine." JP shifted over to the conversation, O'Hara next to him. "Looks like Finn MacCauley wasn't anywhere near this business. That old guy we heard was someone else."

"Still," O'Hara said. "You've done the department a great service, Mr. Angelino. All of you have. My partner's involved in Joshua Sterling's murder, and his participation in organized crime is going to be a huge black eye for us, long after his trial's over and he's in prison. But he will be there, along with Keegan Kennedy, who we are certain orchestrated the timing of Samantha's being a witness to a crime. We've endured worse." He reached out his hand to shake Zach's. "We're grateful to your entire family."

"Just as long as my entire family is alive." Zach glanced at the closed doors that led to the OR.

O'Hara put a hand on Sam's shoulder. "Thank you," he said simply. "We'll see you very soon, I'm sure."

But Zach wasn't sure of anything that moment. The whole family settled in to wait for word after the contingent of cops left.

Chessie and Nicki huddled around Aunt Fran, a trio of tissues and tears. JP and Uncle Jim stood silently next to each other, staring at a TV someone had muted long ago. Behind Uncle Nino, Marc rubbed the older man's shoulders and stared ahead. Sam put her head on Zach's shoulder.

The clan was quiet, scared, and united. Strangely enough, he had never felt closer to or more protected by any of them. At any moment, they could be all he had.

"Let's get some coffee," he whispered to Sam, taking her hand and ushering her out too fast for anyone to say they'd come along. Anyway, no one would leave that waiting room until those doors to surgery opened and a doc said what they needed to hear. And if he didn't say what they needed to hear, they'd still want to hear it together.

Because like it or not, that's how the Rossis rolled. And like it or not, he was one of them.

At the end of the corridor, the nurses had set up a coffee station, and he poured a cup while Sam leaned against the wall, wan and exhausted, staring into space, her bottom lip all but bloody from gnawing.

"I'm going to do it," he said.

She focused on him, frowning. "Do what?"

"If she...makes it, I'm going to help her build that company."

Her eyes filled. "Are you making deals with God, Zach?"

God? Shit, he'd sell his soul to Satan for his sister's life. "It's a good idea," he said. "And I can do it. I know that now." He didn't lift the cup he'd poured, but looked at Sam. "I can do it well."

"Yes, you can. You'd be wonderful at it. But, what..." She swallowed hard, the tears welling. "What if she doesn't make it?"

His own tears burned. "I'll do it anyway. For her."

Her sob escaped as she reached for him, and he held her as she cried. "I'm so sorry, Zach. I did this. I sent her to Billy's and got her involved and I—"

"Stop." He pulled back and put his hand on her mouth. "She was on fire. This is what she wants, and it's dangerous. Anyway, all of this brought you back to me, Sammi. I would never have imagined you'd want me. Never gone back to you. And now...I have you." He pulled her closer, and kissed the top of her head.

"Yes, you do," she assured him. "And you know, nothing would make Vivi happier. She always had this fantasy that we'd…"

He lifted her face to his, thumbed the tear streaks on her dark shadows under her eyes. "We will."

"You're making promises to God again, Zach."

"I'm making promises to you." He lowered his face and looked directly into her indigo eyes as he pulled her in for a life-sustaining kiss.

"Kill the lip lock! The surgeon's out! He wants to talk to you, Zach."

They both whipped around as Chessie tore down the corridor toward them. They ran around the corner to find the entire family huddled around one slight man in blue scrubs, his hair netted, his surgical mask dangling around his neck. He looked at Zach. "You're next of kin?"

Oh, Jesus Christ, *no*. "We all are," he said. "But I'm her brother."

"Your sister is a very strong young woman. She needed a full transfusion. The bullet penetrated her abdomen and spleen, but did not hit her spinal cord. We were able to get it, and close her stomach walls with silk and stitches. After recovery, she'll be in ICU for at least a week."

After recovery. After *recovery*?

"She's going to live." It wasn't a question. It was never a question.

"Yes, she is," he said. "And she will walk." The doctor smiled. "From the looks of her, she'll run."

Chessie whooped and Aunt Fran started crying and Nino muttered prayers. Marc and JP hugged like crazy, and Uncle Jim threw his arms around Nicki and picked her up off the floor.

The doctor walked over to Zach and held out his hand, a bloody bullet in his palm. "You want this? She's quite a little bullet catcher, your sister."

He smiled and nodded to JP. "Give it to the cop for ballistics. And she's not a bullet catcher. She's a Guardian Angelino."

All of the noise and celebration and relief just faded into a blur as he wrapped his arms around Sammi and let the tears fall.

CHAPTER 25

Drink it down, Sammi." Uncle Nino set the thick-rimmed juice glass brimming with near-black wine in front of her. "We're celebrating."

"Vivi's recovery?" she asked. Vivi had been out of the hospital for over a month, gaining strength every day. She wasn't skateboarding around Boston anymore, but she would be.

"Among other things," Nino replied.

"The end of the Joshua Sterling mess?" The week before, Detective Larkin had cut a sweet deal with the DA; his prison sentence was reduced to twenty years in exchange for the names of everyone involved with Joshua Sterling's murder, as well as the killings of Teddy Brindell and Taylor Sly.

Detective O'Hara had been far more forthcoming with information now that he'd discovered the weak link in his department. After Taylor Sly's murder, the whole story unfolded, revealing that she had been quietly and successfully building up a newly formed Irish mob, structured like the crime organization that gripped Boston in the 1970s.

While digging into some story leads about police department corruption, Joshua Sterling had met Taylor and begun an affair with her, passionate enough for him to plan to end his own marriage. But Taylor's reason for the affair was merely to keep Joshua quiet about her burgeoning business and the insiders in the Boston PD she already had on her payroll.

When he shared with her the revelation that his wife was the biological daughter of Finn MacCauley, Joshua wanted to take that story public to help his career go to the next level. But Taylor was already planning to kill her lover, and he inadvertently gave her someone to blame for a high-profile murder. She hired Levon Czarnecki, and sent her lover to the cellar for a secret rendezvous with plans to set Rene up as the witness. She apparently didn't think Marc could be manipulated, and sent men after him after she learned he had the jump drive, but obviously her own men were more than willing to betray, and kill, her.

"There's more than that to celebrate," Nino teased. "Isn't there?"

"The fact that I'm starting law school tomorrow?"

Nino tsked and shook his head, as if she was being dense. "Look at that."

She followed the thumb he pointed over his shoulder, her gaze moving through the panels of the French doors. JP and Zach stood head to head, the first of the turning leaves like a red and gold frame around them as they talked. At one point, JP put his hand on Zach's shoulder.

"They're mending bridges, aren't they?" Sam mused.

"Even better," Nino replied, his dark eyes moist. "They're building new ones." He lifted his glass and clunked it against hers. "You've changed my Zaccaria, young lady. And I'm forever grateful."

She felt her own eyes fill, with love and gratitude and a joy that had settled around her heart and refused to leave.

"I love him," she said simply, the truth of it making her smile.

"And he loves you," Nino said. "So it is time."

She looked at him. "Time?"

"To give you the letter."

"What letter?"

"From Rossella Angelino. Zaccaria's mother."

She almost dropped the glass. "You have a letter from his mother?"

Nino sighed, leaning on the counter with his oversized hands. "Those kids arrived here with some clothes, some pictures, and two letters, which Rossella wrote with instructions that they were to be given to Vivianna's and Zaccaria's...intended."

She smiled at the old-fashioned word, and the old-fashioned zing it sent through her. "I'm not..."

"Ehh..." Nino gave his signature wave of dismissal. "He was waiting for Vivi to be a hundred percent and all this criminal business to be over."

Was he? Sam hoped so, because for the first time she had absolutely no doubt about what she was doing, and knew there'd be no second-guessing this decision...if he asked her to make it.

"I had to read the letter," Nino continued. "Because it's written in Italian. So, I translated her message for you."

"What does it say?"

"You'll see. I'll give it to you the very moment I know for sure." He smiled, his teeth a little yellowed, his eyes crinkling like spiderwebs. "The very moment that we all know you are going to become part of this family."

She nodded, then took a drink of wine to cover her reaction. She'd never wanted anything so much in her life, but Zach had to want it, too.

"You want to be part of this family, don't you?" he asked with a sly smile. "We could use you around here."

Sam didn't speak, but looked down at her own reflection in the dark glass of homemade wine. "I love this family," she said honestly. "As much as I love Zach."

Behind her, slender arms wrapped around her waist, and soft hair brushed her cheek. Vivi's spikes had grown in a little; getting a haircut took a backseat to getting healthy.

"Samantha Fairchild, we love you, too."

Sam turned and pulled Vivi closer. "I thought you were outside listening to those two argue it out."

"I was, but it got to a point where they just have to work it out on their own. JP says yes, Marc said yes weeks ago, Nicki says yes, I say yes."

"Nino says yes," Nino added.

Vivi laughed. "Of course he does. But Zach says…"

The doors opened and Zach walked in, the shadow of a smile on his lips. "What the hell, okay."

"Yahoo!" Vivi reached for her brother, still moving at less than the warp speed she used to, but fast enough to get a good hug going. "Aunt Fran! Uncle Jim! Where the heck is Marc? It's time to make this official."

"I chilled the champagne," Chessie announced, coming in from the dining room with her sister Nicki and their parents. "We were just betting on it. Three-to-one odds he'd agree."

"You bet against me?" Zach gave his youngest cousin a tap on the shoulder as he came around the granite counter to Sam, his slick leather patch blocking his eye and most of his scar, but still looking breathtaking. "Welcome to the nuthouse," he whispered in Sam's ear.

Nino's discussion was so fresh in her mind, she almost imagined Zach could read her thoughts on her face. His mother's letter. His intended. *Part of this family*.

"So you agreed?" she asked, settling into his side, comforted by the arm around her.

"Evidently, I can be bought with flattery and promises of unquestioned authority."

Chessie popped the champagne with a signature shriek as Aunt Fran lined up flutes along the granite bar, and they all gathered around Sam and Zach.

"We'll need ten, right?" Fran said. "Always ten in this family."

"Gabe's not here, Ma," Chessie corrected her.

"But Sam is," Zach said. "And she's prettier."

"And swears less," Fran added. "Although I'd put up with all that cussing just to see his face again."

"He'll be back, Aunt Fran," Zach assured her. "He's invincible."

"You always say that…" She smiled at him. "I hope you're right."

"He's always right," Vivi reminded her. "Just ask him. Now where in God's name is Marc?"

"He had a meeting with Lang," Zach said.

The name of FBI agent Colton Lang had become a

familiar one to the entire family once Finn MacCauley's name became remotely attached to the case—even though all the evidence said he'd been nothing but a fall guy. Still, the FBI got involved and had interviewed Sam and Zach numerous times, as well as Marc and JP.

The front door slammed, and in a minute, Marc ambled in, a wry look moving from the fizzing glasses being filled to Zach. "Yeah?"

Zach lifted a shoulder. "Yeah."

"All right," Marc said, offering some congratulatory knuckles. "Then you're going to love my news."

"Not yet." Vivi was grinning broadly as she handed out champagne and ten glasses were raised, along with a lot of voices. "Quiet down," she called.

They got louder. She put two fingers in her mouth and whistled.

Silence.

"Thank you," she said, her eyes twinkling like the tiny diamond in her nose. "Please raise your glasses to the staff of the newest security, investigation, protection, and crimefighting company in Boston." She shifted her glass toward Chessie. "To our director of information systems in charge of technology and hacking and general noise-making and definitely Friday afternoon parties."

"Suweeet!" Chessie giggled, and clinked.

Next, Vivi lifted her flute to Nicki. "To our head psychologist and criminal profiler."

"Part-time," Nicki qualified, her brown eyes glimmering at her cousin. "I still have a shrink practice to run."

"We'll take it," Vivi said, and stepped to JP. "To another part-timer, our special consultant from the Fraternal Order of Police."

JP's expression was serious. "In charge of making sure you renegades don't break too damn many laws."

"But if we do, you'll save our backsides." Vivi winked at him.

Marc was next. "To our senior weapons specialist and vice president in charge of relations with the Feds."

"Good relations," he promised, tapping Vivi's glass.

"And, of course, our incredible team of support staff, Aunt Fran and Uncle Jim. And..." She looped an arm around Nino's thick neck. "Our chief cook and bottle washer."

He waved a hand, but the pride in his expression was hard to miss. "I'll keep you all in ziti."

"That leaves you and Zach," Chessie said, glass poised. "Co-owners?"

Vivi tilted her head in acknowledgment. "It's a joint venture, yes, but I'm taking the title of vice president of investigations." Then she turned to Zach and lifted her glass higher, the shimmer in her eyes a common sight these last few days. "And ladies and gentlemen, meet the chief executive officer of the Guardian Angelinos!"

A cheer went up, followed by a lot of crystal clinking, laughter, and sips of bubbly.

"Are we done doling out titles?" Marc asked. "Because before you all get too looped and happy, we need to have an inaugural staff meeting to discuss our first..." They all looked at him expectantly, and he rewarded them with his heartbreaking smile. "Paying client."

"What?" At least three people asked the question at the same time.

"Joshua Sterling's widow is missing. I've agreed to consult for the FBI on a mission to track her down and bring her in. And this will be an official Guardian Angelino assignment, with me in the field and you as my backup."

"Does the FBI do that?" Chessie asked. "Hire outside consultants?"

"All the time," Marc assured her. "Sometimes for budget reasons, sometimes for manpower, sometimes because they want a particular individual to handle the job. That would be the case this time. They want me and since I won't go back to work for them, they have to hire *us*."

"I like it," Vivi said. "The FBI at the top of the client list is going to go a long way to attracting more work."

"I better add that to the website," Chessie said.

"We have a website?" Zach looked incredulous.

"All we need is an office," Nino said. "The Jamaica Plain house is off the market now."

Jim put his glass down with a little more force than necessary, the patriarch having been very quiet up to this point. "As you know, I have a law office in Boston that I never use, but won't sell, since I can't get my arms around the fact that I'm truly retired. I'll give it to the company."

Fran smiled up at him. "That's very generous of you, honey."

"Generous?" Vivi almost crawled out of her skin to throw her arms around her uncle. "Those offices are freaking gorgeous! Thank you! Zach, isn't this perfect?" She beamed at her brother, then focused on Sam. "But what about Sam? You need a title and a job, even if you are going to law school. Until you can be our chief counsel, of course."

"I'm the CEO," Zach said, looking down at her with love and affection. "I'll give her a title."

"I trust it'll be a good one," Sam said, reaching up to kiss him. As she did, she saw Nino slip a thin envelope into her handbag on the counter.

Red-hot shrapnel cut his skin. Daggers of pain shot through his eye. Misery stabbed his face like a thousand prickly fireworks, slashing pain from brow to bone.

Zach pulled himself from the nightmare, automatically turning to find the comfort of Sam's silky hair and body, the ease for his ache.

She was gone.

He sat up, blinking into the darkness of her bedroom, used to the shadows of her apartment, the lingering scent of her fruit-flavored shampoo, the welcome sensation of being where he belonged. Mostly, he was used to her being in his arms at 4:00 A.M., but she wasn't there.

Nerves, he guessed. Night before law school nerves.

He threw off the covers, grabbed the pair of boxers she'd taken off him when they first got into bed, and went looking for her. Searching her apartment, he ended up in the kitchen, where he heard a noise from the balcony.

Nudging the door, he spied her sitting on the deck, leaning against the wall, papers in her hand.

"Sammi?"

She looked up at him, stunning him with her tears. He was next to her in an instant.

"Honey, what's wrong?"

"Your mother..."

His mother? He folded in half, getting next to her. "What about her?"

"She wrote this letter and I..." She held an envelope to her lips and closed her eyes. "Want to read it."

"She wrote a letter?" He reached for it, but she didn't let go. "And you can read Italian now?"

"Uncle Nino translated it."

"Who is it written to?"

She let out a soft breath. "I guess that remains to be seen."

"I don't understand," he confessed.

"It's written by your mother for..." She picked up an envelope. "*La...fidanzata.*"

The pronunciation hurt. "I don't speak much Italian anymore and you butcher it beyond description. What does Nino say that means?"

"Your...intended."

He took her chin and turned her face toward him. "You're my intended," he said. "I intend to drag you off this balcony and back into bed in five minutes. Does that count?"

"I don't think that's what she meant." She smiled. "But I like the idea."

He pulled her face to his and kissed her, slow and sweet, savoring her taste and the sensation that always rolled through him when their mouths met. "Then don't make me drag you."

"I want to read this letter, but don't know if I should."

He kissed her again, threading his fingers through her hair. "I think you should come back to bed so I can spend about an hour letting you know exactly how I feel about you."

She breathed into his kiss. "I know how you feel about me, Zach."

"Then what are you waiting for? Read the letter." He dragged his hand through her long hair, gliding over her shoulder to her chest to caress her breast. "Then come back to bed." He stroked her to a peak. "But whatever you do, don't come back and try to speak Italian."

She laughed into his kiss. "Wait for me."

The whispered words hit him much harder than they should have. He leaned back and stroked her face, pushing her hair back to look at her. "If I had said that to you when I left your bed that morning I went to Kuwait, you would have waited for me."

"Yes, I would have," she said.

"I wanted to," he said softly. "I just thought it was too soon to tell you how I felt, and then... all that happened."

"It's history, Zach." She searched his face, her eyes wide and blue and sincere. "The same things would have happened to you over there, and you don't know what you'd have done. Those three words don't matter anymore."

"These three do." He cupped her chin, held her face steady. "I love you."

She just looked at him.

"I love you, Samantha Fairchild," he said. "I love your brain and your body and your face and your heart and your soul. I love you."

He saw her work to swallow as she touched his face. "I love you, too. I love all of those things about you and more that I haven't even discovered yet."

"Then you should read that letter, *mio fidanzata*." He kissed her on the forehead, the nose, the mouth. Then pressed his cheek against her hair. "Just don't take too long."

Back in the bedroom, he opened the drawer of the night table, reaching to the back where he'd placed one item the day he moved into this apartment.

In a few minutes, he heard the kitchen door close and lock, her bare feet padding down the hall, her whisper of a sigh as she reached the door.

"What'd she say?"

Her face was glistening with more tears as she approached the bed. "She just asked that I love you as much as she did." Her voice cracked. "And asked if I could be a sister to Vivi."

"Done." He smiled, reaching for her hand. "That's it?"

"One more thing." She unfolded the single piece of paper, revealing the scratchy handwriting of the woman who gave him birth. He waited for a jolt of emotion that, oddly, didn't come. "This was in it."

In two fingers, Sam held up a slim gold band.

And there was the jolt. "Her wedding ring," he said, taking it from her, the gold warmed by her touch. "I always wondered what happened to it. There was a diamond ring, too."

"She says that one is in Vivi's letter."

He fingered the ring, his mind's eye remembering the slender, olive-skinned hand where it had once resided. The image was a blur. "You know, I don't remember much about Rossella Angelino, except…" Roses. She always smelled like roses. "Her hands were…soft." He looked up at her. "Like yours."

He put the ring on the nightstand and pulled Sam against him, leaning on the pillows. "What else did the letter say?"

She laid her head on his chest and settled into her

place, half on him, half on the bed. "That if we ever have a baby boy, we have to name him Giovanni."

"My dad's name." Why did that make him so damn happy? "Are you okay with that?"

She looked up, smiling. "Beats Nino."

Resting on him, their heartbeats synchronized, their breathing slowed, he reached over to the nightstand.

"I have one more piece of mail for you," he whispered.

He handed her the postcard, the picture of the hills of western Massachusetts and the Wachusett Reservoir.

She smiled. "Is this the...*ahem*...postcard I've been complaining about not getting?"

"Yep."

She sat up and took the card, clearing her throat, and taking her sweet time about turning it over as she studied the picture on the front. "We were at the bottom of that reservoir. I hope you didn't write 'wish you were here' on the back."

That made him laugh. "Read it."

"I want to guess," she said, teasing him with a smile. "You wrote that you love me."

"Read it."

"That you're sorry you made me miserable when you went off to war."

"Read it."

"That you want to..." She turned the card over and read it, a soft sigh shuddering through her. "Give me my title."

"Do you like that title?"

She bit her bottom lip and nodded. "Mrs. Angelino. I like it a lot."

He reached over and closed his fingers around his mother's ring. Taking Sam's left hand, he threaded the ring onto her finger. "From one Mrs. Angelino to another." A tear rolled down her cheek, and his own eyes burned. "I believe this was meant for you."

She gave it a kiss, then pressed her palm against his war-torn cheek, cooling and soothing. "I believe it was."

"You're sure? No second-guessing?"

"Never." She laid her head on his chest, and he stroked her hair, finally at home.

She has something he wants.

He has something she needs.

But first they have to survive . . .

———————

Please turn this page

for a preview of

SHIVER OF FEAR

Available in April 2011.

Did I hear you say you were looking for a Dr. Greenberg, miss?"

For the first time since she'd started her search, Devyn Sterling felt a surge of hope. She blinked at the smooth-faced concierge and hesitated a second, making sure she understood the thick Belfast accent. "Yes, I am."

He notched his head to the side and sent his thumb in the same direction, silently telling her to separate from the other guests lined up for help in the lobby of the Europa Hotel.

"She's here, but she's not here," he said, youthful eyes wide, a sweet flush of color on his pale cheeks, as though getting that close to a woman didn't happen every day. "What I mean is she's checked out, but left bags."

After all the B&Bs, hotels, and hostels she'd tried throughout Belfast and the surrounding area, this was the first time someone had given her anything concrete on the whereabouts of Dr. Sharon Greenberg. She had to fight the urge to grab his arm and demand more. But since she'd arrived in Belfast, she'd made every effort to stay low and quiet, giving no one her name, paying in cash, and changing hotels after a night or two. Just to be on the safe side.

"Are you certain it's Dr. Sharon Greenberg, an American?"

He flickered his fingers around his cheeks. "Lots of silver hair, kinda curly?"

Sharon's shock of white waves was a distinctive look, so this time, hope took a stronghold in Devyn's chest. "She's coming back?"

"Thursday," he said. "She told me herself."

Two days and she'd be here? She almost kissed him. "Did she say where she was going?"

He shrugged, but something about the gesture indicated he knew more than he was telling. "Are you family?" he asked.

This time, she was the one to hold back. "Would you tell me where she's gone if I were?"

His blush deepened. "I don't know where she took off to, miss, but she is coming back. Are you staying here, too?"

"I can check in this afternoon." She'd chosen a smaller inn, but the marble and wood feel of the Europa appealed after all the days and nights in less luxurious accommodations. She didn't need much more encouragement. "Will you call me when she shows up for her bags?"

"Of course. I'm Patrick."

"Thank you, Patrick." She automatically reached for her bag to tip him, but he gave a sharp wave off.

"No, not necessary, miss. I'm happy to help you find your friend, as she was real pleasant to me."

"Did she seem okay, then?" It would be an enormous relief to know Sharon was fine, off on another adventure or vacation or microbiology conference, but safe. The chilling memory of what had happened in Sharon's house hadn't disappeared, not during the days she spent in North Carolina trying to find out where she was, and not since she arrived in Great Britain to follow her trail.

"She was more than okay," he assured her. "A lovely lady, right down to the bone."

"Can you turn her bags over to me?"

"I'm afraid I'd lose my job in a heartbeat if I did. But she'll be back. So be patient and look around. There's plenty to do in Belfast while you wait."

"I've seen every inch of this city, I think," she admitted on a sigh.

"Go up the coast then, lass. I can arrange a car for you, if you like, and you can see our sights. The Giant's Causeway is quite famous, and the Rope Bridge at Carrick-a-rede."

His thick lilt slurred the words, but not the sentiment. She'd love to get out of Belfast and see the coast, but since she'd arrived in Northern Ireland, her entire focus had been on finding Sharon.

Now it seemed she might have done that, giving her two days to kill. "I may do that, but I'll get my own car, thank you."

"Be careful if you get a private driver. They'll rip your pocketbook round here."

"I think I'll rent a car," she said, making the decision right then. Freedom in a car, up the coast, knowing she'd found Sharon—it all suddenly appealed to her. "I'll be back this afternoon. Will you be here?"

"Until six tonight," he said. "Then again tomorrow. After that I'm on the graveyard, so you'll only see me if you're an insomniac."

"Patrick!" Another concierge called from the desk with a dark look and a gesture to the line. "We need you, man."

"Go." Devyn gave him a friendly nudge. "And thank you."

Feeling lighter than she had for days, Devyn turned to survey the hotel she'd just impulsively decided to move into, heading to the front desk to make a reservation and hold it with cash. It had been pretty easy to do that at the B&Bs. Most, but not all, had taken her cash as long as she showed a passport. Still, she wondered, since this was a swankier, more international place.

Not at all the hotel she'd have imagined Sharon would pick.

But a sweet-faced young girl helped her, promised her a room without taking a credit card to hold it, and then iced the cake by nodding and clicking a keyboard when Devyn asked if she could check on the status of another reservation.

"Yes," she said, eyeing her screen. "Dr. Greenberg is due back on September 14, holding a reservation until the sixteenth."

Life was suddenly all sunshine and roses after weeks of doubt and dead ends. "Thank you so much," Devyn said, hoisting her handbag over her shoulder, clicking off her mental plans. She'd go back to the Windermere, gather up her bags, get a rental car, get some air and scenery and relaxation, then come back and wait for Sharon.

She grabbed an Antrim Coast brochure from the pockets

of a tourist information rack and opened it, instantly enchanted by the glossy photos of cliffsides and classic, rolling emerald hills. All these weeks in one of the most beautiful countries on—

She smacked right into the back of a man. "Oh, I'm sorry." She backed away, feeling a heated flush rise along with a bump where her ankle had slammed the corner of his luggage.

"Excuse me," he apologized as he turned and quickly rolled the bag away.

"Not at all," she assured him, holding the brochure as evidence of her clumsiness. "I wasn't . . . looking." And she should have been. Because he made the Irish coastline pale by comparison.

"Not very smart of me." His voice was melodic, warm. And so American. "To stop in the middle of the lobby," he added in explanation, probably because she was staring, her jaw somewhere in the vicinity of her chest.

"No, no, my fault." She took a step back, a natural move from anything that . . . hot. "I had my face in a tourist brochure, I'm afraid, and just . . . pow. Right into you."

He melted her with a smile that lit eyes the color of ripe black olives, revealing straight white teeth that stood out from a sexy shadow of whiskers. "You're from the States. Where?"

"Boston." The truth was out before she could think, but then her brain had flatlined the minute he'd turned around. "You?"

"New York." He winked at her. "We're practically neighbors."

"Imagine that." Imagine what? Kissing him? 'Cause

that's where her brain had just gone. "Well, sorry, again…"

"Are you staying here?" He said it with a little hint of hope, just enough to pull her right back in.

"I am. But I haven't checked in yet."

"You're off to the Antrim Coast?"

She drew back, reassessing him. How did he know that?

"Don't worry. Just a lucky guess." He tapped a long, strong finger on the brochure, the words of her destination in giant red letters. "Heard it's pretty up there."

"Looks like it's…" She fluttered the brochure. "Pretty."

He smiled again, a tease in his eyes that made her stomach flutter. Then he reached out his hand. "I'm Marc Rossi."

She took it. Warm, strong, dry, big. "Devyn…Smith." She remembered to use the fake name, so her brain hadn't completely imploded with a hormonal burst. Someone from New York might easily have seen a story on the murder of Joshua Sterling. "It's nice to meet you, Marc."

One more flash of a smile, a hint of not-quite-dimples embedded in chiseled cheeks, warmth in his remarkable eyes. "You're not going to invite me along on your day trip, are you?"

She withdrew her hand slowly. "No. But I'll take a picture for you."

"I'll look for you this evening, then. In the bar, right over there?"

Was he asking her out? "I have no idea what time I'll be back. Maybe. We'll see." She gave him one last smile, stole one last look at his face and broad shoulders. "Sorry for walking right into you like that."

"I'm not." The flirtatious tone gave her an unexpected jolt, making her laugh softly.

"You're good at that," she volleyed back. "But still not getting the invitation."

"Then I'll work harder next time." Flirtatious rolled right into seductive, and the jolt she felt was farther south than anything she could remember for a while.

"Bye." She turned away and headed to the door, her mission and objective momentarily washed from her mind.

Outside, the sun threatened to break through a gray sky, underscoring the sense that she'd just breathed clean, sweet air and wanted more. More warmth. More flirting. More...of a man like that.

After the last few years, especially the last few months, of ice and misery and daily disappointments from the man she'd married, that little shot of flirting with a stranger was like downing a glass of Irish whiskey.

And it left her just as...warm.

She hesitated at the curb, looking for one of the London-type cabs she'd been using to get around Belfast, already used to the low-rise, open-air feel of the city, although the Europa and the few modern buildings in the little square were taller than most. But she was familiar enough with the main streets and some of the neighborhoods that renting a car and taking a trip seemed like a brilliant and beautiful plan.

Speaking of brilliant and beautiful...she glanced behind her through the glass doors to the lobby, somehow not surprised to see the man she'd just met watching her from the front desk. Their gazes met and he zapped her with a smile again.

"Cabbie, miss?"

She was about to say yes, but then shook her head. The B&B wasn't that far, and for the first time in a while, she didn't feel like hiding in the back of a cab, cornered and considering her options. She'd found Sharon, sort of, she had time and a place to go... and maybe had a semi-sort-of rendezvous that night with what was quite possibly the best-looking man she'd seen in a long time.

Was it too soon to talk to a man, too close to Josh's death to think about kissing someone else? After four years of marriage to one of the coldest cheaters in the world, no, it wasn't too soon to at least think about having a drink with... Marc Rossi. Beautiful name, too.

He was probably in town on business, she decided as she headed around the building toward Great Victoria Street. Lonely, looking for company... married? Undoubtedly a charmer like that had a wife and three kids back in New York. He didn't look young, mid-to-late thirties, with a sexy kind of fierceness under that charm, as if he could slam you up against a wall and pin you there... right before he kissed the living hell out of you.

She almost stumbled on the uneven sidewalk. Was that why she'd turned him down so quickly? Because what was wrong with a little distraction—assuming he wasn't married and really was just a friendly, charming guy from New York looking for company on his trip to Belfast?

Maybe she'd have that drink with him. It couldn't hurt, and it might feel... really good.

She had paused at an intersection, reorienting herself

to the left-side drivers, when a dark sedan slowed down, inching closer to where she stood. Out of habit and for safety, she stepped back, until the window rolled down and Marc Rossi smiled at her.

Delivering the same little bolt of lightning through her blood.

"It's a long walk up the coast, Ms. Smith."

She smiled, her hair lifted by a cool breeze that did nothing to reduce the heat level of his gaze. "I'm on my way to rent a car."

"Now that's just a waste of time, money, and gas. I've already got one, and I can't check in until later this afternoon, so I'm going sightseeing. My offer still stands."

She hesitated, but not long. The thoughts of the last few minutes still echoed in her head. Why shouldn't she have just one afternoon of enjoyment on this mission?

Still…she wasn't sure. She took a step closer. His right hand rested on the window, but that wasn't the one that mattered. The left was on the wheel, and she took a surreptitious dip to see it.

"Looking for a ring?"

So much for surreptitious. "Actually, yes, I am. I'm suspicious that way."

"Suspicious is smart." He held up an empty hand. "Truth in advertising. Divorced and traveling alone, wildly attracted to honey hair and blue eyes, and on my way to kill a day sightseeing. Would you care to come along?"

She laughed, surprised at the dip her stomach took. This wasn't the reason she'd traveled across the ocean and traipsed all over Northern Ireland. This wasn't in keeping with her plan to lie low, talking to no one unless that person might know where Sharon was. This wasn't...

"If it's that tough a decision for you, Devyn, I'll back off." There was nothing but sincerity in his tone, no more flirting, no more seduction. Just consideration and kindness.

And, God knew, she could use some of that, too.

"That's not necessary," she said, tucking her hair behind her ear and smiling back. "I'd love to go sightseeing with you."

Giving her one more knee-weakening grin, he hopped out to walk her around to the opposite side of the car, moving with an easy grace. As he stepped in front of her to open the door, she stole a look at his back, lingering on the jeans over a taut backside and a narrow waist.

She was going sightseeing, all right. And the view was spectacular.

She wasn't *that* suspicious, or following Devyn Sterling—now Smith—around Belfast for two days and orchestrating an accidental meeting that appeared to be entirely her fault could never have happened.

For that, Marc was grateful.

He glanced at her through the windshield as he rounded the car, still amazed at how different she was in person than in two dimensions. Gorgeous, yes. Prettier in fact, because he'd expected an ice queen and gotten a surprising blast of heat. He'd expected bland and bored, uptight and withdrawn, but discovered a woman with a smile that came from her heart, a laugh that sounded like chimes, and windblown hair that was ten different shades of milk chocolate and caramel. Not to mention a lithe, lean body that moved with a magical mix of grace and sexiness.

For that reason, Marc was on guard.

He didn't want to like the woman he was about to play, although he had to admit, it made his job a hell of a lot easier.

"So what brings you to Belfast?" he asked as he climbed in and tugged on his seatbelt. "Business or pleasure?"

"Both," she said. "You?"

"Same, but mostly pleasure." He threw her another look. "Pleasure today, definitely."

"What do you do?"

"Invest," he said easily, the cover story he and Vivi had concocted ingrained in his head. "How about you?"

"Invest in what?"

He maneuvered through a roundabout, at ease with the left-side driving after a few days of following her cabs around from neighborhood to neighborhood, waiting while she went into various inns, hotels, and hostels. "Companies. I invest in companies."

"Like a venture capitalist?"

"Something like that, but a little more in the background. Angel investments." A business he knew quite a bit about after the securities fraud he'd spent a year undercover investigating…the same case that had ended his marriage to a woman who worked for the company. "You didn't answer my question," he reminded her. "What's your business here in Belfast?"

"It's personal," she said, the tone not inviting another question, but at his look she added, "I'm waiting for a friend from the States who gets back on Thursday."

"From where?"

She made a show of opening the brochure she'd been holding in the hotel. "There's a map on the back of this. Pretty scenic."

"So you're secretive as well as beautiful."

A lock of hair tumbled down, covering her expression. Stopping at a light, he reached over and lifted the errant strand, brushing her cheek with his knuckles. "Am I right?"

They locked gazes for the duration of the light, hers sky blue and well guarded.

"I'm private," she replied, turning her head just enough to escape his touch. "There's a difference."

"Still beautiful."

"Thank you." The softest flush rose to darken her translucent complexion, accentuating the defined lines of her cheekbones. She pointed to a main highway. "That's the M2, I believe, that circles Belfast. Take it a little west, then go east up to Ballyclare." She smiled at him. "Sounds pretty, doesn't it? Have you been to Ireland before?"

If it took the day, and the night, to get around her evasiveness, so be it. Nothing about this job would hurt. "I have, actually, but spend most of my time in Dublin. Never been up this far."

"Me neither."

He knew quite a bit about this woman, but he was looking forward to seeing how easily he could get the truth out of her. "I guess it's only fair for me to ask what you asked me. I don't see a ring. Single, too?"

"I am now," she said, looking over her left shoulder, out the window.

"Ah, divorced, too, then?"

She waited a beat. Was she going to lie? "No, actually, I'm a widow."

"I'm sorry," he said, easily genuine. "How long has it been?"

"About a…" *Month*. "Year."

A year? So she was going to lie. Interesting. "Kids?"

"No," she said quickly. "You?"

Maneuvering onto the highway stole his attention momentarily, the wrong-side driving forcing him to think about what was usually instinctive. "Not yet," he replied, the answer quick and honest.

"But you want them?"

He glanced at her. "What was the clue?"

"The word 'yet' and a little bit of wistfulness in your voice."

He laughed. "Private, beautiful, intuitive. Look how much I learned about you in just this little bit of time."

"We're even, then. I've learned you're open, charming, and, oh, let me guess, the oldest in your family."

He laughed at that. "You got all that out of 'not yet'? Second out of seven."

"Seven!" She put her hand on his arm in surprise. "That's a huge family."

"There were five kids and two cousins raised with us. Plus a grandfather, Uncle Nino."

"You call your grandfather Uncle Nino?"

"Long story."

She turned a little toward him. "I think it's a long drive. Rossi, right? So this must be an Italian family. Where in New York?"

Now she'd caught him in a lie, and if he said the family was in Boston, then there'd be a host more questions.

He stole his glance from traffic to look at her. "Wait a second. I only have a day with you; I don't want to talk about my family. Just getting through the lineup would take all day and I only have until...Thursday. Is that when your friend gets here?"

"That's what the concierge said."

He seized on that. "You don't know?"

She shifted again, clearly uncomfortable. "I'm pretty sure it's Thursday. It's two more miles to the turn to Ballyclare. You know, I just like saying that, such an Irish word. Have you noticed how different the accent is up here? More British than brogue, don't you think?" She toyed with that strand of hair again, catching his gaze. "What?"

"You don't want to talk about yourself, Devyn, do you?"

She shook her head a little.

"Why's that? Oh, wait, I know. Private, not secretive."

"And someone as charming and gracious as you, Marc, would respect that and stop asking questions."

He nodded, threading some cars to the exit, sliding onto the more countrified road that headed toward the haze hanging over the coastline. "Why don't we make a deal, then?"

"A deal. Okay. What do you propose?"

He reached over and took her hand, which was as warm as when he'd touched her before, slender and soft and feminine, the feel of her skin giving him a tug of attraction.

Making his suggestion the most natural thing in the world. "Every time you don't want to answer, kiss me."

"Kiss you?" She half choked.

"Yeah, it's Ireland. Blarney Stone and all that. Everyone kisses here, don't they?"

Her chuckle was low, and a little sexy. "I don't know about that..."

"Doesn't have to be on the lips, Devyn. Just...like this." He lifted her hand to his mouth and barely breathed a kiss on her knuckles. "Then I'll know that you don't want to answer me, for whatever secret, er, I mean, private reason."

"But you'll just keep asking." She didn't slide her hand out of his.

"You can answer, or you can kiss. In the investment business, we call that a win-win situation."

"In some businesses, they call it a bait and switch."

"What business are you in?" he asked.

She leaned over the console, a soft whiff of something floral preceding a whisper of her lips against his unshaven face. "That's private."

He just smiled. She wasn't going to be easy, but sticking by Devyn's side was going to be fun. Maybe too much fun.

Want more sizzling romance
from Roxanne St. Claire?
Don't miss the third book in
her Guardian Angelinos series!

———————

Please turn this page
for a preview of

FACE OF DANGER

Available in May 2011.

When Vivi Angelino closed her mouth over a wide straw and sucked hard enough to hollow her delicate cheeks, Colton Lang almost got a boner.

Almost.

The state of damn-near-hard was status quo around this woman, so in the few months he'd been sending consulting jobs to her firm, Colt had learned a couple of tricks to ensure that *almost* didn't become *obvious*.

He would focus on her outlandish black hair, made even more so today by the helmet and what appeared to be yesterday's hair gel. Or he'd let his gaze settle on the diamond dot in the side of her nose, concentrating on how much that puncture had to hurt instead of how it would feel to...lick it.

Or he'd simply remind himself that this skateboard-riding, sneaker-wearing, guitar-playing tomboy happened to have some of the best investigative instincts around, and he wanted to keep the Guardian Angelinos in his back pocket for certain jobs, so acting on a mindless surge of blood to his dick would be unprofessional and stupid.

That was usually enough to quell the erection. Sometimes. Today, finding her in this skate park with a little sheen of perspiration making her pixie-like features glisten and her coffee-bean-brown eyes sparking with unexpected interest, the boner might win this battle.

But look at that outfit, Colt. A long-sleeved cotton T-shirt that dangled off her narrow frame and faded green cargo pants frayed at the cuffs. He could never be attracted to a woman who cared so little about herself she rolled around Boston dressed like a teenage delinquent.

He preferred a woman who looked like a woman, who wore a little makeup, had hair falling to her shoulders, and maybe strolled—not *rolled*—through a park in a pretty sundress. He'd bet his bottom dollar she didn't own a dress.

"All right, I'll tell you," she said after swallowing. "But I swear to God, Lang, don't try to talk me out of it, because I want this job."

"What job?"

"You've heard about the Red Carpet Killer, of course."

He held his Coke, frozen midway to his mouth. "You don't buy that malarkey, do you?"

She smiled. "Lang, *malarkey* hasn't been sold for forty years. Can you get with this century? And two Oscar-winning actresses in a row are killed in two consecutive years, weeks after winning? You really think that's a coincidence?"

"Accidents, both of them. But I do know there's an

FBI task force out of L.A. with an eye on the possibility of a copycat killer."

"Exactly." She pointed at him. "Even if the first two deaths are mere coincidence, there are five women in Hollywood who are scared spitless right now. They are ramping up security like you wouldn't believe."

"You think they're going to hire your firm for protection?" He tried not to scoff, he really did. But it was ludicrous. "A brand-new firm made up of an extended family of renegade Angelinos and Rossi cousins?"

No surprise, her espresso eyes narrowed in disgust. "We are not renegades, for God's sake. I'm a former investigative journalist, in case you forgot, so getting a PI license was a natural move. Zach's thriving in management, which frankly shocks the shit out of me after all those years as an Army Ranger. And, yeah, our core employee base happens to be a few cousins my brother and I were raised with—"

"Don't forget Uncle Nino, providing pasta and daily encouragement."

"Don't knock my Nino," she shot back. "And, for your information, we're interviewing protection and security specialists, including some top-notch bodyguards. The Guardian Angelinos are in a growth spurt."

He acknowledged that with a tilt of his head. "I know that, Vivi, especially since I keep throwing FBI consulting jobs at you. I just think the actresses who are worried about being victims of a curse or a killer will hire the biggest and best in the protection industry."

"Maybe." She took another drink, her eyes dancing with some untold secret. "What do you think of Cara Ferrari?"

"I think I wouldn't kick her out of bed for eating crackers."

She looked skyward with a loud tsk. "I meant of her chances to win."

"I don't follow Hollywood too closely, but I did see that remake of *Now, Voyager*. She couldn't touch Bette Davis's original, in my opinion."

"Fortunately, your opinion doesn't matter. She's got a chance." She gave him a slow smile, revealing that tiny chip on her front tooth. He'd thought about licking that, too. "So I think I do, too."

He just shook his head, not following, but maybe because his body was betraying him again.

"Look at me," she demanded, leaning back to plop her hands on her hips and cock her head to one side.

"I'm looking." That was the problem. She was so damn cute he forgot what they were talking about.

"*Look*, Lang."

At what? The way her position pulled the T-shirt just tight enough to outline her breasts? They weren't big but perky and sweet, just as spunky as she was, and, well, even on Vivi some things were feminine. Is that what she wanted him to look at? Because, if he eyed them any longer, his hard-on was poised to make a reappearance.

"Don't you see the resemblance?" She turned her face to give him a profile, lifting her chin, closing her eyes, and easing her head back in a classic movie star pose. His gaze dropped over her throat, which was...just another fucking thing he wanted to lick.

Jesus, Colt. Get a grip.

She whipped her face around, and for one insane second he thought she'd read his mind.

"I look exactly like Cara Ferrari," she insisted.

He let out a soft hoot of laughter. "Are you as stoned as half these other skaters?"

She scowled at him. "Real skaters don't get high, posers do. And look at this face," she demanded, pointing to her cheeks with two index fingers. "Is this not Cara Ferrari's twin sister?"

He just laughed softly. "Speaking of posers."

"Lang, *damn* it." Frustration heightened her color, making her even *cuter*. "Everyone says I look like her. I mean if my hair were longer and I, you know, had some makeup on."

"Like a truckload." He chuckled, shaking his head.

"I get stopped and asked if I'm Cara Ferrari all the time," she insisted.

"And you believe what drunks say to you in bars?"

"Jeez, you're as bad as my cousins. Quit teasing me and take this seriously."

He worked his face into the most humorless expression he had, and he had many. "Cara Ferrari is a movie star, Vivi."

"So?"

How deep was she going to let him dig himself? "I mean, she's a gorgeous icon…"

Deep.

"Not that you're not really attractive in your own way…" This was getting worse, but on he went. "It's just that she's all glitz and glamour and gloss and you're…"

Not.

"I can glam up."

Now, that he'd like to see. "All right," he relented, not wanting to hurt her. He squinted at her, and made a camera viewing box with his fingers. "Yeah, I can see the similarity. You both have dark hair and dark eyes."

She swiped his hands down. "Never mind, Lang. I should know better than to hope you could think outside the box. I should expect you to be all linear, trapped by your rules and the way things are supposed to be done. I shouldn't ever dream that you might approach something creatively. That would just be asking too much from your structured, formulaic, *uninspired* brain."

All right, he deserved that after the insults he'd just heaped on her, but something was really off in this conversation, even for them. "What the hell are you getting at, Vivi? What creative thinking are you looking for?"

"A body double."

This time he just stared at her, a slow realization dawning. "You're not serious."

She let out a grunt of frustration. "I knew I shouldn't have told you."

"Told me what?"

"C'mon, Lang, it's the oldest form of security in the world. Put a fake—a *professional* fake—in her shoes until the killer is caught. Bait the killer with the body double and you—"

"Stop it," he said, his voice low and harsh, not having to pretend seriousness at all now. "For one thing, all kidding aside, you'd need an extreme makeover to pass as Cara Ferrari."

"Not from a distance."

"Second, if a decoy or bait was used, the job would go to a trained professional, not an outside consultant, ever. And third, good luck getting to Cara Ferrari. It's easier to get an appointment with the president."

A flicker of arrogance crossed her face. "Maybe I already have."

"What? How?"

She shrugged. "What do they say, everyone is six degrees of separation from someone."

"You are not six degrees of anything from Cara Ferrari." Was she?

She picked up her drink and then set it down again. "Forget it, Lang. You're right; she sucked in that role. She should stick to the trashy stuff that made her real money."

"Absolutely," he agreed. "Like the one where she played the pole dancer. I liked that."

"Of course you did. What man doesn't love the raw acting talent it takes for a woman to be able to unzip thigh-high boots with her teeth while giving a lap dance?"

He laughed softly. "You have to admit that was a memorable scene."

"It didn't get her an Oscar nomination."

"But think how many college boys she made happy."

"Were you one of them, Lang?"

"I was already through the FBI Academy when that movie came out, but..." He fought a smile. "It was a pretty sexy move."

She blew out a breath. "Yeah, whatever. And can we just forget we had this conversation? It's moot anyway. They say Kimberly Horne has the Oscar in the bag."

He relaxed a little as she accepted the truth. "Vivi, you don't seriously think you could convince Cara Ferrari to let you *be* her for however long it takes to trap a killer, who, by the way, greater minds than yours don't think exists. So I think you should forget this cockamamie idea of yours."

She snorted softly and grabbed her drink. "*Cockamamie*, Lang? Who says that?"

"I do."

She sucked the straw again, this time looking up at him with wide eyes as her mouth closed as if she were looking up from a blow job.

God damn his dancing dick.

"Just forget it," he said, as much to his disobedient organ as to his sexy little consultant. "It's a cute idea, but—"

"Fuck you, Lang," she shot back.

"Sorry, I know you hate anything cute."

"You just don't get it, do you?"

Evidently not. "Get what?"

"What I'm trying to do with this business my brother and I started."

"How can you say that?" He pushed his drink aside to get closer. "I've given your firm more business than any other outside consultant the FBI Boston office uses. If I'm not careful, my boss is going to start questioning just why you guys have had, what, four or five assignments in as many months? We're supposed to spread the outsourcing wealth, not focus on one firm."

She just shook her head. "This isn't about you and your office. This is about *me* and *my* office."

"Seriously, Vivi. You only started this business last fall. What do you expect?"

"Greatness," she replied without pause. "There are companies doing what mine does and making millions. They've got multiple offices and hundreds of investigators and bodyguards and security specialists on their payroll."

"And that's what you want?" Somehow, the dream of big business just didn't fit this skater girl. Like so many things about Vivi, it surprised him.

"I always want to be the best," she told him. "I don't like to do things half-assed."

"I respect that. But you're not starting with Cara and your body double idea." He underscored that with the look that had gotten him to a supervisory level at thirty-eight years old and placed both his hands over hers, damning the electrical charge he got every time his skin made contact with hers.

"Give me one good reason why not." She slid her hands out from under his, evidently immune to the electricity *and* the look.

He laughed softly. "The debate's never over with you, is it?"

"Not until I win. One good reason, Lang." She put up both hands to stop him before he spoke. "Other than the fact that I don't look like a movie star, as you've pointed out with great relish and ruthless candor."

"It's dangerous."

"My job is dangerous," she replied. "Your job is dangerous. Where's the fun if there's no danger? If we get the job, Zach's found three top-notch bodyguards who'll come stay with me twenty-four seven."

Three guys with her twenty-four seven? Something unfamiliar rolled through him, stunning him. Jealousy. "Doesn't matter. With all those nutcases out there, it's too risky."

She pushed back with a disgusted breath. "You are so…*careful*."

"You say that like it's a detriment. I'm an FBI agent, Vivi. Cautious is my middle name. And if you're going to make it in the security consulting business, you'd do well to adopt the same one."

"Well, my middle name is Belladonna," she informed him.

"A poison."

"A beautiful woman in Italian," she corrected him, and held up her hand to halt any response. "Don't. You've dinged me enough for one day. My point is *cautious* doesn't always work in business, Lang."

"It does in the security business." Three big bodyguards? Shit, he hated that.

"Nobody gets ahead being safe. It's like that half-pipe over there." She tipped her head to a big cement bowl where skaters spun and rolled and flipped. And fell on their asses. "You gotta go big and go wild or go down."

"Yeah, well, I've gone big and wild, and went down hard." No, *he* hadn't gone down. The one and only woman he'd ever loved had gone down. All the way down. Six feet under down.

"What happened?" she asked.

He shook his head. "Just don't take crazy risks, Vivi."

"Too late. I live for crazy risks."

And that right there was why he should squelch every thought he ever had about her, including the ones that gave him a goddamn erection.

Vivi got up, kicked her board out from under the table, and hopped on it. "See ya, Special Agent in Charge Colton Cautious Lang."

"Bye, Private Investigator Viviana Poison Angelino."

She rolled a little, tugging on her helmet and sliding him a rueful look. "Thanks for the slurpee and the vote of confidence."

She zipped off, giving him a perfect shot of her ass as she kicked into high speed.

There went his cock again.

To make the blood flow north to his brain, he forced himself to think about her stupid, foolish, crazy idea. Okay, shit. It wasn't entirely stupid, but the last time he took a risk like that, he lost *everything*. Which was why that would also be the last time he let a boner get in the way of his work.

Never again, not to either one.

THE DISH

Where authors give you the inside scoop!

From the desk of Roxanne St. Claire

Dear Reader,

I'm the youngest of five, a position of little power but great benefits. Yes, it meant I got the car floor on road trips (seriously, the floor!) but that position also allowed me to reap the rewards of parental guilt for sometimes treating #5 as an afterthought. On my tenth birthday, that meant the ultimate gift for a budding writer: a typewriter. I think I've had my fingers on a keyboard ever since. ·

So when I decided to launch a new romantic suspense series, I knew I wanted to anchor the stories around a big family. I hoped to translate the always-fascinating sibling dynamics into complex relationships and unforgettable characters. Since I married into an Italian family, I'd been given a window into one of the most colorful of all cultures, and choosing that background for my characters was a natural move. But this couldn't be an ordinary Italian family, since I like extraordinary characters. To work in my stories, they'd have to be fearless, protective, risk-taking, rule-breaking, wave-making heroes and heroines, willing to take chances to save lives. Oh, and the guys must be blistering hot, and the ladies? Well, we like them a little on the feisty side.

Thus, the Guardian Angelinos were born. They are the five siblings of the Boston-based Rossi family and their two Italian-born cousins, Vivi and Zach Angelino. The security and investigation firm these two blended families form is created in the first book, EDGE OF SIGHT. When soon-to-be law student Samantha Fairchild witnesses a murder in the wine cellar of the restaurant where she works and the professional hit man has her face on tape, she seeks help from her friend, investigative reporter Vivi Angelino. Sam gets the protection she needs, only it comes in the form of big, bad, sexy Army Ranger Zach Angelino . . . who stole her heart during a lusty interlude three years earlier, then went off to war and never contacted her again.

I had fun with Zach and Sam, and just as much fun with the extended family of renegade crime-fighters. One of my favorite characters is eighty-year-old Uncle Nino, who is grandfather to the Rossi kids and great-uncle to the Angelinos. He joins the Guardian Angelinos with typical Italian passion and gusto, carrying a spatula instead of a Glock, and keeping them all in ziti and good spirits. Oh, and Uncle Nino is a mean puzzle solver, a trait that comes in handy on some special investigations. But what he does best is Sunday Gravy, a delicious, hearty meat dinner in mouthwatering red sauce that the family gathers to enjoy at the end of a hard week of saving lives and solving crimes. He's agreed to share his secret recipe, just for my readers . . .

Uncle Nino's Sunday Gravy

Ingredients

- 1–2 pound piece of lean beef (eye of round)
- 1–2 pounds of lean pork (spare ribs)
- 2 pounds of hot or sweet Italian sausages
- 4 tbs. olive oil
- 4–5 garlic cloves, sliced
- 1–2 Spanish onions, chopped
- Pinch of dried chili flakes (optional)

- Pinch of sugar
- 1 can tomato paste
- 2 26 oz. cans whole, peeled San Marzano tomatoes
- 2 cups dry red wine
- 1 tsp dried thyme
- 1 tsp dried oregano
- ½ cup torn fresh basil leaves
- Salt and pepper to taste

Instructions

1. Cut and trim the meats into smaller pieces; halve the sausages, cut eye of round in four sections
2. Heat olive oil in large pan or Dutch oven (deep, heavy casserole) over medium heat
3. Sear meats in hot olive oil until golden brown; may be done in batches and removed from pan, set aside
4. Sauté onions in the same pan until translucent
5. Add garlic and continue to sauté until garlic turns golden (spicy Italians—and these guys are—add the chili flakes here)
6. Add tomato paste and constantly stir until paste reaches rich, rusty color
7. Add thyme and oregano and stir
8. Deglaze the pan with red wine, using spatula to scrape all bits of charred meat (Uncle Nino says this is the key to success) until reduced by half
9. Crush whole, peeled tomatoes (by hand!), then add to sauce
10. Season sauce with salt and pepper and—this one from Grandma Rossi in the old country—a pinch or two of sugar to balance the acidity of the tomatoes
11. Add seared meat into the sauce and simmer for two hours, stirring occasionally

12. Serve over pasta (Uncle Nino recommends rigatoni)
13. Sprinkle fresh basil on top just before serving

(Note: With one pound of pasta, this recipe serves six. Hungry heroes may want more to keep up their stamina, so feel free to add homemade meatballs. Sorry, but Nino's recipe for meatballs remains a family secret. Stay tuned for future books to unlock that and many more mysteries.)

Mangia!

Roxanne St. Claire

www.roxannestclaire.com

♥ ♥ ♥ ♥ ♥ ♥ ♥ ♥ ♥ ♥ ♥ ♥ ♥ ♥ ♥

From the desk of Caridad Pineiro

Dear Friends,

I want to thank you for the marvelous reception you gave to SINS OF THE FLESH! Your many letters and reviews were truly appreciated and I hope you will enjoy this next book in the Sins series—STRONGER THAN SIN—even more.

From the moment that Mick's sister, Dr. Liliana Carrera, walked onto the scene in the first book, I knew she had to get her own story. I fell in love with her caring nature, her loyalty to her brother, and her inner strength. There was no doubt in my mind that any story where she was the heroine would be emotionally compelling and filled with passion.

Of course, such an intense and determined heroine demanded not only a sexy hero, but a strong one. A man capable of great love, but who needs to rediscover the hero within himself.

Jesse Bradford immediately came to mind. Inspired by the many sexy surfer types I encounter on my walks along the beach, Jesse was born and bred on the Jersey Shore. A former football player who had to leave the game he loves due to a crippling bone disease, he is a man who has lost his way, but is honorable, caring, and loyal. Jesse just needs to meet the right woman to guide him back to the right path in his life.

Together Jesse and Liliana will face great danger from a group of scientists who have genetically engineered Jesse, as well as the FBI agents entrusted with his care. The action is fast-paced and will keep you turning the pages as you root for these two to find a way to be together!

If you want to find out more about the real-life Jersey Shore locations in STRONGER THAN SIN, please visit my website at www.caridad.com where you can check out my photo gallery or my Facebook page at www.facebook.com/caridad.pineiro.author@Caridad Pineiro!

Wishing you all the best!

♥ ♥ ♥ ♥ ♥ ♥ ♥ ♥ ♥ ♥ ♥ ♥ ♥ ♥ ♥

From the desk of R.C. Ryan

Dear Reader,

My family and friends know that I'm obsessively neat and organized. I work best when my desk is clean, my office tidied, and my mind clear of all the distracting bits and pieces that go into being part of a large and busy family.

And so it is with my manuscripts. When I created the McCord family and started them on their hunt for their ancestors' lost fortune, I had to find a satisfying ending to each cousin's story, while still keeping a few tantalizing threads aside, to tempt my readers to persevere through this series until the very end.

My editor remarked that, until reading MONTANA GLORY, she hadn't even been aware that the family needed the balance of another generation. Cal and Cora provided the narration for much of the family's history, and a steady anchor for these three very different cousins. Jesse, Wyatt, and Zane provided enough rugged male charm to stir the heart of even the most unflappable female. The women they love brought excitement and fresh flavor into the family dynamic. But it was four-year-old Summer who changed each member of this fascinating household in some way. It is the ultimate gift of a child. They touch our lives, and we are forever changed.

In MONTANA GLORY, I was free to delve even deeper into the McCord family's history to reveal long-held secrets. I made a point to reveal a bit more about Cal, Cora, and the things that shaped them and the other members of this family. And, I hope, we learn things about ourselves in the process.

I hope you fell in love with this diverse, fascinating family as much as I did while writing their stories. And I hope you're as satisfied with the ending as I am. Like I said, tidy, organized, with all the loose ends neatly tied up. I'm a sucker for a happy ending.

Happy Reading!

R. C. Ryan

www. ryanlangan.com

Want to know more about romances at
Grand Central Publishing and Forever?
Get the scoop online!

GRAND CENTRAL PUBLISHING'S ROMANCE HOMEPAGE

Visit us at www.hachettebookgroup.com/romance
for all the latest news, reviews, and chapter excerpts!

NEW AND UPCOMING TITLES

Each month we feature our new titles
and reader favorites.

CONTESTS AND GIVEAWAYS

We give away galleys, autographed copies,
and all kinds of fun stuff.

AUTHOR INFO

You'll find bios, articles, and links to personal
websites for all your favorite authors—and
so much more!

THE BUZZ

Sign up for our monthly romance newsletter,
and be the first to read all about it!